SPELLS WOVEN, BATTLES FOUGHT. . . .

When a dryad answers a dragon's plea, the fate of kingdoms could rest on their trial by sorcery. . . .

Wolf magic can make a warrior strong—but will the power of even such ancient magic be enough to topple a lord of evil?

She came to the inn cloaked by night. Was the enchantment she worked one of love—or some far darker spell?

When a legend wakes to lure her boat to its doom, can a weary warrior fight free of perilous enchantment?

These are just four of the twenty tales of battles fought with sword and spell by the valiant women who people the many worlds of—

SWORD AND SORCERESS

MARION ZIMMER BRADLEY
in DAW editions:

DARKOVER NOVELS
DARKOVER LANDFALL
STORMQUEEN!
HAWKMISTRESS!
TWO TO CONQUER
THE HEIRS OF HAMMERFELL
THE SHATTERED CHAIN
THENDARA HOUSE
CITY OF SORCERY
THE SPELL SWORD
THE FORBIDDEN TOWER
THE HERITAGE OF HASTUR
SHARRA'S EXILE

DARKOVER ANTHOLOGIES
DOMAINS OF DARKOVER
FOUR MOONS OF DARKOVER
FREE AMAZONS OF DARKOVER
THE KEEPER'S PRICE
LERONI OF DARKOVER
THE OTHER SIDE OF THE MIRROR
RED SUN OF DARKOVER
SWORD OF CHAOS

OTHER BRADLEY NOVELS
SWORD AND SORCERESS I
SWORD AND SORCERESS II
SWORD AND SORCERESS III
SWORD AND SORCERESS IV
SWORD AND SORCERESS V
SWORD AND SORCERESS VI
SWORD AND SORCERESS VII
SWORD AND SORCERESS VIII

SWORD AND SORCERESS III

An Anthology
of Heroic Fantasy

Edited by

Marion Zimmer Bradley

CHAMPLAIN COLLEGE

DAW BOOKS, INC.

DONALD A. WOLLHEIM, FOUNDER

375 Hudson Street, New York, NY 10014

ELIZABETH R. WOLLHEIM
SHEILA E. GILBERT
PUBLISHERS

DAW Book Collectors No. 678.

First Printing, July 1986

4   5   6   7   8   9

DAW TRADEMARK REGISTERED
U.S. PAT OFF AND FOREIGN COUNTRIES
—MARCA REGISTRADA.
HECHO EN U.S.A.

PRINTED IN THE U.S.A.

TABLE OF CONTENTS

THE EVOLUTION
OF WOMAN'S FANTASY

Welcome back! I'm happy to say that these anthologies have proved so popular that your editor has made an informal agreement with DAW to make them a yearly occurrence.

The selection from an ever-increasing flood of manuscripts has made the choosing of the final line-up ever more difficult. This year, stories which I would have bought without hesitation for the first of these volumes had to be rejected; just as a novel about the first visit to the moon would now be obsolete.

This is one of the reasons why I ask—no, *implore*—that any writer, no matter how professional, send to me a stamped-self-addressed envelope for my guidelines *before* submitting, because every year the parameters *change*. For instance, I constantly receive stories that are perfectly good but the plot is obsolete: a strong woman successfully challenges an anti-feminist society and is finally allowed to take up her place as a warrior or wizard.

Now there is nothing wrong with this story except—that it should by now be taken for granted; yet I still receive many stories where the writer drags out all the old perfunctory anti-feminist arguments ("In this society/town/country we don't send a girl to do a man's work." . . . "Who ever heard of a woman warrior" . . . etc. etc.—for equally perfunctory rebuttal. The conclusion is all too predictable, especially by now, and in this particular anthology, we *know* she'll win; there's no suspense, no *real* conflict.

After three years of strong-female-protagonist stories we should be able to take our heroines for granted, in fantasy if not in real life. I know that there are, regrettably, still enclaves within various churches and groups where women are supposed to live as if they were soulless helpmates to the

7

(male) Lords of Creation. Without wishing to denigrate any-one's religion, we do not intend to give aid and comfort to these prehistoric attitudes; "We hold these truths to be self-evident," that women are created equal to men; your egalitar-ian heroine is *necessary but not sufficient* to a modern story. The story must, to adapt the words of John W. Campbell, "grant your strong woman and go on from there."

(Campbell created modern science fiction when, after many stories in the Gernsback days, many of which merely dis-cussed some new technological wonder, or gadget, with no *story*, he said, "grant your gadgets and go on from there.")

Heroines in S&S must *start out* as strong, liberated, and enlightened; I don't demand that they all be fully grown; they can, should, and *must* undergo further change, growth, or self-realization during the progression of the story. But they should not have to prove their right to existence/equality. I don't want to print dozens of stories proving and re-proving the right for women to do things on their own. Re-fighting battles already won in a sane society could get very dismal.

This is why I almost automatically reject any story in which a woman is controlled or even helped by a Big Brave Male Mentor who protects and guides her. Granted, some women discover their own strength through the support of some man—nearly all women my age did—but in this mod-ern world where young readers live, that at once marks the women as an unfit role-model for today's girls; we don't need Daddy's permission to grow up as adult human beings; not anymore.

Stories where the protagonist is a housewife, a harem girl, or a slave don't thrill me, either, unless—and this is a big *unless*—the story immediately captures my interest to the point where I *can't* stop turning pages and when I finish reading, know I *must* share it with my readers. In fact, almost any story which captures me so quickly that in the end I realize regretfully, "Yes, but that's science fiction," or, "Yes, but this is just a romance in fantasy trappings," will at least be strongly considered for exception to the rules.

Some writers feel distressed that I can't make an exception for *their* particular work, when I did for another's. An edi-tor's job is to know what people want to read in general; if she makes too many mistakes the books stop selling. One sure way to insure that you *never* sell to me is to write a whining letter, when I reject your story, about "But you didn't *understand* what I was trying to do." Or worse: "I do not accept your criticism because you misused a semi-colon in your rejection letter, and therefore I have no respect for your editorial judgment." (Yes, I really got that one once.)

Kids, for your information, it's a tight market for fiction, and it's not my business to "understand" your story; it's *your* business to communicate to me what makes the story you've written exciting and real to you. I *know* you were telling a story which meant something special to you, but if I don't get, from your writing, just *what* made this story interesting to you, you are not an efficient storyteller and so your story is just another failure. If your story bores me—if I can put the manuscript down long enough to go for a cup of coffee and, when I get back, not care whether I ever find out what happened to Our Heroine—that means the story wouldn't hold my readers. Good stories mean that when I get the coffee, I can't wait to pick it up and find out what happened—or more likely, I'll finish it *before* I take my coffee break. Lisa, my secretary, has already learned that when she tells me I ought to go to lunch, and I call, "Wait, I just *have* to finish this first," it's probably a sale.

There are usually so many manuscripts piled on my desk that I have no hesitation in putting down a doubtful manuscript; there will always be more. If I think a manuscript is ultimately salable but just doesn't turn me on, I say so. Often in harsh words; if you can't stand rejection you are in the wrong business. I can't always take the time to be tactful. ("Dear, you have a lot of talent, don't take this personally, but this particular story bored me to tears.") I try to be constructive, but if I think the story in its present form is hopeless, I recommend a good book on fiction technique. I don't use printed forms, because I remember my own desperation when I got one—"But what was WRONG with it?"

I try always to give some clue to why the story didn't reach me, and this is why I often say something like, "This story just doesn't fit our format; good luck with it elsewhere," or, "This story is too slow getting started."

One of the major mistakes novice writers make is to send me a long analysis in their cover letter:

"This is the story of a very unusual heroine, laid in the days of Alexander the Great. Tasha finds herself up against entrenched prejudice against women as camel drivers, but she finally finds her true will in the Temple of Eternal Fornication."

When I read something like this (and they come in oftener than you can imagine—this is not an actual letter, but very similar ones do really come in every day or so) I know that the writer is an amateur. How? Because she doesn't trust her own story to stand alone. "Listen, honey," I want to say to her, "I *can read;* that's my job. If the story is any good, I will know on the first page that your heroine is named Tasha and that she's living in the days of Alexander the Great. And if the story is any good *at all,* I will want her to find herself, and want to keep reading till she does."

That's what writing is all about . . . to make me *care* whether Tasha finds herself. And if the story succeeds, I'll care—and I'll follow her even into the Temple of Eternal Whatevers.

This is why I often say, "This is a good idea—but stories aren't about ideas; they're about *people.*" If the people in your story interest me, I'll put up with anything.

One admonition, though. Some people send me stories of frontier days in the Old West, of modern witches on a college campus, etc. These may be fantasy or science fiction; they are not sword & sorcery.

The first rule is, tell a good story. The second is KNOW YOUR MARKETS. Don't send fantasy to *Analog,* or hard science to me, not even with a female heroine.

And if you aren't sure after reading this anthology just what sword & sorcery is, go back and read #1 and #2.

I couldn't give a glib verbal definition of what sword & sorcery is, either, but by golly, I know it when I see it. Or when I read it.

—M.Z.B.

DRAGON-AMBER

Deborah Wheeler

Deborah Wheeler, who sold me her first story, is one of the four writers who appear in all three of these volumes (you can find the others for yourself). All of Deborah's stories reflect a strong affinity for animals; this is no exception.

I received about twenty stories about dragons for this volume. Most of them were rejected almost automatically, since their dragons were handled in a manner identical to the dragons made world-famous by Anne McCaffrey. Since Anne has *done* that, it doesn't need to be done again.

This, however, struck me as being quite different and really having something new to say about the relationship of human and dragon.

Deborah is a chiropractor by profession, and by avocation a martial-arts expert; now I think she can also call herself a writer.

M erren woke gasping, her dawn dream shattered. The dying night lay unnaturally still around her, the air heavy with dew. She lifted her head cautiously. The wards she had set the evening before had not been activated, nor was there any sign of physical violation of the sanctuary.

11

Merren gathered her legs beneath her, glad that she had slept in her breeches with no heavy forest robes to slow her movements, and reached for her staff. The ritually carved bronzewood felt cool and reassuring beneath her fingers. She stood alone in the clearing, a stocky young woman with a cloud of unruly curls dark against her russet skin.

From the south, her ears caught a puff of air cascading into a rumbling breath. She focused on its source, a velvet black eddy in the auric fields. No ordinary prowler would create such an imprint, and the wards would have alerted her to the supernatural.

The growl came again, and a tug at her inner senses. A beast stepped from the shadowy forest to the clearing, its outlines visible in the strengthening light.

A dragon—neither natural nor supernatural, but born of a fusion of mortality and magic from the deep times before Light had twisted into Form. They possessed wisdom without language and an honor so convoluted that humankind could only guess at its elements. Generally they avoided humans, even nature-wizards like Merren's folk, keeping to their mountain retreats.

A dragon—sighing at her threshold! It was dull black in stillness, but the iridescent linings of its scales gleamed in rainbow glory with the slightest movement. She could see the outlines of its dorsal crest and the complicated knobs of its vestigial wings. It fixed her with its pale amber eyes and rumbled again.

I must not fear. It is a child of the Light like any of us, Merren told herself. She held out one hand, fingers outstretched and palm toward the dragon as if it were a creature of magic and not mere flesh.

I greet you, O-Brother-Dragonkind

The dragon rustled its scales in a profusion of prismatic light. Its deep thrumming escalted to a musical cry. A spasm of urgency reached Merren, clawing at her guts.

She said aloud, "What is it?" and stepped closer to the barrier established by the wards. The dragon had made no move to enter the protected zone, and she was not sure whether that was because it could not, or for some reason would not. She knew so little of dragonlore. Perhaps its present behavior was a lure to draw her forth to her doom.

But Merren did not believe so. She suspected that if the dragon had intended to harm her, it would already have done so. She spoke the rune to dissipate the wards. It was a risk, yet the texture of the dragon's plea urged her to it.

The dragon shook its heavy head and dropped, belly to the grass. Merren tightened her grip on her staff and approached it. She had not appreciated before how massive it was. Prone, the beast reached to the middle of her thighs. Even as a purely natural beast, its power would be formidable.

The dragon reared up, balancing its bulk upon its hind legs. The exposed scales of its belly glistened like honey, like watered silk. Gleaming talons arched above her head, then subsided.

"Cooommm," came a ragged sound from the beast's throat. Layers of nictitating membranes flickered across its glowing eyes like rare gems—amber, ruby, emerald. Merren felt herself half-ensorceled by the sheer beauty of the creature.

Whatever has driven you to me, O-Brother-Dragonkind? It must be a worthy cause. *But what challenge can I meet that a dragon could not?*

The dragon turned, a swirl of darkness and sparkling color, and strode into the forest. It led her south and a little west, angling through the airy groves toward the ancient heart of the forest. Merren trotted along, tapping the familiar maytrees and bronzewoods with the tip of her staff. Their branches quivered with her passing.

The forest thickened as they turned west, climbing above the sunlit bowl of Merren's sanctuary to craggy hillocks where angry old trees shouldered their neighbors aside.

It needs taming, this wood, love and taming.

Merren did not realize she had used thought-speech until she felt the dragon's flash of agreement. Neither of them liked this territory, where the bones of the land jutted out like half-formed weapons, ungentled by sun or blossom. The underbrush forced them to a walk.

She knew they were near their destination when the dragon surged forward, heading toward the densest twist of forest. Until then she had felt the spirits of the trees neutral at best, but now she could sense an eerie miasma streaming from the tangle before her. The wood was not actually evil, only degenerate toward the alien, the tree-spirits drifting further and further along their own strange dreams. Merren shied away from prolonged contact with them, fearing to carry their taint to her own familiar trees.

Overlaid on the burgeoning separateness of the grove was a residue which was in no way innocuous. Fear, shock . . . a violent warping of natural energies.

Merren slammed her mind-senses closed, grasping her staff in both white-knuckled hands. The dragon had nearly disappeared in the thick growth. She ran to catch up with it.

The residue of wrongness peaked sharply in the little clearing. A man lay face down, sprawled like a child's poppet over the root of a huge ashleaf. He wore leather vest and pants, laced woodsman-style above soft boots. Even in the dim light, his tousled hair gleamed like fine gold.

The dragon padded to the man's side and nudged him gently. Merren knelt by his head and touched his shoulder cautiously, relieved to find it warm and resilient. The left side of the vest was stained deep blue.

Merren checked the man's scalp and back, but could detect no other wounds. He might still have a fracture or internal bleeding which could kill him if she moved him. For a moment she paused, trapped between her own ignorance and the demanding need emanating from the dragon.

The dragon thrummed a command and bent his nose against the man's hips, lifting as Merren turned his head and shoulders. Finally he rested against the slope of the tree roots, head and torso slightly elevated. Merren's eyes went first to the livid bruises around his eyes, then to the seeping indigo stain on his right side. It stank of sorcery.

She studied his face for a moment before inspecting the oozing burn, curious to know what manner of man had entangled himself with such evil. He was well-built, graceful rather than muscular, his features a shade too generous for regularity. The bone structure was clean, the flesh overlying it firm despite the hint of sensuality in his mouth. On a heavy silver chain around his neck he wore an amulet of carved amber. A twist of dark light deep in the heart of the gem reminded her of the dragon.

Merren bent over the wound, drawing back the crisped edges of the vest for better exposure. Fumes swirled with the auric residue of the attack, blurring her vision. She picked up her staff and used its tip to trace a safe-field:

> "*North to the pine,*
> *West to the palm,*
> *South to maytree,*
> *East to bronzewood,*
> *Sun and stars, moon and dew,*
> *Be cleansed, be cleansed. . . ."*

The fumes dissipated with each ritual phrase, leaving a fading corona of green light—green for forest, green for healing. The dragon, relaxing, stretched at her side. The blue exudate shimmered, darkening to near black. Beneath it, the man's ribs moved softly.

Merren sighed in relief. The glancing blow had scorched skin and muscle without shattering internal structures. She touched the pulse point at his neck and felt his heart beat, slow but steady. No shock, then, but he might remain unconscious for hours, or even days.

"I'll need my water pack and remedies," she said aloud, as much for herself as for the great beast. *Guard him well, O-Brother-Dragonkind. I shall return.*

Merren found her camp undisturbed, the serenity of her familiar trees like a wellspring of strength. She leaned against the ancient bronzewood which had been the focus of her meditations. Her heartbeat altered, coming into subtle harmony with the tree. Bronzewood was her own, the touchstone of her wizardry. Her staff was not a piece of dead wood, but a tangible link between her physical manifestation and her spiritual growth. She drew away from the tree, still restless.

Mother-of-Trees, why have You set this task on me? I never sought power or fame, hearthside or human companionship. All I asked was to learn Your children and their wisdom. And how do I even know this is a quest, an ordinary man alone and injured in a patch of weirding forest?

Merren closed her eyes, leaning her forehead once more against the bronzewood's solid comfort.

He is no ordinary man, not guarded by a dragon and reeking of sorcerous assault. It cannot be anything but a guest. . . .

The dragon's cry reached her before the clearing was in sight, a brazen howl that rattled her bones. Merren felt the bronzewood staff quiver in resonance as she dropped her pack and plunged forward.

She was nearly thrown on her back as she entered the space between the deviant trees. The man still lay as she had left him, but the dragon was now a blur of rainbow glory, whirling to attack—

Green. . . . Not the color of life and growth, but the sickly hue of putrescence—a ball of livid light, it threw out tentacles that stank of evil. It whipped through the molten air, reaching past the dragon for the man. The dragon shrieked again and leapt to intercept the streamers. A tip of degenerate green touched its shoulder and disappeared in a shock of thunder. Merren's nostrils filled with the stench of sulfur and lingering decay.

She had never battled sorcery before. As a natural wizard, Merren was pledged to harmony with all living things. Even the leather of her boots and belt came from animals which had died without violence. What had she to do with creatures of death and artifice?

And then she saw the trees, the alien-dreaming trees of the twisted grove. Their spirits dipped toward the green light, curious and . . . hungry.

"No! The Mother gave me guardianship of all trees when She took my oath! You too are my children, strange though you may be—and that thing shall not have you!"

Fire pulsed through her veins as she hurled herself toward the ball of green light. Fire met the answering throb from the bronzewood staff, catalyzing Merren's fury into a point of focused power. She swung her staff at the ball and felt the node of righteous anger arc out, clipping the glowing sphere.

Sparks burst from the green ball, fading into sulfurous ashes. Merren staggered under the impact, her shoulders aching in protest. A tentacle of deadly light whippped toward her. She raised the staff to deflect it as the dragon leapt to protect her. The ball swerved violently, avoiding contact with the bronzewood.

Thunder boomed again as the dragon intercepted it and fell back to guard the man. The sphere began to rotate, throwing off sparks of poison-green light. The dragon cried out and jumped again, but the ball, spinning rapidly now, evaded it easily.

Merren choked back her own upwelling sense of failure. She might swing at the sorcerous device, might even stun it with her bronzewood, but neither of them could destroy the thing now. It was too fast, too powerful for them. It feared the staff, true, but she could not get close enough to it alone.

Not alone! Together! Together, now!

The dragon swung into action as if it were an extension of Merren's spirit and will. It swept alongside the ball, intercepting its path, diverting its attention . . . until the crucial moment when Merren leapt at the sphere and plunged the tip of her staff into its heart.

The thing died in silence, a faint, nauseating hiss through the auric fields and then hot ashes falling amid a horrendous stench. Merren dropped to her knees at the dragon's side, their brief synergy fading into calm. The trees leaned toward them, shaken into a semblance of awareness, strange but no longer alien.

Merren set up her camp in the little clearing while the dragon lay vigilant by the man's side. She sang to the trees as she worked, feeling them grow gentler under her care. The familiar chores helped dissipate the echoes of turmoil from her mind. She had not chosen this quest, it had been chosen for her. She had no time for anger now, nor any energy to waste on useless yearnings.

The man regained consciousness the next day, although his strength still seemed fragile. Merren nursed him with herbs and her own vegetable foods. The dragon disappeared into the forest from time to time, and she assumed it was hunting.

She called the man Ahr, the first letter of the mystic alphabet, because he had no memory of his own name. Nor could he recall why he was companioned by a dragon, or how he had fallen afoul of black enemies.

"You're clearly important," she insisted, keeping her eyes carefully from his. She found his intensely masculine energy disturbing. "Somebody wants you dead or captive, somebody very powerful."

Ahr nodded, sipping Merren's tisane brew. "I remember a little—the dragon fighting at my side. And a face, carved like a mask out of gray ice. Black pits for eyes. As far as I know, I myself have no magic. . . ."

"Mine does not deal with such things," Merren said sharply. "You've described a rune-face, and there's no question of the source of your burn. If you're asking for advice on such matters, I can't give you any. I deal with living things and the natural order, not the obscenity that attacked you."

"I'm grateful for your help, tree-maid."

"Merren. My name is Merren."

"Merren, then. Perhaps my memories will return to me in time. I'll be well enough to travel in a few days. I can go south and seek work in Chi-y."

Merren thought of Ahr stumbling about the countryside, ignorant and unprepared. The dragon, catching her mental image, rumbled and lashed its tail in protest.

"No," she said, her voice breaking. "I can't let you do that. If I cannot help you myself, I must guide you to someone who can. You see, the dragon agrees with me."

"I won't permit you to risk yourself for me."

"Ahr." Merren forced her gaze to meet hers and laid one hand upon his shoulder. "Even with a dragon at your side, you cannot go blindly on your way. You are too vulnerable—"

"Then that is my own business. You need not involve yourself."

"I have already become involved by powers greater than either of us. I am not indifferent to you, I . . . must find my own way through this quest, just as you must. You have been placed in my care and I would not serve you with any less than my best."

"No prince could ask for greater," Ahr replied, smiling.

"You say that as if—"

"I were one? Who knows? I don't feel particularly princely, just aching sore."

"I'll change the poultice on your burn. You could be a monarch's son, you know, stripped of your memory and sent to wander. Our village bard sings of such things. That would explain the dragon. . . ."

"Yes, the dragon. I feel it bound to me as if by magic, yet you seem able to communicate with it much better than I."

Merren bent over Ahr's healing wound, shadows hiding her blush of pleasure.

Rauch, the Elder of Merren's clansite, looked at Ahr's hair and said, "This young one needs help. *Beware, O-Daughter-Spirit* No true magic is this wound, but sorcery born."

"I know that," Merren murmured, restless even in the familiar protection of the living shelters. "He ought to go to his own land-sage, but he has no memory of where he was born. The dragon serves him—that must mean something."

The old wizard stroked the feathery edge of his beard. "You've gotten yourself in a fine tangle here, meddling with artificial magic instead of sticking to your own trees. There's nothing we can do for him, and we can't send him to an ordinary charlatan. Much as I mislike the idea, you'll have to take him to Heävyth and see the Mage."

Merren stared at him. Outside, the dragon resonated with her emotions and rumbled a protest. Ahr asked, "What's the matter?"

"The Mage will never see me, Rauch! She has never had friendly dealings with us, nor we with her. She abhors natural wizardry!"

Yet for Ahr's sake she will see thee. Whatever attacked him belongs to her realm of sorcery, not ours. I have heard of late that she wishes nothing greater than to fuse natural and synthetic magic. To do that, she needs one of us under her control. Were it not for the dragon, I would suspect a trap.

Merren nodded and withdrew from Rauch's shelter, bringing Ahr with her. Outside in the dappled sunlight, the younger clan children stared at them shyly, murmuring and pointing at Ahr's bright hair. Most of the adults and older children were hidden, more comfortable with their trees than with human strangers.

She cleared her throat. "I must go to my foster father's tree and visit my kin. I haven't seen them since I began my journeyman's foresting, nor have I sat in Motherhall. You and the dragon will be comfortable enough at the questing house while supplies are gathered and forest ponies caught for us."

"We're going to Heävyth, then. Do you think it holds the key—?"

"To your past? Perhaps one who lives there does, if she will tell us. The Mage. . . . Elyng."

He looked at her, capturing her with the intensity of his eyes. "You don't approve?"

"There are old quarrels between the trees and the Mage."

Ahr nodded, respecting her reluctance to give further details. "Heävyth. How long a journey?"

"On foot, ten days. Less, of course, with the ponies. Rauch will also see that we have food and a few coins for the city. With luck we won't be there long. . . ." She paused, frowning. "But we can't take the dragon. Here at the clansite, he's a wonder to the children and we have no need of secrecy. Once on the road, or in the city . . . we could draw no greater attention to ourselves."

"And you think we need to stay hidden?"

"What do you think? You've had your name, your past, your purpose ripped from you by some unspeakable sorcerer who found you even in the depths of the forest! Do you think he's going to let you march up to Elyng's door without another attempt? Until we find out who you are and why he wants to destroy you, we dare not risk it."

"I—I cannot leave him. Any more than he could leave me."

Merren heard the ring of truth in Ahr's stammer and lowered her eyes, saying nothing.

They saddled the restive, newly caught forest-ponies at dawnbreak, fingers clumsy with cold on the complicated knots. Merren had not ridden in years and Ahr, although he sat his mount with assurance, was unfamiliar with the gear.

Rauch and the others of the village had given their road blessings the night before. They rode easily the first few days, letting their muscles become accustomed to the stresses of riding hour after hour.

"I haven't seen the dragon," Merren said. They sat by the ashes of their small cookfire at the edge of the thinning forest.

"Not since yesterday, no." Ahr touched the amber at his throat. "I can't understand—I suppose I took it for granted, thought it would be with me all along."

"Not like me."

He smiled, looking up. "You I couldn't drive away, but I don't—hold you the same way. Merren, I would not take you from your forest unwilling."

"I'm not unwilling."

"So you said before. Your words say one thing and your spirit another. No, Merren, look at me. Whoever I am, you must do this thing for me, not for my name or title. I may be the Lost Son of Chi-y that your village bard sang of. It may be my father who battles at the Last Door, holding on to the shreds of life lest the land pass leaderless into chaos. Or I may be none of these things. I would have a deeper bond with you than mere speculation."

"I serve the Mother in all things. Her roots are my roots, Her sap my heartsblood. Whom do you serve, Ahr of no name?"

"I do not know what gods I used to call upon. By my will, I am now of the Light."

"We cannot face the Mage with any division in our hearts. I've held you from me, true, because I did not seek this quest. If I have been harsh or unkind, I ask your pardon. I would not leave Her groves for any man's name or rank, but—" she cupped his chin in one hand so that his eyes met hers—"I would be your friend and ally for your own sake."

"Does your wizardry bind you to celibacy also?" He laid his hands over hers, surrounding her with warmth.

"No." She smiled. "Nothing which partakes of joy and life is foreign to my craft. And it has been a long time since I had a lover to warm my bed."

*   *   *

They rode south as they passed through the placid farmland surrounding Heävyth, the forest-ponies growing fatter and less wild. Merren felt uneasy in the open spaces with their few trees fettered, almost comatose. Even the lush hedgerows were mute and docile. As they went on, Ahr grew more confident, as if his identity were returning with the change of countryside and the healing of his wound.

Merren could not be sure exactly when she knew they were being followed; the subtle hints, a twist of shadow just beyond her sight, a tugging at her inner senses, all gnawed at her intuition. She could not detect any threat, nor did she ever see any actual physical evidence of their trailer. She set her wards at night, as usual, and the only intruders were natural vermin, harmless and easily deflected. She did not speak of it to Ahr, to add to his fears when they stood before the Mage.

Heävyth at last. The city assaulted Merren's senses, acrid stone dust clawing at her throat. She stood in the marketplace just inside the heavy gates, feeling like a child ripped from her homeland forests. *Mother-of-Trees, be with me now!*

"A room, a bath, and then to our mission." Ahr's voice was buoyant, and it helped to steady Merren's nerves.

"No, first we go to the Mage. That's her tower, there on the white hill."

"We can't present ourselves to her covered with trail dirt," he protested.

Merren smiled. Her worn clothing and gear smelled healthy and familiar against the stench of the city. "We are not seeking her approval, to come before her ornamented and perfumed. The day is yet young, our strength good and purpose firm. Why should we wait and give her extra time to plan a counterattack?"

"I thought we were asking her for help."

"Ahr. Listen carefully, for both our sakes. There is no path for you that is not laced with peril, certainly not the road to Elyng's door. If she gives us aid, it will be for reasons of her own, not from fascination with your bright hair. She may tell us true, or lie to us. Or she may refuse to listen and attack me as her enemy. We must not bend our wills in a vain effort to please her before we have even tested her temper."

"Merren." And she felt her heart move with the intensity of his voice. "You risk that danger for my sake, and I a blundering fool in your care. I don't know that I deserve—"

"The dragon thought so."

"Dragons can be bound," he replied.

"You take much upon yourself, dryad," Elyng hissed. Her long black hair gleamed with feral light next to her pale skin. Pale skin, pale eyes, shining against the pale stone of the tower's highest chamber.

"I do not come for myself, Domina," Merren answered politely. She held her bronzewood staff in both hands so that it did not rest upon the cold floor. "I ask you to set aside our old differences and look upon me only as a neutral agent. Wrong has been done this man, wrong by sorcery. Unless you have turned from the Light. . . ."

Elyng hissed again, tossing her head in a river of jet.

". . . you cannot let it go unrighted, not such evil perpetrated by one of your own."

"You are so righteous, you tree-people, always telling others what to do, always thinking you have the right of it! Why should I believe you? Why should I not drain your essence right now and discard the husk?"

"Because," Merren said steadily, "I bear the Mother's blessing, and am no trifling plaything. Nor would you say these things to me if I were."

"This cannot go on," Ahr interrupted. He stepped forward, facing the Mage, dwarfing her slender height. "The tree-wizard does not ask this of you. I do. If she has put herself in jeopardy, it is for my sake. I must be the one to bear the risk."

"You?" Elyng moved toward him, her hips swaying under the sensuous folds of her silk gown. "And who are you to dare to say such things to the Mage of Heävyth?"

"I do not know who I am. That is why I stand here before you."

The Mage touched his face with one pale finger, her eyes upon his gold hair. She reached for the amber which hung at his neck, then drew her hand back as Ahr reflexively avoided her touch.

"But I do know who you are, or I can find out easily enough. You say it is your affair, not the dryad's. Very well, what will *you* give me for this knowledge?"

Ahr paused, confused for the first time. "I have nothing of any value to offer you."

"Nothing?" She sweetened her voice. "You have the amber."

"No!" Merren thrust her staff forward like a weapon. "You must not—"

"Silence, dryad! He was renounced your aid! The choice must be his!"

"He doesn't know what it means!" Merren retorted. "An unfair bargain, without knowledge of its worth!"

Elyng smiled, her lips curving in a poisonous arch. "Fairness and justice are two different things. Which do you seek, O man of no name?"

"I seek what is mine by right."

"No matter what the cost?" The Mage's eyes glittered in the tower's gray light.

"I do not know what you offer. Would you tempt me from the Light for the sake of a kingdom not justly mine?"

Elyng threw her head back and laughed. "Well said, stranger. Keep your dragon-amber for now. I shall give you your name, and the price I ask. You can judge for yourself whether it is worth the cost. Your father named you Dyveth."

Ahr gasped, trembling suddenly. His face washed ashen.

"And the price?" Merren demanded, watching the smile on the Mage's lips.

"A night with me. A small price for such a lusty lad."

Ahr shook his head as if to clear his senses. "Dyveth. I am Dyveth of Chi-y. She does not lie, Merren. I know not what has happened since my abduction, but Chi-y is mine on my father's death."

"To find out you are a king's son and heir to a great realm," purred Elyng, "is that not worth a small moment of pleasure for a lonely woman? A little companionship for a single night?"

Dyveth looked toward Merren, who kept her eyes carefully shielded and said nothing. "I am not free to do so, nor do I trust your motives."

"Is the dryad your mistress to chain you to her laces? But she is of no account, and a man need not be scrupulous about such things."

"But a king must be," Dyveth declared. "Truth for truth, loyalty for loyalty. It is the only way."

Elyng raised both arms above her head, her loose sleeves billowing like a daemon cloak. "You have had your chance, king's-son. Now I will take *mine*!

The room filled suddenly with pungent smoke; flames that were impossible crimson lapped at the walls. Merren drew Dyveth to her side and thrust her staff aloft.

"North to the pine! South to the palm!" Dew, sweet and cool, wet their skins. The fires hissed as they died.

The Mage's howl of anger distorted into an inhuman shriek. Her body began to elongate, her nails and teeth glowing metallic in the darkening room. The shadowy bulk loomed over them, bloated and reptilian.

Merren shouted again and pointed her staff at the transforming sorceress. "South to maytree! East to bronzewood!"

With a clap of silver sound, the staff was torn from her grasp to send her spinning to the floor. Merren's sight cleared to show Dyveth kneeling above her, his face flushed. Her knees were two bonfires of pain where she had fallen on them. "Don't risk yourself, prince. It's me she wants," she whispered.

"No." He straightened up to face the Mage, his hand closing on the amber token. The golden gem flashed, sun-blinding Merren's eyes as Dyveth cried aloud in a hoarse, unreasoning voice, "Dragon, come!"

The dragon bounded from dimensionless space just as the creature which had been Elyng reached taloned claws toward Merren's heart. It roared, shouldering the attack aside without visible damage. Blue flames replaced the red ones Merren's forest dew had extinguished. The dragon swiped at the Mage with one massive paw, and suddenly the room lay silent.

Merren coughed as she rose, clearing the lingering stench from her lungs. Gladness rose in her throat as she beheld the dragon, shimmering in strata of iridescent splendor. It had followed them, faithful even in its invisibility, and on the trail she had sensed its shadowy presence. The bundle between its forefeet stirred, moaning.

"Elyng. . . ." She touched the hair, now dull brown instead of jet, sweeping it back from the Mage's pale face. The sorceress curled into Merren's arms, sobbing weakly.

Dyveth touched Merren's shoulder. "Don't trust her tears."

"No, they're real enough. If there had been more contact between her and my clan I would have realized at once . . . but as it was I could only suspect. I didn't think she had voluntarily forsaken the Light. See, the dragon has broken the geas upon her; its ancient power runs deeper than magic."

"You mean she was being controlled by another, that she did not attack us of her own will?"

"I think that when we discover who, we will also find your enemy. Elyng, open your eyes, look at me."

The Mage stirred, responding like a child to Merren's words. Her eyes were faded blue, her face soft and bewildered. She no longer wore silvery silk, but plain gray wool, tied with an intricately knotted belt of her own hair. There were no traces left of the polished siren, only a pale-skinned, youngish woman with unkempt hair.

She whispered, "The tree-maid . . . and the dragon." There was no fear in her as she looked at the great beast, only wonder and bone-deep fatigue. "Then it was not all a dream. . . ."

"Would that it had been," Merren said, helping her to sit upright. "What do you remember?"

A spasm of grief contorted the Mage's face. She cried aloud and hid her face in her hands, her unbound hair falling forward like a curtain.

Merren seized her by both shoulders and said sternly, "Then you owe us, Elyng of Heävyth, you owe us dearly for your unlawful assault. You have been an instrument—"

"I know! The stars above bear witness that I know!"

"I demand payment now! Who did this thing?"

"I dare not tell you—it would bring doom crashing down on all of us!" The Mage threw her head back, white ringing her eyes, but she could not tear free from Merren's hold.

"The name, Elyng, the name! Or shall I have the dragon rip it from you by force?"

"Merren, you are so harsh with her," Dyveth protested. "If she did this thing against her will—"

Elyng shook her head. "No, the tree-maid has the right of it. The only way I can redeem myself is by undoing the wrong I have aided. Evil does not come into our lives unasked; the weakness is mine and I must bear the payment for it." She turned trembling to look Dyveth in the face. "Your enemy is Zyborn."

"Zyborn Rainbow-hand!" Dyveth exclaimed. "He has always lusted for power, true, but my father banished him from Chi-y after the magician Cathlamet discovered him dabbling in the darker arts."

"He has mastered those arts and is Zyborn Black-hand now," said Elyng, getting slowly to her feet. "As I have discovered to my sorrow. A wily one he, full of false hopes and broken promises."

"And my father? And Cathlamet?"

"I do not know. My memories of Zyborn's dominion are . . . flawed. Were your father dead, the loyal Cathlamet would hold Chi-y in regency for you. He would not betray you with a futile search, for he knows that if the dragon cannot defend you, then surely no mere mortal can."

"I remember. It was Cathlamet who bound the dragon-amber to me. He must have guessed—"

Merren silenced him. "The dragon's power protects you now, and that is enough. We must go to Zyborn and end his menace without delay. He will seek new allies, perhaps ones even our combined strength cannot withstand. When you summoned the dragon and freed Elyng, we lost any hope of secrecy. Best to finish the thing quickly."

"I don't know where he is," said Dyveth. "After he fled Chi-y he could have gone anywhere."

The Mage said, "He is here in Heävyth. The black onyx palace on the Amorath Hills just south of the river. It was the home of a rich man once, with gardens all around and many servants. Now it's a shell of stone, beautiful but sterile. They say that even the bronzewood house-tree in the courtyard is dead."

She paused as Merren cried aloud as if in pain. "I would go with you, if you will have me. My powers may be somewhat diminished, but Zyborn will not take me lightly again.''

Dyveth said, "Should we trust her?"

Elyng had drawn herself up in simple dignity and patted her hair back from her face. Merren realized that the Mage was not much older than she, a slight woman with traces of prettiness and fever-bright eyes. She remembered Rauch's warning and said, "You have not shown us any great friendship. . . ."

"I will swear by your staff!"

Merren touched her forehead with the tip of the bronzewood and felt the quiet pulse of clean power. She nodded as Elyng whispered, "I was not long under Zyborn's influence."

"Have we any hope of defeating him?" Dyveth asked.

The Mage replied, "I would not, not alone. But remember this, King's-son. It takes greater strength to conquer with mercy, as you and the tree-maid have shown me, than to destroy utterly. And Zyborn would not lust after dragon-amber so fiercely if it did not have the power to defeat him."

They are alike, these two, prince of one city and mage of another. I belong with my trees, not in even the finest palace. It is one thing to share my bed with Ahr the nameless wanderer, and quite another with Dyveth King's-son. Merren suppressed a sigh, feeling small and cold in the belly of the stone tower with no green anywhere, no earthy tang of life singing in her throat. . . .

The dragon rumbled, its voice laced with heartsick yearning. Merren touched the fiery hide of the creature and felt it tremble. It had sensed her homesickness for the forest and responded with its own profound longing. She could feel its memory of wild icy mountains, crystalline air, and freedom.

Elyng brought food and drink for them, fish cured with peppers, deer-tongues in aspic, and a cold casserole of tubers and mushrooms. Dyveth downed it all with relish, even the sour fruit wine, but Merren would not touch the flesh dishes and drank only water.

"You have scruples about such things, tree-maid," the Mage observed. "Does your discipline prevent you from enjoying other good things the world has to offer?"

"None so good as what I gain by it. No one who dines on the misery of other creatures can hear the rapture of the trees."

"Or you the sighing of the spheres. A truce, then, for a common cause cannot heal our differences so easily," said Elyng.

Dyveth added, "I have never heard either—"

The sudden, choking darkness ate the last of his words. Merren, her vision blurring under the impact, grabbed her staff and felt the pulse of heat within it. Her eyes steadied enough to make out Elyng huddled on her knees and the dragon in one corner, its eyes gleaming palely in a well of velvet black.

Heat and ice ran together in lightning flashes down the stone walls, filling Merren's nostrils with the smell of ozone and something unnameable, far less clean. Above them, in the exact architectural center of the tower, shimmered a ghostly parody of a human face. Lurid silver were its cheeks, fleshless lips curling in a sneer, its eyes smoldering green fire. Merren recognized the deathly hue of the ball of light which she had battled in the weirding grove.

Dyveth had scrambled to his feet and stood, legs splayed wide apart for balance, fists raised shoulder high. His words came tight and ragged, as if torn from his throat. "Black-hand! Zyborn Black-hand! This time you have met your match!"

The metallic grin widened farther, eyes narrowing into slits of amusement as Dyveth, maddened, leapt for the image. His hands passed through it and he fell heavily, his breath coming in a sob. The dragon swept to his side.

Elyng looked up, her face ashen behind her twisted hair, and cried, "It's his rune-face! You can't touch him!"

"Then none of his own essence is here?" Merren asked.

The Mage shook her head.

"Can he be brought here," Merren asked, gesturing with her staff toward the leering visage, "focused in that?"

"I—I think so. Anyone of master rank can use a projection as an anchor to far-traveling. You do not mean to lure him to us—"

"Shall I let him stay safe in his palace while he toys with

us, until fatigue or luck finish the battle? He tried that once, but he will not get a third chance," Merren said. "We will drive him to us with magic his death-sorcery cannot withstand, and then we will be able to deal with him."

The lightnings, now glowing silver and green, began to spark from the walls, lashing out at the three humans. As they drew into the center, Elyng began a protective chant. Merren watched her, sensing the pattern of the Mage's craft. It was not so unlike her own, except that it drew power from changes and differences, not harmonies as did natural wizardry.

"Elyng . . . Domina, do you know the art of parallels?"

"Parallels? We do not use that word. Ach! That bolt was close. I do not know how long my barrier can hold!"

"As above, so it is below. As in summer, mirrored in winter. . . ."

"Yes, I can partner you in that. Do you need me as anchor here or—"

"As it is here, so be it there! In the courtyard of the onyx palace . . . facing the house-tree."

Elyng nodded, her face grim.

Merren held her staff before her like a sword. The bolts of greenish light were coming even closer now, sparking off the edges of the Mage's safe-field. She could feel the walls of protective power shudder and knew they would crumble under a determined attack. It did not matter, for they would buy her the time she needed.

"Dyveth, get between us. Elyng and I are going to—to work some magic together. Do not look at the rune-face; the more successful our counterattack, the more threatening it will seem. Keep your temper under rein and trust in the dragon." She felt rather than saw his nod of agreement.

The bronzewood between Merren's fingers began to pulsate as she focused her concentration upon it like a lens. She felt the vibrations as a choir of voices, wordless and blending like branches in sunlight, like running water. Interwoven in that harmony came a light tinkling of bells, as delicate as birdsong or the petals of a solitary wildflower. The Mage made a formidable ally, with the power of such control.

A deeper rhythm joined them, a beat like the planet herself, forcing the two humans down, down into their roots.

Merren saw the dragon's hide alight in ripple after iridescent ripple.

Even as Elyng freed them from the dissolving safe-field, Merren felt the earth beneath the tower reach up to them, cradling their spirits through the crystalline smoothness of the stone. The echoes of Elyng's song told her that a similar process was happening at the onyx palace on the Amorath Hills, living joy as an antidote to the searing green poison of Zyborn's art.

Merren remembered then, remembered the chant begun during her brief battle with Zyborn-in-Elyng, and not yet completed. She had called to her the four dimensions of the forest, had gathered their energies but not yet released them.

North, pine . . . West, palm . . . South, maytree . . . East to bronzewood, east to my own! She felt the dormant spirit of the massive house-tree at the Amorath palace stir in response.

Stamp! Merren brought the staff down on the pale stone floor. "Sun and stars!"

The rune-face tore in agony, an inhuman howl raging from its mouth. Dyveth cried out and pointed to it, where a single bead of white light shone in the twisting green of the mask. It began to glow, hotter and fiercer, a spearpoint of fire to ignite the coolest forest, to singe metal and vaporize living flesh . . .

The dragon shrieked, but Merren heard its battle cry only as a deepening of its song, the bass rhythm now surging dense and exultant. The white beam tore through the last traces of Elyng's safe-field, but Merren smiled as she lifted her staff again. "Moon and dew!"

Bronzewood touched stone, stone linked to earth and the seed of life. Merren's inner eye could see the myriad tendrils of healthy green envelope the mage-tower in a celebration of life. The white beam crackled into a shower of stars. In the distant onyx courtyard, the aged house-tree burst into bloom.

"Be healed! Be healed!"

The scent of flowers filled the air, wild and heady, swaying to the dragon's roar. The rune-face wavered, falling. When it touched the stone floor it disappeared, leaving the shrunken husk of an elderly man robed in poison green. He lifted his ravaged face toward them, lips drawing back from yellowed teeth, and whispered, "Never!" He looked toward the dragon with avarice and loathing as the triumphant forest-power stripped the evil from him. Then he collapsed in on himself until only a wisp of dust and tattered cloth was left.

The three-fold song in Merren's heart faded as her vision cleared. She could see the new green which adorned every crack and seam of the pale stone of the tower. Dyveth, breathing heavily, went over to the pile of ash and prodded it with one boot. Elyng clasped her hands before her, laughing soundlessly. The dragon curled in on itself, a ripple of glory and then dead black, a well of sadness.

"I will not go with you to Chi-y, Dyveth King's-son," Merren repeated. "You speak from gratitude of the moment and not from sense or rightness. Once back in your familiar city, you would find me as strange and lost as you were in my forest. You are no longer my woodsman lover Ahr, nor could I leave my trees to be your court lady. If you seek an ally in magic, look to the fair Mage. . . ."

Elyng, sitting across from them, her hair dressed with moonstones and turquoise, bit into another grape and smiled. "You are as generous as ever, tree-maid. But I have much to do in my own tower. You've left me with a formidable housekeeping task, tending all that green."

Dyveth said, "You ought to claim a reward. It's not fair to leave us with that kind of debt." He reached down absently to stroke the dragon's hide and the beast, its amber eyes almost lifeless, did not respond.

"I have already said that I want nothing," Merren said wearily. The rapidly burgeoning green of Elyng's tower only intensified her longing for her trees. "Domina, you have given us the grace of your good will; there is no greater gift I can return to my village."

"But for yourself, Merren, for all we've been through together," Dyveth protested. He shook his head in the soft morning sunlight, the gold of his hair like a nature-given crown. "Please. Let me give you something."

She met his eyes for a moment, measuring the intensity behind them, and then dropped her gaze to the dragon. *He won't accept my answer. He wants to tie me to his memory with presents of gold or gems, like the dragon-amber.* She found her voice suddenly trembling. "Release the dragon."

"What?" Dyveth asked, and Elyng's head shot up.

"The dragon. Its freedom. That's what I ask for."

"But I can't. Cathlamet promised there was no way it could leave me as long as I held the amber. It is bound to me."

"As was I, by the will of the Mother. Your magician captured its spirit within the amber. Zyborn knew it, and wanted control of the dragon as much as he wanted your death. With his destruction, you no longer need the dragon's protection, or mine. Return the amber to its source, and we shall both go free . . . or are you, prince, no more than a pale shade of Zyborn's tyranny?"

"No, I . . ." he began, visibly shaken. "I would be just with you, Merren, and honorable. I would have you remember me as a man and not a figurehead." He fumbled at his throat for the silver clasp.

The dragon, which had been lying like a lump of carbon at his side, sprang to its feet, vestigial wings spread wide and flaming like a cascade of demented rainbows. Dyveth laughed and tossed the amber into the air. The dragon, singing, leapt to meet it, and Merren knew that not for worlds of glory would she have missed that moment of elemental joy.

O-Brother-Dragonkind!

ENTER THE WOLF
A. D. Overstreet

A.D. Overstreet's "Enter the Wolf" was actually accepted for *Sword and Sorceress II,* but when I wound up with over 10,000 extra words, it was trimmed from the final cut. When she discovered that I was preparing a third volume, she sent it back to me with a rewrite giving the story even more sorcerous power; a story of love, strength, and revenge that embodies all the qualities wanted in a sword and sorcery heroine.

This is her first published story.

"**I**t is time," said Mother Wolf, "for you to join The Pack."

Out of love for the old blind woman, Megarin stifled the objection somewhere behind her tongue. The time was not right! She was too young and not yet fully trained. In five years when she was thirty— the proper age— Megarin might have tested her skills against her teachers to win admittance to The Pack. But none of the teachers still lived. Only old Vivien.

Waving aside her two devoted acolytes, the gaunt old woman approached the altar with steps so firm they belied her age and blindness. Megarin winced, angry at the sudden stinging in her nostrils and backs of her eyelids. All younger even than she, the others must not see her tears. Surely old Vivien was dying. Why else command her to join The Pack except to take over as Mother Wolf to the cubs?

Only Megarin was left to care for the children. Only Megarin. And only because she had led a hunting pack that dreadful day six years ago. Filled with joy over her success in her first lead, she had brought the exuberant juveniles back to Wolfhaven. All joy died for her forever. They found The Pack and all the aspirants beaten and raped. The smaller girls had vanished save for three toddlers hidden in an oven. Among all the ravaged bodies, only one moved, moaning softly. Before Garm had struck her blind with the black light from his eldritch sword, Mother Wolf had seen it all. But live she did and told them all that had happened while they hunted. Through the years Vivien trained them all as well as she could alone. Now her failing strength was spent. Now Megarin must become Mother Wolf. Long ago abandoned or sold by parents, the girls must not be orphaned again!

Suddenly weary with the knowledge of the burden that must pass to her, Megarin sank to her knees before the altar. Through the thin but sturdy doeskin leggings she felt the smooth stone polished by so many generations. Bracing her shoulders, she vowed she would not ruin this solemn moment for the Mother or the others. She hurled a silent prayer to the Great Wolf that blind Vivien would not stumble.

As if she could see—but such a thing was not possible, was it?—Mother Wolf raised her hands toward the empty niche and offered the salute.

Against her will, Megarin shuddered. *Please, O Great Wolf, don't let her old mind forget that the crystal cup was stolen by that traitor Magda.*

Mother Wolf completed the reverent gesture. Then she lowered her hands surely to the wolf's-head design on the pedestal below the niche. As soon as she touched the stone nose, the front of the pedestal slid aside. She withdrew a clear crystal, the center of a larger crystal that long ago had been hollowed out to form the sacred cup. Turning toward Megarin, the old woman extended the object toward her so the young woman could see clearly the wolf's head etched in its flat end. With the other children in the back of the temple,

Megarin had seen the crystal before; she had not seen the design.

Softly, Megarin murmured, "I am here, Mother Wolf."

"I can see that, my child."

Surely those dull and sunken eyes could not see! Yet, on the wrinkled forehead, between the grizzled eyebrows, the eyes of the wolf brand were open and glowing a warm red. Megarin blinked, not believing what she saw. Then all she could see was the crystal before her eyes. It glowed with a brilliant, scintillating light. The wolf's-head design gleamed a bright and bloody red. Already she could feel the heat from it. Grinding her back teeth together, she refused to flinch when the brand burned into her own forehead exactly on target.

The pain was so brief that the tears of agony had no time to spill over onto her cheeks. She waited for Vivien to replace the crystal; then, as was proper for the simple ceremony, she rose. Mother Wolf turned her to face the twelve assembled young women and girls. "Behold!" cried out Mother Wolf. "The newest leader of The Pack! Now our beloved Megarin sees with the eyes of the Wolf."

Because she had not been tested, Megarin knew no elation in this supreme achievement of her childhood dream. When she tilted her head back and howled, no answering howls came from The Pack so long dead. Only Mother Wolf's soft growl led Megarin into the second howl which others in the vaulting temple answered wildly.

Released from the old woman's embrace, Megarin looked again at the wolf's head on Vivien's forehead. Now it was simply a brand, lifeless, the eyes closed. Already the old woman's short and shaggy silver hair, worn in the same close-cropped style all of them wore, was falling into place to conceal the mark of the wolf. Yes, that was all it was! A mark of belonging and no more. Yet The Pack had always been so secretive about the mark, especially after each new member returned from First Quest.

"Blow out the candles," ordered Mother Wolf. The acolytes rushed to darken the temple. "Go now, Wolf Woman," Vivien said to Megarin. "Find the prince. Take the crystal cup from Garm and return it to its rightful place."

Grateful for both the old woman's blindness and the darkness, Megarin lowered her jaw in astonishment. "How will I know the prince if he even lives? He was only five when Garm's warriors attacked."

"He lives. The cup will show him to you. Always remember. It was treachery as well as sorcery that let Garm defeat us."

She could sense Mother Wolf turning away. The two acolytes stumbled to assist the old woman in a darkness as full for them now as it must be for her always. Megarin's shoulders drooped. Her own First Quest! Not now! She must not be sent away now, not now that Vivien might be dying. Surely the old woman's mind must be failing. How could she know aught of prince and cup? Yet the footsteps Megarin heard moving away were firm, more sure than the faltering sounds of lighter steps on either side. Megarin sighed. Even now, she could not break tradition; she could not disobey the Mother Wolf. She must go.

Smoothing her unbelted doeskin tunic, Megarin turned around and waited for her eyes to adjust fully to the darkness. Dimly she could make out the outline of the temple door. Outside the windows the sky seemed lighter. Edging carefully toward the dawnlight, she tripped over an uneven stone. The eyes of the wolf, indeed! She was as blind temporarily as Mother Wolf was forever. Finding the door at last, she slipped into the courtyard.

The first faint brush of white radiating from below the eastern horizon greeted her. She smiled at the Wolf's tail, the zodiacal dawn light. "Good morning, Great Wolf. If quest the Mother commands, then quest it must be." For a moment she looked with fierce longing at the stone buildings inside the wall. Shrugging, she strode resolutely through the gate.

When Megarin entered the lush forest surrounding Wolfhaven, she felt the Wolf's morning-breath, that current of air nearly indetectible except by the slight increase in the night's cold. She offered her own early prayer; "Let me soon complete my charge. Mother Wolf is old and I must return quickly."

As silently as any true beast, Megarin moved on bare feet through the dense forest. She suspected Garm was still quartered at the old castle. If not already sold by that vandal or his horde of mercenary terrorists, the sacred cup might be there; but the prince must be as dead as the rest of his family. The sky brightened, and sudden hope filled her heart. Mother Wolf believed he lived; and Vivien did have strange ways of knowing what happened beyond Wolfhaven. The boy might be only wishing he was dead as he endured Garm's special cruelties. She tried to remember the boy, a pert and lively lad with sandy, wild hair. What was his name? Oh, yes, Duer. Prince Duer. If he lived, he would be King Duer of the line of the Corsac to whom The Wolf Pack had, eons ago, pledged their loyalty and their skills at unarmed combat.

Megarin paused, relaxed but ready. Not quite in hearing range, the presence of others around her somehow impinged on her senses. Placing her back near a broad tree trunk, she strained to listen.

A wolf stepped into the small space between the trees where Megarin waited. Standing four feet high at the shoulder, he was black as deep night itself; a sheen of silver glistened from his fur. Megarin swallowed slowly. This was a wild forest wolf, not like the half-tame brownish pups that often wandered into Wolfhaven. Somewhere she found a sprightly grin she offered. "Fellow wolf, I hope you'll honor the fact I'm part of a pack myself."

The huge beast snarled, showing fangs still young and strong and white. Although he seemed to be looking at her eyes, Megarin decided his right eye was aimed more at her forehead. Her eyes crossed when she thought of the wolf's head branded there.

Suddenly she straightened to glare intently at the forest beast. "You will let me pass, brother wolf. I have a quest put on me." In the back of her mind she formed a desperate prayer to the Great Wolf.

The black wolf's eyes shifted; his own fierce gaze averted slightly. Megarin stepped forward. "You've nothing to fear from me, my brother; nor I from you." Training her glance on him, she moved one more step. The brand felt warm. She could smell the wolf more clearly.

Too clearly. Her human nose was not meant to decipher the myriad smells that all at once assailed her nostrils from his fur. Also her ears now picked up sounds she had missed before, sounds of many paws padding lightly against the ground all around her. Then her vision parallaxed. She was seeing nearly double, the second image slightly above the first, although it lacked the color richness of the first.

The wolf backed. A small whine slid through his nose. Concentrating on the second image, Megarin moved toward him. He sat, rolling over onto his haunches, then onto his back. The first image blurred and lessened as the second grayshade vision grew stronger. Growling softly, she knelt to bend over the wolf's exposed and vulnerable belly. Placing her right hand gently on the soft belly fur, she stroked all along his chest. "I won't harm you, my brother." When he rolled back over, his ears were still clamped back, mouth open and tongue lolling out. She bent down to grip his muzzle between her teeth. Firmly she bit down to show her affection; then she filled the empty spot behind each ear with her fingers. He growled his pleasure as his plumed tail flopped against the ground.

Presently other wolves sidled out to greet her and accept her loving touch on their bodies. The black leader leaped up and planted his forepaws on her shoulders. He nipped at her nose—an invitation to play. Delighted with her acceptance into this pack, Megarin romped and wrestled with her new comrades on the forest floor. "I'm hungry," she said at last; and they hunted. As one of the pack sharing the kill, Megarin relished the still warm and bloody venison. Idly, she thought how Mother Wolf would enjoy the liver.

The giant black wolf batted aside several smaller males and himself bit out the liver. Holding it in his mouth, he aimed his right eye toward the brand on Megarin's forehead. As clearly as if he had spoken, she heard his intent. "I'll take this to Mother Wolf and tell her you are one with us." He leaped away. Megarin sat quite still. Now she knew how Mother Wolf kept informed and how the old blind woman saw when she could not see. Gingerly, she brushed her fintertips across the wolf's-head brand.

Megarin rested only briefly. She left the wolves sleeping off their gorging. When she approached the forest road to town, the hairs on the back of her neck lifted. Reading the wind, she detected the rank scent of men having passed recently. She stayed in the trees, moving parallel to the road until she saw the north gate of Oakden at midafternoon. The broken gate hung on bent hinges. Beyond the opening, she saw buildings in need of paint and repair. Curious to see how badly the once pleasant town had deteriorated under Garm's rule, she stepped onto the road. She shivered, feeling her hackles rising again. "I am wolf. But I am human, too!" She strode toward Oakden.

Too well she remembered the last trip here with Mother Wolf four years back. Too well she remembered the catcalls and the hurled clods of mud and other refuse. Although she and three other aspirants fought valiantly, it was Mother Wolf's sonorous voice that struck terror into their tormentors. After that, none from Wolfhaven ever returned to a town that once welcomed them as friends.

No one now watched the gate or waited to welcome weary travelers. Oakden looked deserted and forgotten; yet muffled noises told Megarin it was still inhabited by more than rats. In the town square three scruffy men lounged, drinking from a dusty bottle. Pausing, she studied the bedraggled representatives of the once prosperous town.

One rose and lurched toward her. The others followed, probably because the first held onto the bottle's neck. His voice was only slightly slurred. "What are you doing in town?"

"Care for a toss?" The second moved around her.

"She will!" The third lunged toward her.

Before, no man of Oakden would dare to so accost a lady from Wolfhaven. They must learn that respect again! Megarin stood quite still until they were actually laying hands on her. Then she jabbed two still left fingers into one pair of eyes and her right elbow into a sternum. Following the line of flow, she chopped the edge of her right hand across the third man's throat. Because she intended to teach, not kill, she pulled each lethal blow short of full strength. When they lay screaming on the ground, she announced, "The Pack is back." Proudly she stalked through the main street of Oakden; she noticed heads quickly withdrawn into houses.

She was glad to be through the dank town. The stench was

nearly unbearable even for her limited human sense of smell. While she did wonder how it might smell to a wolf, she decided not to try to find out. She touched the brand and grinned. On the south side of town, the road seemed more traveled but no better tended. The hard-packed dirt would raise no dust from the passage or horses, but the forest was thin enough here for her to see some distance ahead. Twice she moved off the road and into the concealment of trees to let groups of hard-riding warriors pelt by her. Perhaps the townspeople would let Garm's men know of her presence. When one rider, obviously an officer of sorts, galloped madly back, she watched him from the shadows. She nodded once. Garm would know one from Wolfhaven was about. He would not be concerned. No, Garm would be confident. Too confident. She smiled, letting her lips pull back in a snarl.

Approaching the sprawling castle at first dark, Megarin crouched in the shrubbery to watch the raucous security guards. Their attention was slack. No doubt Garm had so terrorized the countryside he and his men feared no one and no attack on his stronghold. Taking a few moments, Megarin slowed her breathing and forced her concentration into the mark of the wolf on her forehead. When the area warmed, she shook her hands to loosen any remaining tension. Her breathing rate slowed, deepened; but her heart sped faster. Now she could clearly hear the inane natterings of the guards.

Also she heard soft pawfalls and quickened breathing of wolves who must have run swiftly after their feeding naps. Sorting out the exquisite scents, she knew the black leader was nearest her. As the wolves moved to circle the castle, Megarin stalked toward the back. Hearing no movement behind the ten-foot wall, she leaped to the top to scan the inside. When she saw no one, she jumped down and ran toward the main building. Still not accustomed to the double vision, she stumbled once over one of the many pieces of trash littering the courtyard.

Another leap took her to a broad window ledge. Slowly easing open one shutter, she peered into the dead king's once luxurious dining hall.

In the king's oak throne lolled Garm, laughing and stuffing various large chunks of food into his mouth. His lank blond hair looked greasy and dark; his once lean frame now showed signs of thickening. His soiled and matted fur garments were crusted over in spots with some blackish stains.

The woman beside Garm drew Megarin's attention. Long and tethered with gold ornaments, hair as black as Megarin's gleamed beneath a tawny fur cap. A fur cloak of the same tawny sheen rested on her shoulders. She ate daintily, not bothering to hide her disgust at Garm's manners. Besides obvious slaves, she was the only one in the room who wore no weapons.

Megarin hissed. Magda! Magda who had favorably achieved all her tests by the teachers of The Pack. Yet—and no one outside The Pack ever knew why—Magda was denied acceptance. Then she stole the sacred cup. Garm came with his wailing sword. The Pack died, all but Vivien.

Megarin glared at Magda. No Pack Wolf would wear the pelt of a predator, especially that of a brother wolf! Did Mother Wolf know the traitor consorted with Garm? If the wolves knew, she knew. Now Megarin knew, and Magda must pay for her treachery. *No.* Mother Wolf had sent Megarin to rescue cup and prince, not for revenge. Not this time.

Scanning the gloomy hall, Megarin ignored activities in dark corners though the shrieks of servitors hurt her wolf-enhanced hearing. Someday these people enslaved by Garm would be freed. Today Megarin must free only prince and cup.

"Boy!" bellowed Garm, and Megarin cringed at the harsh sound. "Bring my wine. What's taking you so long, you miserable cur."

A filthy boy scuttled from the far doorway. In both hands he bore a soiled goblet. In spite of the grime obscuring its beauty, Megarin saw a cup of crystal with a fluted foot. While she looked through her wolf's eyes, the cup began to glow. She blinked and shut the wolf eyes. She could see no glow through her human eyes. Breathing even more slowly, she let the wolf eyes open. Again she saw the warm, red glow. Looking more closely at the boy, she could not distinguish his features beneath layers of dirt; but bruises and whip welts showed on his bare arms and legs. His tangled hair looked as if it had been hacked off with a dull blade.

Trembling, the boy thrust the cup into Garm's hands and ducked. At once, the glow vanished. Megarin smiled; the cup had shown her the prince. Cup and prince were together, but how could she rescue either?

"Hey, you up there!"

On the paving below her, two warriors aimed lances at her. Megarin growled deep in her throat, and the growl was answered at once. Two massive black forest wolves hurtled over the wall. Before the men could even begin to turn, each wolf had struck, hamstringing the warriors of Garm. The wolves paused only to howl before they leaped back over the wall.

The wood shutters rattled on their hinges as Megarin hurtled into the dining hall. Striking the stone flooring, she absorbed her forward movement in a somersault and uncoiled to leap into the air and land on the main table. Her bare feet landed solidly on the unscrubbed planks. Startled, Garm banged the crystal goblet down with brutal force. As wine slopped out, the crystal rang and the table shuddered under the impact. Any lesser crystal, even diamond, would have shattered; but the sacred cup held firm. Swiping at his mouth with the back of one grubby hand, Garm recovered. Laughing, he leered. His lascivious temperament leaked from his teal blue eyes. "One more she-wolf to toy with. My men'll treat you as they did the rest!"

"You'd have to kill me first." She snarled softly.

"Like the others?" His callous smile angered Megarin. Striking as fast as a wolf slashes, she snatched the sacred cup from his grasp. "No, Garm. Never again." She hurled the sour-smelling wine into his face.

"Let me handle this, Garm." Magda thrust off her fur cloak and leaped onto the table.

While his drunken warriors leaned forward in their chairs, Garm rubbed his ragged sleeve over his wine-drenched face. "Go ahead."

Turning to face the black-clad woman, Megarin growled. "I remember you, Magda. Traitor. It was you who stole the sacred cup from its holy place in the temple."

"Of course, child. How else could anyone have successfully attacked Wolfhaven?" Magda crouched, her hands loose and out from her sides. "No one was left to teach you. You've branded yourself but it means nothing."

"Nothing?" Megarin brushed her shaggy hair back from the mark of the wolf. She felt the warmth increasing. Now she could actually see the red glow emanating from her forehead.

Magda gasped but darted forward. Megarin realized this woman was her superior. The traitor had accomplished the entire range of wolf training while Megarin had concentrated chiefly on the lightning-fast method. Planting her left foot, Magda struck out a low kick. The force focus of the blow was in her heel which smashed into Megarin's left knee.

Instead of falling back, Megarin loosened her leg muscles and coiled over the blow. She jabbed her left hand into Magda's solar plexus. Or tried to. Magda twisted around the strike and aimed a blow at Megarin's throat. Parrying with the sacred cup, Megarin felt the ringing vibrate on her flesh when Magda's hand smashed into the cup. The woman yelped and scowled.

Megarin moved in close-range to initiate three straight punches with her left hand. The short lightning blows rocked the other's head; her eyes unfocused. Taking one twisting step forward, Megarin brought her other foot up in a low kick targeting Magda's kidney area.

Magda sagged. Already Megarin's muscles were hurtling her forward. *Always move in toward your opponent.* Her mind fought the nearly instinctive action. She dared not continue the fight; she could not allow the other to regain strength. While her skill had surprised the traitor, Magda would no longer estimate her. Her First Quest was more important! First Megarin must rescue prince and cup. She ran, bending over to snatch up the boy for whom the cup glowed. Garm's sword was in her way.

"Magda's tricks don't stop you. This will." He yelled, "Skarn!" The sword flared a black light brighter than all others. The flash of unearthly light narrowed to a hot, thin line.

Squinting, Megarin sent all her concentration into the hand holding the sacred cup. "Help me, Wolf Cup!" As she thrust it before her like a shield, it glowed fiercely. The overbright light streaming from Garm's sword was trapped. Though the sword wailed loudly, the light kept flowing into the cup. The eerie wail rose to a shriek and Garm bellowed. He tried to haul his sword free, but it was held by its own light tether to the cup. The light faltered. It thinned. It became a darkened smoky stream as the cup absorbed and consumed the fiery energies that fired the sword. Abruptly even the smoky black path from sword to cup vanished. The sword screamed, a piercing ululation that hurt Megarin's wolf hearing. The pitch rose until only she and the wolves could hear it. Then the sword shattered in Garm's hand. Pieces of shiny dust darted fitfully in the shaft of light from the open window. Now the sacred cup was bright and clean.

Raging, Garm snatched at the shiny dust particles. Megarin grabbed up the prince. Running with cup in right hand and boy dangling under left arm, she darted into the courtyard. Her desperate howl called the pack. The forest pack ran through the gate and scattered the astonished guards. In spite of furious outcries behind her, the guards were too busy trying to avoid wild-wolf fang and claw to try to stop her.

She did not stop running until she was deep in the forest and surrounded by chortling wolves. The massive black leader aimed his gaze at her brand still flaring its red glow. His thoughts were sharp in her mind. "The men were so confused! What fun! Shall I run ahead and tell Mother Wolf?"

"She isn't dead yet?" she said though she realized he heard her thoughts more clearly through the brand.

"Of course not, sister wolf."

"Then go and tell her, please."

Certain of the older females crowded around the boy and licked his face. "He needs a bath," said Megarin. "And protection." She found the leader's mate fastening her gaze on the brand.

"He'll have both from us," came the thought.

"Keep him safe and out of Garm's way. He must not be at Wolfhaven should Garm come looking for him. Nor should any of us."

The wolf grinned, her tongue hanging out far. "Could be Garm and his men might find it hard to travel through the forest with so many wolves about."

Megarin nodded. She had not realized how many wolves roamed this country. Had she missed them, or had they not been there before? No matter. They were here now. She cupped the boy's face between her hands. "Prince Duer." When he nodded, tears flooded his face. "King Duer of the Corsac. I, Megarin of The Wolf Pack, am pledged to serve and protect you. Do you remember when you were a small boy and played at Wolfhaven sometimes? How friendly the wolves were to you? Even the fierce forest pack now serves you. Trust them. Stay with them. Soon one from Wolfhaven will come for you. You will be king, Duer. This I promise you."

When she hugged the boy, he suddenly tightened his arms around her. She waited, stroking his head and back, as years of grief and abuse prompted his wild sobbing. When he finally slept, she gave him over to the wolves' gentle care and began her run to Wolfhaven.

When the moon came out from behind glittering clouds, Megarin stopped at the spring in the clearing behind Wolfhaven. She closed her human eyes to study her reflection. The eyes of the wolf on her forehead were open. They glowed, but she could detect the red color only through her human eyes. "Yes, I do see with the eyes of a wolf. I am one with the wolf. I am one with the Great Wolf." She sat back on her haunches. Other wolves joined her salute to the moon. Soon the vast forest echoed and re-echoed the howling of wolves so that it seemed no other creature dared exist.

Megarin dipped the sacred cup into the water. Lifting it filled to the brim with the clear and icy spring water, she saw the full moon held within its holy depths. "Someday, Magda and I shall meet again. She and that vicious Garm will pay for their crimes against the Corsac and against The Pack." Closing both her wolf's eyes and her human eyes, Megarin drank the moon from the sacred cup to bind her pledge.

VALLEY OF THE SHADOW
Jennifer Roberson

One of the greatest—if not *the* greatest—pleasures of an editor is to discover a new writer and see her advance to full strength. Jennifer Roberson, like Charles Saunders and Diana L. Paxson, other writers who made their first appearances in my anthologies and have become well-regarded novelists, writes that her second volume of the Chronicles of the Cheysuli, *The Song of Homana*, has recently been released and that she has just "quit the job at the bookstore for full-time writing . . . seven novels so far, three out of the sf field . . . I think all those years of sweating blood at the typewriter and collecting rejection slips are beginning to pay off."

That's what it's all about: writing, like all other artistic callings, is 10 percent inspiration and 90 percent perspiration.

I tell people, when they ask for the secret of success, "Apply the seat of the pants to the seat of the typewriter chair, and STAY there until you get results." Jennifer did.

She came in on a gust of wind and rain. He saw how she struggled to keep the wooden door from being snatched out of her hands and slammed against the tavern wall. All the lanterns guttered, splashing distorted light

47

over the faces of the men as they drank and diced and dallied with the whores. Hard faces, every one; some scarred, some lacking an eye, teeth, even an ear. But he doubted the whores cared; their faces were as hard.

A gust of wind drove rain into the room. He saw how it splattered across the two men seated at the table nearest the door. Cursing, they spun around on their stools and shouted for her to shut the door before they all were drowned. And then they saw what he did; that she was a woman, and they closed their mouths on curses and simply stared.

With two hands, she pressed the door closed and set the latch. She was heavily cloaked; black, he thought, and glittering with diamante raindrops that spilled off the wool and splashed against the earthen floor. But then she moved into the sphere of lantern light and he saw the cloak was not black after all but blue. Deep, deepest blue, the color of a night without stars, except he thought the crescent moon brooch fastening the cloak would lend enough light to them all.

The hood had slipped. Black-haired she was, with it cut straight at shoulders and again across her brows. Dry, it shone almost blue in the yellow light. Like silk. He wanted to reach out his callused hand and put his fingers in it.

Hardly a step did she take before a man blocked her way. Ugo. He knew Ugo only in passing, for upon occasion—as now—they shared a roadside tavern. Not friends. But not enemies, either. They bore one another no loyalties. In the code of their mutual profession, they did not dare to.

Ugo was an assassin.

But at the moment, Ugo was no more than a man taken by a woman, and intent upon having her.

"Drink?" Ugo asked. Big-voiced he was, to match his bulk and ego, and yet now there was an undertone of something akin to desperation. Well, he could not blame Ugo. A man had only to look at her to want her.

Not a beauty. No. Her edges were hard and sharp as glass, with no softness to them. No blurring of the lines between fragility, femininity. No pliancy. No complaisance in her, either; he knew it almost at once. But there was a keenness to her sex that put him in mind of a knife blade, honed to a sharpness that would bring no pain, none at all, even slicing into the soft belly of a fat merchant who had, perchance, *neglected* to pay his creditor.

She was, in essence, more masculine then feminine, and yet—strangely—it only increased his desire for her.

And Ugo's.

Of course. Ugo's.

"Drink?" Ugo repeated, and the woman slipped by him with silence in her mouth.

Ugo turned. Heavy brows drew down, shrouding his glittering eyes. Brown eyes, peat-brown, glaring after her, with the hot light of need. And pride. Pride roused by her mute refusal; pride smashed down into pieces.

Silence filled the tavern. The men watched with their whores perched on knees and laps, watching also.

"Woman!" Ugo roared.

In the echoes of his shout she stripped leather gloves from her hands. She unfastened the moon brooch and slipped her cloak. It slid off black-clad shoulders; no, blue again. He saw it more clearly now. She dropped the wet cloak to a second stool and sat down at a small table near the roof tree. One hand dipped into a belt-purse and came up with a single coin. It glittered silver in the light.

"Wine," she said into the waiting silence of the room. "Red wine."

The tapster, like all the others, looked at once to Ugo. Ugo showed his strong yellow teeth and took three long strides to the table. In his fingers was a coin. But its patina was merely copper. "Woman," he said, "put your silver away. *I* will buy this wine."

She looked at the copper clenched in his thick-fingered hand. She looked at his face. She looked at the ferocity of his desire. She did not move except to set her coin down upon the table. "No," she said softly, and the word rose up to strike Ugo in his face.

He bared his teeth in a feral display of contempt. "What is it, then—a woman who lies with women?"

Silence.

"*Woman*—" Ugo roared, and reached out to trap her wrist in his hand.

Smoothly, swiftly, she rose. Silver glittered in her hand. But it was not the coin. A knife, and the blade drove home into his belly.

She let Ugo fall across the table even as she pulled the knife free of flesh and muscle. His weight buckled the table; he fell again to smash upon the floor, and she cleaned the blade upon the fabric of his jerkin.

When it was done and the silver coin retrieved, she looked again to the tapster. "Wine," she said. "Red wine."

He brought it in a pewter tankard, stepping carefully around the body on his floor, and when she offered the coin he took it. The tapster's fingers shook.

The woman, still standing by the body, drank. The others did not. To a man, they watched her. To a woman, they judged her. And found themselves lacking, no doubt.

He smiled. Quietly he rose and crossed the tavern to step into a sphere of lantern light. "Lady," he said calmly, "you lack a table. Perhaps you will share mine?"

She took the tankard away from her mouth and he saw how the red wine stained her lips. Closer, she was no more beautiful. He saw nothing of softness in her. But the intensity of her spirit was such that she overshadowed man or woman.

She looked past him to his table. Empty now, for he had beckoned no whore to join him. Even now he did not; of that he was quite certain.

Her eyes came back to him. He saw they were pale blue, almost colorless; in the dimness of the tavern they were very nearly white. Except for the black of the irises.

She smiled. And preceded him to his table.

"Mattias," he said, and sat down. When she did not answer, he knew better than to press her. She drank her wine; he drank his, and when the tankards were empty she bought the next two with shining silver.

"Thank you," he said, "for the wine. And for Ugo's death."

Her eyebrows were straight across the smooth curve of her forehead. "Ugo," she said. "Was that his name?"

"Ugo. No loss."

"An enemy?"

"No. A business acquaintance." Mattias smiled. "His loss is my gain."

She said nothing. She drank.

He wanted to ask her her name, but he refrained. In business, names were only rarely exchanged. A name known gave a man claim on another man's life; he knew better than to lay any claim to her. Though he wanted to.

Her tankard was empty. She did not signal for another. She set it down upon the table and looked at him, and Mattias saw the smile in her eyes though it did not touch her mouth. "Mattias," she said, "have you a room?"

His own tankard, half-full, thumped against the table. "A room. Yes." His tongue felt thick in his mouth. "A room, yes."

This time the smile touched her lips. "Then let us retire to it."

He led her there, to the tiny room under the eaves, and took her clothes from her even as she took his. And there in the tiny room they made the beast with two backs as he had never known it before, in power and passion and helplessness, until he could only lie in the bed and quiver in the darkness.

"Mattias," she said. "Yes."

When he could, he smiled. And asked her who she was.

She shrugged. "Does my name really matter?"

Perhaps not. But there was a need in him to know. "And have you killed men before?"

"Oh, yes."

Her flesh was cool. He felt a chill upon his own. "Many?"

Another shrug. "I have not counted them."

Assassin, he thought. An unusual occupation for a woman, but he had heard of it before. Mattias smiled. "And Ugo thought you preferred women to men."

Yet a third shrug. "Sometimes. I do not discriminate."

He stiffened. Colder still, he sat up. He looked down upon her nakedness. "Like *this*?"

She did not smile. "And do you inquire after mechanics? Or is it a question of simple passion?"

The breath was noisy in his throat. "The last," he said, and said it harshly, because he remembered how much they had shared.

She looked up at him out of the darkness. "Sometimes," she told him clearly.

He looked away from her.

"Judge me not," she said. "What gain is there in that?"

His head snapped back around. "And have you killed *women* as well as men?"

"Oh, yes," she said. "I do not discriminate."

He could not hide the curling of his lips. "At least *that* I have never done."

She shrugged. "When the Book of Life is closed, do you think it will really matter what you have and have not done?"

"And children," he challenged. "Have you killed children as well?"

"Men, women, children." Even in the shadows, he saw a strange serenity in her face. "I do not discriminate."

"Ugo," he charged, "because he wished to buy you a drink."

"I *am* sometimes capricious."

"Woman," he said, "you sicken me."

"Man," she mocked, "I am part of you."

And before he could move to get out of the bed, she placed a hand upon his arm. It stopped him. It stopped him dead.

She knelt beside him. One hand she placed against his left breast. Her palm was cool to the touch, but not cold. And yet he felt a coldness deep within.

Pain sprang up in his chest. He could not draw breath.

"Mattias," she said, "yes."

Her palm was gone from his breast, and yet he felt the grinding pain. It crushed his chest and sent numbness down his left arm, until it touched his fingertips.

She withdrew from his bed of pain. Naked, her shadow lay upon him.

"How much," he gasped, "did they pay you? And name me the name of the man."

"No payment," she said. "No man. What I do, I do for myself."

"Woman!" he cried. "Assassin should not kill assassin!"

Her answer echoed in the room. *"I do not discriminate."*

And as he began to climb down into the valley of the shadow of Death, he knew who she was at last.

THE SONG AND THE FLUTE

Dorothy J. Heydt

Dorothy Heydt appeared in S&S #I with the first of Cynthia's adventures; she submitted this for #II, which was already full. So we were happy to accept it for #III.

I'm not sure whether this falls into the category of "sword" or "sorcery," but it's a magical story anyhow. Enjoy.

Dorothy lives in Berkeley with her husband and two children, boy and girl, plus assorted typewriters, cats, and computers.

The bowl of the sky was the deep blue of Punic glass, and blue as glass was the flat sea beneath. All morning there had been not a breath of wind, not a dolphin arcing out of the still water, not a seagull overhead. The whole of the Mediterranean, as it seemed, had been holding its breath.

Now the sun was nearly overhead, toasting the air to a pale rich gold. And low down, almost flat against the water and close enough for the dolphins to hear, there was a sound: a whisper of music, and the creak of ancient wood, and the rustle of canvas under a single breath of air.

"Next time," Cynthia said, "we must be sure to steal the boat with the new *sails*, not the one with the new paint. I think the owner of this tub had just finished painting her in order to sell her, quick, before she sank under his eyes.''

Demetrios nodded his head "yes" without speaking. He was playing on a little flute of olive wood, playing a strange melody in the Lydian mode, a long strain with many variations. His brow knotted, his head bobbed with childlike earnestness not to make a mistake.

"The wind's picking up," Cynthia went on. "I think your spell has worked. You can stop now."

They sat in a tired old grandmother of a fishing boat, broad-bottomed and creaky, one that had better been left home to nap in the sun. Her sails were patched and worn, and her sheets had grown long frayed hempen whiskers. Her red and white paint, fresh and cheerful, had concealed her age till it was too late. Now it was flaking away as the timbers creaked. The caulking was lavish in her seams, though the way it was working loose promised easy come, easy go.

Still, they had covered two-thirds of the distance from Margaron to Syracuse already, and luck or the gods' favor might see them to landfall yet.

There was no land visible now but a vague smudge to the northwest that might have been Croton. With the wind blowing, even that would soon be out of sight.

"I said, it's worked. You can stop," Cynthia said sharply. She was four years older than Demetrios and had made it clear in their two days' acquaintance that she would take no nonsense from him. But the youth shook his head "no" and went on playing.

"This is the third time through. I think once would have been enough."

The cloudy smudge on the horizon was growing, not shrinking. Plainly it was a real cloud, blowing toward them on the wind as it rose upward from the sea; it was making for a thunderhead.

"Demetrios, too much is as bad as too little; you are blowing up a *storm*! Give me that thing."

But the boy turned around, holding the flute out of her reach while he played the last phrases, playing faster and faster like a tavern dance, tapping his foot to maintain the rhythm. The tune finished, he turned around. "It's dangerous to interrupt a spell, any spell, in the middle," he said with dignity. "I know you don't think much of me, Cynthia, and I admit Father hasn't taught me much about the business. But the first thing I ever learned was never to interrupt him." He tucked the flute into a fold of his bedroll where it lay cushioning the sternpost behind his back.

"All right, all right, I sit corrected," Cynthia muttered.

In the uncomfortable silence they heard a voice murmuring,

"But when we were as far from the land as a voice shouting carries, lightly plying, the swift ship as it drew nearer was seen by the Sirens, and they directed their sweet song toward us: 'Come this way, honored Odysseus, great glory of the Achaians, and stay your ship, so that you can listen here to our singing;' " Palamedes the mage, the father of Demetrios, chanted softly as he sat in the prow and trailed his fingers in the sea, *" 'for no one else has ever sailed past this place in his black ship until he has listened to the honey-sweet voice that issues from our lips; then goes on, well pleased, knowing more than ever he did; for we know everything that the Argives and Trojans did and suffered in wide Troy through the gods' despite. Over all the generous earth we know everything that happens.' "* *

"Go on," Demetrios urged, but the old man was silent, and both his listeners sighed. It was the longest speech Palamedes had made since the Roman ballista stone had taken away his wits at the siege of Margaron, and nothing passed his lips now but quotations: his will had been stunned, leaving only his memory.

"We had a vase once, when I was little, with Odysseus and the Sirens on it," Demetrios said. "A red-figured stamnos, it was as old as Teiresias. The ship had only one bank of rowers. There was Odysseus tied to the mast, and his men rowing away with their ears stopped with wax. There were two Sirens, like birds with women's heads, perched on the rocks above, and a third one falling to her death in the sea. She was fated to die if any man escaped her, so it's said."

*This passage from the *Odyssey* is taken from the translation by Richmond Lattimore, pubished by Harper & Row, 1965.

"That's not in the *Odyssey*. Anyway, Homer had only two Sirens."

"Did he really? I'm not much good at Homer; he talks funny."

"'The isle of the two Sirens,' he said, 'néson Seirénoiin,' not 'Seirénón.' Don't you know a dual when you hear one?"

"Whether I do or not doesn't matter; it's plain the vase-painter didn't. He knew how to paint, though. The vase was my mother's. It was after she died that we started traveling, and I don't know what became of it."

"My mother died when I was born," Cynthia volunteered, "and if she left anything to me I never saw it. Motherhood! what a business."

"Oh Zeus, Cynthia," the boy said, turning pale, "do you have children? You never left them in the city!" He turned and looked anxiously backward over the miles of water that lay between the boat and fallen Margaron. The thundercloud was very high now, boiling outward as they watched into the flat shape of an anvil. The wind was growing cold.

"Don't be a fool, I was only married for six months, before poor old Demodoros got himself killed in a skirmish, in a bean field, with a Roman. Then I miscarried, so I had nothing to show for my six months at all. Your storm-wind is coming up nicely, we'll have enough rain to fill the waterskins, if not swamp the boat."

"Cynthia, I'm sorry. I shouldn't have asked. I didn't know."

"Of course not. Anything we already know, we don't ask about. Don't worry about it." She stared over Palamedes's head into the southwest, and drew in a deep breath. "Worry about that, instead."

It was a ship, just on the edge of the horizon, its masts dark against the sky, its hull half-hidden by the sea. A large ship, to be seen at all at this distance, and moving swiftly northward on a course that must surely cross paths with the little boat within a few miles.

"Well, I don't know who they are, but we don't want to meet them," Cynthia said. "Lean on the steering-oars, I'll shift the sail. We'll tack to the south and sneak behind their backs."

But at this moment the storm-wind reached them, filling the little boat's sail with a jerk and nearly knocking Cynthia overboard. She angled the sail as far to the south as she could, its sheets wrapped round her wrist and her other arm clutching at the sternpost, but the wind was steady and powerful and pushed them almost due west, ready to fall into the great ship's lap. The mast creaked, and the waves slapped against the boat's sides, and the wind whistled through the rigging.

"Who are they?" Demetrios shouted.

Cynthia shrugged as well as one could while holding for dear life onto the sheets. "Roman warship. Roman merchant. Punic warship. Punic merchant. Nobody we want to be known to; even odds if they'd drown us or sell us at their next port of call."

"We should've—" an energetic wave dashed itself in Demetrios's face, and he spluttered and wiped it away. "We should've stuck to the coast."

"*They* stick to the coast, generally; that's why we crossed open sea, to avoid them. This is just pure bad luck."

Steadily the wind carried them westward. The sea was broken into white-flecked waves, dull green now under the gray clouds overhead. At the horizon the sky was still blue, behind the golden shell of the ship that drew steadily nearer. They could see a faint mistiness of spray around her hull far-off, and a fringe of oars, tiny and delicate as the legs of a millipede. There was an eye painted on her prow, round and pitiless and unblinking, and a thin beak before it like the sting of a mosquito. And still she came nearer.

"Jason!" Demetrios said suddenly.

"Jason what?"

"I've just remembered. It was Jason who met the Sirens when he went to Colchis; we used to have a book that told about it. Three Sirens, and they had names which I forget. Jason had Orpheus on board, and he defeated them at singing, and so they escaped."

"And did one of the Sirens fall into the sea?"

"I don't remember; it's been a long time. The book got left behind somewhere, like the red-figured stamnos."

Now the first drops of rain fell, fat and juicy as grapes, and very cold. The wind grew stronger, and the rain thicker, and the drops stung like hail against the skin, skimming along almost parallel to the waves. In moments they were all soaked through, and only Palamedes seemed not to care. Cynthia cursed in Attic, the Koiné, and Egyptian. Demetrios listened with respect.

They were watching when it happened. The great ship, now plainly a Punic warship with three banks of oars and a wicked-looking ram on her prow, seemed to stop dead in the water, as if all her rowers had backed water at once. Then slowly, slowly, like someone getting into an overhot bath, her stern settled into the water. It would take her some time to sink altogether, but her voyaging was over. Demetrios and Cynthia exchanged glances.

"Rocks," he said, half-shouting over the howling wind. "Or shoals at least."

"All right," she said, and pulled the sheet about. "Maybe the wind will let us go *north*." The sail flapped once as she turned it, and filled with wind again, drawing the boat a few points north of west. They could see the Punic ship clearly now, her prow in the air, a few tiny man-figures clinging to her decks or dropping into the sea to swim for shore. There was an island, a small one, no more to be seen above water than a stretch of beach and a spire of rock, indistinct in the mist.

The wind was slacking off now; the thundercloud had passed overhead. Cynthia glanced upward. There was another mass of clouds behind them, but for the moment no rain was falling, and the howling of the wind died away. And in the stillness they heard, faint and sweet as the last fragment of a dream clutched at on waking, a fine thread of song.

A single voice, pure and clear like the voice of a silver flute, singing words that tugged at the edges of the mind, teasing, almost familiar like the memory of a fragrance. The shifting air blew the voice away from them, toward them again, away again. And Cynthia and Demetrios looked at each other and said together, "Sirens." And again, "No, it couldn't be."

"They're supposed to be north of here, anyway," Demetrios added. "Up around Neapolis. I read it somewhere."

"Have you been in Neapolis? I have," Cynthia said. "Good cheap wine, great shellfish, sulfur fumes, thousands of people running around making money. Interminable noise, and no Sirens. And I don't believe in Sirens anyway— Just the same, it's a strange thing, such a great ship to break on such a little island."

The wind shifted again, and blew the voice to them, and she heard faint but clear "Come, Cynthia," and "rest," and then a thin harsh sound like the mew of a seagull, the crying of a tiny child.

Cynthia stood still, her hands clenched on the mast, but Demetrios leaped up and made a dash for the oars lying at his father's feet. But at that moment the east wind picked up again, and the boat jumped forward, and Demetrios fell on his face on the deck. The rotten halyard broke, and the wet sail fell and lay heavily over the deck, and over the boy and his father. From underneath the canvas she could hear him cursing and struggling to get free.

Even with the sail down, the force of the wind was enough to drive them steadily toward the island. It was wreathed in stormcloud now, and the air round about was growing dark. Thunder rumbled overhead, but the voice floated above the noise of air and water. Cynthia clung in misery to the foot of the mast and listened. The song was a lullaby. "Come here, dear child," it sang, "so long abandoned and sadly wandering. No longer vainly ruin your lovely skin with weeping, Beautiful Cynthia; here lives everyone who loves you. For as in the country the lowing calves come running around the cows their mothers when they return from pasture, and bleating kids crowd near the goats with milky udders, so here on shining meadows every mother embraces her own child in her arms, and every child her mother."

The singer paused as if to take breath, and in the pause the infant cried again, an intolerable sound, the child was hungry, or cold. Scarcely knowing what she did, Cynthia fumbled under the sail's edge for the oars. The tears were cold on her cheeks. *Who is that who sings, who cries? My mother, or my child? I never knew either, and they are both dead!*

She couldn't shift the oar; the sail and its wooden yard lay too heavily on it. She crawled to the stern and with the steering-oars guided the boat as best she could toward the island. Her arms ached, her heart ached, and her nose was dripping like a sponge.

Thunder rolled overhead again, and a bolt of lightning split the darkness ahead, burning an instant's vision onto Cynthia's sight. Atop the highest spire the figure stood, her talons gripping the rock, her feathery tail spread out behind, her breast like a dove's breast and her great wings outstretched, all covered in plumage like pure gold. She shone in the darkness like the aureole of the sun. Her hair was bound upon her brow with silver ribbons, her eyes were dark and bright; and her face was no mortal woman's face, but pitiless and serene, indifferent as the stormwind, the face of an immortal.

And beneath her feet, along the beach at the base of the rock, lay the bones of men. Some lay clean and white, picked by the wind and bleached by the sun; some still with the leathery skin stretched taut across them. And one dazed Carthaginian had dragged his broken body this far, to lie beneath her rock, his face lit up with longing, and reached upward with one good arm into the promise and agony of her song. For the Siren sang to each one his own heart's desire.

But the vision was gone in the lightning flash, and Cynthia crouched weeping on the deck, saying, "Liar, liar." The Siren sang her lullaby. The baby cried.

"Liar!" Cynthia screamed, rising to her knees. *"Lying mimicking mocking drab, I'll give you music!"* She put her hands to the deck and began to crawl. It was now raining hard again, and the old wood was saturated and slippery. She spread her arms like a lizard and crept close to the deck, not to be tossed to one side as the boat rolled. The steering-oars beat loudly against the sternpost, a vicious clacking sound like a broken shutter. Her nose bumped against Demetrios's sodden bedroll, and her fingers searched it till they found the flute. She got it to her mouth somehow, found the fipple end, and began to play.

She felt no certainty of getting all the notes right, let alone the variations in proper order. The storm did not seem to care. Hearing its music sounded in its very heart, it exploded into joyous rage, screaming like an eagle, lashing the boat back and forth till Cynthia thought surely the mast must break, the waves wash in, the boat be swamped and the three of them drowned before ever they reached the island. No matter, if the noise drowned out that music.

Something scraped under their bottom; they had run aground on the shoals. Cynthia dropped the flute and reached for the oar again: the yard had shifted and freed it. She planted the blade in the sand and bore against the shaft with all her weight; on three successive swells the boat crept forward and clear of the shoal. The wind flung them forward again, and the oar was wrenched from her hands. She seized the mast again and listened, holding her breath.

For a moment there was only the howling of the wind. Then there sounded a sharp crack, like a tree snapping in a gale, and a rumbling sound sharper than the thunder, building up, rattling and crashing, not dying away. And there came one more sound from the voice, a long descending note, not a cry of pain or grief or any human passion, but the departing cry of an ageless spirit. Cynthia thought she heard some great soft thing fall into the sea, but she could easily have been mistaken.

Then there was no sound but the wind and the thunder and the rattle of falling rock.

It was an hour later, maybe, that the storm cleared away for good and the sun shone again. Gripping the mast and standing as tall as she could, Cynthia could just see what remained of the island: flat beaches nine parts awash that the sea would soon rub into nothing. Of the Punic ship there was no trace but broken wood, and a few shapes floating face-down in the water. Of the Siren there was left nothing at all. Cynthia turned her back on it and began to search the baggage for the waterskins.

The canvas heaved, and an arm emerged between the fallen yard and the prow. "Cynthia?" came a muffled voice from beneath the sail. "Please let me up, we're shipping water down here." Cynthia found the broken end of the halyard and tugged till the sail slid backward and Demetrios could work his way free. "O gods, my head," he muttered. "Father, are you all right?"

Palamedes, emerging from the bottom of the boat, smiled

and settled in the prow again, looking out over the sea. *"Come this way, honored Odysseus, great glory of the Achaians,"* he murmured. *"Come this way, honored Odysseus, great glory of the Achaians,"* as if he had forgotten all the rest.

Demetrios made his way over yard and sail into the stern. He stood there for a long moment, elbows on the sternpost, looking back over the ruin of the island. "I was never so cold in my life," he said. "The sun feels good. Is is still the same day? It felt like forever. I shouted for you, but you never answered."

"I was busy."

"Hard to hear anyway, with the wind and the singing. And now I know how Odysseus felt—Cynthia, what did you hear?"

"Don't ask me, and I won't ask you."

"Oh, I don't mind telling," he said. "She told me I could go home."

"Ha, there you are, waterskin."

"Not that I suppose I'd know Corinth if I saw it now; not the port, or the agora. I remember our house, though, and the street it was on . . . do you know, the Siren knew the name of every tree in our garden. And now she's gone at last. Good riddance. What did she look like?"

"Like a bird—like your vase. Like a spirit of the dead. Whose children were the Furies?"

"Night and Aether's, I think," he said, sitting down beside her. "It doesn't matter. Was she very beautiful?"

"Beautiful, oh yes. So is the Sun, but if you look at him you go blind and lose your way. One for Orpheus, one for Odysseus, one for us. Beautiful lying wretches, they'll never down another man. Oh Demetrios, the last Siren is dead, and now my heart will never break again."

Demetrios by now had his arms round her, trying to pillow her head on his shoulder, but this brought him up with a start. "Don't say that, Cynthia! Some god will hear you and take steps to make a liar of you. Cry if you like, but don't tempt fate."

Cynthia shook free and sat up. "Hmph! Don't let's both behave like fools. Can you splice a rope? Then start mending the halyard, while I empty these rain puddles into the waterskins. After that—'' she picked up her sodden hem and tried to wring it out— "I'd better start bailing."

Classical Note:

The oldest mention of the Sirens is in Homer, and he definitely uses the dual number for them. Later writers, however, seem to have decided that since there were three of everybody else there must have been three Sirens, and gave them various names derived from their qualities: Thelxinoe, Molpe, and Aglaophonos; or Peisinoe, Aglaophe, and Thelxiepeia; or Parthenope, Ligeia, and Leucosia; or maybe just Flopsy, Mopsy, and Cottontail . . . anyway, Apollonios Rhodios puts them into the story of Jason and the Argonauts; he says that when the Argo sailed past the Sirens' island and they tried to lure the Argonauts onto the rocks, Orpheus (who happened to be on board at the time) out-sang them and the Argo escaped. Only Boutes, son of Telson, was seduced by their song and threw himself into the sea, where he would have perished except that he was saved by Aphrodite.

A little creative rationalization—the kind that generally gets applied to Sherlock Holmes or Star Trek—would indicate that there were originally three Sirens, whose names were anything you please, and they made their living by steering ships onto the rocks, rather like the ancient inhabitants of Cornwall. It was fated that if anyone escaped them one of the Sirens would fall to her death. The Argo came and went and one of the Sirens died, leaving two to be met by Odysseus. The single Siren who survived his visit lingered on into early Roman times, when she made the mistake of taking on Cynthia daughter of Euelpides.

The red-figured stamnos is in the British Museum (E.440, C. H. Smith, Catalog of Greek Vases in the British Museum, 1898). It shows Odysseus, tied to the mast of an archaic ship with an eye painted on her prow, double steering-oars, sail tucked up the yardarm, rowers pulling deafly at half-a-dozen oars. Overhead are two Sirens (in the form of birds with women's heads), perched on clouds, and another falling to her death (and about to get tangled in the rigging). One of the survivors is given yet another name, Himeiropa.

Incidentally, the Sirens were the daughters of the river Acheloos and any one of several people, most likely Gaea the Earth. Their physical form was probably derived from old figures on grave monuments, representing spirits of the dead. The Sirens were the companions of Persephone, and when she was abducted by Dis they took the forms of birds to go looking for her, but retained their human heads so as not to lose their lovely voices. All of this is in various sources, mostly Apollonios Rhodios (late 3rd century BC).

JOURNEYTIME
Dana Kramer-Rolls

Dana Kramer-Rolls, a fighter in the SCA, combines authentic battle scenes with sorcery in this gripping story of a young woman priestess in search of her power in a changing society.

From Dana, too, came one of the major members of our household: a mixed-breed German shepherd/wolf, named Signy. Although wolves, contrary to popular folklore, tend to be timid rather than aggressive, their very size makes them appear ferocious—prospective muggers and burglars look at Signy's powerful teeth and jaws and never try to call her bluff.

T he ivory and gold Baton glowed rose in the late sun. Ezme watched it bob with the gait of the pony. She wished she could untie it from the saddle horn and stuff it in her saddlebags. Tax collector indeed! Why couldn't the Silent Ones who guarded the Stone Well do it and save her the trip? The Well lay far above the pass which guarded the border, and it protected something far more precious, the snow pure waters which rushed down every streamed each spring to feed the valley which was the Trencher of the Kingdom of Tremain.

The pony's hooves clopped along sounding out *Ezme-ne*,

Ezme-ne, the honorific of her new rank. She drifted into half-sleep in the saddle. She was again sitting outside the Lady Mother's chamber waiting while the Lady chatted with that stupid oaf who had visited the temple. How could she stand him? A crude Cheval-Priest, more mercenary than Cheval, getting their priestcraft wherever they could pick it up!

Priest indeed! She and Briket had laughed at how he had botched the morning office. Now Briket must be laughing at her. Smug bitch! Briket was assigned to the novice mistress, and she had been Tested and she would begin training in the Great Work, and she would . . . *oh, I hate her*.

She snapped awake as she began to slide from the saddle and looked around, but her escort took no notice. *Thank the Guardians*. It wouldn't do to lose dignity. And after all she might not yet know how to raise the Blue Flame, and healing didn't count, but she *was* a Lesser Priestess of a great House. The endless shocks of the pony's footfalls brought back the pain in her body and heart. *That's what I really am. A sturdy mountain pony like this one, stock, brown-haired and not too important*.

That night stiffness kept her awake. She slipped out of the small tent her escort had set up for her, wrapped herself in a fur against the bitter mountain cold and approached the guard fire.

She had acquired a new escort from the last garrison in the foothills. Two soldiers sat drinking herb tea. "Who passes?" one challenged.

"Lady Ezme-ne." Her voice sounded hollow in the night. The older guard, a sturdy woman with cropped gray hair, rose to her feet.

"Lady, would you honor us? Perhaps some willow bark tea? It does wonders for sore muscles." She added, "At my age I need it, even after a life in the saddle." The young man who sat with her smiled warmly at her. Ezme accepted the transparent attempt to spare her feelings. Summer hunts had been no preparation for this journey. She accepted the tea, and drank in silence. The dark liquid was bitter. What could these folk know of the high things to which she had dedicated her life? She stared at her empty cup and wished she were home.

Who may I thank for this service to the Star Goddess?'' she asked as she got to her feet. Her words sounded thin and pretentious. The Lady Mother Korine-ne would have made them sing like a benediction.

"Lady, thankee," the woman said easily. "I am Sheela, and this here cub is Hrolf."

Ezme nodded, turned abruptly and sought her tent. *I'm here because they don't want me at home. I'm here because I have no Power. And I never will.*

The next afternoon the party arrived at the garrison gate. Yeomen lined the walls with their bows strung, but not nocked. They were challenged, despite the garrison pennants which they flew. The woman who had given Ezme the bark tea rode forward. She was even more formidable in daylight.

"Cheval Sheela-an-Karla, Subcommander of the Third Legion of the Sky Lady, attached to the Fifth Mountain Garrison at Stone Wall, accompanying the Baton-Priestess of Taxes, the Lady Ezme-ne, Lesser Priestess of the House of Eternal Radiance."

She beckoned to Ezme, who rode to her side. "Lady, do you have the Baton ready?"

"Oh, of course." Ezme fumbled for it flushed with anger. Who did this rough woman think she was?

"Easy does it, Lady," Sheela chided gently under her breath. "No point to drop it now."

Ezme steadied her fumbling hands, untied the offending cord and held the Baton aloft. A cheer went up from the yeomen, and the tension drained.

"I never knew the outposts were so glad to pay taxes."

Sheela laughed. "It's not the giving, it's the getting. It's nice to know the Queen hasn't forgotten us out here."

The party moved through the massive gate into the courtyard of the keep.

At Evenmeal, where Ezme had been obligated to say the opening blessing, she formally met the Commander, a sallow beanpole of a woman named Gretchen-an-something-or-other. Outside of that she saw little of the woman, who had made it clear that Ezme should be about her business so that they could get rid of her, only in nicer words. Ezme could see the reasonableness of this. She had no desire to stay anyway. Besides, there had been border raids again.

The Northern Alliance had chosen a new king. Folks said Sismund was brutal. He worshipped the Sky Father, Zor, who was really the Winter King of the Tremain pantheon. But Sismund claimed, or his priests did, that Zor had come to him in a dream and told him that all other God worship was an abomination, and Goddess worship was even worse. The Northerners had always favored boychildren, and held some very quaint ideas about women. Many fine women soldiers, merchants, and artisans had come to Tremain from the north to find new homes. This had long been a sore point between the two nations.

Now Sismund had found an elegant way to "deal with the goats and hens," as the farmers say "with one fodder." A holy war against Tremain would also put his "brother" lords from his alliance where he wished them, subservient to his Kingship, only (of course) until the common enemy was crushed. Ezme had heard Cheval Barak go on about this when he had visited the House and she served at table. How dull it had seemed to her then! Now she wished she had listened. Rumor had it that Priestesses and even village seers of both genders had been killed. There were more rumors that units were marching up to the pass.

One night at Evenmeal Ezme sat beside the Subcommander. It was that disgusting pea and porkfat stew again. She had hardly eaten since she had arrived. The beer, what little was left in this no-season between winter and spring, was sour. The pudding, of grated old bread and fat seasoned with what few dried fruits the cooks had managed to squirrel away, was not much better, but her hunger and the coaxing of her tablemates had allowed her to force down a portion. The Great Hall was the only warm place in the garrison, save for the Commander's study. After supper those who were not on duty would spend their evenings gambling or gossiping. It also gave those who wished to couple a chance at some privacy in the corners of the barns or sleeping quarters.

Sheela was telling some loud story about the day's practice melee, while the subject of the story writhed in humiliation at his table on the low end of the Hall, to the amusement of his mates.

"Then he picks up his mace, by the bumpy end, mind ye, this after he had sat on it." Yelps and howls filled the hall. "And then he turns to Jace, over there, and yells, 'Roll the flank,' and Jace yells back, 'That's your own flank, herd breath,' and then Jace yelps, 'Look behind you!' and Arold turns, and there is the whole Blue Squad just standing there tapping their swords and maces on their shields and grinning."

Ezme was blushing. She could feel the humiliation of the cadet radiating like the stifling heat in the hall. She staggered to her feet, and reeled to the door. She was sick in the snow. She stood shivering in the cold night. Would it never be warm up here? Was there no escape for her from the cold, from these soldiers. She felt someone come up behind her. *Good,* she thought, *let them see me. Let them leave me alone.*

"Need some help, Lady?" It was Cheval Sheela.

Ezme shook her head.

"Are you ill? Are you with child?"

"No, no, no." Ezme was shaking. She stepped back when Sheela tried to hold her.

Sheela shrugged. "I'll be here, if you need me, Lady." She turned to go.

"Why worry about me? No one cares about me. After what you did to that boy in there how dare you?"

"How dare I? You stupid little bitch! That's my job. If that idiot loses his head in battle, real battle, he will lose his life. And the lives of more of my young'uns out there. I did him a favor. I do my job. You see to yours." She spun away, leaving Ezme shaken beyond tears.

The next morning Ezme begged off sitting at breakfast. Great rolling sobs had convulsed her like the orgasm of mourning most of the night. She had tried to say her office to the sun, but the words wouldn't come. She moved with the jerkiness of the undead as she dressed, and walked to her makeshift study in the barracks hall. She stared ahead, not seeing anyone, and continued counting and recounting endless notations about grain, goats, chickens, births, and deaths. She would do her job.

But she refused audience with a small flock of petitioning

farm folk. She was ill, they were told. Tomorrow certainly. And she started taking meals in her room.

After a few days she painfully returned to her place and table, but she kept to herself.

It was on the first morning of spring's warm promise that a garrison scout returned from the Alliance side with reports of troop buildups. They could expect an attack. Ezme had left the door to the barracks open to invite in the new warmth, and relieve the damp, acrid soldier smell of the large room.

"What is the commotion?" she asked of a passing cadet.

"Signal fire, Lady."

"What is that?"

"We are sending a message to the capital. And asking for reinforcements."

"The capital. How? Don't you have a Mindspeaker?"

The lad looked at her, his eyes widening. "Oh, no, Lady. Can you do it? Sweet Mother! Sometimes the message doesn't relay. A rain can dampen the smoke. Or anything. Oh, please, Lady, can you Mindspeak?"

"No, of course not. I'm only a Lesser Priestess." she snapped. The lad stiffened at her answer.

"I beg your pardon," he said formally. "I meant no offense. If my Lady will excuse me. . . ."

"Yes, of course, go." She watched him leave and saw the signal party ride out the courtyard gates. Her stomach ached again. Would she pass the autumn tests? She fought back tears. *I will be empowered by a chosen priest like everybody else. I will pass the Test.* She clenched her hands until they were white.

In the long four days that followed, Ezme watched listlessly from her desk as soldiers prepared armor, arrows, and the like. Wagons rumbled in and out of the courtyard with barrels and sacks of foodstuffs.

Ezme toyed with her peas and fat stew. The High Table was now merely another place for a Staff Meeting. It made it easier for Ezme to avoid conversation with Sheela. Not that Sheela seemed to remember that horrible night in the snow. It took Ezme a moment to realize that Sheela was talking to her.

". . . would be useful, Lady. Can you do it!"

"Pardon, I didn't hear."

"We don't know if they will have a Priest with them. Doesn't happen often up here but you never know. Can you set Wards against Spellwar?"

"No."

"Control elements? Weather? Douse fires? *Start* fires?"

Ezme shook her head at each item.

"Heal?"

"I am not to be trained for that. I am to go to a High Temple at the capital to finish my training, if I can pass the Tests."

"And what the Gods use is that?" Sheela snapped.

"You wouldn't understand." Ezme shot back. There was a short silence. Then the fear of their common danger overcame Ezme's desire to leave for her room.

"Lady Cheval, I have met Sovereign Legate Cheval Barak. Perhaps if I sent a message to him. . . ."

Sheela looked at her with a puzzled half smile. Ezme's stomach lurched. *Can't I say anything right,* she thought.

"Barak. I would to all the Battle Goddesses and Gods he were here! Don't they tell you anything at your temple? Barak is under house arrest. The greatest strategist since Krak the Mighty has been locked up for heresy for offending one of those ever-so-holy priests of yours. A declared heretic for saying no more than what every farm lad in Tremain says morning, noon, and night."

A moonturn ago Ezme would have argued, or sat in smug silence, but now this struck her to the heart. He was Reverend Mother's friend, wasn't he? Perhaps Mother was also a heretic. Or his jailer? Did someone else watch them all? The aridness in her soul crystallized into the dark of the Queen of Death.

The door to the Great Hall slammed open, as a yeoman rushed in with a message from a lookout. Sheela strode down the hall to him, listened, nodded and returned to the table.

Her voice vibrated through the hall. "My Lady Commander, reinforcements are coming. Sharpsighters have seen a scouting party of five."

Cheerful cheers shook the hall. The garrison was under strength. Many yeomen had left to prepare for the thaw and early planting, or to move herds to spring pasture. Most had not yet been located and called back.

Within the hour the small band had arrived. Ezme thought the Cheval who commanded seemed oddly familiar.

"Welcome, Lord Cheval Merkor," Gretchen greeted him. "How far behind is the main party?"

"Lady, we *are* the main party." His rough voice carried throughout the hall. Silence screamed in the air. "Your request was denied."

"Why? Is there fighting elsewhere? Where?"

"No, Lady. Some damn lowlands priest decided you were being hasty, and aid would cost too much."

Ezme remembered. This was the same Cheval-Priest who had visited her temple. How could he say those things? It was heresy! The word struck her like a chill.

". . . don't like letting their troops out of sight," someone was going on.

". . . enough to fear from their own flocks."

Ezme shrank back, feeling their hatred. Was she even safe here?

That night a sergeant was dispatched to try to round up a few more able bodies. And then they again waited. Next morning there was still no enemy in sight. Ezme sat staring mindlessly at a scroll.

The first faint thunder came around midday. She had never heard it in this life but she knew—an army on the march. The sound was drowned out in moments as everybody in the compound scurried to report to units and battleplaces.

"Open the portal, open the portal," shouted a lookout. Ezme pushed back her desk, spilling the scrolls to the packed dirt floor, and rushed into the courtyard.

A frenzied pony galloped through the gate. A short spear shaft danced drunkenly from the back of the body tied to the saddle. Sheela and a few cadets danced in a crazy counterpoint trying to halt the terrified beast. A parchment snapped like a banner from the shaft. Sheela reined in the pony, and snatched the paper. The fury in her face melted away the crowd of onlookers more surely then her famous battlefield voice.

Ezme shouted in frustration. "What does it say?"

Sheela thrust the note at her. "You might as well know now as later."

"Send out your Goddess whore. I have a thousand spears to ram her where she likes it!"

"Holy Mother," Ezme gasped, "But how did anybody know a priestess was here?"

"There must be spies," Sheela sounded chillingly matter-of-fact.

The body slid from the saddle, hanging from the ropes which bound it to the pony like a broken branch, the contorted face swaying back and forth, dead eyes staring at Ezme in accusation. Her temples pounded. The clammy sweat stung her eyes. She could see nothing but those dead eyes, tunneled in the sparkling swirling blackness. Voices in her head screamed, *It's your fault, you will kill them all. You can do nothing. No Wards, no Battlefire, nothing. You will bring death.* "No, no," the moan burst from her as from far away. "I'll go to them. Then you will be safe."

Sheela's voice was almost gentle. "That's very brave, child, but it would do no good. They have to take the garrison to move down the valley. If they get in here we are all dead. Cadet." She paged a passing lad. "Over here. Take the Lady Ezme-ne to her rooms." She addressed Ezme. "Stay there."

Ezme felt drained. She had been prepared for martyrdom, and now she was being led to her room like a naughty child.

The cadet had her by the arm and was force-marching her to her quarters when Sheela shouted something after them.

"You spoke well, Priestess. You said the right thing."

When they were around a corner Ezme shook off the cadet's hand. "I can go myself, thank you. You are dismissed."

"Please, Lady. That was an order."

"Oh, all right, all right. Let's get it over with."

Another cadet brought her dinner of cold fat and peas, and also some rough clothes. "The subcommander thinks it were better if you didn't stick out like a white crow in case—"he faltered—"well, in case something should happen."

The tramping continued for a while, until she could hear the distinct sounds of ponies, feet, and the clank of armor plate on armor plate. And the terrible rumbling of a war engine. Then it stopped.

At daybreak the siege began. The sky blackened with whistling arrows again and again. The defenders refused the attack and let the enemy expend their fire power, collecting what arrows they could to fire back when the time came. Then came the tarry balls of swamp fire which stuck to and seared away living flesh. Ezme looked for the signs of a blue glow which would mean they were Power charged, but there were none. At least the dead would stay dead.

She knelt at the hearth gate. Her brow furrowed with intensity, she tried and tried to light a fire, but the cold kindling mocked her anguished attempt. It was no good. She knew she could not help.

All night she tried to pray, but all she could hear was the whistle of arrows, the screams of the hellburned and arrow-struck, and the shouts of command. The new daylight was a hazy bloodblack as when the Skyhawk swallowed the Sungoddess. Ezme couldn't stand the not-knowing, not-helping any longer. She flung open the door. There was no guard. Of course not. Why waste a soldier on one unimportant Priestess?

She ran out into the courtyard. The sight staggered her. The cookhouse and stable were burning, although the barracks and the commandhouse were still intact. A pile of bodies, partly covered by oilskins, lay stinking by a wall, while an improvised tent was propped up nearby for the village healers. She gasped with shame as she remembered how she had mocked Healers. But she had studied herbs. Perhaps she could do some good there. A fireball whizzed overhead, and she ran with terror. It was almost dusk.

"Here, girl, you too," someone shouted at her. "Are you deaf? Over here. Take this end." She was roughly pushed toward a cot where a wounded yeoman lay. She lifted her end and trudged where she was told. Then she was ordered to load a wagon with wounded. Although some flanking action had been taken, the main force was on the northern gate. There was still an escape route, not for the soldiers who would have to hold this post to their deaths, but for the dead and wounded.

"Can you drive a team, girl?"

Automatically she said yes, remembering the festival wagon rolling garlanded through the streets on holy days. But as she took the reins, suddenly she wondered if she could drive a team down these mountain roads. But she had no choice, now.

And so Lady Ezme-ne, Lesser Priestess of the House of Eternal Radiance, left the garrison driving a wagon carrying the dead. The procession of wagons and ponies clattered in the pitch black, even these mountain folk trusting to the Godseeing abilities of their beasts to guide them. They halted at the village of Ishapass. Ezme mutely helped unload the cart, and then drove it to the stabler. After attending to the chores at the stable, the work party was permitted to go to the inn for a meal. At least here a few gray root vegetables swam in the endless sea of pea and fat stew. She fell asleep at the table.

Someone was shaking at her shoulder. "Hey, girl." She looked up and saw the sergeant who had come and gone time and again to sweep for recruits.

"What's a healthy one like you doing here? Runaway? You know what they do to runaways in wartime?" The guardsman with him jerked his thumb over his throat with a nasty grin. They didn't recognize her. Perhaps she should tell them. What was the use?

"I was driving a deadcart."

"Well, you're not anymore. Over there with the rest."

She joined a ragged handful of locals, was marched into a cottage, and issued an armored gambison, an iron battlebonnet, a bow and a quiver with a few arrows. She was also given wool trews and a short tunic in exchange for the dress she wore. The holes and blood stains were still evident on the armor. It was clear who had supplied them. Zor, Lord God of Winter, King of Death, Hope of the Northern Alliance and Quartermaster to Tremain.

It was breaking dawn when they slipped into the Stone Well Garrison. "Barracks over there." How well she knew where the barracks were. She found an empty cot and fell into it, and was asleep instantly. It seemed like moments or perhaps years when she was roused again. Her unit was marched to the wall and assigned to a sergeant. They were ordered to nock an arrow, draw and hold. In the gentle green meadows around the House of Eternal Radiance she had been thought an excellent archer, picking off small game for the table with her light bow, but here her arms burned and quivered.

"Please, Goddess," she implored with the simple logic of battlefield theology, "just one more moment, let me hold it one more moment, oh, please, Goddess."

But her arrow shot off before the command to volley. The sergeant strode over to her position, cursing.

"If you loose early again I'll flog you, girl. I'll flog you myself. Understand?"

Ezme, white-faced, tight-lipped, nodded.

They pulled again. Ezme managed to hold and fire with her mates, again and again. Finally satisfied, the sergeant ordered the group down.

As they sat huddled by the foot of the wall eating a meager meal of soaked bread, an oak of a man, his red hair shot with gray, came and sat next to her.

"You're not from around here," he stated, but she knew it was a question.

"No, um, er, I was here visiting a friend."

"Oh." His eyebrows shot up.

Ezme groaned to herself. Perhaps farmfolk didn't visit far-off friends. She wouldn't know.

The man went on pleasantly enough. "Name's Alfrit. You?"

"Ezme." Perhaps he's just in a mood for coupling.

"You look like my young'un, Saria. If she hadn't been with child she'd be here."

Ezme saw the pain in his eyes. *And probably died here,* she thought. She had no answers.

Alfrit and Ezme's mates sat at meal as long as they were allowed, taking advantage of the cookfires. By now they had accepted Ezme's quietness for shyness. One of the lads was holding forth on the sexual tastes of the enemy to the guffaws of the others, but Alfrit was quietly staring into the fire.

"It makes no sense," he said suddenly. "They are praying to Zor without Zek. How can the world balance? Who would fire our loins in the spring or cause the goats to mount? Oh, Zor is a good friend on the Battlefield or in winter, but one without the other—it's like asking me to choose between my Saria and her baby.''

Ezme sat in wonder. These simple folks believed in the old stories. They even used the Ancient Names, as if the gods were friends from the village. She tested her Names of Power. Winter King, Summer King. She felt the thrill of sovereignty. What could these people know of such Gifts of Power? She surveyed the rough faces. The thought stabbed her, *but what do I know of the need to breed herds so that all may eat, and live, and love?*

Alfrit had warmed to his topic. ''They don't want to pray to any of the Goddesses. Can you think of sowing the fields, or for that matter a pretty little thing like Ezme, here—'' he winked at her—''without the Mother!''

''Aye, the Mother for you, old man, but Starti for me,'' a young yeoman replied, grinning suggestively at Ezme. She felt a blush rise. Was this the same Love Goddess who in the Great Temple stirred such passion in Her chosen ones that the priests castrated themselves for Her and the priestesses gave themselves in ecstasy to all comers?

''Don't you be rushing her, now, Ulf,'' Alfrit answered. ''She's got the work of the Ezmeid to do yet.''

Ezme was puzzled. ''The Ezmeid?''

''Your namesake, Ezme. The three white crow sisters who serve Morgul.''

''She's the Battle Lady of the Sun, isn't she?''

''You don't call the Gods by their real names, then?'' Alfrit's sharp eyes stared at her. ''That clears the beer! Visiting a friend, eh? You're a runaway, all right. You're a temple runaway.'' He mistook her shock for agreement and scooped her up in his arms. ''Don't fear, child. None of us will tell, even for the reward. There is not one here who hadn't a cousin or child who showed a Gift and was taken away. You can stay with my oathmate Brekke and me, if we live. You can help with Saria's chores with the new one coming. Once you're oathbound they'll not take you back.''

''Maybe there is hope for you yet, Ulf,'' a girl teased.

But Ulf's eyes glistened with tears. ''My ma's a Healer. They took my sister. I never saw her again . . .'' He choked back a sob. ''Maybe ma can teach you if you have the Gift.''

Ezme sat frozen in Alfrit's fatherly embrace. Nothing was as it had seemed. "I didn't know—I was temple born," she confessed. "Why do they take your children?"

Alfrit released her and poured a bowl of herb tea from the pot on the cookfire.

"Near as I can tell, it's to fight with each other. All the Temples want the biggest army of Priests. If they were minding their stalls, Sismund would never be able to get over the border, but they sit in council and they fight like bad neighbors over a stud fee. And if we have needs, we have to beg, not do for ourselves."

That night Ezme dreamed that Briket was chasing her down a black cave scourging her and screaming "Heretic, heretic."

The next day action was sporadic, but in one last burst tarballs lit up the dusk. As one flew over Ezme's head, it dropped spots of its burning death on her arm. She screamed, her cry scarcely heard among the screams throbbing through the compound. She beat on her arm with clots of dirt as she had been taught, until the fire ceased eating her living flesh. She did not leave her post.

She drew at command, held, the tears of pain streaming down her face, her stomach lurching. "Fire at will." She spotted movement in a bush below, lit up the rainstorm of fire arrows. She aimed and loosed. A figure, like a child's Winterday toy, fell from the bush. A cheer went up from her companions.

"Good shooting, Ezme."

"A Sharpsighter for sure."

"You shoot like a Guardian, child."

Soon after, the sergeant came down the ranks, calling for the wounded.

"Over here, sergeant," Alfrit called. And then, "Ezme, show him the arm."

It was aching in earnest, but she said, "No, it's nothing."

"Don't be stupid, child. If you lost it you'd be no good to anyone."

The sergeant's lantern revealed the swelling and weeping wounds.

"Go down to the Healer's tent," he ordered. "And good shooting, lass."

Ezme flushed and quickly turned to obey, as the tears welled up. She was sobbing by the time she got to the healer's tent.

"I'm sorry. I'm sorry." She babbled through her tears. "It's not the pain. I'm all right. There are others so much worse."

"It's all right, dear." The healer was a huge woman with the face of the Mother.

"But, I'm not really crying," Ezme protested miserably.

"Hush, child. It's all right. Cry, child. Cry for all of us."

Ezme rocked back and forth, the moans coming from the well of fear and pain, as Bessie-the-Healer's deft fingers cut away burnt flesh and packed the wound with powdered herbs.

For the next days, Ezme helped in the Healer's ward, her arm still too swollen to return to the wall. It was there they took Arold "Mace Sitter." He had never had the chance to try his training. He had been hit by tarfire while supervising the last evacuation of the ponies. He died the same day. Ezme looked for her "family" with each new casualty, and prayed thanks each time she did not find them, until she realized that the dead were not brought here. She prayed for Alfrit and Ulf and the others with simple prayers.

Three days later Sheela found her sitting by the cookfire. "Wondered what became of you. Guess I figured you had abandoned the Baton and run off."

"The Baton. Oh, Sweet Goddess! I had forgotten." She told Sheela all that had happened.

"Just as well. We need archers more than we need priestesses. You've changed, you know."

"I dear say." Ezme smiled. "What will you do with me now?"

"Do? Nothing. If we get out of this alive, which I doubt, I guess you'll ride back with the Baton."

Ezme began thoughtfully. "I don't want to leave. For all of it, the dying, the hunger. I don't want to leave you all. I don't know anything anymore."

"Well—" Sheela wearily pulled herself to her feet—"that's

a good start.'' As Ezme watched her leave she thought *What did that mean?*

The next morning the siege ended as suddenly as it had begun. The enemy melted into the hills like late frost. After a while the troops were called from their posts. Sheela sought out Ezme. ''Time to become a Lady again, I'm afraid.''

Ezme listened with rapt attention at the staff meeting. Was the retreat a ploy to lure out sally parties, mop them up, and then hit the undermanned garrison at leisure? But outriders had seen no signs of the enemy so it was probably safe to send out parties to survey damage and announce the restoration of civil order. Their final decision was to send Lady Ezme-ne to the Temple of the Stone Wall to finish her duties, as the tax records at the garrison had become problematical after the barracks burned down. Cheval Sheela would head the party. Cheval Merkor would accompany them.

Ezme breathed the astringent pungency of the evergreen forest, heard the splattering of the spring meltwaters, saw moss-covered rocks hiding ferns, with a newness she had never known.

''Glad to be alive?'' Sheela drew up beside her.

''Oh, yes.'' Ezme's eyes sparkled.

''Me too. Every time I live through one.''

Sheela moved off up the line to where Merkor rode.

Ezme watched them. *Odd how much less clumsy he looks.* The thought flitted through her mind unbidden. She blushed. How stupid she had been.

But as they approached the Temple the day darkened. Ezme felt a wave of nausea for the first time in weeks.

Merkor rode to her at a fast clip. ''Have you been Tested yet?'' There was urgency in the question.

Ezme faltered in confusion, the doubts bringing color to her face. ''No.''

''Can you shield yourself?''

''Of course I can.'' *Every temple child can,* she felt like adding.

''Then do so.'' He rode back to the front of the column.

The sweet sickly smell of rotting meat struck her. She breathed into her heart and began the visualization of light around her, but the agitation clawing at her was too strong.

Sheela led the party off the path. She motioned to her scouts, who dismounted and silently disappeared into the forest which clung to the slopes lining the road. They soon returned. The Temple had fallen to the Alliance, but was not well guarded.

"Not the Well." Ezme moaned under her breath.

"Merkor, take half the force, yeomen too, and flank the rear," Sheela ordered. "The wall is breached in a number of places. You'll have no trouble getting in. Horn blast is the signal. When you hear it, hit them."

He rode off with his party through the forest.

"Archers, to the cliff over there. Cover fire. And watch what you aim at when we get in there."

Sheela paced by, giving the two parties time to position. "Move out." she hissed.

The horn screamed shrilly. They hit the gate at a charge. The guard, mostly untrained and untried, fell back. But the few veterans in the courtyard had been warned and the fighting broke down in the chaos of the melee field. Merkor rode in from the rear, herding the rest of the Alliance force, who had tried to escape. The enemy was surrounded and the net drawn around them. It was soon over.

There was no sign in the now silent yard of the Silent Ones who guarded the Sacred Waters, nor of the handful who served their few worldly needs. The uneasiness in Ezme's heart had solidified into a breath-choking oppression.

Sheela barked, "Hrolf, you and two cadets to the stable. Sam, you and two others to the cookhouse. Alrik, you have the main party. Do something with them." She gestured at the captives lying hands over head in the courtyard. "Mark, Will, and you two, with me. Lady, I'd wait out here if I were you."

"No."

"As you wish."

They entered the Temple. Knowing what they would find did not prepare them. What was left of a bloated corpse had been staked out, gutted, and flayed. That was probably not all that they had done to her. The brutal violation of the others was more obvious. The Temple had been smeared with their entrails and the body of an unborn child was found floating in the Well.

The sight left even Sheela gray-faced and shaking. She bellowed, shattering the cold silence. "All right, all right. Let's get them up. Will, bring oilskins. We'll burn them in the courtyard."

Merkor softly whispered, "They're not all dead."

A cadet was shouting something from the doorway. "Cheval, Cheval, come see what we've got!"

Sheela, Merkor, and Ezme strode out. Hrolf and several others were wrestling to subdue a writhing figure. As Ezme approached, it was clear the man was a priest, probably a Zor Priest. His once white robe was blotched with dried brown blood. He shouted obscenity after obscenity at them.

"Whore, bitch-lover!"

Hrolf prodded him roughly with a spear. "Says he was the one who ordered this."

The priest ranted on. "I'll cleanse your well of sin by the blood of the whore goddess. I fixed them. They'll never be free. I bound them here. Never die, never go away."

Ezme watched as if she were miles away. His meaningless gibber spat from his mouth moistened with sunflashing spittle.

"What shall we do with him, Lady?" Sheela was asking her.

Do with him? He was insane, probably beyond the help of the Mindhealers. Do with him! Then he spoke his death. He looked into Ezme's eyes, the lust of his hate stripping her flesh from her bones, and screamed. "I'll ram the pike of Zor up you, bitch. Then I'll do it to this man-woman here. Then I'll sweep down the mountain and valley and ram the holes of all your sister whores."

Ezme shook as if lightning had hit. She saw in a still crack between the motion of time, this beast ripping out the unborn child from Alfrit's daughter, and the tear-bathed face of Mother Korine staring at her from the mutilated body which lay crawling with maggots, staked to the temple floor. And she saw something to pall the rest. The tortured spirits of the Silent Ones oozed screaming bound by the power which defiled the place. She never knew when she pulled Sheela's sword from its scabbard. She only felt its thrust into the Zor Priest's chest.

It was a clumsy kill. She twisted her wrist as the blade hit bone. He was still screaming when Merkor finished the job. Ezme watched the thrill of Merkor's arm thrusting forward, the sunbleached hairs on his arm outlining the muscles flexing and twisting as his blade bit and slid liquidly in and in and into the Zor Priest. Time and life resumed with the thud of Merkor's crossguard against the corpse's chest.

Merkor said the office for the dead, which he knew only too well. But both he and Ezme knew it was an empty gesture. What had been done would need more than ''God's speed and farewell.''

Ezme wandered the compound that night, drawn by a dream of half memory, while the streaming strands of what had been Silent Ones swirled and screamed. She saw Merkor sitting by the cookfire. She felt pulled toward him, by something she did not understand. Perhaps it was only that she had shared the kill with him, like two mated mountain wolves. She invited him with her eyes, letting the hunger guide her.

He rose and followed her to the stables.

There was no tender fondling nor exploratory groping. The power of the battle Goddess Morgul came on them, and he was Zor. As he thrust his power into her she was transformed into victim and victor as she was claimed by Arzgul, the Queen of Death. They were swept into the rape and horror of this defiled place, into the act of vengeance, the punishment of the vanquished to pay for the killed and maimed sword brothers, the unequivocal claim of the conquered land. They climaxed together in sacrifice to the power of death.

Like a bridegroom, Merkor hardened soon again, as the Lady Starti empowered him and they coupled with the hot insistence of Zek—the King of Death not replaced but transformed into the brother was was not other but self, pounding new life into the body of the Spring Queen, Izmael, as the rape of the conquered turns soon to the marriage bed and the birthing chamber.

By morning they spent the last of the gift of the Gods in the sweet, gentle, slow joy of the power of the Mother of the

Groves, he the stag, she the doe, he Kroth the Smith, she Brekid the Weaver, savoring the nectar of lovers as oathmates, caring and equal.

In the darkness of their final consummation, a veil parted and the streaming screaming souls sighed in ecstasy and slipped beyond, unfettered, unbound.

Before dawn, Ezme rose quietly to seek the privy. She pleasured in the stiffness of lovemaking. The calm stilled her. A shaft of the new sunlight illuminated her face. The words of the Hymn to the Morning Sun, words denied her all these days, months, years, lifetimes since she had come up the mountain flooded unbidden to her consciousness.

"O, Mighty Warrior, Sovereign, Maiden of the Sun,
Who splendid shines in Battle heat."

How often had she mouthed these words thoughtlessly?

By whose Blazing Spear the enemy is undone.
Whose Righteousness knows no defeat."

The words hummed in the very shafts of light hurtling through the mountain vista.

Now the Holy One was Sovereign, burning away injustice with her searing fire of Truth. And now Mother, Creatrix of the World, the fire of the loins, the renewal of spring, growth of summer, She who nurtured forgave, and healed. And then She was the Comfort in Death, the dark womb of knowledge, and finally again the young Battle Queen closing the endless circle of creation. And Ezme stood at the Center of All Things, and the veil parted once more and this Place was again Sacred, its ground holy, its air pure, the sunlight blazing in the cool deep waters of the Well.

And Ezme knew beyond knowledge what it was that filled a man of peace like Alfrit and a woman of war like Sheela, so that all who walked in this life with them were oathmate, sibling, and "young'un," one in She Who has Many Names, and that no temple office made a preistess, but it was her own body, spirit and soul, her love—no, *Her* love!

And Ezme gave thanks for the terrible blessing of the Goddess.

*   *   *

The next day they questioned the prisoners. The dead priest had raised a small army to attack the main garrison. He was the type of fanatic Sismund encouraged. The priest supposed that his troops felt as he did and neglected to pay them. When the local pillaging had run out, they deserted to return to their farms and herds and Spring planting. The priest had used the siege as a diversion to take and ravage the Well. It had been his only objective.

Ezme had been uneasy at how to behave toward Merkor, but he had indicated that he welcomed her more conventional company as well, and they remained blanket-companions.

Sheela ordered a halt early the last day down the mountain so that they would arrive at the garrison midmorning of the next day. Merkor sat on a log cleaning his sword and watching a yeoman lay the cookfire. Ezme sat beside him, watching butterflies.

"Merkor—" she felt uneasy suddenly—"you are a Priest. Were you tested?"

"Yes."

"Well, did you pass . . . I mean . . . do you?"

"Have the Gifts?"

"I'm so afraid I don't . . ." she said.

He grinned at her. "I do."

She sat up and looked at him. "Then why didn't you use them?"

He sighed heavily. "The Temple Adepts make such a damnable game out of it! If I had Warded the garrison I would have lasted maybe one tenth of a day turn. Then I would have been as crisp as a Midsummer fruit tart. Sweetheart, if I had had to give you time to get out I would have done it, but for day-to-day fighting no. I'm more useful alive."

It was growing dark. He rose and stood behind her. He spoke to her in a voice of command, the command of the temple, not the battlefield.

"LIGHT THE FIRE!"

Ezme sat, not comprehending.

"LIGHT THE FIRE."

She put out her hands to the neat pile of damp wood. She withdrew deep into herself. Suddenly she could feel the warmth, the glow of the Sun. It rose in her heart. And she could feel it warm her back as she felt the warmth of it swell in Merkor's heart, the heart of her lover and friend. She drew it to her. And then she felt Sheela, going about her business somewhere in camp, and she could feel the love this warrior held behind her testy manner, and she drew it to her.

In an orgasm of wonder she reached with fiery fingers to the cold damp pile of kindling and she embraced it with the Sun. A spark! It distracted her. It went out. She reached for it again, more easily this time. And it sparked, and fired, the whole cookfire adance with little sparkling flames.

She was laughing and crying all at once.

"Fun, isn't it?" Merkor was smiling and holding her.

There was much remarking that night on the superior quality of the food, although it was still only gruel and jerky. Even the young'uns taken prisoner had formed a chorus and were bidding to outdo the southerners with their famous talent for singing in harmony.

Ezme, Merkor, and Sheela sat apart. "Merkor, why didn't you use the power fire on the wall?" Ezme was still puzzled by this newness.

"Don't you know by now what dying by magic like that does?"

The specter of the undead chilled her. The strains of the prisoner came to her. "I guess I would rather take my chances with a sword than do that to any of those poor lads."

"Power is a tricky thing." Merkor stared at the dancing flames.

"They always told me at the Temple that I would need to be tested and initiated by coupling according to the proper rituals in the Temple chamber. With us it just happened."

"They tell you that so that they can control the Power, but it is there for all."

Sheela growled, joining them. "That's why the Temple elite are taking away all the young village healers. Damn their eyes, how do they expect us to go on? Are we supposed to crawl to them every time a young'un breaks a bone?"

"The yeomen I fought with on the wall said that, too. They know the Gods so well—probably better than I do. Zor without Zek. What are the Northerners up to? It's not right."

"It's not just the northerners. It's us too," Merkor said. "When I came from the capital I had heard that Zor worship was to be banned in Tremain. They will have Zor without Zek, we Zek without Zor. Power needs harmony and balance. We have lived with Harmony in the realm of the Gods since the first man and woman. And now it will be gone. I am afraid but I go on trying to be a priest and a soldier. Maybe I can do some good out here."

"I don't want to go back to the Temple. I will never trust priests again. I have seen too much." Ezme told him.

"There is another way, you know," Sheela said, "You could come back to us."

"Be a Cheval-Priestess?"

Sheela went on, her eyes boring into Ezme's, "You could 'Cross the Spear' with the fall cadet class. You'd probably be ready to be elevated to Candidus in a year or two. I'd wager a yearturn's pay there would be one or two Cheval-Priests and Priestesses who would combat happily for your company on your Journeytime after that."

"I think I have begun my Journeytime out of season." Her brows knitted. "Merkor, do I have the ability?"

Merkor guffawed. "Love, you have more battle experience than most Chevals. As for sword work, what the Gods don't provide Sheela will beat into you. Trust in that."

"But what of the Temple. If I go back they will insist on Testing me. They will know I have the Power. They will know everything." Tears glistened in Ezme's eyes. "I could get you all killed."

"Merkor, can you shield her, or block her mind?" He shook his head, "I could but I won't. She is still too fragile in the Power. It could destroy her."

Ezme rose and went to her saddlebags. She reverently pulled out the chamois pouch which held the Baton. Deliberately she walked back to the fire. She unwrapped the Baton, held it aloft as an offering is held aloft. Then she cast it into the fire. Merkor leaped to stop her, but she flung out her arm to block him. Then she stretched out her hands to the singeing wand.

"Go to the Temple of the Mother. Serve as you should have served all this time." The fire blazed and cracked, its fury sending sparks and dancing patterns to the trees around. When the blaze died back there was nothing but ash and slag.

"The Lady Ezme-ne died in the Siege of the Garrison of Stone Wall." Ezme said in a voice of authority. Then she added, sounding suddenly like a child, "What did I do? I suppose someday I'll have to explain all this." She shrugged, and went on. "I know my path now. I have no regrets."

Her voice had regained its sureness. She had chosen a steep and twisting path, but it was clean, like the mountain streams bubbling in the dark forest beside her. Merkor rose, kissed her tenderly on the brow and knelt before her.

"When you Cross the Spear as a cadet, I will be honored to place it at your feet."

"And when you cross, I will place the Sword in your hands." Sheela stood behind her, the warrior's rough hands placed tenderly on Ezme's shoulders. Ezme reached out and embraced them both. She breathed the words softly. "So be it."

And so it was.

ORPHEUS
Mary Frances Zambreno

Mary Frances Zambreno made her writing debut in an anthology of Darkover fiction, *Sword of Chaos* (DAW, 1982) and recently sold a story to the Hubbard Foundations's *Writers of the Future*, receiving more in prize money for her short story than I got for either of my first two novels.

One of the characteristics of heroines in sword and sorcery fiction is that they tend to travel in pairs. However, I'd venture a guess that very few S&S heroines have a werewolf for a partner.

H ellmouth.

Jennet the Berserker stared into gray mist and felt her own mouth go dry. She'd never been to Hell before, but a job was a job. Servia Eodis wanted her lover Cerinthus brought back from the dead, and Jennet from Ybaria needed money.

"Ready?" she called to her werewolf-partner.

"Almost. It's harder with a new moon." Sylvia folded her tunic. "I did warn you about looking for work in Cilia. I was born on this island. I left because of jobs like this one."

"Let's start clear. We go in by the hole the old witch told us about. Then you turn wolf and get us past the Hound."

"And after that you're on your own. Wolves don't talk much. Are you sure the spell will take us to the Throne?"

"It should, once we're past the barrier behind the Hound." Jennet took a deep breath. "Let's go. Change."

Sylvia dropped to all fours. Her form blurred, face lengthening—curly black hair rippled. Then a green-eyed wolf looked calmly up. Jennet took a firm grip on her partner's mane. The things they did for money—

Hellmouth was a dark tunnel extending off into infinity. Dripping rocks, small insects—something fluttered past her hair. Jennet repressed a shudder. Give her a good open sword fight any day. Ahead the sense of bleak distance narrowed to a point of burning darkness, black fire: the Gate, and the Hound who guarded it. He had three heads, all jawed and slavering, but the one in the center held the only mind. Its eyes alone were open, burning red. Jennet loosed her hold on Sylvia's ruff.

"Mind you be careful," she whispered. "We don't want any hell-puppies to raise."

The she-wolf flowed smoothly forward. Her black fur gleamed in the dim red light. Flirtatiously, she lowered her forelegs and whined. The Hound's three heads turned with a certain masculine interest. Sylvia slipped to the right, taunting. Jennet edged left.

Now! He had her—the right head took the impudent female's neck in its jaws, while the left and center bayed in ragged chorus. Sylvia squirmed, not too hard. Jennet leaped across the thin barrier of flame behind the Hound's back and groped for her talisman.

"Sylvia! Wolf! I'm across!"

Her partner came toward her, still coquettishly luring, even as the Hound realized their deceit. The great jaws started to close but the right head was smaller than the center. Blindly Jennet reached into the tangle of dog and wolf. She grabbed a black foreleg and hung on.

"*Per me si va nella citta dolente,*" she spelled gasping, "*nel'etterno dolore, tra la perduta gente—*"

The walls melted around them. She could hear the Hound's frustrated, terrified baying even as she clung grimly to Sylvia. A twisting, sickening lurch—a smell unlike anything she had ever dreamed—a heave—

Hound, wolf, and nauseated berserker fell together in a circle of cold light. Jennet looked up. A tall, pale woman with rippling sea-silver hair sat before them: Lycoris, sea and death, Lady of the Night. Beside Her—

And she had thought the Hound had red eyes! Flaming Hell itself glowed in the face of the god. Perdis, the Ever-Changing Destroyer— He raised a hand, and Sylvia snarled, twisting. The Hound yelped like a frightened puppy and ran tail-down, even as the wolf shifted back to a disheveled, naked, but undeniable human.

"I allow no transformations here except My own," the god said. His face flickered. Around Him, a thousand dim shapes bowed and moaned. Jennet gulped, looked away.

"I am wolf and woman," Sylvia said steadily, if a trifle breathlessly. "I pay homage to my Lady Who Sends the Moon."

A faint, cold smile touched the goddess, but her Lord Captor was not pleased.

"Why have you come?"

"On behalf of the Lady Servia Eodis of Tramonta." Jennet stood slowly. Her hand itched for a blade. "Her lover, Cerinthus, died on the second day of the calends of the third month. She wants him back."

"What does she offer?"

"A year of her life for one of his."

Doubt touched the red eyes. One slim hand turned into a snake and hissed at them. "Cerinthus. I do not recall."

"On the second day of the third calends," Jennet repeated. "Of a bloody flux. He's a poet—lyric, not epic."

"Oh, yes. . . ." The snake vanished, replaced by a small ape that chattered and giggled. "He has been Ours more than a moon. If his body comes back, most of his mind will stay here."

"Lady Servia knows. She has plans for his body."

One finger pointed. "He is here."

A tall, slim ghost—Servia had described her lover as fair and graceful, and this one must have been blond in life. He even looked like a lyric poet as he bowed languidly to the Lord and Lady of the Dead. Jennet nodded.

"That's him. We'll take him back the way we came."

Perdis stroked a dove that had appeared on the arm of his throne. "Are you willing to pay the forfeit?"

"Another one?"

Snakes oozed around his shoulders. "A life. To bring back his."

"Servia—"

"Wisely did not come herself. I accept her offer. I can do without this poor fool's body for a year in exchange for her early arrival. But whose life will pay for the effort of bringing him back at all? I see only two here."

Jennet held very still. "Keep him, then."

The god smiled. "But I have accepted the bargain. . . ."

Lycoris looked down pale and far, away from the god Who imprisoned Her. Sylvia growled softly in her human throat, and Jennet felt the werewolf's terror as her own. How dare He! How dare Servia try to take them this way! She must have known, the little bitch—

"A life, eh?" Jennet said thickly, rage choking her. "Come and take it!"

The she-wolf snarled. Lycoris help her! Jennet made the dark throne in one leap, her sword a cold shaft of light in the hell-red blackness. The god raised one elegant hand and a warrior stood before her, deathpale but flesh and blood. Jennet swung. Her sword took out shield, shoulder and all. Another stood behind him, massive with a battle ax. She caught him with knee and dagger—his flesh felt slimy and he did not bleed, but he fell for all of that. Sylvia took the third in the throat. Jennet kicked out at a fourth who melted like smoke in front of her.

"Stand and fight, damn you!" she howled.

"They are all damned, here." The god laughed, but Jennet was beyond sense.

"*One* isn't," she said, and caught Him in a forward rush.

His flesh burned colder than steel in moonlight and His eyes—but she wouldn't look at His eyes. She fastened strong, living hands around His neck.

"A life, is it?" she panted. "Take your own!"

"Jennet!" Sylvia cried between woman and wolf. "You can't kill death!"

"I can if it's not my turn to die!" She squeezed.

The god writhed in her hands. A lion roared at her, teeth dripping blood, but it was not her blood. Then a great serpent bent poisonous fangs toward her breast; desperately, she hung on, rolling as its coils lashed about her. A bloody-eyed stag leaped in her arms, but she had hunted deer before. Cerinthus himself, then Sylvia, with green eyes turned red. Jennet hung on. An eel twisted sleekly in her grasp, a small, delicate ocelot that almost slipped away from her. A god again, enraged beyond all divine power, raged, beautiful and terrible beyond seeing or belief—

And then she was grasping nothing, and they were in the open air before Hellmouth again, she and Sylvia and Cerinthus off to one side, and the sun was just coming up over the eastern ride.

She rolled onto her back and opened her hands, feeling the anger and fear drain out of her into the new day. The blue sky had never looked so beautiful before.

Sylvia crouched beside her.

"Jennet? Are you all right?"

"I'll live," she said, savoring the words. "How did you start to turn wolf again down there? I thought it took moonlight."

"I had moonlight, with the goddess there. I am Her creature, after all, and I don't suppose She cared for Perdis threatening me. Even if She does have to live with Him half the year. But it took so long, and then when you challenged Him—"

"Is that what I did?"

"Challenge the god to a wrestling match and He has to face you on almost evey terms. I didn't realize at first, but you . . ." Sylvia looked at her curiously. "You mean you didn't know? I thought—but then why did you tackle Him?"

"I just got so damn mad," Jennet admitted sheepishly. "Servia must have known when she sent us down there what to expect. She knew everything else. I was just so furious, I forgot He was a god."

Cerinthus was staring dazedly at the sunrise. He was pale

and alive, but there was no soul in his eyes. Sylvia started to dress.

"What about him, then? Do we deliver him as expected?"

"Not quite." Jennet smiled evilly. "Ever held a looping knife?"

"Jennet! You wouldn't!"

"Why not? Ransom a lover, get a eunuch. Serves her right. It isn't as if he were really alive."

"But she won't pay."

"Oh yes she will. Or if she won't, her husband will. That will teach her to drive hard bargains."

Sylvia looked thoughtful. "Do you suppose the god knew you would think of something like this if He let us go?"

"Maybe." Jennet paused, then grinned. "I wouldn't put it past Him."

She could almost hear the hellish laughter from below.

SCARLET EYES
Millea Kenin

One of the parameters of these Sword and Sorceress volumes is that I do not buy science fiction or stories with a technological "feel," and for that reason I at first rejected Millea Kenin's "Scarlet Eyes." Nevertheless, the story haunted my memory so that I asked Millea to resubmit it if it had not sold elsewhere. A story which I *could* not dismiss from my mind could not be denied to this audience.

And, after all, the great category of fantasy literature can embrace subclasses such as fantasy and sword and sorcery; C.L. Moore especially gave us not only the heroine Jirel of Joiry, but some excellent science fiction such as Vintage Season, a classic of time-travel writing. It is in the spirit of C.L. Moore that I present this story, a splendid blend of adventure fantasy in the sword and sorcery vein and science fiction.

Millea Kenin is a graphic artist who teaches in the Berkeley Adult School and edits *Empire*, the magazine for would-be writers of science fiction. She also edits *Owlflight*, a "small literary magazine," one of the magazines which walk the narrow line between fanzines and professional magazines.

And, of course, she writes—as this story adequately proves.

The girl in the doorway meets my eyes. and I blink and try to focus. Her dark eyes are huge, a little tilted in her pale face—a wide-browed, pointy cat-face. Everything else is hidden by her black, hooded cloak. She enters the inn's common room. weaving her way among the long wooden table set crosswise to the door. She ignores the other dozen or so folk at breakfast and makes her way toward me, as if she's recognized me. I haven't the faintest idea who she is.

Suddenly I'm not even sure who *I* am. My head sinks toward the bowl of porridge in front of me, and I *am* sure that the sight and smell of it will make me sick in another minute. I push it out of the way and swallow hard.

Garnelle lays her hand on mine. "What's wrong, Den?" she asks.

I prop my elbows on the table and my aching head on my hands. "Would say I had a hangover, but I only had three drinks last night. I'm sure of that." I don't claim to be one of the great heroes of the tavern (or anywhere else), but *anybody* has a better head for drink than that. I've had more than that at dinner before old Simarre tried to stop me, and I've never felt like this in my life. . . .

Simarre? I never met anybody named Simarre in my life, either. What have I done to myself? And why do I think this is happening because of something I did?

The girl in the black cloak has reached our table. She stands across from my sister and me, a little uncertain. "Are you Den and Garnelle Scorry?" she asks.

My heart gives a little bound. Den Scorry! That's who I am! The family hero, the founder of my House! To think that I should be reliving *his* life!

Reliving? Hey. I've been Den Scorry all my life. No one with any claim to brains would mistake me for a hero, and I certainly haven't founded any house. No brat calls me father. . . .

Seeing me sitting there and blinking, Garnelle answers, "Yeah, he's Den and I'm Gar. Can we do something for you?"

"I hope so. The people from the caravan said you'd done good work guarding them to Warnford, and you should be available now."

"We are. You're looking for bodyguards?"

"Well . . . sort of." She looks around cautiously. Some eyes have turned our way. It would be hard to pick up a conversation at another table, over the general noise, but it might be possible. "Could we go someplace quieter? You have a private room?"

"Sure." Garnelle swallows the last spoonful of her porridge, drains her mug of cider, and stand up. I rise with her, too quickly, and have to support myself with my palms flat on the table for a moment. I must pull myself together somehow; whatever is wrong will pass quickly, I hope, and I don't want this young person to decide not to hire us because I'm not fit. We need the work too much.

We go upstairs to the room Gar and I slept in last night. Our packs are still there, seemingly undisturbed; our cash and our swords are on us, of course. I turn to close the door behind us, sway, and have to clutch the doorframe.

"What's wrong?" the girl asks. "Are you hurt, or sick?"

I sit down on the bed, prop my head in my hands once more, and think about that. The others sit down at either side of me. In a moment, one thing comes clear to me. "Somebody drugged my drinks last night," I tell the others.

"That explains it," Gar says thoughtfully. "It was only a little while after I came up to bed, when three jolly fellows hauled you up the stairs and slung you in after me. There wasn't enough time, now I come to think of it, for you to get drunk."

"Would you recognize them again? I wouldn't."

"No. I should have realized something funny was going

on, but I just thought you'd been fool enough to get drunk. I was mad at you and hardly looked at them.''

"But why would three strangers drug your drink?'' the cloaked girl asks.

I make a face. "To rob me, of course. They'd have thought I was carrying my half of our pay—actually, Gar was holding all but the price of a few rounds of drinks. No harm done so far; I'll be all right. But if you're looking to hire someone to use their brains, you'll have to rely on Garnelle. Old thud and blunder, that's me.'' I manage to grin, and the girl grins back. Her face lights up; it's the nicest thing I've seen today.

"In any case,'' Gar says, "those three or others just as bad may still be around, and whether or not it turns out we can do the work you need done, you're right not to want your business spread about.''

She nods, murmurs a short incantation under her breath (I try in vain to overhear, then wonder why I should care). and then motions us to silence. She sits still as if she's straining to hear something; presently she nods. "No one's listening.'' I wonder why I wish I knew what sort of a spy-detecting spell she's using.

"Now, why I need your help,'' she says, throwing back her hood to reveal sleek black hair in a long braid. "I'm Lysse of the Ankorries; my father, Lord Ankorry, is a sorcerer in the service of the Light, and since I'm his only child he's taught me as his apprentice.''

I sit up and take notice. If only I'd had a father who'd taught or even encouraged me, instead of one who'd tried to thwart all my efforts to teach myself out of the books I'd had to hide from him. . . .

I don't remember my father. I don't know how to read or write or work spells. Garnelle and I spent our 'prentice-years as slaveys to Red Dargo, practicing every kind of hand weapon known in the Reaches of Aldery till all our muscles were one permanent ache. That wasn't so many years ago, but now we're small-time hired swords looking for work, which is what this noble maiden seems to be offering. I hope I'm not too crazy to do my share.

"Do you know about seek-stones?'' Lysse asks. I nod, and

Gar shakes her head, then looks at me in some surprise. "They light up when the person they're sealed to is in trouble, and they're set so they can swivel, and they always point toward the place where that person is. Since my father must often travel to do his work, he gave me a seek-stone sealed to him. I keep it with me always, and when it began to glow two weeks ago I set out to follow its direction."

"Alone, child?" Gar asks.

"Don't call me child. I'm fourteen. I don't suppose you're all that much older."

Five years—no, why did I think that? Seven. Half again as old. Gar and I are twins.

"Sorry, my lady," says Gar with a rueful grin. I cradle my splitting head and keep quiet.

Lysse replies to Gar with her own marvelous grin. "Just Lysse. Anyway, yes, I went alone, in my boat, following the coast. And I've found where Father is." She rises and goes over to the window, which overlooks the sea. Garnelle follows and sees which island Lysse is pointing toward. I don't feel like getting up just now.

"That island is a stronghold of the sorcerer Valdofor. He and my father have worked against each other before; he must be holding Father prisoner now."

"So what do you want us to do?" Gar asks. "I've heard of Valdofor. If he's powerful enough to hold your father against his will, and all the sorcery you know is what your father taught you, what you need is other sorcerers to help you. What good do you think a sword-fighters can do?"

Lysse smiles wryly. That name—Lysse of the Ankorries—is awfully familiar. I've read it in *The Founding of Scorry's Keep*. Didn't Den Scorry marry Lysse, eventually? No. I'm Den Scorry, right now; I could not have read about all sorts of things that haven't happened yet. Still: a lovely creature, Lysse. But a more skilled sorceress than I, though years younger. . . . Why do I keep thinking I'm a sorceress—I, an unlettered swordsman?

"Have you any ideas," Lysse is asking, "about how to get one sorcerer to help another?" That won't have changed by my time. . . . No. I've got to stop thinking crazy thoughts and listen to her. She's saying, "No, I think you're my best chance. You can ward off material attacks while I concentrate on spells. I can pay ten gold pieces to each of you afterward.''

"That's if we survive. It seems a bit low. Twenty apiece,'' says Garnelle.

"Twenty's all I've got.''

"Kid, you don't know how to bargain.'' Gar laughs. "You should have offered us five each.''

Lysse frowns. "If we do manage to free my father, I expect he'll reward you.'' She clenches her fists till the knuckles go white. "I don't have time to hunt around for helpers. I'm going today, with you or by myself. Take it or leave it.'' She's trembling, stiffening against it.

Gar puts an arm around Lysse's shoulders. "We'll come with you. Won't we, Den?''

"Of course. We're fools for danger.'' That brings a flash of the luminous grin back to Lysse's worried face.

So the two of us buckle on our swords and our packs. Garnelle is still carrying the cash, so she pays our shot at the inn. We follow Lysse out along the shore, and no one follows us as we go past the docks to where a little boat is beached on a sand spit.

It's about the size of a dinghy, and will fit the three of us and our gear with only a bit of crowding. But it's a rather strange boat; it has neither oars nor oarlocks, sail nor keel nor rudder, but it has a carved and painted figurehead of a sea-hawk.

Lysse motions us to stow our gear under the thwarts and then sit down; then she gets in and kneels on the bow thwart. The thing is still sitting on the sand, you realize. She takes a little silver knife from her belt and holds it in her hands over the hawk-head.

"Hear me, my hawk. I who made you
Call upon you now.
Carry me where I bid you go
By my blood upon your prow."

She nicks her left thumb and lets three drops of blood fall on the figurehead. Even as she wipes the knife on her cloak hem and puts it away, the boat shudders, comes to life, slides itself into the water like a seal, and glides swiftly and steadily in the direction of the island on the horizon.

I like this boat. I'm going to make myself one someday. I'll get Lysse to show me how; I'd rather that than gold.

It's not moving any faster than if we were rowing it, so it will take awhile for the boat to reach the island. I'd been expecting to use this time to sort out the crazy thoughts in my head. But I find I'm in no shape to do any clear thinking. The official records never mentioned that Den Scorry tended to get seasick; I suppose that would have tarnished his heroic image. I have never been so miserable in my life. I doubt I'd have risked working the spell that brought me here if I'd known what I was letting myself in for . . .

Official records? I don't usually get seasick, actually; this might be another result of the drug those thieves slipped me last night. I can remember every time I've been in a boat before just as clearly as I can remember learning my stitches, scales and letters from old Simarre in Scorry's Keep . . .

Why do I keep thinking there's such a place? Ma's cottage was hardly a Keep. All this is so confusing that I stop throwing up and sit up straight. The sun on the dancing waves makes my head ache worse than ever. Merciful Brothers, what's happening to me?

I stare down at my arms and hands, knuckles white and tendons tight as I grip the gunwales. The fuzzy blond hair, the freckles, the peeling sunburn are all just the way they were yesterday; all my scars are in the usual places and I can remember how I got each one. Why do I have this dizzy feeling that being Den Scorry isn't at all what I expected it to be? Why do I feel as if my arms ought to be slim, smooth and pale, the hands narrow with long polished nails?

The effort to figure it out makes me queasy again. I have to lean over the side and puke some more. The Brothers know where it's coming from; I haven't eaten anything since last night. Perhaps I should be offering a prayer to the two of Them, that in Their merciful wisdom They will help me get my head straight.

"Are you too sick to try for it today?" Lysse asks. "Shall I put back to the mainland? Now you've promised to help I suppose I can wait another day."

"No, I'll be all right. We won't be killed today in any case, so we might as well go on."

"What? Den, what makes you so sure we won't be killed today?" Gar asks.

"We'll live for years and years and found Scorry's Keep; I read about it—" I break off abruptly.

"What in the sweet Brothers' names are you talking about, Den?"

"I don't know!" I moan, clutching my head. "I'll tell you as soon as I've figured it out. But sail on. It will all work out. Trust me." Though I don't know why she should.

I'm sure it's true, though. I've read *The Founding of Scorry's Keep* so many times that I'd surely remember if it said anything about how Den and Garnelle Scorry met Lysse of the Ankorries, so all this must have happened before the official records begin. Which must mean the three of us will live to be in them.

My memories are starting to sort themselves out. It was only yesterday that Father informed me that I was to marry Bardold of the Kargs, a senile miser who's buried three wives so far. I decided I'd have to work a spell to escape. The problem with being self-taught is that spells which require finesse must be taught in person, master to apprentice. All anyone can learn from books are simple, strong, and often dangerous ones. The only one I was sure I could do properly, with ingredients I had on hand, was one that would enable me to re-live a previous incarnation, one in which I had been a success in life.

The spell has worked perfectly. I reached the mind of my earlier self at a moment of abnormally low consciousness (because of the drugged drink) and now I'm Den Scorry—to think that I had been Den Scorry, of all people, in a past life!—and I'm remembering being Tyrenne of the Scorries two hundred years later. (Remembering? The future? Ah well. So the family became noble! But that's not much to crow about, considering that at least one of my descendants is—will be—a prize ass; I mean my father when I'm Tyrenne.) To put it as straight as I can to myself, I've been Den Scorry all my life, and I've also been Tyrenne, but till just now Den and Tyrenne were two different people.

Just trying to sort it out makes my head throb and my stomach heave. Maybe one human body can't function with this kind of double-mindedness. Maybe I won't stop being sick when I reach dry land, and most likely my coordination will be off, too. I should have told Lysse to put back when there was time; now it's too late. Lysse is beaching the boat in a little cove, murmuring the words that will send it to sleep until she needs it again. Gar is getting her gear together, and I should be doing the same.

People say Garnelle looks like my little brother instead of my twin sister. (Always wanted a sister-it was awful being an only child.) Her blond hair is cut the same as mine; we have the same high-bridged freckled nose and wiry build. Would be vain of me to say I think she looks great. We help each other on with our helmets-it's easy to tell us apart at a glance, I'm the one with a beard. How weird. I'm scratching my chin, confused again, and she's looking at me, worried again.

Just then a small gang of monsters comes crashing through the brush. We have our swords out at the same moment; it sounds like only one sword being drawn. There are half a dozen of them. Each has two arms and two legs and stands more or less the height of a man, but otherwise they're all different, scaly or spiny or squashy and slimy, with fangs and claws or arms like tentacles.

They're also clumsy, not seeming to know quite what to do with their axes and maces. And they don't seem to be quite where they look like they are—strokes of mine that should have connected are off by an inch or two. A sign of illusion. The only illusion-breaking spells I know are far too complicated to attempt while fighting for my life. "Lysse!" I yell, and am surprised by the depth of my voice. "These aren't what the look like. Can you break illusions?"

I hear her small, serious voice begin to chant, and can't help trying to hear and memorize her words. A lizard-type gets too close to me with an axe; I dodge a moment too late, and there's a tiny nick on my left thigh. The weapons are bloody real. Damn! I *am* off my form.

I hear a cry from Gar and pivot, gutting the scaly axe-wielder as I do. She too has felled one, a moment before I did, and seen the illusion break. The creatures that lie bleeding to death at our feet are two scrawny human boys in slave tunics. The sight of the monsters didn't nauseate me at all—in fact, I was just thinking that there's nothing like a good brisk fight to make one feel better—but now I'm glad my stomach is already empty. The remaining disguised slave-boys are fighting for their lives and still outnumber us, unskilled though they are, and Gar and I are at a disadvantage now that we're trying to stop them without hurting them.

Lysse come to the end of her chant with a loud cry: "Va-ohu!" At once four dazed, ill-armed boys stand before us, looking even more confused than I've been feeling.

"Throw down your weapons," I say, and they throw them in a pile. For the first time I realize that being Tyrenne as well as Den is going to come in handy. I don't need to ask Lysse's help this time; I know the appropriate word of power and say it, and watch the four of them slowly sink down, curl up, close their eyes and start to snore.

"They'll be out for a couple of hours," I say off-handedly.

Lysse and Gar are both staring at me. "How in the sweet Brothers' names did you do that?" Gar asks.

"I'll tell you later. It's a long story." She and I wipe our swords, pick up our shields and head inland with Lysse between us, following a rough, overgrown path uphill.

In a little while we come to a tower built of rough stones. We walk all around it but can see no doors or windows. We're on high enough ground now to see that there are no other buildings on the island.

"Well, let's try some opening spells." Maybe it's the relief of not feeling sick anymore, but I'm starting to feel cocky. "If mine don't work, Lysse, you can try."

Garnelle looks at me narrowly, but doesn't say anything. I hear what I'm sounding like, and realize for the thousandth time that she's worth six of me. She's worth six of Den and Tyrenne combined, come to that.

"I really want to tell you what's happened to me, and I promise I will as soon as we can sit somewhere quiet and take the time. Now ssh," though she hasn't spoken. I close my eyes and wait till I have the feel of the place—suddenly feeling almost too edgy to concentrate, but nothing attacks us; we might as well be alone on the island.

Presently I get a sense of where the hidden door is and station myself opposite it. I think about the words and passes for a moment, assuring myself that I've got them right, then work the spell. The stones crumble where I point to them, making a door-sized hole right in front of us, and a huge flame shoots out.

We throw ourselves flat, and Lysse yells, "Va-ohu!" without any of the preparation. The word alone seems to be enough; the flame is gone, and not an eyelash of any of us singed. We sit up cautiously. For a moment all the three of us can do is sit there, clinging to one another, and laugh.

Then we peer in at the doorway. There's a spiral staircase leading up. "Should I—should we," Lysse says to me very politely, showing me up for the oaf I've just been, "put a silencing spell on us all, do you think?"

"If it makes you feel better." I shrug. "Valdofor must know we're here." And if we had any sense we wouldn't be. It's all been *much* too easy so far.

I make sure my sword is loose in the sheath and lead the way up the stairs; the others follow close behind. When we get to the room at the top, it becomes clear why Valdofor has paid so little attention to our small invasion. He's busy.

At least, he is if he's the tall man in the many-colored cloak who stands with his back to the doorway we have just come through. On the floor before him is a pentagram, and in its center several things I don't look at too closely. One is a black cock with its head off—that's about the prettiest of the lot.

There is a naked man chained to the wall opposite the door. He looks gaunt, exhausted, and filthy. Lysse, behind me, gives a little gasp, quickly checked, and her father looks up and meets her eyes; as he looks past me I can see his own eyes are sunken and bloodshot. but would otherwise be like hers.

"All is in readiness, despite your hindrance," the cloaked man is saying in a quiet, cold, almost bored-sounding voice. "All that remains to complete the ritual is the speaking of the Name. You need only pronounce it, and you shall have water at once, and all you require for comfort presently."

The chained man bites his lip; that's all he does.

"Oh, yes, I know the children are here," says Valdofor, still detached, still bored, not bothering to turn around and look at us. "But there's not much they can do, and if you persist in your silence, I may have to make things quite uncomfortable for them, beginning with your daughter."

I realize that a chill has been creeping up my body from the soles of my feet for several seconds now, though I didn't see or hear Valdor do anything to activate a spell. Already I can't move my legs at all, and when I try to draw my sword my arm moves more and more slowly and freezes with only an inch of blade outside the sheath. Any instant now the paralysis will reach my jaw. I can think of only one thing to do. I don't stop to think that Lord Ankorry must have thought of the same thing many days ago, and would have used it to free himself if there wasn't some strong reason against it.

I speak the Word of Unbinding.

Several things happen, more or less at once. "Oh, *no*, you fool!" Lord Ankorry cries, even as his chains unfasten themselves and he crumples to the floor. All our belts and laces unfasten themselves. Lysse pushes past me and even past Valdofor (but remembers to skirt the pentagram); I see her hair unbraiding itself as if the strands were living serpents, while she kneels by her father's side. I feel exhausted as suddenly as if I had lifted a weight greater than my own—and then I feel the floor begin to shake and see cracks appear in the walls.

Valdofor turns to face me. He has a hard, bloodless, ageless face like the statue of a handsome man; unlike Lord Ankorry, he has not grown a beard. "You see," he says without much more expression than before, "this whole island was held together by binding spells that took me a good deal of time and effort, as my colleague there was well aware. I think it will take another minute or two for the whole thing to disintegrate, and months for me to build it up again. But meanwhile, I am not sorry to say, I believe you and your friends are doomed—unless you know the art of teleportation." He sighs, and vanishes.

Lord Ankorry lifts his head from Lysse's lap. "It's all right," he says hoarsely. "Now, I can summon the demon—for now he will do my bidding." Gathering all his strength, he sits up, faces the pentagram and clearly pronounces a single syllable—which I will not repeat.

In the midst of the pentagram a misty form appears, grows darker and more solid till it looks like a column of thunder-cloud the size of a large man. From near its summit two huge scarlet eyes glare at Lord Ankorry.

"Why have you summoned me?" it asks in a voice of muted thunder.

"We seek your aid, O demon," says Lord Ankorry.

"If so, then you'd best mend your manners. We adepts of the ninth plane do not appreciate being called by epithets that insult our race."

"I did not know the word I used was an epithet. No insult was intended, and I beg you to accept my pardon, sir." Lord Ankorry inclines his weary head in a courtly manner. The tower is trembling and cracking around us as if there's an earthquake in progress.

I feel like laughing, but manage to control myself.

"Very well. What would you have me do?" asks the scarlet-eyed being (which I mustn't call a demon).

"Take us to Ankorry's Keep before this island disintegrates."

"And the slaves," says Garnelle, bless her. I've always known she was worth six of me. I'd forgotten all about them.

"And my boat," says Lysse.

"That is," says Lord Ankorry, "take every human being now on this island, and the spell-boat, to Ankorry's Keep." He speaks quite calmly, but huge cracks are appearing in the floor and the quaking is getting more and more severe. We scramble to grab our swords and belts and other possessions before they fall through the cracks, and us as well.

"You know my price," says the being.

"Seven years of the sight of my eyes, that you may observe this plane."

I flash on the thought that the being may want to haggle—and don't know whether I feel more like laughing or screaming—but it seems this is the standard fee. At once we are floating in an opalescent bubble of still air: Lysse, with her father, in the little boat; Garnelle and I and the four slaves (still sound asleep) in a circle around it.

Far below us, the island crumbles apart in a last convulsive quake and sinks beneath the waves. There is a whirlpool for a moment, and then stillness behind us as our bubble floats away.

"Lysse," says Lord Ankorry weakly. "introduce me to your companions." he does, and when I look at him I see his eyes have already become two glowing scarlet orbs without whites or pupils. Somehow, I am sure that though those eyes see me, Lord Ankorry cannot; there is something blind and groping about the way he turns his face toward the sound of my voice.

"I'm sorry, my lord. I'm afraid what I did was very foolish."

"No, lad; I'm sorry I said it was. I should have had the courage to speak that word at the very first—I did not because I was sure the island would crumble in an instant, not slowly as it did." He pauses, gathering the breath and strength to go on. Lysse wraps her black cloak around him. "I should have spoken the word anyway," he says bitterly, "even if it meant my death straightway, rather than let my seekstone lure Lysse to share my danger. I am glad it is I who can pay the price."

"No, Father," she cries, tears starting in her eyes as she bends over to kiss him, and he closes his eyelids rather than let her come so close to those scarlet eyes.

The bubble sways, and we hear the muted-thunder voice (or is it just inside our heads? I can't really tell). "Open your eyes so I can see, and think hard of the direction of Ankorry's Keep." Lord Ankorry obeys, and bubble soars steady on course once more.

The four freed slaves are waking up—that voice must have helped to rouse them. Garnelle reassures them that they are safe and free, and Lysse tells them the story of her adventures and ours till this moment. Then Gar gives me a look I've been expecting.

"I think this is that quiet moment we've been waiting for," she says.

So I have to explain what I, Tyrenne, have done to become one with me, Den. This does not make the former slaves any less confused, and Lord Ankorry's energy is so taken up with keeping his eyes open that I'm not sure he's been listening at all. But Lysse is fascinated. "Does that mean that when you die you'll wake up, still both of you, in Tyrenne's body?"

"Sweet Brothers, with all her—I mean my—I mean her problems still to face? How should I know? I don't even know if all I've read that comes between now and then is unchangeable. But I swear this," I add rashly, "from this time on I shall be known as Den-Tyren Scorry, and I shall see to it that if I ever do any deeds worth writing down, that they be written in that name. Then the book cannot be the same as what I've—what I will have—what I won't have read. Oh, Brothers blast it!"

"But that might mean Tyrenne will never be born, and then—" Her slim fingers rake her unbound hair as she grapples with the nonsense I've made of time.

Then maybe I won't marry Lysse after all. That would be a misfortune. I haven't told her that the book says I'm going to, and maybe I'd better not. Maybe *she'd* rather not. Sweet Brothers!

I've been ignoring Gar, and she's staring at me horrified, as if I'd turned into a monster before her eyes. "Den-Tyren," she mutters, and bursts into tears.

I hug her hard, swords and all, clang-bang. "Hey, Gar, love. I'm still your brother. I haven't stopped being anything I ever was. And if I'm your little sister too—that just makes me even gladder to have you. You don't know how much I longed to have a sister when I was Tyrenne."

"I'm sorry, Den." She wipes her eyes and pulls herself together.

Lord Ankorry's voice comes to us, faint but calm, from Lysse's lap. "It would be fair for me to tell my part of the sotry—how Valdofor outwitted and captured me, and why he was trying to force me to summon the—the adept. If I live, I will do so. But I am using a technique which draws on my last strength, to remain conscious and open-eyed till we reach Ankorry's Keep—and since I don't know how much longer that will take . . ." His voice trails off, and his breathing starts to rasp irregularly.

None of us can think of anything to say. We listen in silence as his breath keeps getting weaker and more irregular, then changes to a faint, horrible rattling sound. He makes a motion to Lysse, who bends her head so her ear is to his lips; from the look of earnest concentration on her face. it seems she is hearing and understanding his last words to her. When she raises her head, her face is pale to the lips. His breathing has stopped, and his eyes are once again dark-irised and bloodshot—but they still stare sightlessly.

The bubble rocks wildly and then goes perfectly still in mid-air. The thunder-voice echoes in all our minds—growing more distant with each word. "The bargain must be fulfilled, or you will stay where you are forever. I cannot maintain contact with this plane without eyes . . . without eyes . . . without eyes . . ."

"Take mine!" I cry, and realize I have not spoken aloud. But I have been heard. Everything goes dark, and I can feel the bubble start to move again.

Seven years. What will I do—will I have to beg to keep from starving, and when I've been slack for so long, will I ever get my skills back again? Will Gar have to lead me about? I dare not speak for fear I'll scream—but no one else says anything either. Suddenly I feel as chilled as when Valdofor's spell was on me. What if the others cried out to the demon when I did, what if it has taken the sight of all of our eyes? I dare not ask. I keep my eyelids open. It seems as if ages are passing.

Then there is a slight thump. I look around, taking several seconds to realize that I can see. The bubble is gone, and we are all on a flagstone floor in the main hall of a keep. Garnelle and I and the four skinny youths in slave tunics are sprawled in a circle around the little spell-boat; we look around at one another before, slowly, our eyes are drawn to the boat. Lysse is still sitting in it, and her dead father is still lying with his head in her lap.

And the huge tilted eyes in her pale, pointy face are scarlet.

THE RIVER OF TEARS

Anodea Judith

Anodea Judith lives on a communal ranch near the northern California town of Ukiah. She is—or was first—an artist, whose murals, with flowers and birds, adorn many walls and areas in Berkeley; more recently she has turned to work as a masseuse and healer and has written a nonfiction book, soon to be published, entitled *Wheels of Life*, about the *chakras* or energy centers in the human body.

In addition she has written a handful of charming stories; "Bedtime Story," in *Greyhaven* (DAW 1983) was a whimsical inquiry into the nature of reality, and her story in S&SI dealt with a healer who healed an abandoned house.

The very nature of a healer's work is the confrontation between life and death; but the victory of one over the other is not nearly as preordained as an amateur believes. Compare this story to Dana Kramer-Rolls's "Journeytime" in this volume.

I t was only on the promise of rest that Subhana willed herself to climb the last flight of stairs to her room. Painfully aware of her body, she felt each muscle cry with the ache of overtime. Her breath came slowly, as she deliberately paced herself, yet her breathing wasn't quite real—as if it might stop altogether if it weren't so willfully imposed. Her mind, cloudy with too much input, wandered aimlessly over the day's events.

I'm going on sheer training now. Body . . . mind . . . will . . . If I couldn't make this automatic, I couldn't do it. I guess what I'm getting here is good for something, even if it is grueling. Her feet continued to climb. *But am I really learning to heal?* Her doubt crept in once again and made her exhaustion deepen. Lately her successes had been somewhat questionable. She was always hard on herself when she wasn't "performing" up to par. But her severity tired her too, and so the exhaustion became an endless loop.

The door to her room loomed in front of her, at last, and she heaved her shoulder against it as she fumbled with the key. She flung herself on the bed as if it were a long lost lover.

"Ohhhhh," she groaned, kicking her shoes across the room. "Ohhhhhh, my aching feet, my aching back, my tired hands! When will this ever end? When will they say I have done enough?"

Her training of four years felt like fourteen. It seemed she had always been here; always worked like this; always ached this way. She thought she was near the end—each day looking for a sign that she was ready, yet none of her teachers said a word to her. At the Healing Academy, there was no set graduation date. "They" decided when you were ready. Many left before this recognition, unable to continue. Many stayed afterward, still feeling unready to practice. But at this point in her supposed last year, she felt like a pregnant woman in her tenth month.

Nonetheless, she *had* learned a few things, she told herself. Even as she lay on the bed, exhausted, her mind reached out to the colors in her room, using them to nourish and recharge. Her lungs reponded to the healing incense, still lingering in the air from her morning meditation, and her breathing became more natural. Her hand latched around a crystal buried beneath her pillow and she drew on its strength as well. She lay for a few moments, drinking in nourishment from her surroundings and their blessed inactivity.

When will I get to rest? she thought longingly.

When you let yourself, her inner voice answered.

I know that, but how? she countered back. *When there's always so much to do?*

You will find a way, the voice answered, then echoed inside her more forcefully. *You must find a way.*

As the aches began to drain out of her body, she found the strength to go to the kitchen and make some tea. Ginseng powder, licorice root and echinacea fell into her cup, and she was thankful she had the herbs of her desire on hand. She appreciated daily the learning she had acquired.

Oh, you'll make it, her optimistic self chimed in. *You just need to catch their attention. Do something spectacular. They're waiting for you to prove yourself, and all you see is your own inadequacy. What can come from that?* She sipped her tea thoughtfully, drawing the warmth into her aching hands.

How can I do something spectacular when I feel like this?

You will learn, came the voice. *You will have to.* In the silence, she found one of her clients haunting her. The neediness annoyed her, and she tried to push the image away but it refused to leave, and in her tired state, she found herself linking up detachedly, examining the flows in the life field, running over the information she'd been given.

Susan Brownville, age 42:

Nervous breakdown, followed by a mild heart attack, just as she was seeming to recover. Lapsed into a coma two days ago with weak and irregular heartbeat. Family strife, the supposed mental cause. *On a thin thread that one*, thought Subhana as she broke contact.

She blinked and looked up from her cup. It was getting late. Time for bed, she thought gratefully.

Beneath the covers she slept restlessly, tossing and turning with dreams of failure. She saw herself thrown out of the Academy, the face of Susan Brownville lying in a coma. "Your client died, Subhana. You have failed the test."

She awoke suddenly. the vividness of the images haunting her. *Susan . . . dying. . . . She's in trouble, that girl!* She instinctively clutched at her heart and without even thinking of her own aching body, grabbed for her sandals, robes, and healer's bag. *I've got to get to her*, she thought.

The sky was dark and moonless as her feet ran across the campus. She projected a line of force toward the recovery house, searching for the exact location of her client. She kept the beacon strong as she ran through the building and up to the second floor. She calmed herself as she came to the room. *Easy now . . . you'll snap the threads. Calm yourself. Breathe in . . . out. . . .*

All that is mine, remain behind.
  All that is needed, shall come unheeded.
  I am but a channel, no part is unprotected.
  Balance will return when the evil is rejected.

The litany was automatic and calmed her instantly. She entered the room.

She lit a candle against the darkness and started some mild incense. She opened the window and cleared the air in the room, and turned to the pale and lifeless Susan lying on the bed. Her experienced fingers felt for the pulse, and noticed the hands and the brow were sweaty. *A good sign. The life force is still fighting. The pulses are slow and weak, but still beating. I think she wants to die. But I can't let her. She's beautiful, talented, and I know she has children who need her. She can't be ready to go yet.*

Subhana's left hand grasped the sweaty palm, while her right hand touched the sternum and felt for the heart. Grounding herself well, she willed herself into trance and connected with Susan. Images of Susan's life swam through her consciousness. Her children, her husband. Constant demands being placed on her; the conflict of home and career, her husband hard and cruel, even brutalizing her at times, for not being good enough, for being too proud and independent.

No wonder she wants to die. Subhana shuddered and went deeper. What was in Susan's own consciousness that permitted this intolerable situation?

As Subhana probed deeper. she found her own aching tiredness impeding her abilities. She called on her exercises of recharging, visualizing streams of light pouring into her body, but Susan seemed to drain her energy as quickly as she could find it. She reached deeper.

Go to the source,
follow the course,
find the life force.
Go to the source,
follow the course,
find the life force.

She felt herself being drawn farther, deeper than she had ever gone into anyone. Her tiredness made her barriers weaken and the merging more complete. She knew she was on dangerous ground with no one to monitor her, with her own levels so low. But Susan's need and, subconsciously, her own inadequacy cried for her to reach further, to find something tangible, to seek resolution. Her probing continued.

It's getting cold here, she thought. *And damp*. She monitored the blood in Susan's veins and got an image of a deep, dark river. The river called her. Involuntarily she reached into the stream and touched an icy, shocking coldness that seared through her very being. She faltered, gasped, and felt herself swirling, spinning, out of control, like a long endless fall that never lands. Swirls of grayish threads formed nets to catch her, but when she touched them they gave way like spider webs and she fell unchecked.

A figure swirled before her, serene and dark with cloak and hood. She raised her head to face the eyes in that hood, and found herself frozen by their depth and serenity. She had no sense of landing, but all motion ceased as she gazed into those eyes. She clutched at the sudden wrench in her heart as she recognized the Death Crone. She stopped cold.

"What are you doing here, Subhana? Are you looking for me so soon?" The voice was of rich black velvet, coming from nowhere and everywhere. The face was a fleshless skull covered with tissue-paper skin, and the wrinkles of a thousand faces. The eyes were dark and piercing, cold and distant, yet strangely compassionate.

Subhana pulled her hand back from the river, but the

dampness on her hand seemed to freeze instantly. She pulled her fingers to her face to breathe on them. They tasted bitter.

"Lost your way, my little one? Pushed too far? Do you need someone to help you?" The Crone reached across the river and touched Subhana's cold hand gently, soothingly. The deep set eyes spoke of total understanding as she took in Subhana's aches and fears, loneliness and pain. There was no threat or challenge. Only a calmness and peace, that Subhana found irresistibly seductive. She craved to throw herself across the river and be nurtured by this woman's hands, to speak her troubles into those eyes. But some part of her lashed out in protection. *This is the Death Crone! Don't give in to Her! Be strong, Subhana, fight back!*

She pulled her hand free and stepped back, fury glazing her eyes. She stared back at the Crone with the hatred of the powerless against their master, but the Crone's eyes returned only kindness and understanding.

"It is nighttime, Subhana. Come, you must sleep." A bony hand brushed a stray hair across her brow, and moved her with its tenderness. "I see you are tired."

The very words accented her exhaustion, seducing her into sleep. Subhana felt herself slipping. But memory of her earlier dreams jolted her awake and she fought frantically.

"No, no, I can't!" she cried, cold sweat pouring down her face. Her mind raced chaotically, reaching for things of the world she knew and loved—things of life and light. of passion and warmth. But they quickly dissolved into nothingness as her strength faltered and her certainty waned. The icy water poured over her feet, and threatened to sweep her away.

The Crone sat quietly. Her dark robes were unmoving, and cast a blackness without shadow. The eyes were still while their depths of eternity watched the young girl struggle with calm detachment.

Subhana felt herself losing her desire to win this battle with death. She was losing everything—her sense of self, her mind, her body. And it didn't seem to matter. Was she Subhana, or was she Susan? She had merged so completely, she could not tell, nor could she finds the threads of logic that could sort it out. The Crone's eyes held her completely, and there was no part of her that was left for wondering about Susan. Her own life was clearly at stake, and if she couldn't save that, she certainly couldn't save Susan. Involuntarily, with fear and the immense sense of failure, Subhana began to sob. First slowly, then with massive heaves of her chest, her cries deepened and the Crone's gentle hands opened to her, receiving her gently, soothingly.

"Your tears add to the river, my child, and it is this you must cross. You may not keep your tears. To me, you must come dry and still, leaving behind desire or will. This river of tears is what you must cross to find the peace you so desperately seek. In death, all tears are left behind."

Subhana looked at herself in the river. The water was rising and pushing faster and more passionately as she cried harder. She felt it creep up her legs, its icy coldness touch her genitals, and creep up her belly, across each breast, to her heart. She felt herself being swept away by this river of pain and loss, this passionate stream of men's souls who long for things beyond their reach. She saw the reflection of her face, twisted with rage and fear, and saw the weakness in her own eyes.

"No, no, this isn't me!" she cried, and when the Crone reached out to give her a hand she grabbed it and forded across the river against the waves of her own despair.

She stumbled up the bank and collapsed. The Crone reached out and Subhana entered the beckoning arms, and lay her head upon the bony shoulder. There were no more tears.

Stillness overtook her, and her body no longer fought what it craved. She gave in to the Blessed rest and peace. She merged with the Crone, with Death, with her client and all who had dared to cross this river of tears . . . and felt nothing.

"Sleep, peace, rest, awaken.
In the dark, your soul be taken.
Life and death be not forsaken.
Tomorrow, you shall reawaken."

The Crone chanted over the sleeping girl who could no longer move, who did not want to move, who finally let go of life, and felt nothing.

Time passed. Nothingness stretched to infinity. Subhana became nothing and everything. She was without will or desire, but she did not cease to be. What she was, she did not know, but nor did she wonder. It was enough to feel this infinite peace. She rested as she had never done in life.

And with the rest came the dreams. At first a mass of confusing images, and then into blackness as the images faded into the long, dark, river of tears. Subhana felt the peace of the limitless night sky descend upon her, and a new kind of strength and understanding take hold. And with this strength, she dreamed *she* was the Death Crone, standing motionless as she watched the river of tears flow by. Faces in multitudes appeared to her, struggling in agony, pleading to get away from her, crying, sobbing passionately, fearing her completely.

She watched dispassionately. *Away from this peace? These tormented souls fear this infinite rest? What fools make humanity! How little they know! How truly they long for me. if only they knew.* She wanted to reach for them, but even desire was dead in her. She laughed instead.

"You fools! You silly, living fools, cradling your thin moments of life so dearly! *I* have let go, while *you* torment yourselves! *I* have found the secret! *I* have entered the kingdom and solved the mystery. And I will wait for you, for I am that which is attained at the end of desire!" Her laugh was a cackle, bittersweet. She raised her arms to the kingdom of darkness that surrounded her, and expanded to meet its depths. She reached beyond the stars, away from life, away from light, and found herself limitless.

A small part of her regarded the Subhana she had been with coldness. She saw how she had struggled to achieve, her ego leading the way, her worries over small things, her understanding limited. She was glad she had finally let go.

"Oh, but have you let go?" came another cry, this time with the voice of a young child, innocent and serene. It jarred her, shattered the stillness, broke the darkness, and tormented her curiosity. The child was familiar somehow, but she couldn't make out who it was. She saw herself as a child. Still unhurt, unbroken and innocent. Thinking not of death or life, but still peaceful and trusting and kind. And she recognized the face and voice of her own child, not yet born or even conceived, but one she knew she would bear and raise in the years to come. It beckoned her with light and with grace, and she knew that infinity held no destiny compared to this task.

Subhana's heart began to turn. Having lost her will and desire, she followed the images effortlessly. Other faces appeared. Faces needing healing—not fighting death, but craving it, yet living because the time had not yet come for them to stop. The face of Susan appeared, calmer now, content.

And then other faces came to her. Faces filled with light and another kind of peace. She saw flames of candlelight illuminating gentle faces of friends and teachers she loved, calling her name. They were light and happy, not dark and dead, and a conflict arose within her and sparked new life in her cold stillness. A silver thread appeared and grew wider and brighter. It enveloped her with warmth and love and she felt herself pulled by it, floating through layers of time to reemerge she knew not where. But she was powerless to resist.

The candleflames grew to fires that warmed her chilled and numb body. Sensation began to return—first of pain, and she wanted to retreat, but she was pulled effortlessly through the fires, her body responding of its own will. Silver threads wove into a web that cradled her and carried her to a different and smaller destiny.

She lay quietly in the candlelight, feeling a new found serenity and sense of wholeness. She was still cold, but she felt warmth around her and drew on it as her healing training has so thoroughly taught her. She did not need to open her eyes to know that her friends surrounded her, that they were calling to her, that she had fought death and won—only because she surrendered, and only because love and the strength of others had called her back. She was enhanced and humbled simultaneously.

"You must nourish and rest in order to heal. You must take in order to give. You must die to understand life. You have proved yourself selfless, and have now found your true self. You are now ready to leave this place and go out on your own. You have learned the final lesson and learned it well. We bless you, sister."

Subhana finally raised her head. She looked at her friends' loving faces and took them inside her, unable to speak.

She looked over at her client, Susan, still lying on the bed, silent and still. She could see Susan's time was not yet up, the tendrils of her life threads still firm and clear, yet perfectly still. She knew now she could pull her friend back, but neither client nor healer had yet entered fully the rest so needed.

With the new found peace within, Subhana smiled and rested. She was content to wait.

FRESH BLOOD
Polly B. Johnson

Polly Johnson was for many years a nun in an Anglican order. She has written for many years, but her fantasy was largely limited to children's stories. When she sent me this I was reluctant to read it; one of the most painful tasks for an editor is rejecting the work of close friends, and what I had read of Polly's work made me doubtful that it could be suitable for these volumes.

However, the first sentence intrigued me: "Her foot had never touched the ground. Not even her small gilded sandals had touched it, nor the floor where the mortals walked."

I kept my eyes glued to the pages, and when I had finished reading I asked my second reader, Lisa Waters, who serves as my secretary, to read it and give an opinion; was I simply prejudiced in favor of a friend?

Lisa read through the story without even coming up for air. When she finally surfaced, she handed it back and said "Buy it. Now you see why I've been nagging Polly for two years to write something for us."

Polly lives in San Antonio, Texas, and hopes one day to write illustrated children's books.

Her foot had never touched the ground. Not even her small, gilded sandals had touched it, nor the floor where the mortals walked. Everywhere she went, slaves scurried to lay mats of woven gold for her to walk on. Only in her own apartments could she move about freely. Ceremony and ritual attended her movements everywhere. She was the Ruling Princess of Tlascan and one of the Immortals. For the spirit of the rulers of Tlascan passed from one to another and did not die.

But what matter? Naila mused more than once. *You die anyway. Grandpa did, here in the palace. And Father died in battle with his head chopped off.*''

Now that the rule had passed to a girl-child, she must marry her cousin, to have children of the pure blood. For all her incessant questioning, Naila accepted these things. It was *whom* she was to marry that angered and puzzled her. Her cousin was a year younger than she, only thirteen, a boy feeble in body and in mind.

How could he rule? she wondered crossly. He would smile vaguely at her, or shrink away if she moved quickly, for he was afraid of her. He was, she thought contemptuously. afraid of most things. He would fidget and whine during the long ceremonies, or turn around on the Dragon Throne to trace the carving with his finger. He had hysterics the only time he had been present at a sacrifice, so ever since Naila had presided alone.

Standing now in the robe of quetzal feathers, she made the sign of clearing on her brow and let her women set the headdress in place. It was three feet high and looked too heavy for such a slender neck to carry, but it was not, being made mostly of feathers. She lowered her hand and shook it before raising it as a fist and opening it to receive the quetzal fan. Closing her hand upon the jade handle she moved it up and down, turning slowly and touching each of her attendants as they bowed and touched thumbs to lips. All her women wore clogs to keep their common feet from defiling her apartment. In the doorway she made the opening gesture that clears away spells and passed through, stepping carefully on the gold mats.

Sometimes Naila wondered what would happen if she were to step on the ground. Would anything *really* happen? The slaves would be sent to the altar-stone for carelessness but beyond that, what? Sometimes she wondered how she really was different from the mortals. Old Maruha was mortal, and she was so wise. It was Maruha who explained things to her. Naila had long ago learned not to ask for explanations from the priests. Even so, many of Maruha's answers were the same, no matter what the question:

"It is determined by the Plumed Jaguar, Princess. These things are in the minds of the gods. We cannot know them. We can only practice the ritual, seek its meaning in the depth of our hearts and understand a little of the truth as it is revealed in the ritual."

Naila knew the words by heart but they did not content her.

Maruha, a slave from nearby Netzatal, had attended Naila's mother and had promised the dying queen that she would care for her newborn daughter. Little did Maruha care for the Jaguar or his bloody cult, but she saw that Naila was to be immersed in it and did her best to reconcile the girl to it. But this was becoming more and more difficult.

Those about the Princess learned that anyone who crossed the old woman came to no good, sometimes consigned to the altar-stone itself. Maruha did not abuse her power—it was enough to remind others occasionally that she had it. She knew too well that had she nursed heresy in the heart of the Princess, the child she loved would have been the first to suffer at the hands of the all-powerful Jaguar priests. At times however she watched the erect little figure in the trailing robes and shook her head.

No one ever knew why Queen Nailasihuatl took a running

horse for her crest except Anole, for she told him once about the sight which might have started it all.

On her way to the mid-month sacrifice, walking along the upper terrace, Naila came to the foot of the temple steps and heard a shirll cry from below the walls. Down the road that curled past temple came a herd of horses, driven by three naked, hard-riding youths. Naila stopped to watch and her attendants had to stop too, although had she not been concentrating on the horses she might have sensed their disapproval.

The reach of the legs, the swirl of manes and tails delighted Naila, bringing tears to her eyes. It was as though there was a beauty and a joy in being a horse, in running, that a mere human could not imagine. All at once Naila wanted to be one of those herders. She heard Lady Horta's sibilant, the word full of her disapproving impatience, and fully aware that she herself should be mounting the steps to the temple, Naila stared deliberately at the older woman before turning back to watch the horses. Only when they had pounded out of sight did she move and by then she had forgotten Lady Horta.

In the temple she went automatically to her place, her mind still on the running horses. She gave the salutation to the kneeling sacrifice, gorgeously appareled even as she in feather robe and gilded sandals, except that under the robe he was naked. As she set the kiss upon his brow, recited the exhortation and stepped back, she looked at him, realizing he had no topknot, that this was a foreigner, not a criminal from the city. She wondered where he came from, who he was, and whether any among his people shared the kind of thoughts she had.

They made him stand with his back to the stone. All the while they were stripping him of robe and sandals Naila was wishing she could talk to him, a preposterous thing for a Ruling Princess to do. He stood still in the drugged calm of the holatl juice they had made him drink, and he would not have answered her anyway. Neatly from long practice they hauled him backward across the stone, four of them holding each a wrist and an ankle. There was no chance to struggle, and this one did not cry out, though sometimes they did. Old Tascoc raised the obsidian knife and struck. He was quick and neat about that, too, and the heart was still beating as he held it up. Some of the younger priests were not so neat. Naila watched the heart being placed between the stone teeth of the Jaguar and through the rising chant her rebellious impatience returned.

Why? What did the Jaguar do with it? Nothing. He was made of stone. Leaving the temple, Naila wished again that she had been able to speak to the man.

The remnant of her frustration roused in Naila a perverse desire to do something out of the ordinary. She decided to see the horses. As Ruling Princess her word was law, but she admitted to herself that old Cacmool, the Chamberlain, was the real law. This time, however, he looked sour but made no demur. Attended by her ladies, and as always by Maruha, escorted by Cacmool and preceded by four slaves laying mats, she came to the stables. Cacmool had already informed the head groom that the Princess wished to inspect the horses taken in battle. The groom was an aged, bright-eyed gnome of a man who winked at her and turned to snap directions at his handlers. They paraded the horses for her, rode them in circles and wheeled them to stand in a line before her. Last of all two grooms led out a stallion. He was small, with a neat, sharp look to him, as though he might have been carved from a block of jade. He was dark red with a white spot between his eyes. He danced when he moved and was to Naila altogether wonderful.

"Ah, he's a beauty, Princess," said the gnome, seeing her delight. "Some fresh blood is what our horses need."

Naila took her gaze from the horse to the groom.

"Fresh blood?"

"Aye, Princess. Fresh blood will give new strength to the colts we'll get from this one. Nothing like some fresh blood to build up the quality of your stock."

Naila went back with her retinue to the palace, stepping carefully on the mats.

We need some fresh blood, too.

That was what was wrong with poor, dim-witted Cooscan—too many generations of the same blood. And the same rituals and the same ideas, added her thought, and then she wondered whether old Cacmool had any more ideas at all.

But if I am to rule, if I am the Princess, I have to consider these things. The welfare of the people, that was the concern of rulers, was it not?

The horses had been taken in battle. Some kingdom had been raided and those were part of the spoils. Prisoners for sacrifice, too—that accounted for the man who had been sacrificed today. But you could not go to battle and capture new ideas the way you could gather men and horses. A new thought came to her: why was no report made to her? She was the Ruling Princess, but there could be a battle, horses and men taken and she knew nothing about it. She was in her sacred chamber, and now she crossed to the door and made the slaves scurry desperately to lay the gold mats ahead of her to the gong in the antechamber. She struck it with a small, determined fist, repeatedly, and then retired into her own room to pace before her state chair. She was thinking, and when Cacmool entered and prostrated himself she glanced at him and remained standing, forgetting to tell him to rise.

"Whence came the man used at the sacrifice today, Lord Chamberlain?"

"He was a prisoner, Exalted."

"I know that. Have the goodness to answer my question." Hearing her own imperiousness, Naila knew a moment of alarm. Then she tilted up her chin and waited.

"It was a tribe—a kingdom which raids our borders."

"Its name?"

"Netzatal it is called, Exalted."

"Netzatal? But that—" Naila stopped, realizing that the Chamberlain would care little that Maruha, a slave among the many palace slaves, came from the raided country. She dismissed the Chamberlain and went to call Maruha, leaving the Lord Cacmool to crawl out on hands and knees, for in her excitement she had forgotten to touch him with her fan.

The stately old serving woman touched the doorposts and sketched the gesture of opening before kneeling, and Naila touched her and began to speak before Maruha had risen, but Maruha interrupted.

"Is it fitting for the Ruling Princess to show discourtesy to her Chamberlain? They have already whispered it to me. To make an aged man go on hands and knees is unfitting in the

Immortal.'' In a softer tone she added, ''And to humble the
Lord Cacmool is dangerous to you, my flower. He is an old
serpent and he can sting, child.''

''I—I am sorry. I will make amends to him, but oh Maruha,
the prisoners—they are from Netzatal. From your country!''

''Do I not know that?'' The old face had the withdrawn
dignity of one long disinherited but still proud, and all at once
Naila saw behind the attentive servant a woman once free,
still free in her heart, and with a fierce love of her own
country. Naila sat silent, staring at her friend with eyes that
grew wider as her inward vision sharpened. Maruha, wise
beyond the wisdom of the Plumed Jaguar. Fresh blood. Prisoners from Netzatal, from Maruha's own country, men who
might have the same wisdom. Fresh blood. Fresh thoughts.

''Mara, I want to see the prisoners.''

''It is impossible, Exalted.'' The answer was swift and
flat, and Maruha's use of the title underscored it.

''But Maruha, listen. Did you hear what the groom said
today? About the horses needing fresh blood? Well, we need
some fresh blood. too. I mean some fresh—fresh *life*! Some
fresh thoughts. They want me to wed Cooscan, but he's a
baby, Mara. He'll always be a baby. And my brothers. They
were just like Cooscan. That's why I used to tease them,
because they were so stupid, even though they were older.''

Maruha sat down cross-legged. She had to lift her head
only a little to look into the eyes of the girl sitting in her low
chair, and she gazed at Naila sternly.

''The Lord Sassoo would have been Ruling Prince had he
lived, Princess. Because he is dead, there is all the more
reason to speak with respect of him.'' She made her tone
severe, but Naila was not impressed.

She leaned toward Maruha and spoke more earnestly.

''That's just it, Mara. Ruling Prince! He couldn't rule me,
how could he rule a kingdom? And as for his death—Remmi
told me how he really died—went blind and mad after sneak-
ing into the cellar to drink honey mull, and you had to tie him
to his bed. Yes, and they sacrificed fifty hearts to the Jaguar
and he died anyway.''

'' 'The Plumed Jaguar acts as he will act, he wills as he

wills,' '' Maruha quoted, but Naila heard uncertainty in her tone and hurried on.

"Then what point in sacrificing hearts? He wills as Tlaxcoc and Cacmool will."

"Be silent, child! Let not even the walls hear you say that!"

Naila slid out of her chair and sat before Maruha, clasping both hands upon her own knees. Even in her excitement the habit that she must never touch a commoner except in formal ritual kept her from touching Maruha.

"Mara," she said. "You are the wisest person I know. Cacmool never thinks anything but what he's always thought. What he was taught when he came of age. You are the one who has made me understand things."

"I tremble to think what I have made you understand."

"Naila ignored that. "There might be someone among the prisoners who could tell me what they do in Netzatal. How they rule. Mara—she interrupted herself—"do they worship the Jaguar in Netzatal?"

"No, Exalted."

"Do you worship him?"

"No, Exalted."

"Why not?"

"Exalted, I may not answer that. It is not necessary—it is not important how a slave worships."

Naila beat her fists on her knees and searched in her mind for words to express what she felt.

"But our worship makes us slaves to the Jaguar. We obey for no reason. Because we are told to. They give him men's hearts, but when it's done the men are dead. All those men, and suppose they had wise hearts, even one of them, it would all be wasted. Mara, I have to see the prisoners before they are sacrificed."

"And what will you do with them, Princess?" The tone was wooden.

"*Talk* to them!" Naila almost shouted. "Can't you understand either? I want to talk to them, learn if they have wisdom!"

Maruha sat still, looking down at her folded hands. She had little faith in the wisdom to be found among battered, defeated prisoners. Yet perhaps this was the way to fulfill a promise to a dying queen. At last she raised her level dark glance and looked at the girl keenly.

"Exalted, let me consider this. If you do it, it must be carefully and in secret. Allow me to withdraw."

Even better than Naila, Maruha knew that it was Naila herself who was ruled. She might be called Exalted, the Holy Personified, but let the child Naila defile the image of the Princess and they would not spare her. On the other hand, Maruha was sympathetic to the Princess's desire. She had tried to teach the child to think clearly and now it seemed she had succeeded. The kingdom needed an enlightened ruler. The priests of the Jaguar cult ruled through fear, an effective weapon, but a dangerous one. People were learning that no one was safe from the Jaguar, no matter how carefully he lived. Sacrifices were necessary, and if criminals and foreign captives were in short supply, victims must be found at home. Revolution was possible. It had happened in the past, Maruha knew. But was the time ripe to lead the child-princess on such a dangerous course? Maruha remembered the Queen, Naila's mother, and the risks she had taken to get this child. Now it must not go for nothing, what they had accomplished.

That evening, when the lights were put out, Maruha came softly to the Princess's door and was bid enter. Naila was sitting on her bed with one foot tucked under her. The moonlight fell through the window and in her loose cotton robe Naila looked so small and youthful that the old woman's resolve nearly failed her. She began as though it had failed.

"Exalted, I cannot allow you to do this. To go to the prisoners in the dungeon would defile the sacred person of the Holy Personified."

Naila was silent and Maruha waited, not sure of what she hoped.

Very quietly and steadily Naila said. "Very well, Mara. I must do this. If you will not conduct me, I will go alone."

Maruha sighed. "You are resolved, my Princess?"

"I am. I am the Ruling Princess. No matter what Cacmool wants me to do I have to find out what is right. Did you know that if they have not enough foreign prisoners or criminals they take the—the ordinary people? They try to tell them the

Jaguar protects them, but they need someone to protect them from *him*. I have to try.''

"Then," said the old woman, "I am resolved also. If I may not dissuade you. I will accompany you. My Princess, if you would see the prisoners, you must go now."

Naila shrank. "Now? But—but in the dark?"

Maruha smiled grimly. "Where they are, my flower, it is always dark. I have torches."

"But—but it is after the Putting Out of Lights."

At this, Maruha stepped forward, took Naila by the hand, and drew her to the window where the moonlight fell upon them both. There she put both hands on the girl's shoulders and looked down into her face. To touch the person of an Immortal was death for a commoner. When the women dressed her, they held the robes for her to shrug into. Only a relative of the pure blood might have caressed the child Naila. But there had been no one to caress Naila. She was possibly the loneliest child in the kingdom, though she did not know it. Now she was held in stunned quiet, both by the touch and by something which it conveyed: the love and concern and tenderness of another human being. She stood very still and stared up wide-eyed and tense at the shadowed face above her.

"Naila," Maruha said deliberately. "My heart's flower, my little quetzal bird, if you truly intend to walk into the dungeons to look at prisoners destined for the altar stone, alone, with only a slave for an attendant, do not trouble for a small thing like walking after the Putting Out of Lights, or the touch of a slave, or of being called by the names a nurse used to her dearest child." Her voice shook a little, and the hands on Naila's shoulders trembled. "Nor need you doubt that if she defile herself so, a Princess of the royal line may herself be brought to the altar stone. That would be after she had been mated to her cousin, forcibly, drugged and bound, kept a prisoner until the child was born and then sacrificed."

When she stopped Naila did not at first move or speak, only stared at her with the same tense quiet. Then, "I have to do this, Mara. I have to. You need not try to frighten me."

"I do not, heart's flower. But I must warn you what may

happen. If the Jaguar priests—if Cacmool—were to learn of this, nothing could save you from—what I have said."

Naila shut her eyes and swallowed. Tears came from under the lids and twinkled down her cheeks.

"I know," she whispered. "But I have to. It's not just Cooscan. They don't even tell me when there has been a battle. I'm not a ruler. I—I'm a doll they dress up in the proper clothes."

She reached out and took the old woman's hand half shyly in her own.

"I don't know why, but I think there is a secret among these—these prisoners that I have to learn."

Tears came suddenly to Maruha's eyes. She knelt, took Naila's hand, and kissed it.

"Thus do we salute our rulers in Netzatal," she exclaimed huskily. "Now you are my ruler and lady in truth. I will do what you desire, Crowned Head."

Naila felt a new dignity then, and a little fear: not of the adventure before them, but lest she not live up to the honor bestowed upon her.

"Rise then, Maruha. You are my chamberlain now. What do we do?"

Because of the grip of superstition upon the folk of Tlascan, it would have been possible to go all over the palace at night without meeting a soul. After the Putting Out of Lights, even the Jaguar Temple was given over to darkness and silence. But darkness is for dark deeds, and there were a few who walked in secret on their own errands. This Maruha bore in mind when choosing their route. In their dark cloaks they passed silently through halls and passages and at last into the temple itself and down the stair to the dungeon. The moon gave enough light so that only at the end of a passage where they felt their way along a rough stone wall did Maruha light their torches. Naila held them while Maruha slid the bolts on the heavy door. They slipped through and Naila gasped.

"Mara, that smell! It's awful! What is it?"

"It is the prison smell, my flower. It will be worse where they are. If you cannot bear it—"

"Go on," Naila said, swallowing hard.

The stench was thick, like drawing filth into the nose and

mouth. Compounded of death and fear and the refuse of closely packed men, it had lain in this hole all the days of the palace, while kings and priests walked the terraces in the sun.

At the end of this passage Maruha unbarred another door. They entered and raised their torches and Naila at once wished they had not. There were legs and arms tangled, packed, dumped together. There were heads and bodies too, but at first they seemed to have no relation, one member to another. There was a leg with a foot missing.

From among the bodies a man stood up. The others moved only a little, raising hands or turning heads to save eyes outraged by the sudden light. The one who stood was tall, dark, naked like the others, with chains on his wrists and an angry, defiant glance. There was a welt on the side of his face and others on his shoulder and side, but he held his head up and spoke, short and angry, hoarse with thirst.

"There are wounded men here. They need care, even though you give them to your jaguar. How long do you think we can stay alive in this hole?"

Naila had wondered whether she would be able to understand him and found she could, for his accent was like Maruha's.

Maruha said, "The Ruling Princess desires speech with you. Tell me your name."

He drew himself even straighter and moved his head impatiently, trying to throw the thick tangle of hair back from his brow, and his tone was proud and still angry.

"I am Anole, Crown Prince of Netzatal."

Maruha's hand shook the torch. Naila clutched at her shoulder.

"Mara, he—they—must go into the Inner Court. Where my father held Remeque. They cannot stay here, oh they *cannot*. I will find a way to speak to them. Crown Prince, I must speak to you.'

His eyes appraised her with a level stare and one corner of his wide mouth tightened in what might have been a grim smile.

"Yes, Princess," said the husky voice. "And will your Plumed Jaguar speak with me afterward?"

"No." She sounded puzzled. "I need to—you must come out of this darkness. I need you."

Maruha said, "Crowned Head, the Chamberlain must give the order. No one must know that you have been here."

In her eagerness, both to have the men out of here and to quit it herself, Naila had forgotten. Struggling to clear her thought in the horror of this place, she nodded.

"Very well. I will ask the Lord Chamberlain to ascertain whether there are any persons of rank among the prisoners. Only he cannot stay here."

At this the chained prince spoke again. "Bring us all out, Princess. Bring my men with me or I tell you nothing, not under the Black Knife."

"It shall be done, Highness," Maruha answered, speaking for her ruler. "We will find a way. Be patient a little. The Princess will not forget."

"Two of us are already dead. Do not make us be patient too long."

He watched the old woman bow to him, saw the Princess glance back, and then the door closed and the solid sound of the bar settling into place put a period to light and sound. They were again in a world of night: night and silence and stink, through which only the groans of suffering men were real.

Anole thought of the girl's face, knowing it would not be long before he began to forget it, as it seemed he forgot everything in the dark. In an odd way he welcomed the pain in his side and the soreness of his dry throat; by them he knew he was alive. He treasured being alive, even in the horror of this pit. He was still standing, and now he felt a movement beside him. He slid down into his place beside Pau and put his hand over the boy's when it touched his knee.

"Anole," Pau whispered. "What will happen?"

They always seemed to whisper, as though the dark could hear.

"I don't know, little brother." It was not what Pau needed to reassure him, but Anole could not think. Suddenly he was tired, drugged with weariness as the reaction to the brief visit, the light and surging hope and anger, came over him. But the boy would not be still and Anole forced himself to answer as the whispered questions came at him.

"Why did they come down here? Who were they?"

He knew Pau was doubting his senses, wanting to be sure the vision was real. You started seeing strange things in the dark.

"I do not know, little brother," he said again. "The little one was called Princess. But—" He frowned over it, wondering why a princess should be creeping into dungeons with only a slave for company. A slave who spoke as they themselves did, moreover, not the slurred drawl of the Tlascano dialect.

"She spoke of taking us out of here. Let us hope she does."

"Take us out," Pau said. "To—to their sacrifice?"

"Perhaps not. She said she wanted to talk."

He remembered her words, almost a cry for help: "Crown Prince, I must speak to you."

In the morning which they did not know was morning two more men were dead. But the guards flogged and kicked to their feet all those who still lived and herded them out, up the stairs to a courtyard where the air was as sweet as new apples and the pale dawn light cruel to their eyes. Here an old man, gray, stooped, humped under a robe stiff with embroidery, with a gigantic nose and no chin, like a rat, whined,

"Which is the Crown Prince?"

And when the others drew aside and let Anole step forward, spoke to him with an obsequiousness which Anole felt at once was a mask for venom. They were given water and, later, food. When Anole demanded water for washing they were presently brought that as well, and clean cotton garments, loose ponchos embroidered in blue which they could drop over their heads, for their wrists were still chained. Anole was given an apartment which he demanded Pau be allowed to share with him. There was only one door and there were guards outside. They could not escape, but they could breathe and see the light. Pau looked at his brother and said, "They cannot sacrifice you. You are the Prince."

But Anole said, "Little the Jaguar cares for our princes, little brother," and he paced the floor, though his head ached furiously.

Pau watched him, more concerned for his brother than for any fear of his own. He was fourteen, two years younger than Anole, a gentle boy, content to follow and worship his heroic older brother. Pau was a warrior, but only because Anole was a warrior and because that was what a prince of the royal house was expected to be.

They slept most of the day. Anole was not allowed to visit his men, but food was brought to them in the evening. Afterward Pau fell asleep, to Anole's relief, but he himself lay awake, telling himself he was a fool for fretting to escape, but fretting anyway.

He slept at last, for he found himself waking at the sound of stone grating on stone. He sat up aware that Pau had roused also.

This time the old woman brought wine and maize cakes and the girl wore a high silver crown with dangling pieces that hung beside her face and spread down the dusky mass of her hair. She was a diminutive thing with a childlike air that would have charmed him had he been able to forget that she was a priestess of the Plumed Jaguar. She presided at the sacrifices, watched calmly while men's chests were slashed open and their hearts torn out. Had she been an aged woman, obviously steeped in evil, she would have been less horrible than this creature of outward sweetness. He stood rigid and silent while the older woman set the wine and cups upon the stone ledge and pulled a stool forward—for him, since the young Princess had already seated herself on the ledge. Pau's eyes were wise and he forgot, for the first time in his life, to look at his brother to see how he should react. He could only stare. The Princess did not notice, but the old slave did.

The torch, set in a socket in the wall, gave a smoky glow, making of Naila a figure half light, half darkness. She gazed up at the Netzatalian Prince, seeing him similarly divided, shadow and light. He loomed above her, silent, with nothing of the abject attitude which she usually saw in those before her. But he was her source of wisdom and she would not be daunted.

"You—you are a ruler too," she began timidly, and then with an attempt at greater assurance, "Will you not be seated?"

"Is it not customary for a prisoner to stand when being interrogated?" he asked coldly.

Again she hesitated. "But I do not desire to interrogate you as a prisoner. Then I should have had you brought to me in council. I desire to learn from you as from—from an old man."

He did not relent, and he wondered where this was leading.

"And what would a Jaguar Priestess learn from one soon to be a victim of her sacrifice?"

His tone rejected her and her plea and he saw her eyes fill with tears. The old woman made no sign. The girl leaned forward, swallowed, and spoke with a strange, earnest humility.

"But that is the only way I know. That is why I wish to hear how things are done in your country. I do not know how to rule and I wish to learn from you as you are a ruler also. I command you to answer me."

The last sentence was a mistake.

He lifted his head and gave a short, mirthless laugh.

"You command me, Jaguar Lady? And what if I refuse?"

She started to answer but his angry tone whipped at her.

"What will you threaten me with that is worse than what I already know awaits me?"

She said, "But that is our custom. You must have customs of your own that would be as strange to us. I want to learn about your customs. Why can you not tell me what I wish to know?"

For a long moment he was speechless, unable to say any of the things that rioted through his mind. She spoke of sacrificing men in a way that not even a sheep would be sacrificed in Netzatal. There, even the lowest peasant had a right to demand the King's Ear if he could not obtain justice. This girl's life was ruled not by any appeal to truth, but only by the everlasting ritual. The saying in Tlascan, "Rite is right," was used as an expression of derision in Netzatal. She might demand answers of him, but she would never understand because she could only hear from within the Jaguar cult. When he spoke at last his tone was no longer harsh.

"Lady Princess, there is nothing I can tell you. Your way is different from ours. You—"

"But that *is* what I want to know!" She broke in excitedly. "I know that your way must be different. I need a different way if I am to rule a people who are terrified of the Jaguar."

He knew the power of the priests as well as Maruha.

"The way of the Jaguar is the way you must rule, Princess," he said gently, and his eyes pitied her.

Naila came toward him holding out her hands as though he were vanishing in darkness and she must grope for him through the murk.

"The Jaguar!" she cried. "Yes, it is all the Plumed Jaguar. I preside in the temple when he is given men's hearts and the wisdom in men's hearts. They are put into his mouth but he does nothing with them. The priests eat them and they are not wise either." She paused, thrust her hands down at her sides and went on, more quietly but rapidly, a kind of calm desperation in her tone,

"When I was twelve, right after I was crowned, I used to try to hear his voice from his mouth in the temple. I waited there all night, many nights, after he had been given hearts. I commanded more hearts be given him. But he was silent. He—" She hesitated, for superstition was ingrained in her even though she fought it, but she lifted her chin and blurted,

"He is only a piece of stone!" She covered her face and wept.

Never before had she spoken openly the truth she had long felt, so deep inside that she hardly knew it. Now she knew she was betrayed by the god she had trusted and there was a dark and empty place within her.

They were all silent. Pau looked at his brother now, and his eyes were pleading, but Anole stared down at the huddled little figure and frowned. Pau might wish he could help the girl, but Maruha knew that if Naila could not do this for herself, there was no help that could be given her from anyone else.

Anole sighed. He was still skeptical, but with his toe he dragged up the stool and seated himself before her. Gently he took her by the shoulders, making her sit straight. With the edge of his poncho he wiped her eyes. Maruha handed him a cup of wine which he took and held for Naila, telling her to drink it. Pau stood, hands clenched, his eyes devouring Naila.

Anole told her about the worship of the Sun, the giver of life and growth, who in his wisdom retired at night to give his children rest and thus taught the value of opposites, of that-which-is and that-which-is-not, of the necessity for sun and shadow, death and re-birth. Much of what he told her was familiar: the warrior clans, the peasants who tilled the fields.

"But we hold the peasant as important as a warrior, for without the man who grows the food there would be nothing to nourish the man who fights."

Naila nodded, asked questions, and understood.

They talked through the night until Maruha called them to an awareness of where they were, reminding them that the Princess must be in her apartments at dark-ending. Anole drained the cup of guava wine which had stood untasted beside him all the night, and Naila watched the movement of his throat as he swallowed. He had picked up the cup and drunk from it with no sign, and he did not lay his hand on it as he set it down.

"Do you do that in Netzatal?"

"Do what?"

"Make no clearing sign before you drink?"

"What does that do?"

"Clears the cup of poison or evil."

He laughed. "If you had poisoned the wine and I had drunk it, I should be writhing in my death-agony whether I made any sign or not. And anyway, why would you poison me if you wanted to ask me all these questions?"

She smiled shyly, still unused to this kind of exchange.

"I might, anyway."

"It wouldn't make any sense."

Naila sighed. "Does everything make sense in Netzatal?"

"Not everything, Princess," he answered gravely. "But you see, if most things make sense, it makes nonsense more fun."

She considered that, equally grave, and at last shook her head.

"I do not understand that. You will have to explain it."

He laughed softly, and as she rose to go, took her arm.

Startled by the touch, she put out her hand as though to hold him off and as she did, felt the beat of his heart against her palm.

His heart.

"Oh!" she gasped. "No! They shall never have your heart!"

She turned and vanished through the hidden door and Maruha followed, swinging the slab of stone into place behind them.

Cacmool, Lord Chamberlain of Tlascan was sure, the last week of his life. that his Princess was bewitched. She demanded reports. Reports on everything—the horses, the prisoners, the state of the markets, the water in the cisterns. She ordered raids across all their borders to cease. When he protested that there were victims needed for the sacrifices, she pointed out that there was not a sacrifice until the Rite of the Full Moon and they had ample prisoners for that, now that they were not dying in the dungeon before they could be used. She gave orders for rationing water. This was in defiance of tradition, whereby when the water sank to a certain level, the common people were simply denied its use. For the drought was now severe. Jaguars had been seen in the city, driven down out of the hills by thirst. She asked why they were not killed, for three people had been killed by them and, when she was informed in horrified tones that they were sacred, had snapped, "It doesn't make sense!"

"Is the Ruling Princess the protector of her people?" she demanded of Cacmool one day.

"Aye, Princess."

"Then why may I not protect them from jaguars?"

"It is the Plumed Jaguar who protects all, even the person of the Holy Personified," he told her sternly.

"But who is to protect me and my people from him?" Naila insisted. "It doesn't make sense."

At night she and Maruha met with the two princes. Naila asked questions of Anole and listened and said, "That makes sense." Sometimes she did not understand, and patiently he would explain. But on one point they came to no agreement.

"It doesn't make sense!" she insisted after he had explained for the tenth time that no woman could rule in Netzatal. "You say that I couldn't lead my army to battle, but surely I could appoint a general who could. That is what a ruler does, you said: appoint those who are skilled in various tasks to aid in the rule. Anyway, I could lead an army as well as anyone if I were on a horse."

He shook his head. "Traditionally, a man has always—"

"Ha, tradition!" She rounded on him. " 'Rite is right', then. Is *that* a saying in Netzatal?"

And although they both laughed, Naila was serious, and Anole had no answer.

Maruha and Pau played supporting roles in these conversations, Maruha pointing out difficulties. Pau playing the enthusiast. For Naila wanted to overthrow the Jaguar cult, tomorrow if possible, and Pau was ready to do it for her single-handed if need be, but Anole was skeptical and Maruha said bluntly that there was no way to do it without something which would stir the people sufficiently. Moreover, she realized with growing uneasiness that the longer they kept meeting, the greater the danger of discovery.

"How came that door there?" Naila asked thoughtfully after one of their late visits.

"No one knows, Crowned Head. It was built with the palace, longer ago than any now remember. But I have heard that these chambers were once the King's private audience hall, and he would have used that door to communicate privately with the Inner Court."

"Did my mother know of it?"

Maruha was silent. Naila could not have said why she had asked that, half idly, but now she turned and looked at Maruha, seeing the older woman startled by the question. With her new imperiousness, Naila remained staring at her servant, demanding an answer.

"Aye, Princess."

"Did she use it? Whom did she go to see?"

"The prisoner Remeque, Princess."

"Remeque?" Naila exclaimed. "Who *was* he? My father held him for years in the Inner court. Even I remember him. Who *was* Remeque?"

"He—he was a prince of Netzatal whom your father captured and brought here as a hostage when Netzatal threatened Tlascan with war and you could not withstand them.'' She looked hard at Naila, seemed to make up her mind, and added, ''He was my son. Princess.''

''Maruha! *Your* son?''

''Aye, Princess.'' The dark gaze held Naila's. ''And—he was your father.''

For a space Naila was held dumb, with set face and staring eyes.

A man of Netzatal. The pure blood of the Immortals. Tlascoc, Cacmool, they all think—Cooscan. The reason I am not half-witted like Cooscan is because I have the blood of Netzatal. My mother gave me fresh blood. The blood of Maruha and Anole. Anole. The strange, dark prince, whom she saw only in darkness. Suddenly she stood, her face still set but, Maruha thought, the face of a woman, not a child.

''I will hold audience. This morning, at first light. Summon the Lord Chamberlain. And my women.''

They brought her the robe of audience, black with crimson border, but she looked down at it and signed it away. She would have no darkness about her for this interview.

''Bring me the Rain Robe.''

They looked at her and at each other, shocked, but they brought it. It was earth red, covered with silver sequins the size of pigeon's eggs, the watered earth. Maruha set the silver crown that went with it upon Naila's head, straightened the long silver rain-tassels with an ivory comb. Naila held her hand open and they put the turquoise fan into it and she signed them all and turned to the doors. Maruha, straightening a row of sequins at her shoulder, whispered, ''Fairest, have you considered what you are about to do?''

Naila said, ''I have considered,'' and stepped firmly onto the gold mats.

They followed her, silent and afraid, to the Open Court.

The Rain Robe was a majestic one, but there was something in the face and manner of the Princess that was more than the robe. Cacmool saw it as he prostrated himself and knew its cause, or thought he did. For he had had ashes sprinkled ever so lightly in the chambers of the captive princes and had seen there the track of a small sandalled foot.

So when Naila appeared in the Rain Robe when it had not rained these six months, Cacmool was not surprised. She was defiled, fallen from the Immortals. and anything was to be expected. She touched his head with her fan and he started to rise, but she laid the fan upon his shoulder, making him stay where he was.

"The Lord Chamberlain has been much exercised in my service of late," she said in sweet, clear tones. "It has not gone unnoticed."

As his mind scurried after some double meaning in this, she laid a fold of her cloak upon his shoulder. Even this honor, and before all the court, could not move him now. Not if she had put the edge of her fan under his chin, the gesture by which the ruler "lifted up the head" of one chosen for particular honor, not even then could he have forgotten that she was defiled, and her honors hollow. She was no longer the Princess. It only remained to meet with the old priest and decide what was to be done.

The brassy, relentless sun flashed defiantly on the silver spangles, hitherto only seen glinting softly in the rain, and Naila stalked across the court to her chair. She seated herself and swept the hall with her gaze.

"Send for the High Priest."

Cacmool gave the order and smiled a secret smile. This outrage would simplify his task with the old priest, who could sometimes turn obstinate. At sight of him, blinking and squinting from the darkness of the temple. Cacmool smiled again. The sun blazed, but there was a bank of black clouds in the west and the air was heavy and still. Cacmool watched Tlascoc prostrate himself and felt a malicious pleasure as two attendants had to help his aged colleague to rise.

The Princess began to ask questions: about the supply of water: was it rationed as she had ordered, about the jaguars. Tlascoc hinted that the Plumed Jaguar was angry and special sacrifice might have to be made. Cacmool nodded. The old fool was playing the ring right into his own court.

The Princess said, "It doesn't make sense."

She now ordered the prisoner brought, the Prince Anole.

Cacmool gave that order too, watching Tlascoc, and smiled his secret smile.

When the prisoner appeared the Princess ordered a stool set for him. She asked him questions, too. Was the drought severe in Netzatal? They farmed and raised horses, did they not? What did they do for water? Ah, wells. She must have him explain wells.

She said, "It makes sense."

The prisoner said, "Yes, Exalted," or, "No, Exalted," or, "It is thus, Exalted," but his manner and look were direct, without the humility proper in addressing an Immortal. Not once did he even bow his head. Tlascoc was outraged, but Cacmool smiled.

"You do not worship the **Jagu**ar in your country?" was the Princess's next line of questioning.

"No, Exalted."

Maruha tensed. All this had been discussed in their secret meetings. Naila could only intend to have the entire court hear.

"How do you worship?"

"We reverence the Sun, Exalted."

"Do you sacrifice to him?"

"No, Exalted." Then, when she did not follow immediately with another question, he went on, "Our old men spend their days watching His rising and setting, learning the time when crops must be planted and harvested. He gives life to us all, light for living and darkness for rest. He rules the course of our lives, the seasons of the year, the cold, the heat, the rain—"

A clap of thunder cut him off. The sky was dark. A cold wind blew from the west. There was a blue flash and another crash of thunder. The Princess arose and held out her turquoise fan to the prisoner. She touched him with it, set the edge of it under his chin.

"I thank you for your courtesy, Prince Anole," she said clearly, and her words and gesture completed the stupefaction of the court as the rain came pouring down.

Naila's robe blew around her and the sequins tinkled as she pointed her fan to the sky and let the rain beat on her upturned face. They saw her lips move.

"Oh Father, Sun. Spirit of Life," Naila murmured. "Save

my people from drought. Let me save them from the Jaguar. And let me save the Prince Anole.''

She lowered the fan, gave the gesture of dismissal and passed her ladies out of the Open Court.

When she was gone the Chamberlain ordered the prisoner seized and returned to the Inner Court. He stood in the doorway and eyed the two princes.

"These shall be brought for the sacrifice in the Rite of the Full Moon. Choose three more and bring them when I command."

To Tlascoc he said, "Say nothing to her. Let her attend the sacrifice as usual. Let her see him die. Then let her be mated to the Prince Cooscan. It should have been done long since."

In her apartments, Naila let them remove the sodden Rain Robe and looked at Maruha with shining eyes, triumphant eyes. After she had dismissed her women she said, "The Rain Robe. You see, it truly brought the rain."

"It has brought the chance we need, my flower," nodded the old woman with a touch of grimness. "There are two days before the Full Moon Rite. Let me speak a word to those I can trust, and we may accomplish what you desire."

"In two days?" Naila smiled at her, excited, but surprised at Maruha's sudden optimism. "Now you are more impatient even than I."

Maruha did not smile. "Not impatient, Princess. Desperate, perhaps. Cacmool has learned our secret. But I have not been idle."

Naila was not alarmed. Buoyed up by the rain and her conviction that she was about to become a real ruler, doing for her people the things a ruler should do, she was sure nothing could stop her. Cacmool was a small matter.

Maruha knew better. She went through the palace and spoke to one and another: about the Princess who brought the rain and of the Jaugar who did nothing but kill when the people were in need. She forbade Naila to use the secret door, but she herself spoke to the Princes.

"They will bring you to the altar stone, Crowned Head. Between you and the Princess you must contrive to delay them until I can set my plans in motion. Drink nothing that they bring you tomorrow—it will be drugged.''

To Naila she spoke more specifically. The girl heard her and nodded. She was very calm.

"We will do it, Maruha. We must succeed. The Jaguar devours my people. I will do it somehow.''

Maruha was less optimistic but she kept her manner confident.

"I leave you then, Crowned Head. Tomorrow, wear the Rain Robe under the Robe of Sacrifice, but let no one see it.''

Naila was curled on her cot in her nightrobe. When Maruha left, she slipped out of the robe and into a flowing, embroidered robe of red and white. From a coffer she took a headdress of gold, a simple thing if compared to the ceremonial crowns, but which framed her small face in a spreading circle of glittering petals. She paused a moment to listen and then slipped to the secret door, taking a tiny lamp instead of a torch.

She saw the movement as he sat up. Deliberately she approached him, holding the lamp so that it illumined his face, illuminating her own at the same time.

He said, "Princess?" and then, "Naila. What . . .''

She put up her hand to press her fingertips to his lips.

"We have no time," she whispered. "Listen to me. Tomorrow I may have to kill you." She heard Pau gasp but ignored him. "If we cannot delay long enough for Maruha to bring the people to the temple, I must. I will want to die with you, but I may not. I am the Ruler. You told me that a Ruler must die in battle if necessary, for the people. But I will have to live for them, because I have to use the wisdom you gave me.''

She spoke like a child but her face looked old.

"But if I rule, I will not have Cooscan's child to follow me.''

She stepped back from him, set the lamp on the stone ledge between them, and slipped out of the red-and-white robe.

"I will have yours, as my mother had Remeque's," and she took off the golden headdress and let it fall upon the robe.

Anole drew a long breath and stepped toward her. He put

his hands on either side of her face and looked into the shadowed eyes.

"Yes," he said, low and husky, "You are a Queen indeed."

He slipped out of the poncho and stood before her as she had first seen him in the dungeon.

"I was right," Naila said, and she put her arms around his neck and welded herself against him.

Pau was silent and they did not heed him.

On the day of the Rite, Naila seated herself as usual on her high throne, pulling the feather robe carefully about her. Her women had made no demur about her strange command. She had worn the Rain Robe once before in defiance of tradition and she had brought the rain. She commanded the skies; surely she could command her servants.

The victims, each in their gold sandals and gorgeous feather robes, were ranged before her. Naila held herself very still, maintaining a dignity which would allow her movements the greatest deliverance. Her heart was pounding heavily as she watched to see which victim would be led forth.

Cacmool had got Tlascoc to agree to sacrifice the Prince last, letting him watch the deaths of his men and his younger brother before his turn came. Cacmool hated Naila for refusing to be a puppet; he hated the strange Prince whose counsel she sought rather than his. Now a man was led forward and the Priestess came down the steps to intone the prayer and set the kiss upon his brow. Two priests held the man. Naila saw that he stared at her dully, feigning the drugged stupor induced by the holatl juice. It crossed her mind that they might really be drugged. She stood in front of him, waiting until the priest's chant was ended. Then, instead of beginning the exhoration, she turned to look over the other victims.

Maruha needed time. Therefore Naila must sacrifice the men with Anole and Pau, delaying the chants and prayers as long as possible so that she need not have *him* brought to the stone. Then, as she gazed along the line of faces she met Anole's eyes and remembered what he had said the first time she had faced him in the dungeon.

"Bring my men with me or I tell you nothing, not under the black knife."

She could never face him if she sacrificed his men to save him. A ruler was responsible for the good of all the people. "Princess, the Sun shines on the slave exactly as on the King," he had told her when she had asked how to rule. *He* would die to save his people, even if it were only these four. Now she would have to save them all, not just him. But her heart argued, saying that she needed him, surely she could allow the others to die for the people, to save him. But she could not.

She raised the fan and pointed it at the tall Prince.

"That one." Her voice was harsh, or perhaps it was only a squeak, a child's voice. "Bring that one."

The two old men looked at each other, but Cacmool nodded. It would have been pleasant, but it made no real difference, and Tlascoc would grow difficult if there were any marring of the Rite.

The priests led Anole forward. When they forced him to his knees he toppled face down and they were forced to pull him up, haul him into position before the Priestess.

Naila intoned the prayer in a clear voice, deliberately, making the grace-notes quaver at just the right places, giving the instructions to the victim, bidding him give his life to the Jaguar, the awful, the majestic—she knew the words by heart and she did not listen as she dragged them out. She set the kiss upon his brow at last and stepped back. They stripped him of the feather robe and he moved so fast that she did not see the blow that smashed one man limp against the altar stone.

The priests were at a disadvantage because they had to take him alive. Three he stunned before the rest overpowered him. Back to the altar stone they hauled him while the other prisoners also were captured. Anole drooped in the guards' grip, head hung, gasping for breath. The man on his left stumbled in the gloom over the leg of a fallen comrade, the prisoner's head was flung up suddenly, catching the guard under the jaw. Anole stamped on the other guard's foot, smashed his fist to the belly and it was all to do over again. When they caught him this time he was truly exhausted. He gave Naila one glance before they dragged him down across the stone.

Now the aged Tlascoc approached the altar and Naila, waiting until he was immediately before her, stepped in front of him, paced calmly up the steps to the side of the victim and lifted from its shelf the ancient obsidian knife. Again she felt the two old men look at each other. It was the right of the Ruler to make the sacrifice. She had never done it before, but by tradition they could have no reason to forbid her. Still, if they were sufficiently suspicious, if they wondered why the prisoners were not drugged—Naila set her jaw and stared into the eyes of the old priest. He made no move, only blinked at her. She saw that he would yield and nodded slightly.

Anole lay silent. His chest still heaved with his desperate breathing, the only sound in the temple now that the chant was ended.

How would it sound when the knife was driven in?

Naila wondered this and listened. Listened for the murmur of voices, the sound of feet, anything to tell her that Maruha's uprising was beginning. What if she could not delay long enough, what if after all she had to kill him to gain time?

I cannot, I will die too. I will kill myself, not him.

There was no sound, no way to delay longer. If they suspected that she was hesitating it would endanger Maruha's work. She could not do that. But she must act, a ruler must act to save the people. She looked across at the other prisoners, put down the knife.

"Bring those here. They must come close. Let them see how the sacrifice is done."

She waited until they were ranged, then ordered Pau's guards to change the boy's position yet again. There was a wild, barely controlled horror in Pau's eyes but Naila could not attend to it. Again she surveyed them, ready to note any irregularity which she could order corrected. Anole lay across the stone as though turned to stone himself.

Naila could delay no longer. Now if Maruha's plan failed it would. . . . She grasped the knife again, raising her arm straight up, seeing the hollow between the ribs where it must go, willing herself to hear the sound of voices, of running feet. There was only one way to allay suspicion now, keep Cacmool from suspecting that an overthrow of his power was planned: she must sacrifice indeed, let the Rite proceed

smoothly, until Maruha could gather the people to strike for
freedom from the Jaguar. This was what was important. Not
Anole's life. If she had to kill him she would not live herself.
To drive the knife into her own heart after tearing out his
would be easy. But then she knew she could not do that. She
was the Ruling Princess, she hoped she carried his child. She
had to live, and rule. This was what she had said she wanted,
and what was right for the ruler to do. But she would not
sacrifice him to the Jaguar. They would not offer his heart to
those stone teeth. He would lie in a tomb in honor, and when
she died they would place her heart in it with him.

Naila struck with the black knife.

Tlascoc cried, "Blasphemy!"

Although he had seen the Princess wear the Rain Robe in
defiance of tradition; although Cacmool had told him that she
visited the prisoners, that she was defiled, he himself has
seen nothing wrong with her behavior since she entered the
temple. She had herself ordered the one brought to the stone
whom Cacmool said she visited and she had claimed the right
to sacrifice him herself. Tlascoc was a little jealous of
Cacmool's authority, jealous of his own supremacy in the
temple. If the Chamberlain was trying to tell him, the High
Priest, how to conduct the Full Moon Rite, Tlascoc intended
to show that he would not be stampeded because of the
other's suspicions. He himself had seen nothing wrong.

Until this moment. Her arm raised the black knife and
Tlascoc, standing nearer to her than the others, saw the
feather Robe of Sacrifice open, saw the Rain Robe under it,
the Robe which could never be worn in the temple, which
belonged—Tlascoc nearly gibbered. She would defile the
temple. She had defiled it. Horror at the sacrilege combined
with rage at the flouting of his own authority nearly choked
Tlascoc. He lunged at her, catching at her arm. He tripped
over his own robe, stumbled against her, missing his snatch
at the black knife.

Naila did not know what it was that struck her. With
despairing strength she had struck, determined to kill Anole
quickly if kill him she must, when she felt herself driven
forward over his body. The knife struck the altar stone and
she felt rather than saw it shatter. With some vague idea of

freeing Anole to fight now that she had failed to give him a clean death, she flung herself at the priest who was holding his right arm. Startled by Tlascoc's cry and with Naila's nails at his face, the man let go his hold. Naila went rolling over his head and across the floor, losing the feather headdress.

Bundled in the robes, her hair over her face, bruised and breathless, at first Naila could only lie still and wonder why there was so much noise. Then she knew. She had not been able to kill Anole and now he was fighting for his life and she must help him. She struggled to sit up and saw a strange sight.

The temple was full of struggling men and women but Maruha and Anole stood on the opposite side of the altar stone, talking quietly. Maruha was speaking, and Naila saw Anole nod. Maruha gave him a sword, for which he seemed to thank her gravely before turning to plunge into the battle.

Naila struggled to her feet, still dazed, and Maruha saw her. Watching her nurse and grandmother, Naila did not see another figure coming toward her.

Tottering and bent, with mad eyes and a thin knife in a claw of old bone, Cacmool's one thought was the death of the bewitched Princess, she who had defiled the temple and the Rite and who had dared to try to tear from him the power he had held all his life, he the true ruler of Tlascan. She was a mere slut of a girl and she looked it, hair falling over the sacred robe, her eyes upon the slave, the old woman who had so long thwarted *him*, oh yes, he knew it, her sly manner did not deceive him. And this girl, this child who should have taken advice from him was looking at a slave with such a look as she never gave him, tears filling her eyes. She must die, she was. . . .

Naila saw Maruha's eyes widen, saw fear in them which she had never seen before, saw Maruha point, and Naila saw Cacmool and shrank back. She felt stone behind her, the stone carving with the open mouth where hearts were placed. She shrank away as he came at her, and it was not the knife so much as the glaring hatred, baring his few teeth and convulsing his whole being, which made terror crawl into her throat and choke her. She was alone. Maruha was on the other side of the altar, cut off from her by fighting and by the bloody stone which had cut Naila off from so much else in life. Anole was somewhere among the struggling rebels.

Cacmool's arm went up, Naila watched the knife in fascination, feeling his bony hand clutch her shoulder. Instinctively she put up both hands, shrinking back, slipping aside from the stone jaguar head which would have trapped her. Her hands closed on Cacmool's arm and she fell away, her eyes on the knife, holding her arms out stiffly to keep it from her throat. He was but little stronger than she, he was slower, and her fall executed a wrestler's trick, pulling Cacmool with her and sending him tumbling over her head onto the stone floor. Naila felt his hold loosen and snatched at the knife, a desperate hope awaking in her. She caught the knife by its blade, got the handle at last and twisted away from Cacmool. Wound cocoon-like in her robes she struggled to her knees and saw Cacmool lying on his back. blinking and gasping. He saw her. He had been stunned by his fall but now he moved, trying to rise, hampered as she was by the robes. Naila shuffled toward him on her knees. She had to stop him from getting up. All her life he had been the one who thwarted her: questions he would not answer, orders he only pretended to obey. If he could, he would kill her and Maruha and Anole. She knelt on his belly and she had the knife.

At her shoulder she heard Anole's voice. "Princess, I will—'

"No!" Her voice broke on the word.

Cacmool stared up at her, his eyes cold now, beaten perhaps, but hating still. If she had seen him afraid she might have pitied him. She would not let Anole do this for her. She did not think of what Maruha would say. Because of this thing which so hated her she had been ready, a few minutes before. to kill the man she loved. There was no love in this one. Its heart could only hate. Cacmool *was* the Jaguar. Naila did not know she was sobbing as she drove the knife into his chest. He gave a thin screech and struggled. She hacked at the feather-sewn linen, tore it with knife and fingers. She did not hear Anole telling her to stop nor feel him take her shoulder. She found the gray, wrinkled skin, the bony part in the middle. not there, to one side, between the ribs, so. Then saw through the tough part, where was it, she had to find it, there, it was beating still and it was slippery and hot and stinking but she had it in her hands and put it between the stone teeth.

Then it was Maruha, not Anole, whose face was before her, full of grave concern and Naila sank against her in wild weeping.

For several minutes Maruha held her, letting her cry away some of the horror, holding her in silence. When she spoke it was gently but insistently.

"You are the Ruler, Crowned Head. The people wait for you."

Naila looked up at her. They might have been alone, the three of them, standing over the body of the Chamberlain. A girl came panting up, the silver Rain Crown in her hand, and Maruha took it and set it on Naila's head. Naila fumbled at the clasp of the feather robe and let it fall. Anole watched her, and when she looked at him she could not read his expression.

"I had to do it myself," she told him. "He was more my enemy than yours."

For a moment he hesitated. Then he saluted her with his sword.

"I will be your War Leader today, Crowned Head."

She said "Yes." It was all she could think of.

He turned back to the struggling mob. Maruha made as though to draw Naila toward the high stone seat before the altar, but Naila drew back.

"No, Mara! Not there. I will never sit there again."

"Where will you go, Exalted?"

"To the Open Court. Let them set my chair."

As Naila came out of the temple, the gold mats were laid ready.

"Take those away," the Princess ordered. "I will walk upon the earth, where the rain falls," and she paced across the stones.

In the Month of Horses, in the twenty-third year after the earthquake, Queen Nailasihuatl became the first Ruling Queen of the kingdom of Tlascan. She executed the Jaguar priests, the last sacrifice the Plumed Jaguar ever received in Tlascan, and established the worship of the Beneficent Sun as it was practiced in Netzatal. And she united her realm to the kingdom of Netzatal by marriage.

Anole and Pau and the warriors from Netzatal came with the triumphant rebels to salute the Queen after the Battle of the Temple. Anole laid his sword before her and touched thumbs to lips in the salute of Tlascan.

"Anole of Netzatal salutes the Rain Princess and desires her to become his bride and unite our kingdoms and our hearts."

From her raised chair Naila could look straight into his face as he stood before her. She looked at him in the sunlight, delighted by the straight, gleaming black hair, the warrior's body, slim and powerful, and most of all his eyes, deep, warm brown, that smiled at her as the wide mouth smiled. Her War Leader and her lover. He was dressed now as a warrior of Tlascan, in cotton kilt and leather hauberk.

She looked beyond him to Pau and saw the boy watching her with his heart in his eyes, not a boy, he was her own age, he had been a warrior two years. He had been her supporter in the rebellion even as Anole had, siding with her in their arguments with Maruha and Anole. She looked at Anole again.

"No, Prince. I will not wed the Ruling Prince. Tlascan shall not be subject to Netzatal. But I would ask a favor."

Anole, stunned, said "What?" without thinking about anything but that she had said no.

"Give me leave to wed your brother."

She saw the light in Pau's face and as he came toward her, eagerly like a colt to the trumpet, Naila rose and came down from her chair. Anole took her arm, still with the stunned look.

"Naila, I love you. And you love me. I know you do."

The look in his eyes hurt her, but she remembered his other look, in the temple after she had killed Cacmool.

"I will always love you. But you are the ruler of Netzatal and you would be the ruler of Tlascan also, you that tell me that a woman may not rule.

"I love you," she repeated. "But I will not wed you. It doesn't make sense."

THE MIST ON THE MOOR
Diana L. Paxson

Diana L. Paxson needs no introduction to readers of Sword & Sorceress; she, and her heroine Shanna, have been featured in all three volumes.

This new adventure of Shanna is loosely based on a well-known Norse myth, but Diana has done something new and original with it, not just retold it from a woman's point of view.

Diana lives in Berkeley and has published two novels of an imaginary land, Westria. Her latest book, *Brisingamen*, is a contemporary fantasy about the Norse gods in Berkeley. It's a great book—go read it.

A third Westrian novel is in preparation.

Mist swirled across the path like a tattered shroud, choking the breath as it blinded the eye. Shanna swore and reined in, too sharply—Calur slipped on wet rock and nearly fell, then stood shuddering. The falcon, Chai, mantled with a wild fluttering of wings, and settled back to the saddlebow, scolding harshly.

"Oh be still!" Shanna told her. "We have to get through this wasteland before sundown." She did not allow herself to think what would happen if they did not. She did not allow herself to articulate the fact that they were lost already, going on only because she had always kept going, whether or not she knew her way.

Chai responded with another protest, then her mottled russet feathers folded back into sleekness, and powerful talons fastened once more on the scarred leather of the saddle. Shanna could still hear a muffled grumbling from deep in the bird's throat, and was momentarily glad that the falcon no longer had the power to assume her human form.

The curse of one emperor had doomed Chai's kin, and Shanna feared that the treachery of another had caused her own brother to disappear. After the escort with which she had started her journey had been killed, Shanna had thought that there would be some comfort in sharing her quest with Chai, but at this moment the burden of her own fate was almost more than she could bear. Imprisoned in bird form, Chai was only a mute reminder of an additional responsibility. *Don't think*, Shanna told herself. *Just keep on*. . . .

She stood up in the stirrups, trying to peer ahead, but mist had swallowed up the world. Settling back into the saddle, she took up her reins and squeezed the mare's sides with her long legs to get her moving again. Calur whickered unhappily, took one lurching step forward, and then halted.

"Turds!" Shanna was already swinging out of the saddle as she swore. Swiftly she ran callused fingers down the mare's leg, felt her flinch as she probed the pastern, and straightened with another obscenity. Her mind strained against the fear of being trapped here as her eyes had strained to see through the mist that surrounded her.

They had to keep going, she told herself as she gave a gentle tug to the rein. The moor could not extend forever. Still limping, but not so badly without a rider, the mare followed her. Shanna bit her lip, refusing to recognize the panic that surged within. She was a princess of Sharteyn, and she had sworn to complete this journey. That was the only thing she could allow herself to remember now.

"Holy Yraine," she murmured. "Let me see my way!"

She hitched her swordbelt higher and rubbed at the aching muscles in her lower back, and kept walking. But still the mist curled and eddied around her. The silver light was unchanging—she could not tell if any time had passed, if there was any time, here. One of her boots had burst a seam, letting in moisture with every puddle she stepped in. Shanna's foot slid in clammy leather, and she stumbled, dropped the rein to avoid hurting the mare's mouth, and sprawled in the mud.

"Misbegotten muck!" For a moment she lay where she had fallen, furious and exhausted. Then she felt the mud dragging her down and, panicking, pushed herself upright. Calur took a limping step toward her, lowered her head and butted Shanna anxiously.

"It's your fault, you bay bitch!" Shanna struck out at her. The mare whickered unhappily and shied back, and Shanna felt despair drown her fury and sighed, looking around her. At ground level, the fog veiled a wilderness of heather whose belled blooms were lightly pearled by the air's moisture, but she could not appreciate their beauty. She shivered, and gathered her strength to get up again. It was cold for late summer; at least walking would keep her warm.

Still half-crouched, she paused, staring down, then straightened to her full lean height. Chai called questioningly.

"Did you see it too?" she asked the falcon. "If only you could still talk!" The falcon shifted position on the saddle-bow, and Shanna stroked her bronze feathers gently, still looking down.

She had not imagined it—water was seeping into a human footprint in the mud before her. She had seen no one, but this thick mist could hide anything, and the footprint was fresh . . . Her vision blurred and she twitched a strand of black hair out of her eyes, but it didn't help much. Hope fluttered like a trapped bird in her heart as she tried to steady her voice.

"Come on, girl, whoever made that print can't have gotten very far. We'll find him and he'll set us on the right path."

She tugged at the reins and stumbled down the track, following the footprints. And in a few moments she knew that she had finally done something right, for she smelled the smoke of a wood fire.

But it was hard to say where mist ended and smoke began. A shape loomed before her, she started to hurry and stubbed her toes on an outcropping of stone. In the end, it was not her own senses but Calur's hopeful whicker that told her when they finally came to the house she was looking for.

The place would have been easy to miss—weathered boards and a roof of cut turf overgrown with grass made it look like part of the moor. But the ground was flatter around it, and the wiry growth had been somewhat discouraged by the passage of human feet. A soft, background clucking indicated the presence of fowl.

Shanna threw back the hood of her red cloak and took a deep breath, then she tugged on Calur's rein and, wincing as her weight came down on her bruised toes, marched around the wall to find the front door. She could hear no sound from inside, and there was no response to her knocking. But she did smell something cooking behind that sagging door, and abruptly her stomach would let her delay no longer. She dropped Calur's rein, held out her arm so that Chai could run up it to perch on her shoulder, and pushed the door open.

An old woman was bent, stirring, over a great pot that stood on three legs above the peat fire. On the other side of the cottage, as far away as he could get and still remain in the same room, a man was sitting in a rough chair. His back was to the door, and all Shanna could see of him was one outstretched leg and the top of a balding head, but his foot was about the size of the prints she had seen. She wondered what these two old people were doing out here alone.

She coughed, and took two steps into the room.

At almost the same moment, the door blew shut behind her, and the old man and woman turned and looked at her with bright stares like the avid eyes of birds. These eyes held not the proud gaze of Chai's people, but something more akin to the faintly malicious intelligence of a raven or a swan. Chai shifted restlessly on her shoulder, and she wondered what the falcon thought of their hosts. Such a look in human faces was oddly disturbing, but Shanna had faced worse. She forced a smile.

"My horse went lame, and I need a place to rest her. May we shelter with you for a little while?"

For a moment the old woman said nothing. Then she cocked her head toward the man.

"Yod, you fool! I told you something like this would happen if you went out today!" She wiped her hands on the rusty black folds of her gown.

"You told me to go, you old besom—that's what you told me! It's your stinking herbs I went out to gather, wasn't it? Sitting right there in that basket that someone will trip over if you don't put it away!" The chair scraped as he turned it to face the hearth. His white beard flowed down his chest like an animal's pelt.

"Those herbs grow beside the stream, not on the high moor, and you know it well, old man!" The woman waggled her finger at him. Her hair was still dark beneath its threading of gray, while the man's was pure silver, but as she turned, the firelight flared full on her face, and Shanna saw that it was seamed and crinkled like last autumn's leaves.

"What were you doing up there, leaving footmarks for anyone who came along to follow? Up to no good, I'll be bound!" she went on.

Shanna stared. How did the old woman know that she had followed the man down from the moor? After that first look, the old creature hardly seemed to be aware that anyone else was in the room.

"I know who you've been meeting up there, you old lecher—" The woman gave the pot a vigorous stir. "Enjoy it while you can, for winter's coming, and she'll be gone with the rest of the flock!"

Shanna coughed. "Pardon me, Grandmother, but the day is passing—if I can't stay here, I must be on my way. May I claim your hospitality?"

"Claim?" The old woman looked at her finally, her eyes glittering like dark coals. "You cannot claim anything, child, but you may ask. . . ."

"I ask you then." Painfully, Shanna bent in a court bow. "Lady, of your mercy, I beg shelter!"

The old woman grinned, and her face folded into a thousand creases, like a map of barren watercourses in a dry land. "So—manners are not entirely dead among the young! I am glad to see it. Stable your mare in the shed behind the cottage," she added abruptly. "And you, my daughter, may stay here with me."

Shanna turned her head and met Chai's fixed golden stare. There was some meaning in that look, but the curse upon the falcon's people prevented her from voicing it. However Chai moved onto the old woman's arm readily enough, so Shanna had to conclude that whatever the falcon had sensed about their hostess was nothing dangerous.

When Shanna returned from settling Calur, Chai was perched upon the mantel of the hearth, preening her bronze feathers. Steaming bowls had been set upon the rough table, and the old man was already seated, spooning up stew noisily. It sounded as if he were straining it through his beard, but the white mat remained miraculously unstained.

The woman pointed, and Shanna took a place beside him. The scent of the stew filled the air, redolent of onions, and chicken, and some kind of spice she could not identify. She told herself that she should taste just a little at first; there was too much that was strange here for her to trust what came out of the old woman's mouth or her cauldron without testing it, but her stomach reminded her how long it had been since she had eaten, and once she had taken the first bite, Shanna found herself gobbling as fast as the old man.

Shanna stared at the bottom of the bowl, and realized that she had been looking at it, seeing nothing, for some time. Or perhaps her eyes had been closed—she blinked rapidly, trying to clear her head. She had eaten one bowlful, or perhaps it was more. she could not quite remember, and the room was very warm. She was not used to feeding so well, and digestion was claiming all her energy. In that muzzy warmth, even the aching of bruised feet and muscles made sore by unaccustomed walking faded away.

Her head drooped and she brought herself upright with a start. Why was she so sleepy? Chai was still perched on the mantel, eyes hooded as if she were dozing already. Shanna wondered what the old woman had fed *her*. The old man had disappeared, but she did not think he had gone far, for his staff was still leaning against the wall beside the door. As she looked around, the old grandmother came through a door she had not noticed before, her arms piled high with blankets.

"Here, child, you may make up your bed before the fire.

We old folks need our rest, so you must forgive me for not keeping you company. We will talk when morning comes.''

Shanna stared at her, suspecting irony—at the moment, the old lady seemed to be far more alert than she was. But the woman was already spreading the blankets in front of the hearth. The natural gray wool looked like carded clouds. Soft clouds—so soft—Shanna knelt to feel their texture, and then somehow she was lying down, and the old woman was pulling another over her.

"Thank you," she murmured. "Thank you—what shall I call you?" Fatigue thickened her tongue.

"You may call me Ama—'' The old woman's voice was softer then Shanna would have believed possible, but she had no time to wonder at it. Sleep enfolded her as the mist had muffled the moors while old Ama was still bidding her pleasant dreams.

And as if her words had been a spell, Shanna did dream—confused sequences from her wanderings all mixed in with scenes from her past that came and disappeared just as she was about to understand their significance. She saw her brother Janos as he had looked when he set out to offer fealty to the Emperor in Bindir, eyes glowing like a young god's. But there was something she had to tell him before he left Sharteyn—it was on the tip of her tongue, but before she could speak the scene had changed. Now she was kneeling in the mud beside her servant Hwilos, trying to stanch the blood that flowed from his chest and keep him from dying as the other men of her escort had died. He struggled to tell her something, but, again, before she could understand it, the scene had changed and she was alone in a dim wasteland where ghosts drifted aimlessly. She drifted with them, without home or companion or goal.

Again the dream changed. Shanna was still wandering in the waste, but now something was chasing her. Faster and faster she ran, and still it came after with a great beating of black wings, until she woke with the perspiration beading her face and her heart thudding as loud as the beat of Calur's hooves.

Shanna fought off the blankets and sat up, breathing deeply. She was still shuddering. It was very quiet in the dark room.

Outdoors she could hear the whisper of wind, and the thrice-repeated screech of a raven. Inside, nothing moved, and the only light came from the last coals of the fire. No—it was not quite the only light. As she looked around, Shanna saw a faint radiance shining from the staff that old Yod had left leaning beside the door.

Shanna's head felt as if someone had been using it for a drum; it reminded her painfully of the headache she had had after the first time she had drunk too much country beer. After her dreams, she could have sworn that she would never sleep again, but her eyes had the heaviness that comes of oversleeping, and the light filtering through the oiled leather that covered the window seemed very bright.

Ama's voice cut painfully through the fog that swirled where Shanna's brain should be.

"I want fresh rushes—fresh ones, mind you, and I'll know where you got them by the color and kind, Master Yod—so don't you go trying any tricks on me!"

"Oh aye, you're the mistress here, and I'm just to fetch and carry for you, is that it?" He had wrapped himself in a fuzzy gray cloak that flapped around him as he shook his arm.

Shanna hauled on her boots and got painfully to her feet.

"And wasn't it you who was just complaining that this place was turning to a pigsty and you wanted some order here? Make up your mind, old man, that is, if your mind's not become as empty of sense as your pate is of hair." She turned on him, gesturing with her broom.

Shanna began to edge toward the door, her headache forgotten in a fervent hope that Epona, the horse-goddess, had been merciful and a night's rest had been enough to fit Calur for the road again.

"You flap-dugged hag!" the old man exclaimed, "I'll bare-pate you, I'll stir your cauldron for you, see if I don't—" He picked up his staff, and Shanna took advantage of his movement to slip through the door.

Shanna had cleaned out and examined Calur's hooves as well as she could when she stabled the mare the night before. In the dimming light she had not been able to find anything jammed in the hoof, and she hoped that perhaps the mare had only suffered from a stone bruise. But as she opened the door of the shed, Calur lifted her head and took an uneven step toward her and stood with her right foreleg hardly touching the ground. Her eyes were dull, and her coat seemed to have lost some of its shine.

With a sinking feeling in her stomach, Shanna went to the mare and knelt beside her, gently lifting the foot and tapping the sole and frog of the hoof with the heavy hilt of her dagger to test for tenderness. Suddenly Calur flinched, jerking her foot from the girl's grasp.

"Turds!" muttered Shanna. She picked up the foot again, reversing the dagger and gently scraping at the impacted mud that had looked like part of the inner hoof the night before. Now she could feel heat in the hoof wall and the fetlock too. She finished cleaning out the hoof and washed it, but still she could see nothing. If gravel had gotten up behind the hoof wall, she would have to wait for it to work its way out at the top where she could extract it. And she would need hot water to soak it, and cleansing herbs. She swore again, realizing that Ama probably had just the thing in her cupboard, and that she was going to have to ask the old woman's help and stay here while she treated the mare.

She saw that Calur had scarcely touched the grass she had given her the night before, and realized just how sick she must be. She swore again and went into the house.

"I will treat the mare." Ama's words offered no room for argument. "I have the herbs and the spells that will make them efficacious, but if I am to spend my day tending your mount, you must help me with my tasks."

"Yes, of course," said Shanna. The old woman had fed her a chewy porridge with stewed fruit and some kind of herb tea that almost succeeded in clearing her head, and things seemed much more encouraging than they had when she woke up that morning. "What do you need?"

For a moment the beady eyes that stared into her own grew luminous. "More than you can give me, granddaughter, but enough for me to give you." Then the dark eyes hardened.

"I must make up a special medicine for the mare. You will have to fetch water from the stream to fill my cauldron."

She handed her a wooden bucket, and Shanna nodded. The bucket could hold two gallons, and the cauldron looked as if it would hold about ten. Surely five trips to the stream would be enough to fill it up. She set off almost at a run.

When she returned from her first trip down the hill, Ama was gone. Shanna sloshed the water into the cauldron and detoured to the stable to check on Calur. The mare's fetlock had been neatly poulticed, and although she still moved painfully, she seemed a little more comfortable. Shanna shook her head. Ama had lived up to her part of the bargain—she should get the rest of the water now. The mare butted her gently in the chest, and for a moment Shanna held her. Calur was all that was left to her of her old life—if any harm came to her, what would there be to remind her of who she had once been?

She went out then and made her way down to the stream for more water. But when she poured the water into the cauldron the second time, there was something odd about the sound. She turned back to look into it—the water seemed low, but she had not really noticed how high it had been after she poured the first bucketfull in. Her stomach tightening with an anxiety she would not name, she turned back toward the stream.

When Shanna came back with the third bucketful, she set it down beside the cauldron and looked inside before pouring it in. The bottom of the great pot was black and bare. She looked around her. Ama was still gone, and there were no marks in the rushes to indicate that the cauldron had been moved. Even if the old woman could have budged the thing by herself, she could not have done it without disturbing them. There must be some explanation. There had to be. Very carefully, Shanna tipped the bucket over the side of the cauldron and let the water pour in.

It swirled down the curving sides, but instead of settling at the bottom, it continued to whirl, funneling the water through an invisible opening. Around and around—her gaze followed it until it dizzied her. And then, with a last gurgle, it was gone.

No—she shook her head. That couldn't be! She reached down to touch the bottom, and it was hard and cold. Her throat closed and began to ache as she stared uncomprehending.

She had done what the old woman asked of her—she had poured the water into the cauldron—but there was nothing there! It was like her life, she thought dully. By now she should have been on her way back from the Emperor's court in Bindir as she had promised her father, with her brother by her side. That had seemed a worthy goal, but a year had passed and Bindir was still far away. If she had stayed with Lord Roalt, they would probably have been married by now, maybe with a child on the way. But instead she had nothing— nothing! All her labors had been as fruitless as her attempt to fill the cauldron.

But the cauldron must be filled, or Ama would not be able to brew her medicines, and Calur would die.

Tears stung her eyelids, but her eyes remained dry. She stared at the cauldron emptily.

"Weep—" said a soft voice behind her. She turned and saw Yod, leaning on his staff. The evening before he had seemed faintly comic, but there was nothing funny about him now.

"I cannot weep," she answered him. "I have to be strong."

"Weep," he repeated. "Even the strongest tree will crack if its roots get no nourishment."

"No." she said, "I am a princess of Sharteyn. . . ."

"Let the tears flow," he told her. "Are you too proud to share the common griefs of the children of men?"

And as if the images were flowing directly from his mind into hers, she saw a child weeping beside the body of her mother; tears of rage in the eyes of a farmer who watched warring armies trample his fields; the desolation of a lover bidding her beloved farewell. With a clarity she had not known for years, she remembered her own mother's funeral, and the uncomprehending grief of the child she had been. And finally she saw Calur's hanging head and dull eyes, and her heart ached with a sense of impeding loss.

Her eyes smarted like open wounds, and suddenly the tears began to fall, leaving shining trails down the curving sides of the cauldron and pooling in the bottom. Far more quickly than seemed possible, they covered it. The water rose until she could see her own face darkly mirrored, strong bones sharply defined by months of hard living, brown eyes which had not entirely lost their vulnerability. And still she wept, until the cauldron was filled.

"Taste it," said Yod.

She stared at him. "It will be salty."

He offered her the dipper, and she slipped it beneath the shining surface of the liquid in the cauldron, then lifted and sipped carefully.

It was sweet, but when she turned to tell Yod, he was gone.

The next morning, Ama informed Shanna that in order to make new bandages for Calur's foot, she would need to spin more wool.

"On the moor Yod's sheep are grazing," she said. "Get a bagful of their wool and bring it here to me."

Shanna nodded warily. She had seen it done, the protesting sheep vised by the shepherd's legs while he pulled out great handfuls of long-fibered, strong-smelling wool. It did not look hard, but she had spent too much of the night lying still in her blankets, trying to understand what was happening to her here, and she still did not know. She met Ama's gaze, but the black eyes were as opaque and uncommunicative as stones.

When Shanna came out of the cottage, she saw that swaths of mist lay in the slopes and hollows like wisps of wool and smiled at the analogy. Ama had said she would find the sheep on the hill above the house where the summer's warmth had cured the wild grass to hay. Wishing that she had repaired her boot the night before. Shanna slung the hemp bag over her shoulder and began to climb.

She sighed with relief when she found the flock, clumped at one end of the field as if the clouds had left dirty tatters stuck to the heather as they went by. She started across the slope. The sheep lifted their heads, looked at her suspiciously, and drifted farther up the hill. She stopped with a sigh. They regarded her a moment longer, and then began to bite the tough grass once more.

A familiar feeling of frustration began to curdle in Shanna's belly as every move she made sent the sheep farther away. She tried to get up the slope above them, so that at least she would be driving them downhill, but when she got there half of them had somehow moved even farther above her. And the gray fleeces of those below blended with the fog that still clung to the hollows so that they were almost impossible to see.

I need a dog, or Chai! she thought angrily. But she had left the falcon in the house with Ama. She realized now that this was another test. She did not know why the old woman was setting it for her, but she believed that the life of her horse depended on whether or not she passed. Her thought continued, *I am still lost! If only I could understand!*

She searched the hillside desperately, and as her eyes passed the crest for a second time she saw Yod looking down at her, as still as any standing stone. Shanna raised her hand in salute to him..

"Master Yod, can you help me? I must catch the sheep to get wool for your old woman, and they won't stay still."

"Will a drifting cloud stay still?" he asked as he moved down the hill toward her. "If you cannot pluck them, you must let them pluck themselves." He gestured toward the fold in the slope where a little stream carried the runoff from the moor. "See, there they are—"

Shanna saw the sheep drinking with their feet in the water. She nodded and picked her way carefully through the heather. When she got to the stream the sheep were gone, but with a lightening at the heart she saw what Yod had meant, for where they had passed, the tufts and streamers of gray wool caught in the wiry branches fluttered in the little breeze. She opened the bag and began to harvest it.

Ama was spinning. Like magic, the swift twirling of the old woman's gnarled fingers transformed the cloudy wool into a strong thread. As the thread lengthened, the drop-spindle swung hypnotically. Shanna realized that she was staring, and forced her gaze back to the fire.

A small pot hung from the iron bracket in the hearth. She could smell the acrid odor of the herbs that were simmering there. If all went well, Calur's new medicine would be ready by morning. Already the mare's foot was improving—the new stuff should have her ready to travel soon.

"Keep up the fire. You must keep it burning steadily. That is all you have to do." Ama had said to her. Shanna peered under the round base of the pot and reached for another stick to feed the flames. Across the room, Yod sat in his great chair, making notes in the margins of a tattered roll of manuscript that rested upon his knees. For once, the two of them had stopped their bickering. The scratching of his quill on the parchment blended into the whisper of the fire.

Ama hummed steadily as she spun, the sound as mesmerizing as the movement of her hands. Shanna found her vision blurring and shook her head to clear it. In the dry warmth of the fire it was hard to remember Calur's danger and her own despair. She stared into glowing caverns of flame, following their windings. . . .

"Child—are you asleep there? Look to the fire!"

Shanna jerked upright, blinking. The room was suddenly very dark. Had she been sleeping? Frantic, she snatched fuel from the basket and thrust it ino the hearth.

The fire blazed up as if something more flammable than wood had been hidden in the fuel, hiding the pot and billowing out into the room. Chai exploded from her place on the mantel in a flurry of wings. Instinctively, Shanna grabbed her cloak and began to beat at the flames, but the flapping only served to fan them.

And as she struggled, she saw suddenly a darkly shining figure lift a sword of flame. She dropped her cloak and snatched her own blade from the wall, yanking it from the sheath as the fiery warrior darted toward her.

And then she had her sword free. Her blade came up, she settled into the balanced fighting stance that practice with Lord Roalt had grafted onto the training her brother's swordmaster had given her. Her heart flamed with exultation—at last there was something to fight, a way to strike at all the frustration and uncertainty!

Her sword seemed to move of itself as she turned, back and around in a smooth cut toward the shrouded head behind that glowing blade. But it was the opposing blade that it touched, and as the two weapons clashed, fire ran from her enemy's sword down her own and flared through her.

Pain! She had forgotten what pain could be! She struggled to get up and keep battling. But her nerves were still paralyzed. As she lay gasping, a still voice whispered in her ear—

"This is not an enemy you can overcome by fighting— give yourself to the flames!"

With every nerve twitching, Shanna managed to push herself up on her hands and knees. Her sword was still in her hand. She looked up, trying to penetrate the veil of flame that hid her opponent. As she had not known how to weep, she did not know how to surrender. She could only remember how she had given herself to the dance of death in the fight in which she won her sword.

Dimly she understood that this was a test, too. *For Calur—* she said into her heart's confusion, *to save Calur!*

With a sigh, she sat back on her heels, brought up her blade in a salute, and then very deliberately opened her guard.

The flaming blade came down, searing every nerve with ecstasy; flame billowed around her like a bright cloak opening. And behind that radiance she saw a woman's form, and a face with eyes that shone like twin stars.

My Daughter, a voice spoke in her soul, **Why are you fighting Me?**

Shanna lifted her hands in homage, and her greeting was a prayer—

"Yraine . . ."

As she spoke the name of the Goddess, darkness reversed the light. Shanna blinked, trying to recover her vision. When she could see again she found that not only the light, but the cottage and all it contained had disappeared. The moor stretched away to every side, veiled in ground-mist, but a cold wind was blowing, revealing the stars. She found her cloak beside her and, shivering, pulled it on.

Then she heard the musical "keaar, keaar" of a falcon's cry and, looking up, saw Chai's elegant silhouette against the stars. The falcon circled above her and soared ahead, Shanna got to her feet and, still holding her drawn sword, followed her.

In that dim waste she could not tell how far she walked, for she did not feel tired. She was not even sure it was the common earth she trod, for despite the lack of light she did not stumble. She did not know where she was going, or where she had been, she only knew that as long as Chai flew forward, she had to go after her.

The ground began to rise, and a jumble of stones loomed through the mist. Chai cried out and swooped downward as Shanna climbed toward them. Then she stopped, startled, for the shapes before her were not all stone. Someone was sitting there. With a tightening of the nerves, she recognized the old woman and the old man of the cottage.

"Master Yod, Mistress Ama—what are you doing here?"

There was a long silence, and Shanna felt cold fingers brush her spine.

"You will know that when you know who we are. . . ."

This was another puzzle, like the tests the old woman had set her during the past three days. How could Shanna expect to know them by any names except those they had given her?

"Who are you?" The words pushed past her caution.

"Look at us and see—"

The wind's whisper echoed the word, an infinity of "see," "see," "see," rustling through the heather. Startled, Shanna looked around her, then back at the old woman and man who were regarding her so steadily. She had been telling herself that this must be some dream. But what if the world she had thought she was living in was the dream, and this the true reality? She blinked, trying to change her vision, but the dark world around her remained the same.

"I'm tried of riddles with no answers and games I never asked to play!" she exclaimed. "Now you answer me! Why couldn't I fill the cauldron?"

"How could you have expected to? The cauldron holds all the waters of the sea."

"Then what about the sheep? Why were they so hard to catch?"

"Have you ever tried to catch a cloud?" It sounded like the old man's voice this time.

"And the fire?" she said then.

"The fire is the gift of the sun, to serve, or to slay. Some powers must not be mastered, but understood."

Shanna nodded and, straightening, brought up her sword. "My Goddess sent me to you. Who are you?"

The wind rushed around her in a confusion of voices, but Shanna could not concentrate on what they said, for her vision was altering, or perhaps it was the figures before her that were growing, until they towered like pillars toward the stars.

And as they expanded, they changed. The old woman's skin smoothed and her body firmed until she glowed with a terrible beauty, and the color of her worn robes deepened to the black of the sea on a night without stars. She was hooded, and for that Shanna was grateful, for she knew that if she had been able to see that face fully she would have died of fear.

She turned quickly to the man, but the purity of his countenance was in its own way almost as fearful as the woman's implacable beauty. His beard shone like silver, and his rippling robes shone with the same pale radiance she had seen in his staff.

"You perceive us, mortal, in such fashion as your eyes can see. Are you answered?" The voice seemed to come from everywhere.

"I am answered." she found the courage to say.

"Then you shall tell us what you are doing here, and what you desire."

From some deep place within her, the words of the ritual came to Shanna then—

> *"I am lost, and I would find my way.*
> *I am hungry, and I would be fed.*
> *I am dying, and I would be reborn. . . ."*

And that was the truth of it, she understood then. She had lost all direction in her wanderings. It was not the mist on the moor that was imprisoning her, but the confusion in her own heart.

"As your spirit has spoken so it shall be." came the answer. "You have answered the questions, and passed the tests. You road will never be easy, but when you know what you are truly seeking, it will be found.''

The radiance increased, dark and light, and the air rang.

I'm looking for my brother, came the automatic response. Then Shanna stopped herself—was that truly the answer? Her spirit quested inward, seeking truth, and the faces before her fused with the face she had seen in the fire, then changed to a Glory too great for her consciousness to apprehend.

And then the scene around her was dissolving. She felt herself falling, and knew no more.

Shanna woke still grasping at the skirts of a dream in which she had understood the meaning of all her pain. Dawn was turning the mists to veils of rose-gold, and she lay wrapped in her cloak beside the embers of a campfire upon the open moor. The details of Shanna's dream faded swiftly, but the sense of a friendly presence glowing like a flame in the darkness, and the peace with which it had filled her, remained.

She was still alone in the wilderness, but she no longer felt the desperation that had driven her—no doubt she would have more battles to fight on her journey, but she need not fight the world as well. Shanna sat up, surprised that after such a night she was not stiff and sore, and looked around her.

She could not remember having made camp, but her gear was laid out beneath a weathered standing stone that overlooked a dark pool. Calur was drinking from it, her muzzle trailing ripples through the black waters. Calur! The mare had been in the dream too—there had been something wrong—with a low cry, Shanna reached out to her.

Seeing the girl's movement, the mare lifted her head and moved easily around the pool to butt her soft nose against Shanna's outstretched hand, and for a moment both horse and girl were outlined in gold by the light of the rising sun.

BARGAINS
Elizabeth Moon

One of the pleasures of editing is finding a good story in the floods of unsolicited junk which come in. I try never to be totally destructive of any work which shows a grain of talent, because even a quite hopeless writer may improve with a little encouragement.

It's also true that if a writer cannot stand the heat of well-meant criticism, he should get out of the kitchen. All too often, someone with more sensitivity than brains writes me a hurt letter after I have rejected his or more likely, her story, pleading that I just didn't *understand*. (Kids, how often do I have to say it? It isn't my job to understand their stories, it's their job to communicate what makes their story interesting to me. Or *should* make it interesting if they have done their job properly.) If they haven't, I try to make some constructive criticism; but I have often been tempted to tell them that if they want to be wirters, they have to work; if not, if they want a hobby they should take up crocheting, or collecting coins or Cabbage Patch dolls, and spare me their efforts— and their hurt feelings.

Elizabeth Moon sent me a total of six stories; the first five were all unusable, for one reason or another. In rejecting the fourth or fifth I mentioned that I really needed something short and preferably humorous.

So she sent me "Bargains." I liked it—and I admired her persistence, and her willingness to make use of well-meant criticism.

The horsetrader waved his helper aside and turned to Rahel. "Lady, you can see for yourself this horse would pass for Marrakai—but you, because anyone can see you know horses—I'll tell you the truth of it. His sire was Marrakai; his dam was a Valchai-Marrakai cross."

Rahel said nothing, staring at the horse she'd always dreamed of. A compact bay, not too heavy, short-backed with a long underline. Hard black hooves danced lightly on the cobbles. Wide dark eyes stared at her. Alert ears, a good shoulder, withers to hold a saddle in combat or on mountain trails. The trader took the lead, brought him forward, backed him. Straight motion, a powerful solid hock, spring in the pasterns. Rahel swallowed.

"How much?"

"Well. for you—you see, lady, this horse is special." Generations of horsebreeding ancestors clamored in her head. Rahel ignored them. "He needs a rider, I'll say that for him."

"What about training?"

The trader shrugged. "He's had his ground work—carries a saddle—I've taken him on the road from here to Cestin Var. But he needs a rider, a real rider, lady—like you are."

"How much, then?"

"For you—you were made for this horse, lady—for you, only eighty—"

The price was low; Marrakai halfbreeds went for more than a hundred.

"Here—try him." Before she could answer, he'd scooped the saddle off her hip, and thrown it on the bay horse's back. The horse stood quietly. Rahel watched, eyes narrowed, as the man tightened the foregirth and started to unbuckle the war harness.

"Fasten it."

He stared at her. "But lady, in the market you don't need—"

"I don't need a horse that blows up when you put a crupper under his tail. Fasten it." The man shrugged and bent to the task. The horse accepted the crupper and reargirth. She held out the bridle slung over her shoulder before the trader reached for it, and watched as the horse took the bit quietly. Then the trader held the rein and beckoned.

"Now try, Lady Rahel. The only horse in this market fit for your pleasure. In fighting, you might want to use a different bit—a curb—"

"How'd you know my name?" she asked, turning the stirrup to mount.

"Everyone knows of the lady—and her friend." He managed to bow without loosing his hold on the rein. Rahel swung up, checked her stirrups, and nodded. The horse stood, alert yet motionless. She nudged; the horse stepped forward. Around the square, into the ring at the center. She thought of having that springy stride under her on all her travels and suppressed a grin. Hooves pounded behind her; she legged the horse aside as a loose horse ran by. Her horse—she already thought that—had not spooked.

Eighty natas. Pir would be stunned. This was exactly the horse she'd been looking for.

Pir was waiting at the west gate, a delicate veiled figure standing beside her white mule. She didn't recognize Rahel until the bay horse stopped; then she stared.

"Rahel! That horse—you're broke—"

Rahel grinned down. "I'm not that bad a bargainer, partner. I had enough left to fill my bags with something to eat—so as soon as you're ready—"

"I'm ready." Pir mounted, swinging her veils over the mule's rump with practiced ease.

"I thought you were going to buy some replacement—"

"Hush. I did." Pir nudged the mule, and it stepped forward. Rahel rode after her, frowning. Once clear of the gates, she came up beside her.

"You said it might take all day—"

"But it didn't. I, too, found a bargain." Pir looked around, then pulled a slender black wand a little way out of her sleeve. "See? Fireballs."

"Really?" Rahel stared. "How about that healing spell?"

"Better—I got two copies of clearhead, and a ring of horsecatching." Pir looked smug, and turned to look at the scenery. Their way led up a narrowing valley, into the Westmounts. Traffic had thinned by the time they came to the branch trail to Horngard. Rahel looked back, seeing dust from a caravan they'd passed just outside Pliuni, and a couple of foot travelers headed east. She reined the bay horse onto the Horngard trail, and loosened her sword.

"How did you buy all that, Pir? Are you sure the stuff's real?"

"Oh, yes—I'm as good a bargainer as any horsetrader's daughter."

"Horse*breeder's* daughter," corrected Rahel.

The trail wound upward along a mountain flank. The bay horse stepped out easily, and Rahel relaxed. Soon they were out of sight of the main road. Rahel heard a marmot whistle—then another. The bay horse slowed and stopped. Rahel closed her legs.

"Come on," she said firmly.

The horse shook itself like a wet dog. Pir snickered, and Rahel turned to glare at her as she nudged the horse again and shortened her reins. The horse took a few more mincing steps, and Rahel smiled.

Then the bay horse dropped out from under her and bolted straight down the mountain into the worst-looking brush Rahel had seen since she left home. She heard Pir's cry behind her; she could not look. She had both feet braced, but the horse ignored her pull on the reins. *Might* need a different bit, she thought angrily, yanking one rein to pull the bay horse's head around. He kept running, half-sideways. They crashed through one thorn bush. He jumped the next crooked, landing with a jolt that threw Rahel forward, and pounded on. She looked ahead. More thorn, lots of it, and thorn trees with low limbs.

The horse paid no attention to voice or rein. Rahel ducked sideways; thorns scraped her leather jerkin and raked her arm from elbow to shoulder.

The horse burst through a wall of thorn into a space as large as two caravan wagons side by side. Ahead was a dropoff steeper than the other, great boulders tumbling down to a dry wash. Cursing, Rahel kicked free of the stirrups and swung down, rolling clear of the clattering hooves. The horse veered, running along the edge of the bluff and turning uphill. She clambered up, checked her sword, and peered back into the thorn. It would be a miserable climb back to the Horngard trail.

She had made only half that distance when she heard the voices. Pir's, angry and defiant. Others, heavy and amused. She drew her sword and crept closer. Two men held the white mule. Another held her bay horse. Two more had Pir backed against a thorn tree: Pir pointed the black wand at them.

"Fireballs," Pir was saying. "I will fry you like fishsticks if you don't tie my mule and that horse and go."

The men laughed again. Pir flipped her other hand free of her veils and began to gesture; Rahel ducked. Then she stared. Out the end of the black rod came an orange glowing sphere that rolled sluggishly through the air until one of the men stepped aside; it turned a darker orange and vanished. Pir muttered furiously, swinging her hand, and another ball of orange light appeared, this one slightly brighter and moving faster. One of the men stepped back, but the sphere touched his chest and popped like a soap bubble. He broke into nervous laughter, and came forward with his fellow.

Rahel stormed out of the thorn, sword high, and slammed into the man holding her horse; she was not surprised to recognize the trader's helper. They bay horse snorted and clattered away. Next came the men with the mule. One of them had whirled to meet her charge; she dodged, and vaulted the mule to thrust her sword into the other's neck. The first man cut behind the mule. At Rahel's command the white mule planted both hind feet on his chest and tossed him backward into the thorn.

When she looked, a sickly green cloud veiled the far side of the opening. Someone was choking; Rahel shook her head and turned back to the three she'd fought. One was dead, the trader's helper was unconscious with a flap of scalp hanging loose, and the third groaned pitiably from his bed of thorns. She heard footsteps and looked back. Pir stepped carefully over the rough ground, holding her veils clear of the thorns, and carrying a plump purse.

"Some bargain horse," she said cheerfully.

"Some bargain fireballs," said Rahel. "Do you have anything that works?"

"This." Pir took out the horsecatching ring and thumbed it. In a moment the bay horse reappeared, wide-eyed, and came forward until Rahel could catch the trailing rein. They mounted and rode back up the hill; once again the bay horse moved steadily. Some time later they stopped to count the rest of their loot: all the gold they'd paid in Pliuni, and more.

"How did you know the horsecatching ring would work?" asked Rahel, tucking away the whistle that had signaled the bay horse.

"Oh, that. I don't take chances with important things. You said you'd heard they were using a good horse for this trick, worth spending something on. I paid Guild prices for that ring." Pir resettled her veils. "Our bargain came first, partner."

A WOMAN'S PRIVILEGE
Elisabeth Waters

When I first read "A Woman's Privilege," I felt it one of the most original stories I had ever read; but, as I have said so often, stories aren't about good ideas, they are about interesting people. So I stood over Lisa during two rewrites, which was simple because she works as my secretary.

But there's nothing new under the sun. One week after Lisa had sweated out the final rewrite of this story, and I said, "Now *that's* good. I'll take it," a story came in from an acquaintance which had virtually the *same* plot, a pair of twins, and a most unusual sword-spell. I was honestly sorry to reject the second story, since I knew there was no question of plagiarism or collusion; Lisa and the second writer knew one another, but were not on such terms as to exchange plots or discuss a work in progress. Ideas do seem sometimes to be in the air . . . and if Leigh had been a faster worker, her story might have come in first.

Lisa Waters made her first appearance in the title story of *The Keeper's Price* (DAW 1980) and appeared again in *Sword of Chaos* (DAW 1982), and *Greyhaven* (DAW 1983.) We now regard her as a full-fledged writer, since she has made her first sale "outside the family," in the volume *Magic in Ithkar,* edited by Andre Norton and Robert Adams (Tor, 1985.)

Acila hummed softly to herself and stirred the cauldron to the rhythm. With her father and most of the castle guard away, she had finally managed to get sufficiently caught up on the work of running the castle to steal a bit of time for her own experiments. This one promised to have interesting properties if she could complete it successfully, but the potion still needed another hour of constant stirring. It was still three hours and a bit until dinner time, so she had a good chance. . . .

"Acila!" Her twin brother Briam could be heard halfway down the corridor. "There's an army coming up the valley!" He caught himself in the doorway and stared at her. "What are you doing?"

"What kind of an army? Is Father with them?"

Briam looked bewildered, and Acila sighed inwardly and struggled for calm. She loved Briam dearly, but nobody could possibly claim all his wits were there. Their mother had died during their birth, and while Briam had survived and grown into a sturdy young man, his mind was that of a child. Two questions at once were more than he could handle. She continued to stir the cauldron carefully and tried again. "What did you see?"

"I *told* you. An army. Men, horses—you know what an army is!"

She would have to go see for herself. "Briam, come in and bolt the door." He complied, looking worried. "Good. Now listen carefully. I'm going to go look at that army. While I'm gone, I want you to stay here and stir this cauldron. If anyone comes to the door, don't answer, just keep stirring the cauldron. Don't do *anything* else. Is that clear?"

"But I want to come look at the army with you!"

"Briam, it is important to keep stirring this potion, and if you don't do it, I am going to turn you into a wood dove and use you for hunting practice. Is *that* clear?"

"Yes," he said sullenly, taking the paddle from her and beginning to stir.

She watched him as she stripped off the cloth she'd tied her hair back with and began to unlace her gown. "Good, that's right, just keep it up. I'll be back as soon as I can." She slipped off the gown and laid it on the end of the table, followed by her undertunic and hose. Naked, she crossed to the window and perched on the broad sill. She had chosen this room long ago for its location; it was at the very back of the castle with a sheer drop of several thousand feet into the gorge below. The gorge protected the entire back and most of the sides of the castle, and the climb up from the valley at the front wasn't easy either. The place would to quite defensible—if it were adequately provisioned, which it wasn't. *Damn Father for bringing all those mercenaries here to feed in the middle of winter!*

She dove out the window, concentrating on the feel of the wind rushing past her skin, fluffing the downy breast feathers teasing at the pin feathers . . . she stretched her wings to their full extension and beat them to start climbing, then banked to the south side of the castle and caught an updraft.

As Briam had said, it was an army. Men, horses, baggage wagons to the rear, siege engines; they were obviously determined. The leader wasn't hard to spot, he was riding to the front with several of his lieutenants. His hair was dark but streaked with white through the warrior's braids, and the blue rank circle between his brows was creased by his frown as he replied to something one of his men had said. This conversation might be well worth hearing.

Acila landed on a tree ahead of them, sheltering within the branches while she changed shape again. This transformation was more difficult because she had to make herself smaller than her true size, and her changing talent did not allow her to change her mass. But she did manage to become a small, fairly inconspicuous, and very heavy crow. She hopped carefully to a lower branch and listened for all she was worth.

"But, Lord, you worry needlessly. The man is dead, and

none of his guard escaped to bring warning here; to that I swear with my life. There can't be many men left here, and who is there to order the defense?'' Acila felt faint with shock, only the crow instincts holding her on the branch. Her father dead, and all his men as well? And all the mercenaries?

''He did have children, and they must be near grown by now. Do you think that such a wily old fox would not have shared some of his cunning with his pups?''

''Two children only, My Lord.'' That voice was familiar and Acila stiffened in anger. She had tried to tell her father that hiring foreign mercenaries and bringing them to his own castle was not a good idea. Naturally, he had simply called her womanish and fearful and bade her tend her stillroom. Well, at least she had done that to some purpose—if Briam didn't ruin her potion. She hoped he wouldn't; it sounded as though they were going to need it.

The voice continued. ''It's simple enough: kill the boy, marry the girl, and you are the undisputed owner of a defensible castle, a good quantity of land, and such serfs as survive the fighting.''

''And the pillaging thereafter? I've told you, Stevan, and I mean what I say: keep your men in order. I do not wish my honor further compromised by your actions.'' Honor? Acila wondered. What does he mean by that?

There was uneasy silence for several minutes, during which they came into her line of sight. Stefan looked up, saw her and reached for his bow.

The lord twisted catlike in his saddle at the movment. ''What do you think you are doing?''

Stefan gestured. ''The crow, My Lord.'' Acila tensed for flight, not that she'd get far at this weight with this wingspan.

''Leave it be,'' the lord snarled. ''Unless, of course, *you* wish to eat the dead after the fighting.'' They rode on in silence.

Acila allowed herself one sigh of relief before retreating to an upper branch and changing back to hawk form for flight.

As she headed back to the castle she pondered her options, which were certainly limited. She didn't fool herself that there was any way to defeat this army, the problem had become how to lose with as little loss of life as possible. She dove to her windowsill, reverted to human form and hastily began to dress.

Briam looked up inquiringly from the cauldron. "You were right, brother, it's an army." She hastily checked the potion. "That looks good, Briam. You can stop stirring it now. Just put it by the window to cool."

While he did that, she laced her gown, covered her hair, and slid back the bolt. Then they headed for the walls together. All of the remaining men-at-arms were clustered there, in anxious talk with the castle steward. He looked up in relief at the twins' approach.

"My Lord, My Lady." He bowed—"What should we do?"

Acila chose her words carefully. If she had been a boy, they would have accepted her orders as rightful, but under the circumstances it was necessary to preserve the fiction that the orders came from Briam—even though all present knew it to be a fiction. "We feel that it would be best to bring all the serfs—and whatever they can carry—inside the walls."

"But, Lady," protested the chief man-at-arms, "surely we can't feed all those people for more than a few days."

"We can't feed the rest of us for more than two weeks, but if we take in the serfs, the enemy may believe us to be better provisioned than we are." Not likely, she thought grimly, no doubt that skunk Stefan knows exactly what our provisions are. "And I am determined—we are determined—to lose no lives in this invasion if we can avoid it—not one man-at-arms, not one serf, not one sheep, goat, or chicken. We trust, men, that you have no quarrel with that resolve?"

"No, Lady," the man hastily assured her. "I'll send men to call the serfs in right away." He hurried from the wall.

Acila and Briam followed more slowly with the steward, to whom she gave orders for the housing of serfs and animals and the putting up of a semblance of defense. ". . . oil spouts and barrels, and it doesn't matter if the barrels are empty— but we need to *look* prepared to defend ourselves."

Satisfied that the steward understood and would carry out her instructions, she dragged Briam off the her room to be drilled in his part in the defense. No point to tell him he was the one in most danger; he wouldn't understand that anyone could want him dead. Best to make him think he was doing this to defend her; he'd heard enough stories of gallant knights and fair ladies for that to appeal to him.

By the time the army arrived they were ready. The serfs and livestock were all safely inside, the castle was closed and looking formidable, and Briam, dressed in freshly shined armor, stood on the battlements with a large hawk perched on his shoulder. It was an uncomfortable perch, but Acila consoled herself with the reminder that they looked imposing—and she was close enough to mind-speak to Briam without anyone's knowing he was taking orders from his sister.

Stefan rode ahead of the army to parley. *Good*, thought Acila, *they consider him expendable. At least they have reasonable taste*. "Lord Ranulf of the Mountains comes to inspect his new castle. Open to him at once."

Briam had a good voice for shouting from battlements, a nice full booming bass. "I do not recognize Lord Ranulf's claim to my castle, and I do not speak to scum like you."

"He claims this castle by the death of your father, boy." Stefan pulled a head from his saddlebag and held it up by the hair.

One of the archers on the wall loosed an arrow. The head dropped to the ground, Stefan hastily dropped the lock of hair he still held and checked to be sure he still had all his fingers, to the accompaniment of guffaws from the men of both sides.

Lord Ranulf rode forward and gestured Stefan back to the ranks. The blue circle on his forehead was furrowed to an oval by his frown.

"Lord Ranulf," Briam called out. "Your choice of men does not commend you to us, nor does your proposal of marriage to the Lady Acila."

One advantage of hawk form, Acila reflected, was the eyesight. She could see Ranulf's eyebrows rise in shock. If they were very lucky, he'd think Briam was a sorcerer and would go away. But instead, he was looking thoughtfully at her. No one alive knew that she was a changer except Briam, but Lord Ranulf would certainly have heard folk tales of the existence of the talent. If he had a good imagination, and a good eye for feather patterns, and if he had noticed her as she

flew over his army . . . no. that was really stretching coincidence too far. He couldn't know, and even the suspicion
would be lunatic. But he did not appear ready to leave.

"Lord Briam," he called out courteously, "you cannot
hope to withstand me for long. I have plenty of men and
supplies; even if I can't breach your walls, I can certainly
starve you out, and I am prepared to do so. Yield, and save
us all trouble and grief."

"I will not sell my folk and my sister into slavery so
tamely," Briam returned. "I challenge you to single combat.
If I lose, the castle is yours; and if I win, you hand that
turncoat mercenary over to us for justice and depart in peace."

"A somewhat uneven bargain, Lord Briam," Lord Ranulf
replied. "Why should I risk the castle in single combat when
I can win it by force of arms?" He thought for a moment. "I
propose the following terms: fight Stefan, since you seek his
life, and if you win, you go free."

"And my sister goes with me?" Briam countered.

"What life would the lady have wandering about with you?
I pledge to marry her in all honor; she will have her home and
position."

Agree, Briam, Acila thought at him.

You want to marry him? The thought sounded hurt and
incredulous.

No, but I'll get out of it. Just agree to the terms.

"I will agree to the following terms: tomorrow morning I
will fight in single combat with the mercenary Stefan. If I
win, I go free with my armor and weapons, my horse, and
my hawk; If I fail to kill Stefan, you will dismiss him from
your service and banish him forever from this estate. In either
case, the castle will be surrendered to you, and you in turn
agree to show mercy to the serfs and castlefolk and treat them
well."

"I agree to your terms with the following exceptions: you
may have horse, weapons, and armor, but not your hawk."
But he can't *know!* Acila thought. *Can he?* "And I will marry
your sister."

"If she will have you!" Briam retorted.

"Very well, if I can gain her agreement." Lord Ranulf

sounded much too confident for Acila's taste. "Then we are agreed upon the terms?"

"Yes," Briam said slowly. "We are agreed."

"Until tomorrow morning then." Lord Ranulf bowed in the saddle, then straightened. "By the way, don't try to send out any messages. My men have orders to shoot any creature trying to leave the vicinity." He rode back to his army to begin setting up camp.

Briam ordered the men-at-arms to keep watch, then strode majestically to Acila's room, bolted the door, and set her carefully on the window ledge so she could change back. The last rays of the setting sun still warmed the ledge, but the air was getting cold, and Acila was grateful to scramble back into the clothes she had left in front of the fire.

"Acila," Briam said, worried, "can you change into a horse?"

"A colt, maybe, but nothing big enough to carry you."

"I could lead you, and walk."

Tears came to Acila's eyes, and suddenly she couldn't stop crying. Briam picked her up and sat on the ledge holding her in his lap. "Don't cry, Acila, please don't cry!"

"I'm just overtired, Briam," she sobbed. "Go get out of your armor and have supper served for us here in an hour, all right? No, dammit, we can't do that, if we don't sit at the high table tonight all the castlefolk and serfs will panic." She sat up and resolutely began to scrub at her face with the hem of her gown.

"Do you have to sit at the high table if I do?" Briam asked. "I could have them send up your supper and you could rest."

She considered it carefully. "I guess that would be all right. Just look confident, and then bring your wine and join me after dinner."

"I will." Briam kissed her cheek and set her down. "Don't worry. I'll be good."

Left alone at last. Acila indulged in a hearty cry. She was so tired and so cold and so hungry . . . she forced herself to crawl over the chest where she kept her stash of dried fruit and honey bars and choked down two of them between sobs.

Too much changing and not enough food. she told herself firmly.

Footsteps in the hall warned her of the approaching maid-servant with her supper. She hastily went to check on the cauldron to hide her tear-streaked face as she directed the woman to put her tray on the table. As soon as she was alone again she went to inspect the tray; Briam had chosen well, lots of good hot food and a large bowl of thick soup. She ate every bite, and felt much better afterward. And rest was probably a good idea; she knew she was in for a long night. She lay down on her bed and went into resting trance, waking only when Briam arrived with the wine.

"Better?" Briam asked.

"Much better." She took the goblet of wine he handed her and sipped at it. "Don't drink too much, remember that you do have to fight tomorrow."

"But in single combat the right side always wins." Briam protested.

"Only in stories," Acila sighed. "Have you seen Stefan fight?"

"Yes, I watched the men-at-arms practice. He's not very good."

"Well, that's some help. But he'll be fighting for his life tomorrow, so he'll fight harder."

"If I lose, I'll be dead," Briam said slowly. Obviously he was just now realizing this. "Does it hurt to be dead?"

Acila felt her dinner turning over in her stomach, and reminded herself sternly that this was no time to turn squeamish over what she'd forced her brother into—if he didn't do this, they'd just kill him out of hand. Oh, if only she *could* turn him into a wood dove—or anything else, but her changing ability was limited to herself, and she could only change herself into an animal. Unless the potion she had labored so hard over worked; it was designed to give her the ability to turn herself into *anything*. And it had better work.

"Acila?"

What had he asked her? "No, being dead doesn't hurt; dying does, but the pain stops once you're dead. But you're not going to die tomorrow, not if I can help it."

"And you'll change into a horse and come with me?"

"That won't work." Acila frowned. "I don't know how, but I'd swear Lord Ranulf knows I'm a changer. Remember what he said about not letting any creature leave the castle."

"So what are you going to do? I'm not going away without you."

Acila took a deep breath. "I'm going to turn myself into a sword." It was the first time she'd dared to say the words out loud, and she hoped she didn't sound as scared as she felt. "And you're going to use me in combat, and then walk out of here with me at your side."

Briam looked at her as if she were crazy. "But you can't turn yourself into a sword. A sword isn't an animal. A sword isn't even alive. How can you turn back if you're not alive?"

"The potion will let me turn into a sword." *If I made it right and I do the spell right,* she thought grimly. "And after you get out of here, you will take me to the ocean and put me in the water, and that will turn me back."

"The ocean's a long way away." Briam sounded overwhelmed.

"I know." *Sweet Queen of Life, what am I doing?*

"Okay." Briam had come to terms with it. He trusted her. "What do I do?"

"Go to bed and sleep tonight. When you get up in the morning come here. You should find a sword, the cauldron, and this parchment." She pulled a scroll out of her chest and showed it to him. "Burn the parchment. empty any potion left in the cauldron out the window, and take the sword. Have your horse saddled and get one of the men-at-arms to hold him during the fight. Kill Stefan. Get on your horse and head for the ocean. When you get there, put the sword in the ocean. Do you understand?"

"Burn parchment, empty cauldron, take sword, get horse, kill Stefan, put sword in ocean. Yes, I understand."

"Good." She handed him the packet of dried fruit bars. "Take these you'll want them when you're riding."

His face lit up; he'd always loved dried fruit bars. "Thank you."

She fought back tears and gave him a hug. "Good night, Briam. Sleep well."

"Don't worry, Acila. I'll take good care of you. Good night." He returned her hug and left.

She closed the door behind him, carefully not bolting it. He'd need to get in tomorrow morning. Carefully she spread the parchment on the table and read the spell. The words danced in front of her eyes. She coudn't concentrate; it didn't make any sense. *But it has to make sense; I have to do this spell!*

Why do you have to do this? a voice in her head asked. *I don't want to be a sword!*

Do you want Briam killed? she asked her other self.

Not particularly. But why do I have to be the sword? Why can't he use one from the armory?

Because as a sword I can help him fight. I'll be right in his hand and can link with him. Besides, didn't you hear him? He won't leave the castle without me. And the way Lord Ranulf's acting, I don't think I can turn into a bird and fly to meet him.

You could put a sword here for him and hide someplace. Did it ever occur to you that he just might be able to defeat Stefan on his own? Briam is pretty good with a sword—he does have some ability. Just because he's your "baby brother" doesn't mean that he's totally helpless. Look at his suggestion about dinner; he was right. You're just in the habit of doing everything for him.

You have a point. But even if Briam could defeat Stefan on his own, you know as well as I do that he can't go into exile without someone to take care of him. And I don't see anyone else offering to do it.

Who's going to look after Briam if you're a sword? Are you still going to be able to mind-speak with him? Face it, if you're a sword, you'll be absolutely helpless. How do you know Briam isn't going to lose you someplace? And what if he loses the fight even with you helping him?

Then I'll be a sword forever—assuming, that is, that I ever manage to turn myself into a sword in the first place, with you arguing with me!

Something moved on the window ledge, cutting off the internal dialogue. Acila froze in horror as a spider a full fathom across began to crawl over the sill. Fortunately her paralysis lasted only a second, then she grabbed a torch out its wall holder, lit it in the fire. and used the flame to stop the creature's advance.

It froze on the window ledge, flickered in the firelight, and reformed into human shape. Lord Ranulf!

"Lady Acila." He bowed courteously, apparently quite untroubled by the fact that he was naked.

Careful. Remember you haven't met him. "I fear you have the advantage of me, Sir. May I ask who you are and what you are doing in my room?"

His eyes inspected the room, and Acila took another step toward him, blocking his view of the parchment with the spell as she did so. There was no way to hide the potion; if he stepped from the ledge he'd land in it. He did not, however, seem inclined to get any closer to the torch she held. His eyes moved from it to her face, and he chuckled. "You know full well who I am, My Lady." There was a peculiar caress in his voice. "And may I say that you are even lovelier as a lady than as a hawk—or a crow?"

"Since I am neither a hawk nor a crow, I fail to see any point in this conversation. And I really must request that you leave immediately. For me to entertain a strange man unchaperoned would be unseemly—even were you properly dressed. Aren't you cold?"

"And you therefore use fire as a chaperone? How considerate of you. Surely no such formality is necessary between a betrothed couple?" His face still reflected amusement, but he was keeping a wary eye on the flames.

"So you are Lord Ranulf." At least now she didn't have to pretend not to know his name. "I would remind you, Lord"—*I am* not *going to call this man* my *lord*—"that I have not agreed to this betrothal. Furthermore, with the current unsettled state of the castle, I do not feel inclined to entertain. So just turn yourself back into a spider and crawl right back down that cliff!" She took a step toward him, holding the torch before her.

"But you will agree to the betrothal," he replied confidently. "After all, who else are you likely to find who will understand you so well? And you're exactly what I need for a mate—just think of the children we'll have. Until tomorrow, my wife.'' He shimmered again, and the spider crawled over the ledge and down the castle wall.

She bolted the shutters behind him—at least he seemed to have the same size and weight limitations she did—then leaned against them and shook. *Well, which would you rather be—a sword or a womb to birth were-spiders?*

A sword, and pray the Lady he doesn't figure it out.

He shouldn't; there probably aren't five people alive who have even heard of the spell. And the potion isn't easy to make.

This time the spell made sense. She took off her clothes, folded them neatly, and put them away in her chest, checking it carefully to be sure she hadn't forgotten any more parchments in it. When she was sure that her chest contained nothing but clothes, she made her bed neatly, burned the few papers she had except the spell, and checked the room for anything else she didn't want to fall into the wrong hands.

When she was satisfied that she had done everything she needed to do in human form, she placed the spell on the window ledge next to the parchment, got into the cauldron—with some difficulty; it was rather a tight fit—bathed every inch of her body in the potion—which was very cold—and chanted the spell, with concentration but very softly, in case there was a spider outside the window. As she intoned the last syllable, she could feel herself compressing, shrinking, becoming incredibly dense and colder than she had ever imagined was possible. But to her horror, she was also becoming blind, deaf, and mind-blind. Her last thought was *is this what they call 'cold iron'?*

She was covered in warm sticky liquid and she was looking at Stefan's body as her feet—no, her point—no, her feet—slid out of his chest. *Sweet Lady, it worked! But I'm not supposed to be changing back yet!* She tried to halt the change, but she was too cold and weak. In a moment she was sprawled, naked and bloody, on the field—right where Briam had dropped her.

Briam stripped off his surcoat and wrapped it around her. ''But you said you wouldn't change back yet!''

''You have strange taste in weapons, Lord Briam.'' Lord

Ranulf rose from checking Stefan's body for signs of life and walked over to them. Acila struggled to sit up; she was *not* going to lie down in front of this man!

"Is he dead?" she demanded.

"Quite dead." Lord Ranulf raised his eyebrows. turning the blue circle almost to a triangle. "What chance did he have against so determined a pair of opponents?"

"About the same chance our father had against a troop of treacherous mercenaries," Acila retorted. Unfortunately her teeth started to chatter just then, diminishing the effect she was trying for.

Lord Ranulf dug into his belt pouch and pulled out a bar of what appeared to be nuts and seeds stuck together with honey. "Eat this, there's no sense in your going into shock. As for your father's death, it was not by any order of mine. I would have met him in honorable combat."

Acila chewed diligently and swallowed. "As what?" she asked sweetly, taking another bite.

"As a human," he replied calmly. "I've no hand as skilled as your brother's to wield me where I to become a sword. How did you do it?"

Acila's mouth was full, and Briam answered. "She used a spell. I helped stir the potion," he added proudly.

"You did well," Lord Ranulf said courteously, as Acila choked on a seed.

"But I must have done something wrong," Briam said, puzzled. "She wasn't supposed to change back until I put her in the ocean."

This time Acila had no need of hawk's eyes to see the astonishment on Lord Ranulf's face. "But that spell was lost long ago! Most people think it only a legend."

"Why did she change back?" Sometimes, Acila reflected bitterly, Briam had an extremely limited mind.

"Salt water and blood have the same elements," Lord Ranulf muttered absently, looking at Acila. "It seems I chose better than I knew when I decided to marry you."

Acila swallowed the last bit of honey and decided she'd live. "May I point out, Lord Ranulf, that I am not going to marry you. Stefan is dead, and my brother and I have won our freedom."

"I said I'd marry you!"

"*If* I agreed. I don't agree."

"Whether you agree or not, you were not included in the list of things your brother is allowed to take!"

"Oh yes I was." Acila knew now that she had won. "Your words were 'horse, weapons, and armor'—and you said yourself that I'm his weapon." She rose to her feet and wrapped Briam's surcoat more securely around her. "You'll just have to console yourself with the estate, the serfs, and the castle—unless, of course, you are planning to break your pledged word."

"I hold by my honor," Lord Ranulf said grimly. "I'll console myself with your library—at least for a time. But I assure you, my Lady Acila, I won't forget you. My offer holds if you change your mind—but see to it that your mind is all you change."

"Come, Briam." Acila headed toward his horse. "Let's go." Briam swung himself into the saddle in true heroic fashion, pulled Acila up in front of him, and they headed down the path.

TALLA
J. Edwin Andrews

Most of the stories in this volume are from writers who have become well-known to me over five or six years of editing. It is rare for a story to come in from a total stranger; I know nothing about J. Edwin Andrews except that he gives his occupation as "screen writer," and that the story came in just as I was about to close the anthology, having about enough stories.

I'm glad I could squeeze this little story in; it struck me as a bit gruesome, but perhaps it is necessary to make a bow to the horror-fantasy genre which overlaps the field of sword & sorcery.

T he Dragon Mistress Talla pulled her hands deeper into the voluminous sleeves of the blue robe that draped her frame. She waited patiently beside the dark Solamarian, who was still a strong, powerful figure, though silver streaked his hair and beard. He glanced at her, then sighed and shook his head at the pair of rogues before them. They were young, lean-waisted, and obviously hungry for easy money. When they had jumped from the shadows, the two probably did not expect to face a healer and a desert warrior.

The Solamarian rested the heel of his hand on his ivory-handled scimitar, leaning on it so that the hilt was thrust forward and well in view.

"Don't be stupid," was all he said. But then, that was all he had to say. Reluctantly, the young pair slid back into the shadows of their alleyway.

"You handle yourself well," Talla said. The desert warrior only grunted.

"At my age I have found a good, quick bluff to be as efficient as a sword."

The pair continued through the chilled night until they reached the Krying Kobold Inn. The little inn was on the border between part of the city which was considered respectable and that part called the Web. The Web was not a place Talla would have neared at night, but she was needed. The warrior had ridden two days to find her and, as much as she hated the winter, she also loathed the thought of not helping when she was called. It was, after all, her duty and the payment would make the winter pass swiftly.

Inside, the inn was warm and dark. The smell of old roast and soured wine was faint in the air. Heavy tables and benches filled the room, even if patrons did not. No more than a half-dozen men and women, travelers by their attire, were seated around a robust fire. All of them shot evil glances at the open door and tried to huddle deeper into themselves as the outside chill slipped in. One, however, did not balk at the cold intrusion. He stood and approached.

The twin swords on his hips gleamed dully as he passed the firelight. He was tall without being overpowering, and the Dragon Mistress could tell by the dark under his eyes and the stubble of unshaven beard that his attentions had been elsewhere for at least three days. There was urgency in his eyes and something else, something almost captivating but also frightening. He and the desert warrior exchanged nods, then he spoke.

"Thank you for coming so quickly," his voice was fluid and deep. Politeness was not something foreign to this man, and Talla found that intriguing.

"My friend has explained the necessity of calling you out into the weather?"

"He explained only that I was needed," she responded. The story behind her reason for coming was not important to her, but she knew that those who sought her help thought it was. She waited.

"There were three of us," he began. "I am Barak; Khassen, your escort, and our friend Hartman were gathering the eggs of the Luna spider."

Talla frowned. "Why would you endanger yourselves so?"

Barak cleared his throat. "We were once members of the Circle of Swordbearers, which means that, of late, we have been trying to make a living."

She nodded. The Circle, once the king's peacekeepers, had disbanded four winters ago.

"King Tredan was offering a heavy purse for each egg collected—some festival for his wizards or consorts or some-one." He gestured, as if trying to wave away the reason, "On the way back, one of the eggs in Hartman's pack hatched and she was bitten."

Talla shook her head. There was much pain in a Luna spider's bite, before death.

"Where is this Hartman now?"

Barak motioned for her to follow him upstairs to the rooms. He opened the first door and let her enter. Inside, on a simple bed, was Hartman. Her helmet and armor lay on the floor nearby. Talla could tell that the woman was a Lytrenian by her coloring and the exotic angles of her features. Even in her suffering, she was beautiful. Her sweat-soaked hair was full and long, save for the crown, which was kept short. Though she was in a fevered sleep, her face was pale and twisted from pain. Muscles, strong and well defined along her arms and legs, trembled.

The Dragon Mistress studied the woman for a long moment, then she turned and lead Barak into the hallway.

"What is this woman to you?"

"She is a sword sister, a companion."

"You know my fee is high?"

"I am aware of your payment," he said. The muscles in his neck bulged slightly. There was still that something in his eyes she could not read, some hurt or anger that boiled inside.

"Knowing what you must pay, I ask you again. What is this woman to you?"

Barak's face pulled into an ugly mask. "Damn you, healer, what or who this woman is to me is none of your concern. I will pay your price, just save her!"

Talla watched Barak descend the stairway before she reentered the room. What or who. No man or woman had ever answered with that before. She looked down at the sleeping figure. A single oil lamp illuminated her features.

"All right, my dear," she whispered. "Let us find out who you are."

Talla produced vials of oils and powder from the pockets within her robe. She prepared a concoction in a small porcelain dish and let it trickle past Hartman's lips. The Dragon Mistress ran her fingers through the warrior's damp hair and smiled sadly, then turned and tugged the cord about her neck.

Her robe fell to the floor and the solitary light cast a thousand sparkles along her sleek, scaled skin. She was not a slight woman, her body was nearly as hard and defined as that of the woman beside her. Talla's face was highly angled and attractive. Pale hair the color of a full moon grew like a mane from the middle of her forehead to her shoulders. Her eyes were those of a serpent, glaring and unblinking, frightening yet seductive. She knelt and prepared another mixture. Of this she gave only half to Hartman, drinking the rest herself. Then she rose and slid onto the bed. Her hands carressed Hartman's face, and she turned her mind to the fevered woman under her. Talla kissed the warrior gently, letting herself feel the power within the woman and sharing her own where it was needed. Then, slowly, her mind penetrated Hartman's. The two merged and flowed and wrapped themselves around each other and the flames of passion and poison rose and licked at them with a burning fever.

And neither was willing to let go.

Barak tightened the cinch of the saddle and Khassen handed him a skin of wine, which he tied down.

"I'm afraid this is all odd to me, my friend," Khassen said. Barak sighed and patted the horse's rear. He had not slept during the three days that the Dragon Mistress had treated Hartman.

"The Luna spider's poison affects the mind as well as the body. Only the Dragon Mistress can deal with both."

"But the price—"

"Was worth it."

Khassen shrugged, "I suppose. But to be parted for five years? You save her, only to lose her again."

"But that is the price. Five years of service to the Dragon Mistress for duties performed."

"Why?"

Barak stared off into the distance. "Supposedly, this kind of ritual drains the healer, I guess they need someone to tend them during recovery."

Khassen rubbed his hands together to warm them. Snow was just beginning to fall over the city. "Still, five years without Hartman—"

"Will be an eternity." Barak clapped his companion on the shoulder. "But she is alive, my friend, she is well."

The door to the Krying Kobold opened and Talla, the Dragon Mistress, walked toward them, her face hidden in the darkness of her hood. She looked at Barak, whose face was heavy with sadness. "The horses are ready."

Talla nodded, "She sleeps now, and probably will for three days. She is strong, but her recovery will be slow."

Barak pulled himself up into the saddle. He looked down at Khassen.

"Watch over her, but no matter what, do not tell her where I have gone."

"What am I going to tell her then?"

"Tell her that I will miss her."

The two men looked at each other, then Barak fell in behind Talla and they rode out of the city.

"Do you think we will be caught in the storm?" Talla gestured at the heavily falling snow.

"Not likely, snow's too dry, wind too calm," Barak answered dully.

"Shedding silent tears?"

"You would not understand."

"Oh, but I do. There is a little of your Hartman still with me. I have seen and felt the things you two have experienced together as friends, swordmates, and as lovers. You two share something special. I would like one day to have that something for myself."

"I hope one day you do," he said, and she knew he was sincere.

Talla nodded. "In the meantime, I must deal with you. We have five years together, I would like you to be happy, Barak."

Talla pulled back her hood and smiled. Barak knew that smile, more, he knew that face. Under the sheen of gracefully lain scales, was the face of Hartman. Barak blinked his eyes and stared, "As my friend Khassen would say, I don't understand."

"It is an effect of the healing ritual. I have some of her, she, some of me. It will pass when the memories fade—what is the matter?"

Barak smiled a warm but unsure half-smile and glanced back at the city.

"It suddenly feels a little deceitful."

"Well, it wouldn't be the first time, would it? Remember, I know as much about you as Hartman does."

Barak placed a hand to his chest, "Me? I've always saved my affections for Hartman!"

"The little dancer in Fredesh?"

"That was my cousin!"

"—the silversmith's daughter in Lashar?"

"That was innocent!"

"What about the five sisters, all animal trainers from Spragel?"

"That was a disaster!"

Talla laughed lightly. "I am glad to see some of the warmth, no matter how mischievous, you share with your friends."

"Oh? And why is that?"

"After all, for the next five years, I have to live with you, too."

"Barak bowed his head and spurred his horse on, but a smile stayed with him. Talla knew of Hartman's feelings for the man, and knew the hurt she would face in his absence. But the healer could not really worry too much about the recovering warrior. For the next five years she was going to experience everything that she had felt second-hand from Hartman. She wanted to share that fire.

And, if by some magic, what she and Barak shared proved to be bonding—who knew how long five years could last?

TUPILAK

Terry Tafoya

Trained as a traditional Native American storyteller by his Warm Springs relatives, Terry Tafoya is a Taos Pueblo Indian who has worked as a consultant for Native and Bilingual programs across the Western U.S. and Canada. He is a Family Therapist for the Interpersonal Psychology clinic in the Harborview Community Mental Health Center in Seattle, Washington, where he also serves as a staff trainer for the U.W. Medical School, teaching the basics of Family Therapy. He is a National Humanities scholar, and one of the northwest nominees for *Esquire* magazine's 1984 Directory for Under-40 Leaders of National Impact.

Utilizing storytelling as part of the healing process, he has been active in translating and explaining the use of traditional Native American ritual in treating both Indian and non-Indian patients. His original work was in clinical psychology, he eventually switched to educational psychology to pursue his interest in how people use language to structure reality.

I can understand this; when I applied to the department of Clinical Psychology at U.C. in Berkeley, my own teacher of psychology implored me to apply in educational psychology instead; he said that the Department of Clinical Psychology had "taken six or seven of my best counseling students and made rat-runners out of them." We're glad that no such fate occurred to Terry Tafoya.

It is a shaman thing . . . Tupilak. A construct, pieced together of bone and black magic: the feather of a ptarmigan to give it flight; a piece of human skull so it can think; the bone of a seal that it might swim; the bone of a raven so it can scurry quickly across the ground; the tooth of a polar bear so it can bite. The Tupilak casts a deep shadow that needles the skin like the west wind when the moon hides from the sky."

He said nothing, staring at her with narrow eyes, his hand full of tobacco he had offered her. She was hardly old, though the lines between nose and mouth were deep slashes, and a streak of silver gleamed softly in her night-colored hair. One eye was like milky quartz, sightless, or perhaps turned to inward sight.

"It is an ugly thing," he said at last, running his finger on the small ivory carving, shoving the tobacco forward with his other hand, still somewhat fearful of actually touching her.

"No more than a toy." She laughed harshly. "The one who shaped this has never seen a Tupilak—few do and live. It is Egulik's work from a village two days from here. Some men believe the carving of a Tupilak to be lucky, as though a person's fortune is affected by something filed and sanded. Shape in smallness and control the thing itself. But in truth, it is the blood and power of the shaman that quickens the bits and pieces of the Tupilak . . . opens it so that a spirit inhabits it the way the lemming snuggles into a hole." She began to firmly pack the tobacco into her small stone pipe and sent soft blue-white smoke and a prayer upward.

A faint wind blew a hint of salt that mixed with the smoke, and Tingmiak smoothed his thick hair nervously.

"Now ask me the question you really came for," she said

quietly, so quietly that for a moment the words hung there like smoke, so quietly that he wondered if he had heard her speak at all.

"What question?" he finally blurted out, his voice rough, as though he had spent the night throat singing.

"There's a smell of Power on you stronger than the smell of tobacco. You shine like wet ice. Only those who are chosen are this way. Why else seek a shaman with a toy warm in your hand and tobacco under your nails from squeezing so hard? If you are to walk the path now opening for you, you should learn to speak and ask directly."

"Then I can ask questions?" Tingmiak's eyes widened in surprise. All his life he had heard all knowledge of shamans was secret, handed out over years of apprenticeship in miserly amounts.

"Any man or woman can ask," she said, blue-white smoke misting her words. "Whether I choose to answer is up to me. Tingmiak . . . Tingmiak . . . little seabird. Tell me, fledgling, tell me of what you've seen on your first flight." Then she blew smoke over him, and it seemed impossible that her small body could hold so much, that she could continue blowing without breathing in. The smoke circled him and he relaxed, remembering.

"Tingmiak, Tingmiak," he remembered his mother shaking him so that he felt as if he were shaking apart, until he opened his eyes to see faces of his family all around him.

"Are you all right?" she asked, tears like a seal flowing swiftly down her round face, and then the question she feared to ask and that he sought to avoid: "Did you see?" With the inflection she gave the word, the verb had nothing to do with eyesight.

"Did you see?" The question for someone who did not seek, but was chosen by the Powers to become a shaman . . . or worse. Shaman: Elik . . . "one who has eyes."

"A kayak," he whispered although to his own ears he seemed to be shouting, "tossed on high waves, lost until a seagull landed in front of me. It turned to face the water and the ocean calmed like a surface of new ice, and we sailed. It looked forward, but every now and then it would cock its

head and look back at me. One eye was red and the other was milky like dirty ice.''

And he woke again, startled to see one dark eye and one white eye staring at him. "And so it begins," she said, her words heavy with smoke. She tapped the bowl of her pipe and ashes spilled out onto her hand. "Blow onto my ashes, and let this be your first lesson. Fools see us suck out sickness and think it part of our power, but in truth the strength comes in blowing. Blow your breath on my hand and let us continue."

He blinked, confused, and blew gently over the ashes the way he would try encouraging an ember. He blew gently, but the ashes scattered as though a north storm wind had seized them, falling down with heavy sounds like the lead weights the traders had brought during their last trip.

Black and gray ashes buried themselves into the surface of her caribou skins that lined the floor of her snow house.

"East," she said, puffing her pipe that was now giving forth smoke again, although he had not seen her refill it.

He waited for her to go on, but no words followed; he glanced up, and then back to the pattern of ashes on the caribou skins, only to discover the shaggy fur was clean, showing nothing.

She smiled and her teeth were filed sharp. "Did you think it would remain? Your second lesson: messages to a Shaman do not stay patiently like ice in winter or the black books the traders pack. Blink and you may as well be blind." She exhaled and smoke rose, curling about her head, and for the briefest instant he thought it formed the shape of a polar bear's head.

"What is east?" he asked, his heart pounding, and now he remembered quite clearly hearing the same sound when he had been in the kayak and the seagull had settled in front of him. He had thought it constant drumming, but now he realized it was his heartbeat.

"For some, a place of new beginnings. Did you think becoming a shaman is a matter of sitting at my feet and pretending to listen? Your Power is your true teacher . . . the seagull that pitied you and lifted you up. You did not seek Power, but Power found you. Once chosen, you have few choices. You can complete your obligation, by following the direction that has been shown and doing as you are instructed; you can begin to follow and fail, or you can go home and set nets, trying for the rest of your life to be deaf and blind to the world as it really is. Each choice has a price," she said, resting her pipe in a bowl carved of whalebone, the pitted surface of the bowl in shadow. "Fail and you become a half thing, neither here nor there. The place for a human being is among human beings, not always in the spirit world. Some who fail lack the discipline to choose where they wish to be, and so they shift in and out of the real world without warning, without desire." She set the bowl and pipe aside, reaching for dried fish that she offered to him with no ritual. "Walk away from here without looking back and you will live to a colorless and cold old age, never able to bear responsibility. "The choice is yours."

"And if I succeed?" he asked, chewing, but tasting nothing.

"Then you will be a Shaman," she said simply, and paused so long he thought she had finished speaking. "You will make your own rules. You will choose the direction of your own life. Some will give you gifts out of gratitude, and others out of fear. You will never be welcome in anyone's home save your own or another shaman's. But when you call, people will come . . . or they will die."

At dawn she led him out to meet the sun, walking to a place where the sea was so hard they walked on it, walking out to step into morning. "Here you'll wait," she told him, pressing on his shoulder until he sank to his knees. "Four days," she whispered, "no food. As much water as you can melt in your mouth when the sun rises. If you can empty yourself out enough for a spirit to fill you, you will survive. Take ice into your heart and you will live. Be one with the cold and do not fight against it. Only in this way may you live. Fail and the price is your life for now and three lives to come. Empty yourself out and examine without fears the reason you seek Power."

Before he realized it, she was gone, and cold and hunger began to strip him of his awareness. He woke, and gathered a mouthful of snow that he placed on his tongue. The ice crystals bit into his throat and he began to shiver. He closed his eyes and felt himself melt into the sea, sliding out of himself, while the light began to grow. Brilliance increased, but brought no warmth, and he fell slowly, ice in his heart. . . .

Seeking, you come, and I pity you The Seagull turned its head. The feathers glistened like mother-of-pearl, its body lit with an inner glow that drew out the last of his human warmth, swallowing it. The Seagull was larger than the umaiak, the boat used to hunt walrus. One eye was red, and the other eye milky blue like the core of a glacier.

Blood are you seeking, the blood of the one who led you here, the one-eyed witch The Spirit Bird did not speak as a human speaks, but it was as though Tingmiak remembered the words, rather than heard them.

"She killed my father," he told the snow.

Let the snow drink her blood.

"My mother raised me with the story of his death, letting me know my obligation. How do I fulfill my destiny? How can I kill her?"

You have sought to kill her as she killed your father. She is allied with Polar Bear. Even I with all my cleverness cannot stand against him in battle.

"Then there is no hope?"

No hope in your original plan to become a shaman to destroy a shaman. She must die as a woman dies. Wait until she begins a spell of quickening. Let her split off a part of herself to bring life. At that time the hold on her body will be weakest and you can kill her with sharpened bone or the dark iron of the traders.

The Seagull turned and its feathers darkened and contracted. Wings thickened into arms and the round eyes narrowed, until Tingmiak looked into his own face.

"It is time to learn your song," Tingmiak/gull said. And until the sun rose again, Tingmiak sang and listened to the teachings of the Bird Spirit.

Thirst returned him to awareness of another dawn and the need to let snow melt on his tongue. As icy drops soothed his throat he could feel a force like fire nearing him, and he turned to see her approach.

"So, fledgling," she called, "I hatch a shaman from the shell of a shivering boy. Stand and follow me." Without waiting, she turned and walked back to her snow house, hearing him step heavily as he left the surface of the sea.

She lit a seal-oil lamp by glaring at it, and a greasy flame danced with small movements, brushing the furs with shadows and light. She heated tea and broke his fast with raw meat dipped in fresh seal oil.

"It is unfortunate that the Seagull chose you," she said, pulling his boots off to let them dry. "The Seagull is even less reliable than the Raven. A trickster. You'll never know whether it lies to you or savors truth. It will lie for the enjoyment of it. At least," she said, slicing more meat with quick movements, "it has a pretty enough song."

His lessons from her continued, while he sharpened his knives and his patience.

One day he asked her, "Show me how to shape a Tupilak."

She sat on her furs without speaking while his heart pounded and he worried that she would smell his fear.

"Yes," she said, and the seal oil lamp nearly blew out, "I suppose it is time you learned. You have been learning everything quickly enough." She rummaged through round baskets and pulled out small bundles of red trade cloth that she lingered over, smiling at him with her filed teeth. "What do I look for?" she asked him.

"A piece of human skull so it might think," he answered, and she tossed him a sliver of white, shaped like a flower petal with one rough edge. "A raven's bone so it can scurry quickly across the ground." She laughed and in her left hand there was suddenly a hollow bone tied to a feather as dark as greed that she blew into the air where it spun lazily across the snow house into his grasp. "Feather of a ptarmigan so it can fly . . . Seal bone so it can swim." And one by one these things sprang into his hands, where they moved like worms.

"And what else?" she smiled, her words frozen in the air.

He shivered, his mind blank and he knew that he had failed, but her grin widened at his discomfort and he answered, "The tooth of a polar bear so it can bite."

"Just so," she said, her smile gone. She reached into her mouth and pulled out an enormous bear's tooth that she must have palmed earlier.

"Pieces," she sighed, "just pieces without the blood and spirit of a shaman. Give me your knife."

He handed it to her, and she turned it slowly, reflecting dull light from the small fire of the lamp. She held his eyes with her stare and pulled the knife across her hand. With impossible slowness, red beads grew in a line across her palm and she smeared her blood on the objects in his hands. The beginning of the Tupilak twisted together, bonding into oneness as it fell out onto the furs.

"It is nothing without the joining of the shaman. A sliver of life force, thinner than a slice of raw meat. This is how you separate a splinter of yourself. Watch and learn." She breathed out, and the muscles of her face relaxed and flattened as she withdrew into herself.

His heart pounding louder and louder in his ears like maddening skin drums, he watched her life force flicker and he unsheathed his second knife with trembling fingers. Drawing ice into his heart he leaned across the furs and sank the sharpness into her chest. He struck bone and the knife twisted as her eyes flew open and he stared into black and old milky ice.

"For my father's death," he gasped. "Life for life in payment."

"So many fathers," she said, her voice rough and light, her good eye growing as cloudy as its mate. "No idea which one was yours."

But before he could answer, her eyes lost awareness and he watched her life force tremble and then vanish like the flame of the seal-oil lamp.

"Egulik," he spat, feeling cheated. "Egulik was the one you murdered. But he can rest at last, knowing that life has paid for life." Tingmiak picked up the reddened knife she had used to draw her own blood, but the other blade he left embedded in her body. He cleaned it, wiping it on her furs.

He gathered his things quickly and stepped into the dim coldness, wanting nothing more than to return to his home and let his mother and others know he had avenged his father and cleaned their family. He continued, not stopping to eat or drink more than a mouthful of snow.

As the last shreds of light disappeared, he began to grow

cold and he pulled his furs more tightly around him, his breathing burning his dry throat.

He thought he heard something, but there was nothing he could see. He shifted his pack to ease his shoulder and went on, almost running. Again he could hear something and he stopped, casting out his awareness as she had trained him to do earlier. Nothing. He turned in a circle and this time he heard the sound of something scurrying quickly across the snow like a raven.

Dropping the bundle from his back he began running, numb with a nameless fear. He ran until the ice of his heart melted and bled away. He ran until his legs cramped and he fell, his breathing raw and hot. He struggled to get up and he realized he was no longer alone.

"So, my fledgling has claws," she called from above, her voice shattered almost beyond recognition. He looked up and choked on his fear. It was the size of a ribbon-neck seal now. Monstrous and almost gaudy in color, the Tupilak dug into the snow and smiled at him with sharpened teeth. The long forgotten ivory carving was indeed a toy beside this obscene shape. Two-thirds of its face was jaw and teeth. The eyes were empty holes and it stood on four feet furred like a bear.

"A good teacher doesn't teach everything to her student. The Gull must have told you to attack me physically, since its petty power could never stand before mine. Did it tell you to sheathe your steel in my flesh while I created a Tupilak? Did it trick you, or was it your own stupidity and greed for revenge that led you to choose the one spell to strike where I would be using my own soul to clear a place for a spirit to enter into and animate the Tupilak? Egulik, you called your father. The first man that ever refused my bed. Oh, yes, I remember Egulik. And I'll remember his son." She smiled her deadly smile and the rising moon made the filed teeth sparkle like new ice. It was the last thing he ever saw.

Background on Tupilak

For two years I served as Alaska Field Specialist for the National Bilingual Training and Resource Center at the University of Washington, providing training and technical assis-

tance to Native Bilingual work there, the Canadian government asked me to begin working with similar Innuit and Athabaskan programs throughout the Northwest Territories, since the languages were the same as the ones I worked with in Alaska, although the dialects were different. One of the things that fascinated me when working with the Eskimo people was their feelings toward their Shamans.

We Indians have deep respect for our Medicine People. We strongly distinguish between Medicine People and Witches—although their abilities are similar, their intent is different. The Medicine Person affirms the Harmonies, while a Witch works for his or her own selfishness. The Eskimo people traditionally blurred the line between the two, fearing their shamans with apparently good reason. Undoubtedly more than one shaman took advantage of his or her situation. At least this is the memory shared by the Eskimos I have interviewed, all of whom have happily converted to Christianity, delighted that shamanism is only talked about as something disappearing during their grandparents' time.

On the infrequent occasions when traditional spiritual help is needed, the Eskimo people will seek assistance from their Indian neighbors, who still keep their Medicine traditions going.

While taking some "artistic license," I tried to be as accurate as possible in utilizing Eskimo traditions, although the story represents a blend of Innuit beliefs and customs, rather than one specific group. In terms of the theme of the story, Arima mentions that ". . . the desire for vengence motivates more action than any other emotion (in Eskimo myths) and that the Eskimo hero is 'predominantly an avenger.' "

—*Terry Tafoya*

SWORD SWORN

Mercedes Lackey

I had known "Misty" Lackey as the "gofer mother" for a couple of our Fantasy Worlds Festival conventions; as an expert needlewoman, a creator of beautiful embroideries and costumes, and as a friend who could supply us with opera tapes not broadcast in the S.F. Bay Area. I did not know she was also a writer until she sent me a story for *Free Amazons of Darkover*.

When she arrived for Fantasy Worlds 1985, I was swamped in a flood of manuscripts for S&S III, and began to read hers without enthusiasm: I believed I had enough longer stories for the volume, and was racking my brains for a polite way to tell a valued friend that I had enough stories of this length; I yelled "Damn you, Misty—" because I couldn't think of a single reason to reject it. In fact, it was far too good to reject; I found myself glued to the page. Strong action, a compelling likable character, believable swordplay and genuinely convincing magic—an unbeatable combination. What started out to be an ordinary rape and revenge story quickly developed into a quite unusual story of supernatural vengeance and personal growth.

T he air inside the gathering-tent was hot, although the evening breeze that occasionally stole inside the closed tent flap and touched Tarma's back was chill, like a sword's edge laid along her spine. This high-desert country cooled off quickly at night, not like the clan's grazing grounds down in the grass-plains. Tarma shivered; for comfort's sake she'd long since removed her shirt and now, like most of the others in the tent, was attired only in her vest and breeches. In the light of the lamps Tarma's clansfolk looked like living versions of the gaudy patterns they wove into their rugs.

Her brother-uncle Kefta neared the end of his sword-dance in the middle of the tent. He performed it only rarely, on the most special of occasions, but this occasion warranted celebration. Never before had the men of the clan returned from the Summer Horsefair laden with so much gold—it was nearly three times what they'd hoped for. There was war a-brewing somewhere, and as a consequence horses had commanded more than prime prices. The Shin'a'in hadn't argued with their good fortune. Now their new wealth glistened in the light of the oil lamps, lying in a shining heap in the center of the tent for all of the Clan of the Stooping Hawk to rejoice over. Tomorrow it would be swiftly converted into salt and herbs, grain and leather, metal weapons and staves of true, straight-grained wood for looms and arrows (all things the Shin'a'in did not produce themselves) but for this night, they would admire their short-term wealth and celebrate.

Not all that the men had earned lay in that shining heap. Each man who'd undertaken the journey had earned a special share, and most had brought back gifts. Tarma stroked the necklace at her throat as she breathed in the scent of clean sweat, incense, and the sentlewood perfume most of her clan had anointed themselves with. She glanced to her right as she did so, surprised at her flash of shyness. Dharin seemed to have all his attention fixed on the whirling figure of the dancer, but he intercepted her glance as if he'd been watching for it and his normally solemn expression vanished as he smiled broadly. Tarma blushed, then made a face at him. He grinned even more, and pointedly lowered his eyes to the necklace of carved amber she wore, curved claws alternating with perfect beads. He'd brought that for her, evidence of his trading abilities, because (he said) it matched her golden skin. That she'd accepted it and was wearing it tonight was token that she'd accepted him as well. When Tarma finished her sword-training, they'd be bonded. That would be in two years, perhaps less, if her progress continued to be as rapid as it was now. She and Dharin dealt with each other very well indeed, each being a perfect counter for the other. They were long-time friends as well as lovers.

The dancer ended his performance in a calculated sprawl, as though exhausted. His audience shouted approval, and he rose from the carpeted tent floor, beaming and dripping with sweat. He flung himself down among his family, accepting with a nod of thanks the damp towel handed to him by his youngest son. The plaudits faded gradually into chattering; as last to perform he would pick the next.

After a long draft of wine he finally spoke, and his choice was no surprise to anyone. "Sing, Tarma." he said.

His choice was applauded on all sides as Tarma rose, brushed back her long ebony hair, and picked her way through the crowded bodies of her clansfolk to take her place in the center.

Tarma was no beauty; her features were too sharp and hawklike, her body too boyishly slender; and well she knew it. Dharin had often joked when they lay together that he never knew whether he was bedding her or her sword. But the Goddess of the Four Winds had granted her a voice that was more than compensation, a voice that was unmatched among the Clans. The Shin'a'in, whose history was mainly contained in song and story, valued such a voice more than precious metals. Such was her value that the shaman had taught her the arts of reading and writing, that she might the more easily learn the ancient lays of other peoples as well as her own.

Impishly, she had decided to pay Dharin back for making her blush by singing a tale of totally faithless lovers, one that was a clan favorite. She had only just begun it, the musicians picking up the key and beginning to follow her, when, unlooked for, disaster struck.

Audible even over her singing came the sound of tearing cloth, and armored men, seemingly dozens of them, poured howling through the ruined tentwalls to fall upon the stunned nomads. Most of the Clan were all but weaponless—but the Shin'a'in were warriors by tradition as well as horsebreeders. There was not one of them above the age of nine that had not had at least some training. They shook off their shock quickly, and every member of the clan that could seized whatever was nearest and fought back with the fierceness of any cornered wild thing.

Tarma had her paired daggers and a throwing spike in a wrist sheath—the last was quickly lost as she hurled it with deadly accuracy through the visor of the nearest bandit. He screeched, dropped his sword, and clutched his face, blood pouring between his fingers. One of her cousins snatched up the forgotten blade and gutted him with it. Tarma had no time to see what other use he made of it; another of the bandits was bearing down on her and she had barely enough time to draw her daggers before he closed with her.

A dagger, even two of them, rarely makes a good defense against a longer blade, but fighting in the tent was cramped, and the bandit found himself at disadvantage in the close quarters. Though Tarma's hands were shaking with excitement and fear, her mind stayed cool and she managed to get him to trap his own blade long enough for her to plant one dagger in his throat. He gurgled hoarsely, then fell, narrowly missing imprisoning her beneath him. She wrenched the sword from his still-clutching hands and turned to find another foe.

The invaders were easily winning the unequal battle; despite a gallant defense, with such improvised weapons as rugs and hair ornaments, her people were rapidly falling. The bandits were armored; the Shin'a'in were not. Out of the corner of one eye she could see a pair of them dropping their weapons and seizing women. Around her she could hear the shrieks of children, the harsher cries of adults—

Another fighter faced her now, his face blood- and sweat-streaked; she forced herself not to hear, to think only of the moment and her opponent.

She parried his thrust with the dagger, and made a slash at his neck. The fighting had thinned now; she couldn't hope to use the tactics that had worked before. He countered it in leisurely fashion and turned the counter into a return stroke with careless ease that sent her writhing out of the way of the blade's edge. She wasn't quite fast enough—he left a long score on her ribs. The cut wasn't deep or dangerous, but it hurt and bled freely. She stumbled over a body—friend or foe, she didn't notice; and barely evaded his blade a second time. He toyed with her, his face splitting in an ugly grin as he saw how tired she was becoming. Her hands were shaking now, not with fear, but with exhaustion. She was so weary she failed to notice the circle of bandits that had formed around her, or that she was the only Shin'a'in still fighting. He made a pass; before she had time to realize it was merely a feint, he'd gotten inside her guard and swatted her to the ground as the flat of his blade connected with the side of her head, the edges cutting into her scalp, searing like hot iron. He'd swung the blade full-force—she fought off unconsciousness as her hands reflexively let her weapons fall and she collapsed. Half-stunned, she tried to punch, kick and bite (in spite of nausea and a dizziness that kept threatening to overwhelm her. He began battering her face and head with massive fists.

He connected one time too many, and she felt her legs give out, her arms fall helplessly to her sides. He laughed, then threw her to the floor of the tent, inches away from the body of one of her brothers. She felt his hands tearing off her breeches; she tried to get her knee into his groin, but the last of her strength was long gone. He laughed again and settled his hands almost lovingly around her neck and began to squeeze. She clawed at the hands, but he was too strong; nothing she did made him release that ever-tightening grip. She began to thrash as her chest tightened and her lungs cried out for air. Her head seemed about to explode, and reality narrowed to the desperate struggle for a single breath. At last, mercifully, blackness claimed her even as he began to thrust himself brutally into her.

The only sound in the violated tent was the steady droning of flies. Tarma opened her right eye—the left one was swollen shut—and stared dazedly at the ceiling. When she tried to swallow, her throat howled in protest, she gagged, and nearly choked. Whimpering, she rolled onto one side. She found she was staring into the sightless eyes of her baby sister, as flies fed greedily at the pool of blood congealing beneath the child's head.

She vomited up what little there was in her stomach, and nearly choked to death in the process. Her throat was swollen almost completely shut.

She dragged herself to her knees, her head spinning dizzily. As she looked round her, and her mind took in the magnitude of disaster, something within her parted with a nearly audible snap.

Every member of the clan, from the oldest grayhair to the youngest infant, had been brutally and methodically slaughtered. The sight was more than her dazed mind could bear. She wanted most to run screaming to hide in a safe, dark, mental corner; but knew she must coax her body to its feet.

A few rags of her vest hung from her shoulders; there was blood running down her thighs and her loins ached sharply, echoing the pounding pain in her head. More blood had dried all down one side, some of it from the cut along her ribs, some that of her foes or her clansfolk. Her hand rose of its own accord to her temple and found her long hair sticky and hard with dried blood. The pain of her head and the nausea that seemed linked with it overwhelmed any other hurt, but as her hand drifted absently over her face, it felt strange, swollen and puffy. Had she been able to see, she would not have recognized her own reflection, her face was so battered. The part of her that was still thinking sent her body to search for something to cover her nakedness. She found a pair of breeches—not her own, they were much too big—and a vest, flung into corners. Her eyes slid unseeing over the huddled, nude bodies. Then the thread of direction sent her to retrieve the Clan banner from where it still hung on the centerpole.

Clutching it in one hand, she found herself outside the gathering-tent. She stood dumbly in the sun for several long moments, then moved zombie-like toward the nearest of the family tents. They, too, had been ransacked, but at least there were no bodies in them. The raiders had found little to their taste there, other than the odd bit of jewelry. Only a Shin'a'in would be interested in the tack and personal gear of a Shin'a'in—and anyone not of the clans found trying to sell such would find himself with several inches of Shin'a'in steel in his gut. Apparently the bandits knew this.

She found a halter and saddlepad in one of the nearer tents. The rest of her crouched in its mind-corner and gibbered. She wept soundlessly when it recognized the tack by its tooling as Dharin's.

The brigands had not been able to steal the horses—the Shin'a'in let them run free and the horses were trained nearly from birth to come only to their riders. The sheep and goats had been scattered, but the goats were guardian enough to reunite the herds and protect them in the absence of shepherds—and in any case, it was the horses that concerned her now, not the other animals. Tarma managed a semblance of her whistle with her swollen, cracked lips; Kessira came trotting up eagerly, snorting with distaste at the smell of blood on her mistress. Her hands, swollen, stiff, and painful, were clumsy with the harness, but Kessira was patient while Tarma struggled with the straps, not even tossing her gray head in an effort to avoid the hackamore as she usually did.

Tarma dragged herself into the saddle; another clan was camped less than a day's ride away. She lumped the banner in front of her, pointed Kessira in the right direction, and gave her the set of signals that meant that her mistress was hurt and needed help. That accomplished, the dregs of directing intelligence receded into hiding with the rest of her. The ghastly ride was endured in complete blankness.

She never knew when Kessira walked into the camp with her broken, bleeding mistress slumped over the clan banner. No one recognized her—they only knew she was Shin'a'in by her coloring and costume. She never knew that she led a rescue party back to the ruined camp before collapsing over Kessira's neck. The shamans and healers eased her off the back of her mare, and she never felt their ministrations. For seven days and nights, she lay silent, never moving, eyes either closed or staring fixedly into space. The healers feared for her life and sanity, for a Shin'a'in clanless was one without purpose.

But on the morning of the eighth day, when the healer entered the tent in which she lay, her head turned and the eyes that met his were once again bright with intelligence.

Her lips parted. "Where—?" she croaked, her voice uglier than a raven's cry.

"Liha'irden." he said, setting down his burden of broth and medicine. "Your name? We could not recognize you, only the banner—" He hesitated, unsure of what to tell her.

"Tarma," she replied. "What of—my clan—Deer's Son?"

"Gone." It would be best to tell it shortly. "We gave them the rites as soon as we found them, and brought the herds and goods back here. You are the last of the Hawk's Children."

So her memory was correct. She stared at him wordlessly.

At this time of year the entire Clan traveled together, leaving none at the grazing grounds. There was no doubt she was the sole survivor.

She was taking the news calmly—too calmly. There was madness lurking within her, he could feel it with his healer's senses. She walked a thin thread of sanity, and it would take very little to cause the thread to break. He dreaded her next question.

It was not the one he had expected. "My voice—what ails it?"

"Something broken past mending." he replied regretfully—for he had heard her sing less than a month ago.

"So." she turned her head to stare again at the ceiling. For a moment he feared she had retreated into madness, but after a pause she spoke again.

"I cry blood-feud." she said tonelessly.

When the healer's attempts at dissuading her failed, he

brought the clan elders. They reiterated all his arguments, but she remained silent and seemingly deaf to their words.

"You are only one—how can you hope to accomplish anything?" the clanmother said finally. "They are many, seasoned fighters, and crafty. What you wish to do is hopeless."

Tarma stared at them with stony eyes, eyes that did not quite conceal the fact that her sanity was questionable.

"Most importantly," said a voice from the tent door, "you have called what you have no right to call."

The shamaness of the Clan, a vigorous woman of late middle age, stepped into the healer's tent and dropped gracefully beside Tarma's pallet.

"You know well only one Sword-Sworn to the Warrior can cry blood-feud," she said calmly and evenly.

"I know," Tarma replied, breaking her silence. "And I wish to take Oath."

It was a Shin'a'in tenet that no person was any holier than any other, that each was a priest in his own right. The shaman or shamaness might have the power of magic, might also be more learned than the average Clansman had time to be, but when the time came that a Shin'a'in wished to petition the God or Goddess, he simply entered the appropriate tent shrine and did so, with or without consulting the shaman beforehand.

So it happened that Tarma was standing within the shrine on legs that trembled with weakness.

The Wise One had not seemed surprised at Tarma's desire to be Sworn to the Warrior, and had supported her over the protests of the Elders. "If the Warrior accepts her," she had said reasonably, "Who are we to argue with the will of the Goddess? And if she does not, then blood-feud cannot be called."

The tent shrines of the clans were always identical in their spartan simplicity. There were four tiny wooden altars, one against each wall of the tent. In the east was that of the Maiden; on it was her symbol, a single fresh blossom in spring and summer, a stick of burning incense in winter and fall. To the south was that of the Warrior, marked by an ever-burning flame. The west held the Mother's altar, on it a sheaf of grain. The north was the domain of the Crone or Ancient One. The altar here held a smooth black stone.

Tarma stepped to the center of the tent. What she intended was nothing less than self-inflicted torture. All prayers among the Shin'a'in were sung, not spoken; further, all who came before the Goddess must lay all their thoughts before her. They must be sung, not spoken; further, all who came before the Goddess must lay their thoughts before her. Not only must she endure the physical agony of shaping her ruined voice into a semblance of music, but she must deliberately call forth every emotion, every memory; all that caused her to stand in this place.

She finished her song with her eyes tightly closed against the pain of those memories.

There was a profound silence when she'd done; after a moment she realized she could not even hear the little sounds of the encampment on the other side of the thin tent walls. Just as she'd realized that, she felt the faint stirrings of a breeze—

It came from the East, and was filled with the scent of fresh flowers. It encircled her, and seemed to blow right through her very soul. It was soon joined by a second breeze, out of the West; a robust and strong little wind carrying the scent of ripening grain. As the first had blown through her, emptying her of pain, the second filled her with strength. Then it, too, was joined; a bitterly cold wind from the north, sharp with snow-scent. At the touch of this third wind her eyes opened, though she remained swathed in darkness born of the dark of her own spirit. The wind chilled her, numbed the memories until they began to seem remote; froze her heart with an icy armor that made the loneliness bearable. She felt now as if her soul were swathed in endless layers of soft, protecting bandages. Now she saw, through eyes withdrawn to view a world that had receded just out of reach.

The center of a whirlwind now, she stood unmoving while the physical winds whipped her hair and clothing about and the spiritual ones worked their magics within.

But the southern wind, the Warrior's Wind, was not one of them.

Suddenly the winds died to nothing. A voice that held nothing of humanity, echoing, sharp-edged as a fine blade yet ringing with melody, spoke one word. Her name.

Tarma obediently turned slowly to her right. Before the altar in the south stood a woman.

She was raven-haired and tawny-skinned, and the lines of her face were thin and strong, like all the Shin'a'in. She was arrayed in black, from her boots to the headband that held her shoulder-length tresses out of her eyes. Even the chainmail hauberk she wore was black, as were the sword she wore slung across her back and the daggers in her belt. She raised her eyes to meet Tarma's, and they had no whites, irises or pupils; her eyes were reflections of a cloudless night sky, black and star-strewn.

The Goddess had chosen to answer as the Warrior, and in Her own person.

When Tarma stepped through the tent-flap there was a collective sigh. Her hair was shorn just short of shoulder length; the clansfolk would find the discarded locks on the Warrior's altar. Tarma had carried nothing into the tent, there was nothing within the shrine that she would have been able to use to cut it. Tarma's Oath had been accepted. There was an icy calm about her that was unmistakable, and completely nonhuman.

No one in this clan had been Sword-Sworn within living memory, but all knew what tradition demanded of them. No longer would the Sworn One wear garments bright with the colors the Shin'a'in loved; from out of a chest in the Wise One's tent, carefully husbanded against such a time, came clothing of dark brown and deepest black. The brown was for later, should Tarma survive her quest. The black was for now, for ritual combat, or for one pursuing blood-feud.

They clothed her, weaponed her, provisioned her. She stood before them when they had done, looking much as the Warrior herself had, her weapons about her, her provisions at her feet. The light of the dying sun turned the sky to blood as they brought the youngest child of the Clan Liha'irden to receive her blessing, a toddler barely ten months old. She placed her hands on his soft cap of baby hair without really seeing him—but this child had a special significance. The herds and properties of the Hawk's Children would be tended and preserved for her, either until Tarma returned, or until this youngest child in the Clan of the Racing Deer was old enough to take his own sword. If by then she had not returned, they would revert to their caretakers.

Tarma rode out into the dawn. Tradition forbade anyone to watch her departure. To her own senses it seemed as though she rode still drugged with one of the healer's potions. All things came to her as if filtered through a gauze veil; even her memories seemed secondhand—like a tale told to her by some gray-haired ancient.

She rode back to the scene of the slaughter; the pitiful burial mound aroused nothing in her. Some outside force showed her eyes where to catch the scant signs of the already cold trail. No attempt had been made to conceal it. She rode until the fading light made tracking impossible, and made a cold camp, concealing herself and her horse in the lee of a pile of boulders. Enough moisture collected on them each night to support some meager grasses, which Kessira tore at eagerly. Tarma made a sketchy meal of dried meat and fruit, still wrapped in that strange calmness, then rolled herself into her blanket.

She was awakened before midnight.

A touch on her shoulder sent her scrambling out of her blanket, dagger in hand. Before her stood a figure, seemingly a man of the Shin'a'in, clothed as one Sword-Sworn. Unlike her, his face was veiled.

"Arm yourself, Sworn One." he said, his voice having an odd quality of distance to it, as though he were speaking from the bottom of a well.

She did not pause to question or argue. It was well that she did not, for as soon as she had donned her arms and light chain shirt, he attacked her.

The fight was not a long one; he had the advantage of surprise, and he was a much better fighter than she. Tarma could see the killing blow coming, but was unable to do anything to prevent it from falling. She cried out in agony as the stranger's sword all but cut her in half.

She woke, staring up at the stars. The stranger interposed himself between her eyes and the sky. "You are better than I thought—" he said, with grim humor. "But you are still clumsy as a horse in a pottery shed. Get up and try again."

He killed her three more times—with the same non-fatal result. After the third, she woke to find the sun rising, herself curled in her blanket and feeling completely rested. For one moment, she wondered if the strange combat had all been a nightmare—but then she saw her arms and armor stacked neatly to hand. As if to mock her doubts, they were laid in a different pattern than she had left them.

Once again she rode in a dream. Something controlled her actions as deftly as she managed Kessira, keeping the raw edges of her mind carefully swathed and anesthetized. When she lost the trail, her controller found it again, making her body pause long enough for her to identify how it had been done.

She camped, and again she was awakened before midnight.

Pain is a rapid teacher; she was able to prolong the bouts this night enough that he only killed her twice.

It was a strange existence, tracking by day, training by night. When her track ended at a village, she found herself questioning the inhabitants shrewdly. When her provisions ran out, she discovered coin in the pouch that had held dried fruit—not a great deal, but enough to pay for more of the same. When, in other villages, her questions were met with evasions, her hand stole of itself to that same pouch, to find coin enough to loosen the tongues of those she faced. Always when she needed something, she either woke with it to hand, or discovered more of the magical coins appearing to pay for it; always just enough, and no more. Her nights seemed clearer and less dreamlike than her days, perhaps because the controls were thinner then, and the skill she fought with was all her own. Finally one night she "killed" her instructor.

He collapsed exactly as she would have expected a man run through the heart to collapse. He lay unmoving—

"A good attack, but your guard was sloppy." said a familiar voice behind her. She whirled, her sword ready.

He stood before her, his own sword sheathed. She risked a glance to her rear; the body was gone.

"Truce. You have earned a respite and a reward," he said. "Ask me what you will, I am sure you have many questions. I know I did."

"Who are you?" she cried eagerly. "What are you?"

"I cannot give you my name, Sworn One. I am only one of many servants of the Warrior; I am the first of your teachers—and I am what you will become if you should die while still under Oath. Does that disturb you? The Warrior will release you at any time you wish to be freed. She does not want the unwilling. Of course, if you are freed, you must relinquish the blood-feud."

Tarma shook her head.

"Then ready yourself, Sworn One, and look to that sloppy guard."

There came a time when their combats always ended draws or with his "death". When that had happened three nights running, she woke the fourth night to face a new opponent—a woman, armed with daggers.

Meanwhile she tracked her quarry, by rumor, by the depredations left in their wake. It seemed that what she tracked was a roving band of freebooters, and her clan was not the only group made victims. They chose their quarry carefully, never picking anyone the authorities might avenge, nor anyone with friends in power.

When she had mastered sword, dagger, bow, and staff, her trainers appeared severally rather than singly; she learned the arts of the single combatant against many.

Every time she gained a victory, they instructed her further in what her Oath meant.

One of those things was that her body no longer felt the least stirrings of sexual desire. The Sword-Sworn were as devoid of concupiscence as their weapons.

"The gain outweighs the loss," the first of them told her. After being taught the disciplines and rewards of the meditative trance they called "The Moonpaths," she agreed. After that, she spent at least part of every night walking those paths, surrounded by a curious kind of ecstasy, renewing her strength and her bond with her Goddess.

Inexorably, she began to catch up with her quarry. She had

begun this quest months behind them; now she was only days. The closer she drew, the more intensely did her spirit-trainers drill her.

Then one night, they did not come. She woke on her own and waited, waited until well past midnight, waited until she was certain they were not coming at all. She dozed off for a moment, when she felt a presence. She rose with one swift motion, pulling her sword from the scabbard on her back.

The first of her trainers held out empty hands. "It has been a year, Sworn One. Are you ready? Your foes lair in the town not two hours' ride from here, and the town is truly their lair for they have made it their own."

So near as that? His words came as a shock, ripping the protective magics that veiled her mind and heart, sending her to her knees with the shrilling pain and raging anger she had felt before the winds of the Goddess answered her prayers. No longer was she protected against her own emotions; the wounds were as raw as they had ever been.

He regarded her thoughtfully, his eyes pitying above the veil. "No, you are *not* ready. Your hate will undo you, your hurt will disarm you. But you have little choice, Sworn One. This task is one you bound *yourself* to, you cannot free yourself. Will you heed advice, or will you throw yourself uselessly into the arms of Death?"

"What advice?" she asked dully.

"When you are offered aid unlooked for, do not cast it aside," he said, and vanished.

She could not sleep; she set out at first light for the town, and hovered about outside the walls until just before the gates were closed for the night. She soothed the ruffled feathers of the guard with a coin, offered as "payment" for directions to the inn.

The inn was noisy, hot and crowded. She wrinkled her nose at the unaccustomed stench of old cooking smells, spilled wine, and unwashed bodies. Another small coin bought her a jug of sour wine and a seat in a dark corner, from which she could hear nearly everything said in the room. It did not take long to determine from chance-dropped comments that the brigand-troupe made their headquarters in the long-abandoned mansion of a merchant who had lost everything he had including his life to their depredations. Their presence was unwelcome. They regarded the townsfolk as their lawful prey; having been freed from their attentions for the past year, their "chattels" were not pleased with their return.

Tarma burned with scorn for these soft townmen. Surely there were enough able-bodied adults in the place to outnumber the bandit crew several times over. By sheer numbers the townsmen could defeat them, if they'd try.

She turned her mind toward her own quest, to develop a plan that would enable her to take as many of the enemy into death as she could manage. She was under no illusion that she could survive this. The kind of frontal assault she planned would leave her no path of escape.

A shadow came between Tarma and the fire.

She looked up, startled that the other had managed to come so close without her being aware of it. The silhouette was that of a woman, wearing the calf-length, cowled brown robe of a wandering sorceress. There was one alarming anomaly about this woman—unlike any other magic-worker Tarma had ever seen, this one wore a sword belted at her waist.

She reached up and laid the cowl of her robe back, but Tarma still was unable to make out her features; the firelight behind her hair made a glowing nimbus of amber around her face.

"It won't work, you know." the stranger said very softly, in a pleasant, musical alto. "You won't gain anything by a frontal assault but your own death."

Fear laid an icy hand on Tarma's throat; to cover her fear she snarled, "How do you know what I plan? Who are you?"

"Lower your voice, Sworn One." the sorceress took a seat next to Tarma, uninvited. "Anyone with the Talent and the wish to do so can read your thoughts. Your foes number among them a sorcerer; I know he is responsible for the deaths of many a sentry that would have warned their victims in time to defend themselves. Rest assured that if *I* can read your intentions, *he* will be able to do the same, should he cast his mind in this direction. I want to help you. My name is Kethry."

"Why help me?" Tarma asked bluntly, knowing that by giving her name the sorceress had given Tarma a measure of power over her.

Kethry stirred, bringing her face fully into the light of the fire. Tarma saw then that the woman was younger than she had first judged; they were almost of an age. The sorceress was almost doll-like in her prettiness. But Tarma had also seen the way she moved, like a wary predator; and the too-wise expression in those emerald eyes sat ill with the softness of the face. Her robe was worn to shabbiness, and though clean, was travel-stained. Whatever else this woman was, she was not overly concerned with material wealth. That in itself was a good sign to Tarma—since the only real wealth in this town was to be had by serving with the brigands.

But why did she wear a sword?

"I have an interest in dealing with these robbers myself," she said. "And I'd rather that they weren't set on guard. And I have another reason as well—"

"So?"

She laughed deprecatingly. "I am under a *geas,* one that binds me to help women in need. I am bound to help you, whether or not either of us is pleased with the fact. Will you have that help unforced?"

Tarma's initial reaction had been to bristle with hostility— then, unbidden, into her mind came the odd, otherworldly voice of her trainer, warning her not to cast away unlooked-for aid.

"As you will," she replied curtly.

The other did not seem to be the least bit discomfited by her antagonism. "Then let us leave this place," she said, standing without haste. "There are too many ears here."

She waited while Tarma retrieved her horse, and led her down tangled streets to a dead-end alley lit by red lanterns. She unlocked a gate on the left side and waved Tarma and Kessira through it. Tarma waited as she relocked the gate, finding herself in a cobbled courtyard that was bordered on one side by an old but well-kept stable. On the other side was a house, windows ablaze with lights, festooned with the red lanterns. From the house came the sound of music, laughter, and the voices of many women. Tarma sniffed; the air was redolent of cheap perfume and an animal muskiness.

"Is this place what I think it is?" she asked, finding it difficult to match the picture she'd built in her mind of the sorceress with the house she'd led Tarma to.

"If you think it's a brothel, you're right." Kethry replied. "Welcome to the House of Scarlet Joys, Sworn One. Can you think of a *less* likely place to house two such as we?"

"No." Tarma almost smiled.

"The better to hide us. The mistress of this place and her charges would rejoice greatly at the conquering of our mutual enemies. Nevertheless, the most these women will do for us is house and feed us. The rest is in *our* four hands. Let's get your weary beast stabled, and we'll adjourn to my rooms. We have a great deal of planning to do."

Two days after Tarma's arrival in the town of Brether's Crossroads, one of the brigands (drunk with liquor and drugs far past his capacity) fell into a horsetrough, and drowned trying to get out. His death signaled the beginning of a streak of calamities that thinned the ranks of the bandits as persistently as a plague.

One by one they died, victims of weird accidents, overdoses of drugs, or ambushes by clever thieves. No two deaths were alike—with one exception. He who failed to shake out his boots of a morning seldom survived the day, thanks to the scorpions that had taken to invading the place. Some even died at each other's hands, goaded into fights.

"I mislike this skulking in corners," Tarma growled, sharpening her swordblade. "It's hardly satisfactory, killing these dogs at a distance with poison and witchery."

"Be patient, my friend." Kethry said without rancor. "We're thinning them down before we engage them at sword's point. There will be time enough for that later."

When the deaths were obviously at the hands of enemies, there were no clues. Those arrow-slain were found pierced by several makes; those dead by blades seemed to have had their own used on them.

Tarma found herself coming to admire the sorceress more with every passing day. Their arrangement was a partnership in every sense of the word, for when Kethry ran short of magical ploys she turned without pride to Tarma and her expertise in weaponry. Even so, the necessary restrictions that limited them to the ambush and the skills of the assassin chafed at her.

"Not much longer," Kethry counseled. "They'll come to the conclusion soon enough that this has been no series of coincidences. *Then* will be the time for frontal attack."

The leader, so it was said, ordered that no man go out alone, and all must wear talismans against sorcery.

"See?" Kethry said. "I told you you'd have your chance."

A pair of swaggering bullies swilled ale, unpaid for, in the inn. None dared speak in their presence; they'd already beaten one farmer senseless who'd given some imagined insult. They were spoiling for a fight and the sheeplike timidity of the people trapped with them in the inn was not to their liking. So when a slender young man, black-clad and wearing a sword slung across his back entered the door, their eyes lit with savage glee.

One snaked out a long arm, grasping the young man's wrist. Some of those in the inn marked how his eyes flashed with a hellish joy before being veiled with cold disdain.

"Remove your hand," he said in a harsh voice. "Dog-turd."

That was all the excuse the brigands needed. Both drew their weapons; the young man unsheathed his in a single fluid motion. Both moved against him in a pattern they had long found successful in bringing down a single opponent.

Both died within heartbeats of each other.

The young man cleaned his blade carefully on their cloaks before sheathing it. (Some sharp eyes may have noticed that when his hand came in contact with one of the brigand's talismans, the young man seemed to become, for a fleeting second, a harsh-visaged young *woman*.) "This is no town for a stranger." he said to no one and everyone. "I will be on my way. Let him follow me who desires the embrace of the Lady Death."

Predictably, half-a-dozen robbers followed the clear track of his horse into the hills. None returned.

When the ranks of his men narrowed to five, including

himself and the sorcerer, the bandit leader shut them all up in their stronghold.

"Why are these—ladies—sheltering us?" Tarma demanded one day, when forced idleness had her pacing the confines of Kethry's rooms like a caged panther.

"Madame Isa grew tired of having her girls abused."

Tarma snorted with scorn. "I should have thought one would learn to expect abuse in such a profession."

"It is one thing when a customer expresses a taste for pain and is willing to pay to inflict it. It is quite another when he does so without paying," Kethry replied with wry humor. Tarma replied to this with something almost like a smile. There was that about her accomplice—fast becoming her friend—that could lighten even her grimmest mood. Occasionally the sorceress was even able to charm the Shin'a'in into forgetfulness for hours at a time. And yet there was never a time she could entirely forget what had driven her here . . .

At the end of two months, there were rumors that the chieftain had begun recruiting new underlings, the information passed to other cities via his sorcerer.

"We'll have to do something to flush at least one of them out." Kethry said at last. "The sorcerer has transported at least three more people into that house. Maybe more—I couldn't tell if the spell brought one or several at a time, only that he definitely brought people in."

A new courtesan, property of none of the three Houses, began to ply her trade among those who still retained some of their wealth. One had to be wealthy to afford her services—but those who spent their hours in her skillful embraces were high in their praise.

"I thought your vows kept you sorcerers from lying," Tarma said, watching Kethry's latest client moaning with pleasure in the dream-trance she'd conjured for him.

"I didn't lie." she said, eyes glinting green with mischief. "I promised him—all of them—an hour to match their wildest dreams. That's *exactly* what they're getting. Besides, nothing I'd be able to do could ever match what they're conjuring up for themselves!"

The chieftain's sergeant caught a glimpse of her spending an idle hour in the marketplace. He had been without a woman since his chief had forbidden the men to go to the Houses. He could see the wisdom in that; *someone* was evidently out after the band, and a House would be far too easy a place in which to set a trap. This whore was alone but for her pimp, a beardless boy that did not even wear a sword, only paired daggers. Nor would he need to spend any of his stored coin, though he'd bring it to tempt her. When he'd had his fill of her, he'd teach her that it was better to *give* her wares to *him*.

She led him up the stairs to her room above the inn, watching with veiled amusement as he carefully bolted the door behind him. But when he began divesting himself of his weaponry and garments, she halted him, pinioning his arms gently from the rear and breathing enticingly on the back of his neck as she whispered in his ear.

"Time enough, and more, great warrior—I am sure you have not the taste for the common tumblings that are all you can find in *this* backward place." She slid around to the front of him, urging him down onto the room's single stool, a water-beaded cup in her hand. "Refresh yourself first, great lord. The vintage is of mine own bringing—you shall not taste its like here—"

It was just Kethry's bad luck that he had been the official 'taster' to a high lordling during his childhood of slavery. He sipped delicately out of habit, rather than gulping the wine down, and rolled the wine carefully on his tongue—and so detected in the cup what he should not have been able to sense.

"Bitch!" he roared, throwing the cup aside, and seizing Kethry by the throat.

Kethry's panic-filled scream warned Tarma that the plan had gone awry. She wasted no time in battering at the door—the man was no fool and would have bolted it behind him. It would take too long to break it down. Instead, she sprinted through the crowded inn and out the back through the kitchen. A second cry—more like a strangled gurgle than a scream, which recalled certain things sharply to her and gave her strength born of rage and hatred—fell into the stableyard from the open window of Kethry's room. Tarma swarmed up the stable door onto the roof of the building, and launched herself from there in through that window. Her entrance was as unexpected as it was precipitate.

Kethry slowly regained consciousness in her bed in the rented room. She hurt from top to toe—her assailant had been almost artistic, if one counted the ability to evoke pain among the arts. Oddly enough, he hadn't raped her—she would have expected that, been able to defend herself arcanely. He'd reacted to the poisoned drink instead by throwing her to the floor and beating her with no mercy. She'd had no chance to defend herself with magic, and her sword had been left, at Tarma's insistence, back at the brothel.

Tarma was bathing and tending her hurts. One look at her stricken eyes, and any reproaches died on Kethry's tongue.

"It's all right," she said, as gently as she could with swollen lips. "It wasn't your fault."

Tarma's eyes said that she thought otherwise, but she replied gruffly "You need a keeper more than I do, lady-mage."

It hurt to smile, but Kethry managed. "Perhaps I do, at that."

Four evenings later, all but three of the bandits marched in force on the inn, determined to take revenge on the townsfolk for the acts of the invisible enemy in their midst. Halfway there, they were met by two women blocking their path. One was an amber-haired sorceress with a bruised face and a blackened eye. The other was a Shin'a'in swordswoman.

Only those two survived the confrontation.

"We have no choice now." Kethry said grimly. "If we wait, they'll only be stronger—and I'm certain that sorcerer has been watching. They're warned, they know who and what we are."

"Good." Tarma replied. "Then let's bring the war to *their* doorstep. We've been doing things in secret long enough, and it's more than time this thing was finished. Now. Tonight." Her eyes were no longer quite sane.

Kethry didn't like it, but knew there was no other way. Gathering her magics about her, and resting one hand on the comforting presence of her sword, she followed Tarma to the bandit stronghold.

The three remaining were waiting in the courtyard. At the forefront was the bandit chief, a red-faced, shrewd-eyed bull of a man. To his right was his second-in-command, and Tarma's eyes narrowed as she recognized the necklace of amber claws he wore. He was as like to a bear as his leader was to a bull. To his left was the sorcerer, who gave a mocking bow in Kethry's direction.

Kethry did not return the bow, but launched an immediate magical attack. Something much like red lightening flew from her outstretched hands.

He parried it, but not easily. His eyes widened in surprise; her lips thinned in satisfaction. They settled down to duel in deadly earnest. Colored lightnings and weird mists swirled about them, sometimes the edges of their shields could be seen, straining against the impact of the sorcerous bolts. Creatures out of insane nightmares formed themselves on his side, and flung themselves raging at the sorceress, before being attacked and destroyed by enormous eagles with wings of fire, or impossibly slim and delicate armored beings with no faces at their helm's openings, but only a light too bright to look upon.

Tarma meanwhile had flung herself at the leader with the war cry of her clan—the shriek of an angry hawk. He parried her blade inches away from his throat, and answered with a cut that took part of her sleeve and bruised her arm beneath the mail. His companion swung at the same time; his sword did more than graze her leg. She twisted to parry his second stroke, moving faster than either of them expected her to. She marked him as well, a cut bleeding freely over his eyes, but not before the leader gashed her where the chainmail shirt ended.

There was an explosion behind her; she dared not turn to look, but it sounded as though one of the two mages would spin spells no more.

She parried a slash from the leader only barely in time, and at the cost of a blow from her other opponent that surely broke a rib. Either of these men was her equal; at this rate they'd wear her down and kill her soon. It hardly mattered. *This* was the fitting end to the whole business, that the last of the Tale'sedrin should die with the killers of her clan. For when they were gone, what else was there for her to do? A Shin'a'in clanless was a Shin'a'in with no wish to live.

Suddenly she found herself facing only one, the leader. The other was battling for his life against Kethry, who had appeared out of the mage-smokes and was wielding her sword with all the skill of Tarma's spirit-teachers.

Tarma had just enough thought to spare for a moment of amazement. *Everyone* knew sorcerers had no skill with a blade—they had not the time to spare to learn such crafts.

Yet—there was Kethry, cutting the man to ribbons.

Tarma traded blows with her opponent; then saw her opening. To take advantage of it meant she must leave herself wide open, but she was far past caring. She struck—her blade entered his throat in a clean thrust. Dying, he swung; his sword caving in her side. They fell together.

Grayness surrounded Tarma, a gray fog in which the light seemed to come from no particular direction, the grayness of a peculiarly restful quality. Her hurts had vanished, and she felt no particular need to move from where she was standing. Then a warm wind caressed her, the fog parted, and she found herself facing the first of her instructors.

"So—" he said, hands (empty, for a change, of weapons) on hips, a certain amusement in his eyes. "Past all expectation, you have brought down your enemies. Remarkable, Sworn One, the more remarkable as you had the sense to follow my advice."

"You came for me, then?" it was less a question than a statement.

"I, come for you?" he laughed heartily behind his veil. "Child, child, against all prediction you have not only won, but *survived!* I have come to tell you that your aid-time is over, though we shall continue to train you as we always have. From this moment, it is your actions alone that will put food in your mouth and coin in your purse. I would suggest you follow the path of the mercenary, as many another Sworn One has done when clanless. And—" he began fading into the mist''—remember that one can be Shin'a'in without being born into the clans. All it requires is the oath of *she'enedran*.''

"Wait!" she called after him—but he was gone.

There was the sound of birds singing, and an astringent, medicinal tang in the air. Tarma opened eyes brimming with amazement, and felt gingerly at the bandages wrapping various limbs and her chest. Somehow, unbelievable as it was, she was still alive.

"It's about time you woke up." Kethry's voice came from nearby. "I was getting tired of spooning broth down your throat. You've probably noticed this *isn't* the House of Scarlet Joys. Madame wasn't the only one interested in getting rid of the bandits; the whole town hired me to dispose of them. My original intention was to frighten them away; then *you* came along. By the way, you are lying in the best bed in the inn. I hope you appreciate the honor. You're quite a heroine now. These people have far more appreciation of good bladework than good magic."

Tarma slowly turned her head; Kethry was perched on the side of a second bed a few paces from hers and nearer the window. "Why did you save me?" she whispered hoarsely.

"Why did you want to die?" Kethry countered.

Tarma's mouth opened, and the words spilled out. In the wake of this purging of her pain, came peace; not the numbing, false peace of the north wind's icy armor, but the true peace Tarma had never hoped to feel. Before she had finished, they were clinging to each other and weeping together.

Kethry had said nothing—but in her eyes Tarma recognized the same unbearable loneliness that she was facing. And she was moved by something outside herself to speak.

"My friend—" Tarma startled Kethry with the phrase; their eyes met, and Kethry saw that loneliness recognized like. "—We are both clanless; would you swear blood oath with me?"

"Yes!" Kethry's eager reply left nothing to be desired.

Without speaking further, Tarma cut a thin, curving line like a crescent moon in her left palm; she handed the knife to Kethry, who did likewise. Tarma raised her hand to Kethry, who met it, palm to palm—

Then came the unexpected; their joined hands flashed briefly, incandescently; too bright to look on. When their hands unjoined, there were silver scars where the cuts had been.

Tarma looked askance at her *she'enedra*—her blood-sister—

"Not of my doing." Kethry said, awe in her voice.

"The Goddess's then." Tarma was certain of it; with the certainty came the filling of the empty void within her left by the loss of her clan.

"In that case, I think perhaps I should give you my last secret." Kethry replied, and pulled her sword from beneath her bed. "Hold out your hands."

Tarma obeyed, and Kethry laid the unsheathed sword across them.

"Watch the blade." she said, and frowned in concentration.

Writing, as fine as any scribe's, flared redly along the length of it. To her amazement it was in her own tongue.

"If *I* were holding her, it would be in my language." Kethry said, answering Tarma's unspoken question. " 'Woman's Need calls me/As Woman's Need made me/Her Need must I answer/As my maker bade me.' My geas, the one I told you of when we first met. She's the reason I could help you after my magics were exhausted, because she works in a peculiar way. If you were to use her, she'd add nothing to your sword-skill, but she'd protect you against almost any magics. But when I have her—"

"No magic aid, but you fight like a sand-demon." Tarma finished for her.

"Only if I am attacked first, or defending another. And last, her magic only works for women. A fellow journeyman found that out the hard way. "

"And the price of her protection?"

"While I have her, I cannot leave any woman in trouble unaided. In fact, she's actually taken me miles out of my way to help someone." Kethry looked at the sword as fondly as if it were a living thing—which, perhaps, it was. "It's been worth it—she brought us together."

She paused, as though something had occurred to her. "I'm not sure how to ask this—Tarma, now that we're *she'enedrin,* do I have to be Sword Sworn too?'' She looked troubled. ''Because if it's all the same to you, I'd rather not. I have very healthy appetites that I'd rather not lose.''

''Horned Moon, no!'' Tarma chuckled, her facial muscles stretching in an unaccustomed smile. It felt good. ''In fact, *she'enedra,* I'd rather you found a lover or two. You're all the clan I have now, and my only hope of having more kin.''

''Just a Shin'a'in brood mare, huh?'' Kethry's infectious grin kept any sting out of the words.

''Hardly,'' Tarma replied answering the smile with one of her own. ''However, *she'enedra,* I am going to make sure you—we—get paid for jobs like these in good, solid coin, because that's something I think, by the look of you, you've been too lax about. After all, besides being horsebreeders, Shin'a'in have a long tradition of selling their swords—or in your case, magics! And are we not partners by being bloodsisters?''

''True enough, oh my keeper and partner.'' Kethry replied, laughing—laughter in which Tarma joined. ''Then mercenaries—and the very best!—we shall be.''

(There will be another story of Tarma and Kethry in S&S IV.)

A TALE FROM HENDRY'S MILL
Melissa Carpenter

In the first of these volumes I spoke of the story of rape and revenge as a story which appears and reappears in women's fiction; and because it is such a common plot, variations must be very original.

This is perhaps the strangest such story I have ever read: a story of a woman, a demon, a rape, and a surprisingly original revenge.

When Hendry's wagons threaded back through the Inakforest hills, a stranger followed them. None of the wagon haulers saw him, or noticed his bootprints in the muddy track.

They returned to the village of Hendry's Mill with fewer bolts of cloth and sacks of grain than the last spring, though the wagons had left at first thaw stacked high with inkwood. Hendry greeted them with a tight smile and a ledger. Her elder daughter Trida hugged the baby on her hip and asked them for word of her husband, who would spend half a year in the city. Her younger daughter Roona joined the villagers in begging for news from the rest of the kingdom.

The stranger prowled unseen behind the water-wheeled mill and the shingled houses, waiting for nightfall.

The haulers' tales were different that spring: the mysterious

Maveth appeared in every one. Some tales said he was the king's second son; others said he was a demon. Some claimed one look etched his shape forever into a person's mind; others swore he was invisible. Some said his hands had been burned when he touched the forbidden Borning Staff; others said under his gloves he had no hands.

All the tales agreed that Maveth left no blood; he could paralyze or kill, as the fancy took him, with a single touch. And his eyes, they said, were as violet as a dragon's.

"Now I saw a dragon once, when I was a girl," Hendry said. The haulers paused and gulped their dolberry wine. "Nasty slobbering creature. So I believe in dragons, all right. But this demon of yours sounds a bit too fantastical. I'll believe in him when I see him. Or don't see him, as the case may be. Now, I want to know what price the inkwood brought, and whether the furniture market's still falling."

She refilled the wagon leader's mug and straddled the bench beside him, firing off questions. But the other haulers spun out every demon story they could remember, while Hendry's loggers and their families listened with the amazement they always reserved for news from the world at the other end of the road.

Roona hung at the edge of the crowd, straining to catch every word. She could not imagine what real magic was like, any more than she could picture what Trida and her husband did upstairs on winter nights, or what it felt like to hold Hendry's authority over a whole village. But she drank in the stories, her brown eyes wide.

That evening, after the village had feasted on brottlemeat stew and roundnut cakes, Hendry's family gathered in the warm kitchen of the big house. Hendry pored over her account books, her shoulders hunched. Trida nursed her youngest child while the other four played Pegs and Pockets behind her chair. Roona scrubbed the wooden mugs and bowls, imagining she could smell demon tales among the lingering scents of brottlemeat and wine, pretending she did not have to return tomorrow to the hiss of sawing machines and the dry odor of sawdust.

Roona hated the inkwood that slipped smooth as black ice through the blades. She hated the haulers and loggers who hung at the mill door and made her feel awkward and scrawny and shy. Someday, she told herself, she would walk all the way to the city and find a handsome stranger who would love her at once and make her strong and beautiful. Then she would start her own business and her own family.

"And I'll have a fancy city wedding, like the ones in the stories," she said dreamily, wiping back her thin brown hair with a soapy hand.

Trida smiled indulgently, but Hendry glanced up, eyebrows raised. "Is that so? Haven't noticed any man look twice at you. Or even once. If you don't take more initiative, girl, fix yourself up and start talking to our young men, you'll never even get yourself pregnant, much less married. Unless that so-called demon stops by and plants his seed."

Roona flushed, then found something she could contradict. "Weren't you listening, Mother? The women Maveth rapes—if they live—always miscarry or something. He can't be a father any more than he can be a—a lover. It's his nature. Like in the story about Maveth and the fisherwoman. He never gives, but only takes."

"Hmmph. Aren't you the expert." Hendry stabbed her pen into the inkwell. Under her short gray hair the frown still lined her forehead.

"Yet they say he looks like the king," Roona went on, "except for his dragon eyes."

"And how would you know what the king looks like?" Hendry snapped. "Girl, you'd be better off paying more attention to the mill and less to fancy stories that don't concern us."

Roona slapped down a clean bowl. "It doesn't matter anyway," she muttered. "Maveth will never come here. Nobody ever comes here."

"For which you should be everlastingly grateful. We don't need magic here, and we don't need strangers." Hendry bent over her accounts again. "Wonder if those demon stories could be affecting veneer sales. People are so irrational . . . though you take the prize, girl. Always moping around, jawing about cities and magic and true love. Never taking advantage of what you got right here. It's hopeless trying to talk sense into you."

Roona squeezed her eyes shut. Her mother was right, of course. She never would attract a man, or take charge of anything, except by becoming more . . . more like someone she was not.

She wrung the dishtowel, remembering how once, in desperation, she had tried to seduce the youngest and stupidest wagon hauler. She was not sure he had even noticed.

Hendry slapped her account book shut. "Now I've got to come up with a new way to use inkwood, or all our stomachs will be empty come winter." She stood. "Not done with the dishes yet? Now what are you moping about, girl? You'll never see me or Trida with a face like that."

Roona ducked her head, fighting tears as she dried the last bowl. Then she flung the towel into the sink and ran upstairs.

When she leaned out her window the air was mild on her hot cheeks. But above the dark trees, the stars were cold as snowflakes. Roona pulled her window closed and shuttered it.

Outside, the stranger marked where her face had been.

With the shutters closed and the lamp unlit, Roona's bedroom was black as inkwood. She undressed in the dark and felt her way under the rough, clean sheets, then tried to lull herself to sleep with her usual daydream about the city man who would change her life. Tonight the handsome stranger in her dream turned away from her in disgust. From behind she could see right through him, and knew he was a demon.

She woke to the feel of hands pinning her wrists. Roona shrieked, then bit it off. Whoever this man was, if she scared him away, she would never know. . . .

Then she noticed his fingers were uncallused, smoother than her own. And they were cold as night.

"Who is it?" The words barely squeezed past her growing fear.

No one answered.

Roona kicked then, and twisted and jerked and bit. Nothing shook the man's grip. Numbness spread from her wrists into her fingers and up her arms, into her shoulders, her chest. . . . Soon she was too weak to move, too weak to cry out. Each breath was a labor. Her heartbeat sounded sluggish.

A scream began inside her head, but her paralyzed throat would not let it out.

He moved then, and his touch seared her. When he was through she lay rigid as a lightning-split tree.

Her lamp flared into sudden life. In its light Roona saw the stranger's face, pale as moonlight, and his violet eyes. They held no expression. She tried to look away, but she could not move her head.

"I think," he said quietly, "I will let you recover. Enough to tell them I will be back tomorrow night."

Then he vanished. A moment later the lamp went out.

After a long time the wordless scream in Roona's mind faded. She lay unmoving in the darkness, wishing it had been a nightmare. Then it occurred to her that against all odds, a magical stranger *had* come to her and changed her. It was like one of the old tales, in which a dream comes true and the dreamer regrets it the rest of her life.

Loathing choked her. Roona thought she ought to die—except that she did not want to defile Hendry's clean sheets with her body. She did not know whether she hated herself or the demon more.

By the time dawn drew a gray line between her shutters, Maveth's paralysis had loosened its grip on her. She could turn her head slowly, bend her fingers. She would live—at least until he returned.

And there was still something she could do. Maveth wanted her to tell them he was coming back.

Roona chewed on that fact, trying to ignore her own wretchedness. Maveth wanted her to tell—her family? The whole village? Either way, he wanted her to prepare them, to make them spend the day in fear and dread. He preferred his victims that way.

The first thing she could do, then, was to pretend nothing had happened to her during the night.

Sunlight gleamed through the crack between her shutters when Trida thumped on her door. Roona's voice broke when she answered Trida's call, but it was strong enough. Stiffly, painfully, she pulled her legs to the edge of the bed.

A lightning-split tree was useless as timber, she thought, but it could still bear fruit.

She smiled. It was a strange, proud, unfamiliar smile.

Hot spiced cider kept the family in the kitchen late into the evening. Roona could hardly swallow hers, but she made herself laugh and chatter while she cast about for another excuse to keep them all together. Trida's baby was already asleep in her arms. The other children were starting to whine when a knock interrupted them.

Hendry opened the door to the smell of spring pollen, the buzz of night insects, and a murmuring voice. Roona took a long breath. Surely it was not the demon; he would never knock. She twisted around in her chair.

The visitor wore mud-stained boots and gray breeches, a gray cloak and gray brottleskin gloves. His hair swirled long and loose, reminding Roona of polished black inkwood. His face was pale. His eyes were violet.

Roona waited. But only the children whispered and stared. Neither Trida nor Hendry had any reason to notice the man's eyes.

He shot one look at Roona, and she fought a pang of dizziness. When her vision cleared, she saw Maveth's expression shifting, as if he were preparing to play a different game. He took the mug of cider Hendry offered him without removing his gloves, and sat in the shadowy corner of the kitchen.

"Well, now," said Hendry, "May I ask who you are, and what you're doing here so far from the king's highway?"

"I am, ah, exploring." The stranger smiled into the steam rising from his cider. "And my route is determined by a demon. Even here, I am sure you have heard of Maveth?"

"Until I'm sick of the name," Hendry grumbled. "Tell me, did you happen to pass through the town of—"

"Have you noticed," the stranger interrupted, "that all the stories talk about Maveth eating, drinking, picking up things, knocking on doors, killing with a touch. Yet they say that underneath his gloves he has no hands."

He paused. Trida glanced up at him, then bit her lip, suddenly pale. Hendry frowned uneasily. The stranger set down his mug and touched his gloved fingertips together, drawing out the moment.

Roona swallowed. Her battered body screamed at her to run, hide, get away. She pushed herself up, clenching all her muscles to keep from shaking. She took three steps, and yanked off the demon's gloves.

Shock froze Maveth in his chair. Roona backed away, holding the gloves at arms' length.

Hendry gasped. A child screamed. They all saw Maveth's fingertips, and his wrists. But in between, where the forbidden Borning Staff had branded him, there was nothing.

Only Roona looked at his face instead of his hands. She did not understand the expression growing in his violet eyes.

"Tell me your name," she said. She was surprised that her voice came out louder than her thudding heart.

"I am the—" He faltered. "Maveth."

"The demon, or the son of King Mordan?"

"Both." He wet his lips. Then a sudden fury filled his face. He whipped to his feet and raise done invisible hand. Roona edged back, holding his gloves like a shield.

"You forget my magic, woman. I let you go last night. But you forget that I collect lives. Tonight I will take one." His rage disappeared, and he smiled slowly. "In honor of your, ah, your amusing though utterly inappropriate boldness, Roona, I will let you choose which one, out of all the lives in this room."

He watched her. Roona made her face as blank as sanded wood. She knew Maveth meant to savor her terror if she chose herself, her guilt if she chose anyone else. She also knew exactly what she ought to do. In all the stories the hero sacrifices himself.

She glanced back. Hendry sat stiff as a stump, hardly able to comprehend what was happening. Yet under ordinary circumstances the whole village depended on her. Trida clutched her baby while her other children clung to her legs. Roona knew they all needed each other.

No one needed her. Roona knew she would never have a lover or a child; Maveth had spoiled her for that. She was hardly worth saving. Yet now that her own dream was ashes, she felt a perverse desire to go on and see what else she could make of her life. She did not want to die.

Yet she had to choose death for someone in that room.

Roona let out her breath. "I've chosen. Take your own life, Maveth."

He gaped. Then he began to laugh, a wild noise that made Trida's children whimper. When he was done he plucked his gloves from Roona's fingers. For a moment his violet eyes looked tired and almost human.

"You win," he said. "You make me wish I could just go home tonight. At least I can go. Yes. It doesn't really matter if one tiny village in the Inkforest thinks of the demon as only a bedtime story. Hendry's Mill will not see the demon, or feel his touch, again. You have the word of the king's son."

Maveth pulled on his gloves. He met Roona's eyes, then looked away and vanished.

The kitchen was silent. Trida hugged her children. Hendry sat speechless. Roona stumbled to the kitchen window and looked through the gap where the wagon track parted the forest. She thought she saw the stars between the trees dim, then brighten. But she was not sure.

S.A.R.
Patricia B. Cirone

This is another of the stories I wasn't sure about. I read it
with delight and fascination, but at the end I realized that
technically speaking, it was disqualified, being science
fiction. I designated it "first alternate" meaning I would
use it if there was room, but I finally decided that reada-
bility was more important than category.

Would-be writers for this series, please don't interpret
this as license to deluge me with science or space fiction; if I *know* it's sf, I will NOT read it. But if you can slip
it by me, if I read it with such fascination that I can't
ignore it, then I may decide to ignore categories. I always tell young writers: don't try to give me a hard sell in
a cover letter. DON'T EXPLAIN OR TELL THE PLOT IN
YOUR LETTER; let the story stand on its own feet.

Patricia Cirone is married, with a three-year-old daughter; she has sold non-fiction articles, but this is her first
story sale. Now that her husband is out of the Navy, she
hopes to stay put in New England. She is working on a
novel—who isn't?

Kit inched her way diagonally up the wall, fingers and toes feeling for each crevice in the rough hewn rock. After an infinity of time she reached the niche the carved gryphon called home and slid her lean form within its shelter. Gratefully she pressed her soles against security, and tried to ease the cramps out of the balls of her feet. Then she took the first deep breath she'd dared in twenty minutes. She darted a glance at the silent, dark street below her, then one across to the opposite building, bathed in the cold light of the moon. No glow from lanterns softened the moon's reflection on the diamond-paned windows. Good. Carefully she eased the coiled rope off her shoulder and grasped the three-pronged hook at its end.

With a fluid motion, she tossed the grappling hook through the air toward the roof of the opposite building. Her ears picked up a faint chink as it settled into position. Taking a deep breath, she launched herself, swinging lithely across the narrow street. The building rushed at her. Her feet scrabbled vainly to gain purchase on its smooth side. They failed and she swung to the side. Her shoulder thudded painfully against the wall and she bounced sickeningly. Scrabbling again, she managed to brace the soles of her feet against the stone and steady herself. She breathed again.

Oh so delicately, Kit leaned back against the rope. Her muscles were cramping again; she tried to relax them. Kit gazed into the quiet street below her, checking to see if she had been spotted. She took another deep breath. Time was going on . . . and she was as obvious as a fly at a feast hanging here in the moonlight. Regretfully, she eased herself into action, hitching herself up the remaining four feet to the window, glad she hadn't had to do the whole climb up the slippery side of this building. She wedged a thin metal bar between the casements and pushed against the latch. It snicked open. Softly she eased the windows open and slid through. She was in.

Swiftly she swung the window shut and pulled the heavy drapes. Then she muttered an imprecation . . . she couldn't see a blasted thing once the moon was shut out. Easing the drapes back open, she fumbled open her belt pouch and struck her flint, lighting the candlebox she had carried within. Then, once more, she shut out the moonlight and any curious eyes. Kit eased the curved reflective back of the candlebox against the palm of her hand, running her fingers through the grips, then closed its faceted glass front while glancing around the room. The library. She grinned. As good a place as any to start. She wiggled her shoulders, savoring the mixture of excitement and nervousness that flooded through her. It was like the high she'd always felt before a tournament. Her lips tightened and she snapped back to what she was doing. She got to work, pulling out books, looking under and behind furniture. Now where would Baldour keep his jewels?

She moved on to the bedroom, snorting at the elaborate spread on the huge bed. She bent down. There was something under the bed. Eagerly she put down her candlebox and stretched to pull it out. A sword! Why the devil was Baldour risking imprisonment by keeping a weapon within the confines of the city? Probably for the jewels, she thought ironically, looking down at its hilt: the only booty she had found so far . . . and it unusable.

The sound of voices and laughter broke over her awareness. Baldour had come home! The bedroom door flew open; a laughing couple, suddenly sober, were framed in its embrace. Kit stood there, foolishly, exposed. Her heart and mind raced; her feet stood still, not knowing which way to run. She had to *do* something. An elusive thought whispered: there *was* something she could do—but it was gone just as quickly. She grasped the sword more firmly, wondering if she could learn how to use it in the next ten seconds. At least it was *some* action. Her mind blurred with the need to do something more. Then she found herself falling. Confused, she wondered how she could be falling. She was *in* the

apartment, not still outside perched on that rope and nothingness. Before she could even complete the thought she landed
on purple veined grass, still clutching the sword.

"OOF!"

"Sweet Danu, it worked!" a voice behind her exclaimed
with both astonishment and thankfulness.

"Huh?" Kit turned her head and found herself facing a
woman who looked tired to death. Her cropped gray hair was
disheveled; her right arm and shoulder were bound in a
makeshift sling. Kit stared.

"I'm sorry, Godsend. There's no time to give you welcome and thanks. My name is Ragee. Please, come quickly;
Longire's scouts will have seen the smoke from my petition
fire." The older woman lurched painfully to her feet and
slung a large provision sack onto her right shoulder.

"Please. Carry Prince Luewel. Guard him!" Kit, confusion still spinning her mind, bent over the carry sack the other
had indicated. It was a baby: three, maybe four months old.
Ragee picked up the sword which had been lying beside her
and gripped it in her good hand. Free. Ready for use. She
peered toward the left horizon with a frown, then hurried off
through the knee—high purple grass. Kit followed, not feeling on top of the situation, but not knowing what else to do.
She had no idea where she was, what had happened to
Baldour . . . or anything else. But judging from that anxious
look the other had cast at the horizon, it might be healthy to
follow swiftly, without questions.

The gray-haired swordswoman headed directly for the line
of tumbled hills which lay beneath the mountains ahead.
Once there, she lost their track among the many ways that
wound through and over the rocks. When they had worked
their way far from where they'd left the plain, Ragee sank
down, trembling, by an outlook. Sweat traveled down the
pain lines in her face. "Thank you. Thank you, Godsend."
She stopped to draw her breath. "Thank you for coming to
my aid and thank you for following me so swiftly without
questioning." Kit nodded and lowered herself down beside
the other, awkwardly plunking down Baldour's blasted sword
on the ground in front of her. Ragee noticed her lack of
finesse. She kept staring at the sword as she said:

"When I beseeched the Gods for help, I didn't expect the blessing of a warrior."

"A warrior! I'm no warrior!"

"Then why are you carrying a sword? . . . Godsend."

"I was just stealing it when I fell through to here."

The other stared at her. "You were *stealing* it?"

Kit nodded.

"Leaving someone *defenseless*?"

"No! I didn't. I mean he'd never need a sword to defend . . . He probably doesn't even know how to use it," Kit trailed off before the shock in the other's eyes, wondering why she felt such a need to justify her actions. They had not felt wrong before; Baldour was such a waste it had seemed a good deed to steal from him. But somehow she didn't feel that would hold weight with this gray-eyed woman.

"But you *do* know how to use it," the woman stated after a brief pause.

"No," Kit admitted reluctantly. "It was the jewels in the hilt . . ."

Ragee just stared at her for a moment, then looked up at the sky. "I wonder which God I've offended? First I'm wounded smuggling Satur's only child out of danger and now I'm sent a thief who can't even use what she feels free to steal!" She shook her head wryly, then winced with the pain the movement had brought. "Well, whatever you are and wherever you're from, the gods have sent you, and I'll make use of you. Far be it from me to spurn an offering of the gods." She looked at Kit with a glance so mingled with contempt and weary resignation that Kit gritted her teeth against the vain ache to justify herself. What did this woman know about her life? About how everything she had planned had been swept away?

Ragee reached over with her good arm and clamped Kit's wrist. Startled, Kit broke her reverie. The other was nodding toward the plain. A group of ten, mounted on horses, were milling around the remain's of Ragee's small fire. Carefully, making no sound, the other scrambled onto her feet. "Come. Let's go," she whispered.

"Are you well enough?" Kit hissed, noting that red had started to seep through Ragee's bandages.

The other snorted. "I'll be worse than not well enough if we stay here. I'll be Pik bird feed."

Kit nodded and reached for the provision sack before the other could. She'd show this woman she was no shirker. She threaded her arms through the straps and hoisted it onto her back, then bent and picked up the baby and Baldour's sword. Ragee gave a moue of disgust but acknowledged her weakness by not protesting. She started off, Kit following. Ragee stuck to rocky ledges and boulder strewn paths, reluctantly following dirt paths through the scrub only when necessary, so as not to leave a trail. She soon had to secure her sword in its scabbard; she needed her hand to pull herself up some of the waist-high boulders. She would turn to help Kit, burdened with the baby, scramble up behind, but always silently. As if she couldn't be bothered to talk with the type of person she judged Kit to be. In the silence, Kit watched their progress by the pain lines that etched their way deeper into Ragee's face; by the increasing size of the stain on her bandages and by the deepening set of her mouth as she forged steadily on. Even Kit's well-toned muscles began to protest, from the hike as well as from carrying both baby and sword, neither of which she was accustomed to. Yet Ragee's pace never varied. Her grim determination echoed, for Kit, her own struggle for perfection as a gymnast. Years of practice, of trying again and again, of ignoring pain, of persisting in the face of minor injuries: all for nothing. Judged second rate; unfit for professional tours; finally too old to audition again.

Kit closed her mind to the bitter reflections and wondered instead how she had gotten here. And how she was going to get back. Eventually this paled, too, and she just walked doggedly on, reachieving that blankness she had lived in so often since that final audition failure.

It was dusk before they stopped. The prince had been crying fretfully for some time; Ragee looked gray with exhaustion. Kit ignored her own tiredness and started a small fire concealed in the outcropping of rocks where they sheltered. She sensed approval from the other. Even the silence had, recently, seemed more a product of tiredness than of deliberation. When the fire was going, she looked over and saw Ragee fumbling with the baby, trying to change him one handed. Kit moved to help.

"Thanks. I've never had much to do with babes and this doesn't help any," Ragee said wryly, nodding with her chin toward her shoulder.

"That's all right. I'm not a mother but I've watched my sisters' children from time to time." Kit was glad the silence was broken. She glanced up and found Ragee's penetrating gaze fixed on her.

"What's your name?"

"Kit."

"Why were you stealing?"

"The danger. Something to do," Kit replied off-handedly, resenting the other questioning her, even if she did seem less disapproving, now. She busied herself with warming a skin of milk for the royal bundle.

"Danger! Why don't you learn to use that sword you're carting around? That would give you both danger and plenty to do. And you seem to have enough physical endurance for it. A good sword wielder can always find employment."

"Not on my world."

"You going back?"

"I don't know. I don't know how I got here."

"Hmmm. My petition fire stirred things up and the smoke blew the wrong way, huh? Sorry, but I was desperate, and I always thought godsends knew what they were doing."

"Somehow I can't picture myself as a gift from any god," Kit replied, with a reluctant smile. "Especially not the way I've been acting lately. More likely they wanted to get rid of me somehow."

Ragee gave a commiserative snort of laughter. "Well, don't cut yourself up. Despite everything, you *have* been a godsend today. I'd never have made it this far, with the babe as well as everything else."

"I'm glad I could help." Kit hesitated then continued, not looking at Ragee as she busied herself sorting through the provisions sack for some dried meat. "It feels good to be of some use. I was training for something, but it didn't work out. I'd trained for it all my life, and since I was turned down, well, I haven't felt much good at anything. Not even living with myself.''

Ragee leaned forward and silently gripped Kit's wrist for a moment then, noting Kit's determined silence, changed the subject and began discussing their route for the next day.

"So one more day should do it, then we'll have to get through the town in the pass and down into Gellis's lands,'' she concluded. "He's Satur's brother, and will guard the prince well until Longire's men are routed." Kit nodded, not knowing what the war was about and not really caring. It was enough, for now, to be doing something. To have a goal, rather than seeing life stretching aimlessly ahead.

"Can I help you rebandage that?" Kit asked, looking at the other's shoulder.

Ragee grimaced. "I wonder if it wouldn't be better to leave it alone until I can get to a medcrafter.''

Kit eyed the roughly wound, red-stained bandages uncertainly. "You sure?"

"I suppose not," Ragee sighed. "Put it down to a warrior's reluctance to mess with wounds. You never really get used to them: you have to believe you won't get them. You have any medcrafting experience?''

"You mean like a doctor? No. But I have some aid experience. I grew up among broken bones and strained muscles.'' Kit moved over and carefully unwrapped Ragee's shoulder. She didn't attempt to deep clean the wound; they hadn't sufficient clean water. Besides, she was afraid of doing more damage. Instead she washed the edges, packed some fresh baby cloths hard against the wound and strapped Ragee as if she had a dislocated shoulder. Ragee's tight-lipped expression relaxed when Kit finished jostling the area.

"Thanks," she said briefly. A few moments later she smiled more warmly: "Thanks, Kit. That does feel better, now that things have calmed down a bit there.''

Kit nodded, finished putting everything away in the travel bag and settled down for the night. After Ragee had fallen asleep, Kit lay there, her thoughts wandering: what the devil had happened to her? Had Ragee's gods really plucked her from her own world and hurled her here? She had always wanted to do something . . . oh . . . well, in her dreams, heroic. But reality had to be faced. There wasn't much scope for heroics, at least not in her world. So her dreams had led her to try for the fame of a professional gymnast. But even her "real" goal had been denied her. Maybe this sudden transformation was an answer to her childhood wishes. But those fantasies of desperate deeds and swords and nursery-myth worlds hadn't been as true to life as this place seemed to be. Oh, there was excitement—if you liked the itchy feeling she'd had in her back since seeing the swords those scouts had worn so easily. But what about the crystal clean beauty of the myth worlds painted in her children's books? Kit's mind laughed wryly. Hardly. She had never been so dirty and dusty and sweaty in her life, even when practicing for a tournament. And sore and tired, she thought with a wince. Kit sighed. She wondered if she'd ever get her life in order. Even if she somehow flipped back home, what could she do? She'd have to start over, train for something new. And not the thievery she had so defiantly taken up. That had been childish. Oh, what was the use? She was dead-ended. Washed up and useless at the grand age of twenty-five. She turned over. The pulsing glow of the fire's embers outlined a tired peace on Ragee's face. Kit felt better.

The next morning the cliffs began their slow curve inward and up: toward the pass. The two women could see their destination lying in the distance before them. Torta. The city of the pass. It sprawled in an ungainly V down the sides of the pass, pressing against their restricting sides, petering out toward the valley floor. They both stopped to look at it, Ragee with an assessing grimace, Kit with dismay.

"There's no way around it!"

"No," Ragee agreed. "We'll work up close to the sides, staying as high as we can, but eventually we'll have to go down and through the town streets. The sheer cliffs that front the mountains are impassable unless you climb with ropes and scaling shoes. And lots of experience."

"Will there be problems getting through the town?"

Ragee shrugged. "Depends on how thoroughly entrenched Longire's troops are. We didn't have word when I left the castle with Luewel. But even if they don't have the town completely secure, there'll be scouts out looking. For me, for other swordwielders loyal to Satur.''

"Then what will we do? Disguise ourselves?''

"I doubt it would work. Not with my arm in a sling, both of us carrying swords and my hair in a warrior's cut. Besides,'' she added with a wolfish grin, "my face has become well known to them over the years.''

"Great. So we just go in there and hope we make it through?''

"No other way,'' Ragee replied, looking pleased at the thought. Kit was amazed that she could seem excited by the thought of danger, incapacitated as she was. But Ragee had been moving easier today. She had the quick healing ability born of determination and a warrior's disregard for hurts others would think major. But for all her love of action, she was practical as well. She led Kit along the edges of the cliffs, passing through clefts and up screes Kit would have thought impassable, just to delay the inevitable descent into the town. When they had gone about as far as they could, Ragee hunkered down in a sheltered spot and signaled they'd wait until nightfall. Kit settled down to tend to the small prince, who was getting more and more restless at being cooped up in a restrictive carry sack. Kit was glad he was as young as he was; his weight wasn't much burden and his restlessness stemmed from missing a familiar routine, rather than ambitions to crawl and explore. A few months older and a trek such as this would have been unbearable. Kit divided the somewhat aging milk in two, to stretch it. Ragee handed her a small vial.

"One drop,'' she murmured. "In the second skin, for later.''

Kit raised her eyebrow.

"It will make him sleep, but won't be enough to harm him. We can't risk his waking up in the town and drawing attention.''

Kit grimaced. She didn't like the thought of putting a baby to sleep. Ragee leaned over and gripped her wrist.

"He's dead if we don't,'' she said earnestly, her eyes holding Kit's as hard as her hand did her wrist. "We might be ransomed; held prisoner; whatever. But he'd be killed. Instantly.''

Kit nodded and put the drop in the second skinful of milk. The baby dropped off to sleep after sucking the first dry. Kit settled him against a curve of the provisions sack and leaned back against a rock. To wait. She watched the blue sky; not even a cloud in it to break the monotony. It would be clear tonight; starlight would mark their way. But no moonlight: there didn't seem to be a moon here. Kit sighed and moved restlessly, stretching her neck in the direction of the town. But she couldn't see even the outer fringes. Ragee had purposely picked a spot where they could neither see nor be seen. She glanced over to where Ragee was busily polishing her sword one-handedly, propping its hilt between her knees. The older woman looked up.

"It'll be hours yet. Do you want to get some sleep?"

"I'm not tired," Kit answered crankily.

Ragee's gray eyes assessed her. "You want to learn how to at least grip that sword you're carrying? I can't teach you how to fight, but at least you'd have the appearance of a warrior. It might put off opposition.''

"Gladly!" Kit replied relieved at the thought of having something to do.

Ragee nodded and got to her feet, Kit following suit.

"Here," Ragee said, holding her hand out. "Look how my hand grasps the hilt: thumb so, fingers spaced to hold it evenly, firmly. You hold it as if you think it's going to bite you. Watch.'' Ragee swung the sword around in a few easy swings to demonstrate how her hand moved with the sword. Even right-handed, she seemed sure of herself. Kit tried to duplicate the grip with her left hand but the sword dipped and wavered about on its own.

Ragee put her own sword down and reached over to move Kit's fingers into the proper position and hold them there, moving the sword back and forth to show Kit how it should feel. "Try to keep your hand like that and practice getting the feel of it.''

"Just hold it?"

"I'll show you a few beginning maneuvers. Not that you'll

be able to fight anyone with them, but it'll get you used to the sword.''

Kit practiced on and off the rest of the afternoon, glad of something to do. She had visions of helping Ragee in a fight and then would see the way her sword wobbled and laugh wryly at her pretensions. Still glory seeking, she chided herself.

"Don't tire yourself out," Ragee advised.

"I'm not. I've got strong arms from years of gymnastics. It feels good to excercise them; they've been feeling cramped from carrying the baby." Ragee grunted and showed Kit how the excercises fit together to block and thrust against an opponent.

"You might have a natural aptitude," she said approvingly. "I'd almost think you'd been practicing for two afternoons instead of one." Her eyes twinkled.

Kit snorted.

"No, seriously. If you want to become a swordwielder, I think you could. Even starting this late. A few years of practice with a good instructor and you'd be passable."

"Thanks," Kit said ruefully. Ragee shrugged and sat back down. Kit hadn't meant to hurt the other's feelings. "I just wish I was at least passable tonight. That town worries me."

Ragee looked back up, her lips twisting into half a smile. "Can't have everything. We'll make it." But Kit noticed the older woman was pensive.

They started working their way down the cliffs as dusk deepened into night. Kit was glad she'd had a day and a half scrambling around on these rocks—and had naturally sure feet. It was no joke negotiating them in what faint light was left. Abruptly the rocks stopped: they were in the town, flitting up quiet streets.

Yellow light and laughter spilled from the open doorway of a tavern. They silently went up the side street to avoid it. The town stretched endlessly: narrow streets and cobbled walkways, houses, stores . . . scenes familiar yet skewed with a difference that Kit, a townsperson all her life, felt more deeply than she had the purple grass and the absence of a moon.

She shifted the milk-and-drug-drowsing prince from one

arm to the other and sped up a stonecut staircase after Ragee, to the next level. Again they crept past houses, scurried up slanting streets and flitted with the shadows, ever higher. They paused to let pass a talkative group of townspeople who never noticed the two women, still, against a shadowed corner of a building. After they were by Kit shifted the baby back to her right arm to free the left for the sword. Ragee signaled and they moved on up. They were near the top, a scant street or so away from the straight path to the border, when they were spotted.

"Hoi! Two of them! Guards, to me!" a man shouted. Ragee dived toward him, her sword flickering in the light of the torch he held. The clang as their swords engaged seemed to echo throughout the night, awakening shadows. Before Kit could wonder what to do it was over. Hampered by the torch, the man had been no match for Ragee, even right-handed as she was now. But just as Kit drew a sigh of relief she heard the sounds of running feet coming toward them. She and Ragee took off, running desperately, giving up concealment for speed.

The footsteps gained on them. Light from carried torches nipped at their heels, then spilled across them. The way narrowed. One street wide. The pass was directly ahead. Shouts rose from Gellis's men, manning their side of the pass. Against the flickering torch light, Kit could see archers jumping into position. She realized they must have been keeping this last street up to the pass free of Longire's troops by this means. But the road was too narrow for them to risk shooting with Ragee and her in the way. And Longire's men were gaining too fast.

"Ragee! Take Luewel!" Ragee faltered and shook her head no, urging Kit to come.

"Take him!" Kit thrust the infant at Ragee and turned toward their pursuers, bringing her sword up in the first movement Ragee had shown her that afternoon. She prayed desperately she could delay them the few extra seconds that Ragee needed.

The first man met her sword with a crash that almost knocked her to her knees. She thrust hard, pushing soles to the ground and regaining her balance as if recovering from a bad dismount. She swept her sword up and somehow managed to encounter the other's. The sound rang dully, not a true hit. The man shifted and his sword sped toward Kit. She heard cheers from behind; knew Ragee had made it. Then she fell, pain exploding in her side.

She woke slowly in a brightly lit room. Sunlight streamed in, patterning familiar wallpaper with the scallops of the curtains; keepsakes from her childhood jostled each other on the shelf at the foot of her bed. She was in her own room: the attic, with its own separate entrance, which she rented at the top of her sister's home. The only incongruous note was Baldour's sword, leaning against the wall.

"Hello, traveler!" a man said cheerily.

Kit turned her head to see a perfect stranger leaning against the wall. He was casually dressed, with merry brown eyes.

"How do you feel?" he asked as he lounged forward and straddled a chair.

"Disoriented," Kit answered frankly. "And confused as hell."

"Very common!" he said sagely, belying the tone with a disarming grin.

"How did I get back here?"

"Most travelers return to a familiar place when they leave an alternate reality, especially when they leave it abruptly, as you did. First-timers usually show up in their rooms. A homing instinct, I suppose you might say. Those more experienced usually train themselves to arrive at the center. Control develops with experience."

"What are you talking about?"

"Traveling. Skipping to alternate realities. I'm from S.A.R., the Society for Alternate Realities, here at your service!"

"Society for Alternate Realities! That's a nursery myth!"

"Ah, no. We really aren't. Not that we go around talking about it because, like you, most people flat out disbelieve alternate realities exist. And will regard you as wikky if you go about talking about them. But you: you are special. You've shown you have the ability to travel and so you really should belong to us. Actually, to all intents and purposes, you do belong to us since even if you never come to the center, we will still monitor you, make sure you don't start abusing your talent. Go nipping into alternate realities and wreak havoc, whatever. Any questns?'' he concluded brightly.

"Tons," Kit answered, bemused.

"Come down to the center. We'll teach you all there is to know. Or at least all that we know. And there you'll find people to talk to who'll believe you! No one else will, so don't attempt to try it, Kit. Not family, not friends, not even nursery-myth readers.'' He sounded more serious, toward the last part, but his eyes still twinkled.

"So. I wasn't sent there."

"No. No one sent you. You took yourself. Need on your part responding to need on the part of someone in an alternate reality.''

"I was panicking. I had broken into an apartment and been discovered. And Ragee was petitioning her gods for help.''

"Yes, an urgent desire to be very much elsewhere often activates the talent. And petitions for help would provide access to the world you entered. It's not always as explicit as that.''

"Why? I mean why can we travel?''

The man shrugged. "The gods? Fate? A quirk? No one knows. Some of us like to argue it back and forth. Most just accept it.''

"Is it just people from our world? That can travel to others?''

"Good lord, no! Any world we can travel to has travelers that can come to us. And if there are some who neither send nor receive travelers, well, we'll never know, will we?''

"How did you find out about me?''

"Oh, that was easy. Anything as big as the shock of an inexperienced traveler breaking the barriers will give anyone attuned to the flows between the worlds a headache. You were as easy to trace there and back again as it would be to follow the path a searing hot iron was taking across your back. No blame to you. No one knows what they're doing the first time. They shatter the barriers instead of slipping through. You'll learn. That, and how to feel the pull of a need in another reality when there's no need on your part. Practice. That's all it takes.''

"Why do it?''

"Don't *you* know?"

"Something to do," Kit replied.

The man raised his eyebrow.

"Something worthwhile to do?" Kit amended.

"Close enough." He grinned. "You'll find it feels good to do what needs doing. Help out. Plus you get to see worlds that most people couldn't even dream about. And friends . . . they're the best."

"How soon can I go back? To where I was?"

"Ah. You can't," he said regretfully but finally. "Not to that world. No one's ever been able to return to a world where they've been killed."

"Killed?"

"You died in that world. Or would have, if your essence had belonged there. Instead you were jolted back here, to your own reality. Fortunately, considering what we often encounter, your true death can only occur here. But in that reality you died. So you can't go back."

"But Ragee . . ."

He just sat there, sadness and wisdom showing in his brown eyes, making them seem much much older than they had moments before.

"There had to be need," he said finally, softly. "And you fulfilled the need that was there. Even if you had left of your own volition and not been killed, you couldn't just go back to a place, or a person. Not unless there was a new need to provide the initial entryway. . . . But there are other worlds. Do you think you want to exercise your talent?"

Kit lay there, thinking. Adventure? Perhaps. Hard work? Evidently, if her one experience was typical. But work had never bothered her. Something to work at, to commit herself to. Now that would feel good. And even if she never met Ragee again, or found out what had happened, well, as he had said, there would be others. Others to meet, to help, to become friends with. An ache, a need and a new found sense of purpose burgeoned within her. "Yes," she said decisively.

MORE'S THE PITY
L. D. Woeltjen

This story came in "over the tramsom" from a complete stranger. At first I thought it was just too grim, and put it aside to reject. When I picked it up a few days later I found the story still haunting me. I have a weakness for very short stories which are unforgettable; I feel this is the highest art of the writer.

So we present it here; a grim story and not for the squeamish, or those who like life prettied up. Even fantasy can be realistic.

H old!'' Mongrel bellowed from her left.
Bracer stood straddling her fallen opponent, her sword poised to deal him a merciful death. She glanced toward her swordmate, awaiting an explanation.

"Spare him," insisted the squat, ugly man. "The battle's won and he's just a hired sword, like us."

Bracer shrugged her acquiescence, suspicious of her comrade's motives. She bent over her enemy's body, wiping the gore from her blade onto his cloak. A glint caught her eye. She noticed, for the first time, the hexagonal badge pinned to the cloak. It bore the emblem of a captain in the Hordavan army. Now she understood Mongrel's compassion.

The hyena face grinned sheepishly. "Let's drag him to the

stream. Water'll bring him to long enough to spill what he knows."

Bracer sheathed her sword and surveyed the battlefield before complying with Mongrel. The fighting was finished now, the meadow littered with corpses from her own side as well as the routed army's. She turned her aching back on the looting, and bent to grasp the wounded man's feet while Mongrel hefted his head and shoulders. They lugged him a score of yards to the shelter of some brush and boulders. With luck, the prisoner would reveal information worth a few extra gold pieces to their employer, King Rasperd.

They plopped down the captive in a nest of shrubs sheltered by rocks the size of men. Here no snooping opportunist could see or hear what they were doing. They had no intention of sharing the meager bounty for information promised by Rasperd.

While Bracer caught her breath, Mongrel brought water in his cupped hands, dumping it onto the captain's face. The soldier sputtered and thrashed about, groaning.

"Let me do it, fool!" Bracer said impatiently. Mongrel richly deserved his name. He had not only the face of a cur, but the manners as well. The swordswoman tore a piece of cloth from her victim's tunic and went to dampen it in the stream.

As Bracer dipped the rag into the water, she frowned at her reflection. she had not glimpsed herself since cropping off her auburn hair for battle. Cut short, the gray hairs were more noticeable than ever. She sighed, already resigned to the aging process. Ten more years, at best, before her lean, hard body began to waste away. What then?

She forced her mind back to her task, focusing on the ragged fabric submerged beneath her reflection. Cursing, she jerked her hands out of the water, hurled the soggy rag to the ground, and fumbled with the crimson wrappings which supported her wrists during battle.

—*Damn*—she thought—*I hope they're not ruined*. The strong, blood-red strips which bound her slender wrists were her one admission of slight inferiority to men. Too many sprains during her years as an apprentice swordswoman had made her accept her instructor's advice to wrap her wrists.

Once she had hidden the bindings with ornate silver-plated bracers, booty from an early campaign. The wrist guards had been lost in a card game, but the nickname they had earned her still remained. After spreading the cloths, like red streamers, over a bush to dry, Bracer rinsed the tunic scrap. Mongrel, who had set about making camp, grumbled at her to hurry. She squeezed the rag out and returned to the wounded man.

He was conscious now, but his breathing was labored as he watched her warily. She knelt beside him, wiping his face with the cool rag.

"Let me make you more comfortable," she said gently, continuing to mop his sweaty, dust-caked skin. He looked to be in his mid-thirties, perhaps a dozen years her junior. Still, he was no cub, and under other circumstances, she might have found him attractive.

The bloody gash across his midsection drove any trace of lustfulness from her mind. She soaked again the rag before attempting to cleanse the wound. He was slit from hip to hip and bleeding faster than she could blot. The odor of bowel told her the depth of the injury.

"He doesn't have much time," she whispered to Mongrel, tossing away the useless wash cloth.

A morbid grin crawled across the stocky fighter's face, as Mongrel stooped beside the dying man.

"Well, Captain," he taunted, "what can we do to ease your final minutes?"

The man closed his eyes and said nothing.

"Give me your waterskin," Bracer demanded. She knew Mongrel kept it filled with beer, despite their commander's orders against such unmilitary behavior. They weren't regular soldiers, after all. Mongrel handed over the nearly empty skin and glared at her as she held it near the prisoner's mouth.

"Here," Bracer urged, dripping some of the golden liquid onto the gasping lips. They parted, allowing Bracer to aim a stream of beverage into the soldier's mouth. He managed one swallow before Mongrel yanked away the skin.

"No need to waste it," he accused.

"I only sought to loosen his tongue," was her snarled response. She would not put up much longer with this coarse creature. When this service ended she would find a new traveling companion, or go it alone.

Bracer stroked the dying man's hair, a bit too roughly at first. Finally she calmed herself enough to address him softly.

"We're just mercenaries, like you. We owe allegience only to ourselves. If you want to send a message to your kin, I swear it will be delivered. Tell us where your father's house lies. We'll carry your dying words to him."

"My father cares nothing for me," was the agonized response. "I was dead to him years ago."

"You're wasting time, Brace, let me handle it." Mongrel took a swig from the skin before bending to speak close to the man's ear. He spat out beer foam with his words.

"Now, sonny, surely you've a gray-haired mama somewheres. One who'd treasure a memento of her dear dead son. This badge, perhaps . . . Just tell us what Lord Hordavan plans and we'll promise to carry your leavings to your sweet old mother."

"A curse on the woman who bore me!" growled the man with such violence that his body shuddered. "She was no mother to me. Like an animal in the field, she dropped me, then moved on. No," he sighed heavily, "I insult the herdbeasts. At least they wait to abandon their young till their offspring are weaned."

"All right, bastard, then," Mongrel swore. "We want to know what Hordavan plans. Tell us quickly, and we'll be merciful." He shook the soldier till blood and muck gushed from his belly, but Bracer did not move. She sat, eyes closed, engrossed in disquieting musings.

Once she had abandoned a child. A boy child. Was it really thirty years ago? How odd, to realize that somewhere existed a grown man who was her son. Or had he died by now? Or was he dying, here, by her own bladestroke?

The idea was too preposterous. How could she, who had faith in nothing, believe in such a coincidence?

"Now tell me what you know!" came Mongrel's voice, punctuated by a slap. Bracer roused from her ponderings.

"No more, Mong!" She glared at her partner. "You'll only hasten his death." She stroked the soldier's stubbly jaw, smoothed his black hair. "There, there . . ." she crooned. "I won't let him hurt you." She was aware of Mongrel, leaning forward to catch her words. "I'll help you, but you must cooperate with us. We're more to you than Lord Hordavan, eh? We're kinfolk of the sword. We know what it is to be lonely, to be rejected, cast out. That's the tie that binds us, lad. What's a secret between family?"

Bracer cradled his head in her lap. He twisted his neck in the pillow her knees made, as if relishing the sensation of being held thus. His lake-blue eyes opened, staring up into hers. *Why,* Bracer imagined briefly—*they could be mirrored from my own.*

"No one's ever done that." His words came in soft, slow phrases. "I ached for my father's second wife to mother me. I watched her rock her babes and cuddle them . . . I wanted to know such love. She was so tender with them. Couldn't understand why she hated me so. . . ." He shut his eyes again—"till I was grown. Wanted her own son to be Father's heir." He was silent for a long moment. "Damn me if I cared." He swallowed hard and his body went suddenly limp as he lost consciousness.

—*The stubborn boy must have left home to prove he didn't want his father's estate*—Bracer imagined as she eased his head from her lap—*and become a soldier of fortune. He wouldn't be the first dispossessed youngster to turn anger into a livelihood.* She had seen many such men, and women. The lonely were always most willing to face danger, the angry most anxious to stand and fight.

Bracer retrieved the filthy washrag and went to rinse it. Fires flared against the dusky sky as the army with which she currently served made camp. Mongrel busied himself gathering wood.

—*Is this my son?* Bracer, who had once been called Arista, wondered.—*If he is, I must find a way to explain to him what happened. I can't let him die hating his mother.*

How could she convey to him the dispair that had driven her to abandon her newborn son? Would he understand that she had been only a child herself? Her manipulative mother had coerced her father into marrying off Arista, though she was only thirteen, to one of Baron Venire's most promising aides. Lon, Arista's husband, had been a kind man, and gentle. She had accepted him, even cared for him. War had taken Lon away from home around the time his bride of a dozen weeks began experiencing symptoms of pregnancy.

The following months had been a nightmare for Arista. Always a healthy, active child, she was unprepared for the queasiness and discomfort, or for the changes which distorted her belly and breasts. Her in-laws were cruel during their son's absence, forcing her to work like a servant instead of pampering her the way she knew Lon would have. They also forbade any contact with her own family. So, she had no woman to calm her distress over the changes that were defacing her body. The child moving in her womb frightened her. She did not understand the intricacies of her body, but imagined that her belly would burst when the creature inside grew too large to be housed there.

Reality was horrible enough. The baby had ripped his way out of her body. When her mother-in-law instructed Arista to nurse the child, she could not. All she felt was revulsion for the small, ugly, red infant who had brutally forced its bloody way out of her loins. Once her strength returned, but before her mother-in-law noticed and put her to work, Arista escaped.

She had since learned to see childbirth as the temporary discomfort it was. She had occasionally thought she might want another child, but had never settled down to have one. Fate had led her to a life of travel and danger. She never looked back, or regretted. As Bracer, she had faced death many times, cradling mortally wounded comrades, as she had held this young soldier. Bracer had watched their lives ebb away, sometimes envying them. She was, she realized now, just as alone and bitter as this dying man. Did she dare ask his father's name? If this was her son, could there be a healing between them before he died?

—*I do not think this is my child*—she insisted as she walked back to where he lay. Mongrel, having lit a fire, already knelt beside the still form. The old fighter's stubby fingers lightly slapped the quiet soldier's cheek.

"I can't rouse him," he said, looking up.

Bracer knelt down so that she could put her ear against the man's mouth. She heard nothing, felt no breath on her skin. Running her hands over his chest, shoulders and arms, she sought some sign of life. At last she grasped his hand. It was cold.

"Is he dead?" asked Mongrel.

She nodded, appearing indifferent, then rose and walked off toward the bushes.

The old mercenary began rifling the body. "Didn't tell us a damned thing," he grumbled, "and not even a good luck trinket worth pocketing, more's the pity."

He sat back on his heels and spat in disgust. "You'd think a captain would've had a ring, at least, or a medal," he muttered. "Hey," his eyes narrowed to accusing slits, "where's that badge of his. It's worth something, melted down."

"I have it," Bracer stated firmly. "He was mine."

Her head was bowed as she concentrated on retying the wrist wrappings. Mongrel shrugged, then feeling hungry, scrounged out his rations. It was her kill, after all.

MARWE'S FOREST

Charles R. Saunders

Charles Saunders, and his stories of the African warrior
Dossouye, need no introduction to readers of *Sword and
Sorceress.* For those of you who came in late, Charles
Saunders is a young Canadian of African descent, whose
novels of a "Black Conan" warrior, *Imaro,* have been
published by DAW. So far there are three volumes, and
we all hope there will be more . . . and some day, perhaps,
a story where Imaro and Dossouye meet, as with Conan
and Red Sonya, the warrior barbarian and fighting woman
created by Robert E. Howard.

T he moment Dossouye awakened, she knew Gbo was
gone. She sat up instantly, fully alert, without any of
the lassitude that usually marks the transition from
sleep to waking. In a single, smooth motion, she was on her
feet.

Her eyes swiftly scanned the small clearing she had chosen
for her encampment. Tall, lean, skin darker than midnight,
Dossouye appeared to be an integral part of the rain forest
that surrounded the clearing.

But she knew she was not. . . .

Her war-bull's saddle lay at her feet. The bridle and reins
were looped loosely about the pommel. Dossouye had never

considered tethering her mount; in the past, he had shown no inclination to stray.

She called his name once, then again:

"Gbo. . . ."

The word meant "protection" in the language of Abomey, her homeland. Gbo had more than lived up to his name: his presence alone had often sufficed to ward off predators. The few times they had been attacked, Dossouye and Gbo had fought in a deadly tandem to drive the assailants away.

Although she had wandered the wilderness for nearly two rains, Dossouye had seldom experienced loneliness. The war-bull was her friend and protector, and she had never contemplated what she would do if Gbo were gone.

Concern, anger, and fear chased each other through Dossouye's mind like leaves blown by the wind as she gazed at the broken foliage that marked the place through which Gbo had entered the forest.

Why didn't the noise awaken me? she wondered.

Then she remembered how quietly Gbo could move, despite his size.

Still, I should have heard, she thought uneasily.

She listened closely now, but she heard only the arrhythmic chorus of birds and the screeching challenges of monkeys and the low hum of insects. Dossouye focused her hearing on the two sounds that were the most ominous in the forest: the scrape of a python's scales and the low cough of a leopard. Although neither sound reached her ears, she did not relax her vigilance.

She pulled her long, slender sword from its scabbard and slashed viciously through a morning sunbeam.

"You, at least, have not deserted me," she said to the weapon.

The sword and Gbo had been with her since her departure from Abomey. Both had served her well: without them, she would not have survived her long wanderings through the uncharted wastelands that separated the western and eastern kingdoms of Nyumbani. To ensure her continued survival, she needed Gbo. The trail of the war-bull was clear. So were the perils she would risk if she followed it.

For a moment, she debated the wisdom of leaving the saddle and bridle behind. Then she realized she was only delaying the inevitable.

"Gbo," she muttered bitterly. "Have you decided to return to the wild? You can no more do that than I can!"

But we have both tried, she added silently.

Shaking her head in resignation, Dossouye pushed her way onto the track of the war-bull.

Only a short time passed before Dossouye found Gbo. But for her, moments seemed to stretch into hours of caution. The skin between her shoulderblades crawled each time she passed beneath a low-hanging branch.

Fortunately, Gbo had left a clear trail, and Dossouye was free to concentrate on avoiding the dangers that lurked among the trees.

The clearing appeared abruptly—one moment, Dossouye was slashing her way through a tangle of vines; the next, she was standing in the open. And she saw Gbo.

Why didn't I hear? Dossouye wondered again. For Gbo was not alone in the clearing. There was another horned beast with him.

The war-bull's appearance reflected his ancestry: the Abomeans had bred their mounts from the wild buffalo that roamed the forests and plains. Gbo retained the black hide, sweeping horns, and thick shoulders of his feral counterparts. But Gbo's kind were tractable, trainable. Dossouye could command her mount with a word or a gesture.

Now, though, she doubted that the war-bull would heed her. . . .

The other animal in the clearing was not a buffalo. It was unlike any other beast Dossouye had ever seen. It was of the cattle-kind, but she knew it was not domestic.

It was smaller than Gbo, who was nuzzling the creature's neck. Its hide was a deep brown burnished with red highlights. Ivory-white horns rose in graceful arcs from a head that had the long, delicate lines of an antelope.

A long, tasseled tail flicked at the air while Gbo's rough tongue licked the hide of the strange, beautiful animal that

Dossouye could not quite think of as a cow. The creature was crooning in a voice that was disconcertingly human.

A spirit-beast? Dossouye wondered. In her rare encounters with the people of the wilderness tribes, she had heard stories of animals that had the souls of humans, and humans with the souls of animals. . . .

"Gbo!" she called sharply.

Both animals turned to look at her. Gbo's eyes were clear and alert—the eyes of an intelligent animal, nothing more. The other's . . . *deep, dark, penetrating in a way no animal's could ever be . . . there was a message in those eyes.* . . .

Go, the eyes said. *You have no place in this.* . . .

Gbo returned his attention to what Dossouye now called the spirit-beast. The creature's eyes did not stray from hers, not even when Gbo moved behind the beast and rose to mount her. Dossouye felt the presence of those eyes long after she turned and fled the clearing.

Dossouye lost the next several hours. Later, when she attempted to recall what she had done after she ran from the clearing, her mind remained blank. No sensations, no emotions—nothing other than a rind of green along the edge of her sword. That, at least, was evidence that she had spent some of the lost time cutting through foliage as though the bush were an enemy.

When awareness returned, Dossouye found herself standing once again at the brink of the clearing. Once again, the tangle of vines stood before her. But the sun was slanting through the trees at a different angle now. Dusk was near, and in the dimming light the forest resembled a gigantic temple of a forgotten god. . . .

Dossouye raised her sword to chop at the barrier . . . then she realized the full significance of the green crust along its edge, and a shudder rippled through her.

I could have been killed! she thought in sudden panic. *A leopard or a snake could have attacked me, and all my sword-skill would have meant nothing without my mind there to direct it. How did I survive, hacking away at vines and bushes?*

Calling on the discipline she had absorbed during her training as an *ahosi*, Dossouye pushed her panic aside.

I am jealous of a cow in heat, she chided herself.

She ran her thumb and forefinger down the edge of her blade and wiped the green residue on the leather loinguard that was her only garment. An emerald tinge remained on the steel. But she had no cloth to clean it properly.

Delaying, she thought as she pushed the weapon back into its scabbard. *I'm delaying again.* . . .

She remembered the eyes of the . . . cow. She heard no sounds from the clearing. She pushed her way through the vines; and for the second time that day, she stood wide-eyed, momentarily unable to speak or move.

Gbo was still in the clearing. And another was still with him. But the other was not a horned beast. . . .

The war-bull was lying on the grass. His head rested in the lap of a woman, who lifted her head and gazed directly at Dossouye. The eyes transfixed Dossouye . . . she had seen them before. But her thoughts were clouding over, and she could not remember.

"Gbo," Dossouye said softly.

At the sound of his name, the war-bull lifted his head. The woman leaned back to avoid the sudden movement of his horns. After rising to his feet, Gbo walked toward Dossouye. His gait was unsteady, as though he had awakened from a deep slumber.

Gently, the war-bull butted against Dossouye. She drew a finger across the keratin boss that connected Gbo's horns.

" 'Gbo'? That is his name?"

Dossouye's attention instantly returned to the woman, who was now also on her feet. She was as tall as Dossouye, who was herself taller than many men. But where Dossouye was lean to the point of gauntness, the other was full-bodied, with large breasts, rounded limbs, and wide hips. Her skin was a deep shade of mahogany burnished by the fading sunlight.

Although the woman's words were strange to Dossouye's ears, she still caught the meaning. Her suspicions should have been aroused then, but a dreamlike mist was permeating her mind.

Those eyes. . . .

"Gbo is his name, yes," Dossouye said at last. "And what is yours?"

"Marwe."

Marwe was wearing an ankle-length skirt of softly tanned leather decorated with geometric patterns of beads. Except for a circlet of beads about her throat, her upper body was bare. Above a wide-cheeked face with strong, well-molded features, a *manyoya*, or plumed headgear, trailed down to the middle of her back. The plumes were ivory-white.

But it was Marwe's eyes that held Dossouye captive.

"The cow—" Dossouye began.

"Is gone," Marwe finished. "What is your name, and why do you wander alone here?"

"I am Dossouye."

"Why are you alone?" Marwe repeated.

"I am not alone," Dossouye said sharply. Her hand still rested on Gbo's head.

Marwe looked at her and smiled. Dossouye felt her will slipping away from her, like water trickling between outstretched fingers. . . .

There is sorcery here, Dossouye thought. But the thought caused her no disquiet.

"I am alone because that is the only way for me," she said.

"Do you want to be with me?" Marwe asked. She was still smiling.

No! a voice deep within Dossouye cried.

"Yes," she said.

Marwe stretched out a hand for Dossouye to take.

No! the voice cried weakly.

"Gbo's saddle and bridle are still in the clearing," Dossouye said.

"No one will steal them."

Dossouye took the forest woman's hand then, and Marwe led her out of the clearing. Gbo followed docilely at the heels of the two women as they entered the forest.

Night had nearly fallen when they reached Marwe's dwelling. In the scraps of dusk that remained, Dossouye could see how different the forest had become. Treetrunks no longer grew in straight columns; now they twisted and interlaced like tapestries made of limbs and leaves and hanging vines. Bird and animal sounds were subdued here, as though muffled by the intervening foliage.

Marwe's *kwetu,* or dome-shaped dwelling, seemed almost an outgrowth of the forest. Roots and branches conjoined to form its circular walls, and a canopy of leaves was its roof. A small clearing dotted with flowers surrounded the *kwetu.* The boughs of the trees around the clearing were heavily laden with fruit.

Dossouye and Gbo followed Marwe toward the *kwetu.* Halfway there, Gbo stopped to graze. Marwe beckoned Dossouye to enter the dark, oval portal that led to the interior of the *kwetu.* For a moment, Dossouye resisted the pull of Marwe's hand.

"It's almost dark," she said. "Aren't you going to light a night-fire?"

"We need none."

Still, Dossouye held back: a final twinge of suspicion battled against the lassitude that was claiming her. But Marwe's eyes would not release her. She allowed the forest woman to draw her into the darkness of the *kwetu.*

Inside, Dossouye saw only the pale blur of Marwe's *manyoya.* Marwe's hand released Dossouye's, then trailed lightly up the warrior's arm to her shoulder. After a short pause, the hand descended to touch the shallow curve of Dossouye's breast. Then her mouth met Dossouye's, as if she knew—

—as if she knew that the woman soliders of Abomey did not lie with men . . . as if she knew the full extent of the emptiness inside Dossouye . . . as if she knew what Dossouye needed better than Dossouye herself knew. . . .

Then Marwe's arms were enfolding her, and both women descended to the floor of the *kwetu,* and Dossouye surrendered to the magic of the forest woman.

"Tell me who you are," Marwe whispered into Dossouye's ear.

They were lying together, arms sliding across smooth flesh, legs entwined. Marwe's skirt and *manyoya* lay nearby, as did Dossouye's loin-protector. Darkness and sweat blanketed them.

Although she was drowsy and satiated, Dossouye began to tell Marwe of her former life as an *ahosi,* a woman soldier of Abomey. She told of how she had been chosen in a dream to wield the sacred sword that had saved her kingdom from conquest by the Ashanti, and how she had seen the tree that guarded two of her three souls destroyed by a jealous rival. With only a single soul left, she should have died with her tree. but she did not die . . . in deep confusion, she had exiled herself from her homeland, where she was a spiritual contradiction.

She recounted her wanderings since that time . . . she had gone farther and farther from the kingdoms of the west; deeper and deeper into the wilderness. She told Marwe of the encounters she had experienced in the sparsely populated wasteland: confrontations with spirits, demons, sorcerers, and bandits. She could not say what she was searching for . . . perhaps it was her lost souls. . . .

Never had Dossouye confided in another as she now did in Marwe. The forest woman remained silent as Dossouye talked. Whenever she sensed the beginning of tension beneath the *ahosi*'s skin, Marwe stroked her until the strain eased.

When Dossouye was done, Marwe said nothing for a time. Then she shifted her position until her face lay close to the *ahosi*'s.

"You will stay with me," Marwe said. It was more statement than question, but there was also an implication of choice.

For a moment, Dossouye's mind was clear. The mists were gone; she was no longer under any influence of sorcery. Her response to Marwe's statement was a single word:

"Yes."

Time flowed swiftly, like a flooded stream. Dossouye spent her days hunting in the forest or helping Marwe tend to her flowers and fruits. Gbo wandered in and out of the clearing, but he never adopted feral ways. Dossouye suspected that he was still consorting with the horned beast, even though she had not seen the creature since the day in the clearing. When Dossouye asked Marwe about the mysterious animal, the forest woman only smiled.

Dossouye did retrieve Gbo's saddle and bridle, but the riding equipment remained inside the *kwetu*. The war-bull accepted both women equally, and Dossouye did not begrudge the affection Gbo bore toward Marwe.

At night, Dossouye and Marwe talked and made love. The talk was mostly Dossouye's: the forest woman's curiosity concerning the world beyond her forest was unquenchable. Night after night, Dossouye filled the dark interior of the dwelling with stories of Abomey and its neighboring kingdoms. Much of the *ahosi*'s knowledge of the more distant lands of the west was incomplete, but Marwe still absorbed Dossouye's words with the eagerness of a child.

"Have you ever wanted to leave this place; to see the lands you never tire of hearing about?" Dossouye asked one night.

"No. Would you like to return there?"

"No," Dossouye said after a pause.

Marwe's face was resting on Dossouye's shoulder. The *ahosi* felt the forest woman's lips curve in a smile that touched her skin. Then Marwe's tongue probed the juncture between Dossouye's neck and shoulder. And Dossouye forgot the misgivings that had begun to worry at the edges of her contentment.

What has happened to me? an almost inaudible voice cried within her.

Dossouye, ignored the voice and allowed pleasure to envelop her.

It was when the first rains of the wet season fell that Marwe's pregnancy became obvious. There could be no other explanation for the swelling of her breasts and belly and the sickness that seized her when the sun rose.

On a day when the rain had temporarily abated, Dossouye and Marwe faced each other in the clearing. The sun's rays made rainbow jewels of the droplets that clung to the grass.

Inactivity had added another layer to Dossouye's flesh,

though she was still slender. Her ebony hair was now cropped close to her head, and her indigo-black skin reflected an almost metallic sheen in the sunlight. She was wearing one of Marwe's skirts. Her sword and scabbard were in the *kwetu*. Her eyes were clear, but her emotions were not.

"When did it happen?" Dossouye asked.

"Before I met you."

"And there were others before that?"

"Yes."

"Women and men?"

"Yes."

This time, Marwe did not reply. Dossouye realized then how little she truly knew of the forest woman. Although Marwe looked and felt human enough, Dossouye had seen the branches of trees bend to her will.

If she were indeed a sorceress, Marwe had not done any harm to Dossouye or Gbo. Yet the *ahosi* often found her perceptions clouded, as though she were living a hallucination. . . .

Dossouye felt neither anger nor jealousy because Marwe had lain with others before her. Despite the rigid Abomean strictures against pregnancy for *ahosis*, Dossouye had herself once shared love with a man. But the man was actually a ghost. . . .

What, then, are you, Marwe? she wondered silently.

Will you stay until I give birth?"

Marwe was asking, not demanding. No mystic compulsions were being imposed. Dossouye's decision was entirely her own. She didn't understand why her feelings were changing.

"I will stay," she said.

But she made no move to embrace Marwe.

As the rains washed through the days, Marwe's abdomen grew larger, and Dossouye's desire to depart grew stronger. At night, she continued to sleep at Marwe's side. But their conversations dwindled, and their touching ceased.

Sometimes, Dossouye would stand naked in the rain, hoping that the warm sheets of water could eradicate her discontent. Her life was no longer dreamlike. The happiness was gone. And she could not understand why. . . .

Her early training as an *ahosi* would not release its iron hold. *A pregnant* ahosi *is a dead one* . . . it was more than merely a saying. All of the women soldiers of Abomey were wives of the Leopard King, who never touched them. If an *ahosi* became pregnant by another man, both she and her lover were beheaded. Thus, *ahosis* turned to each other for love. And the thought of pregnancy was repellent to them.

Dossouye was torn between her love for Marwe and the deeply ingrained customs of her people. The rain did not wash the conflict out of her.

Marwe's hand touched Dossouye's shoulder, and the *ahosi* snapped into wakefulness. She opened her mouth to speak, but she could not. Nor could she move. Marwe's touch held her immobile like an insect in a spider's web.

"It is time, Dossouye," the forest woman said. "The birthing will soon come. Then you and Gbo will be free."

Darkness pervaded the dwelling; Dossouye could not discern even an outline of Marwe. But she sensed Marwe had more to say.

"I am not human, Dossouye. And I am not a ghost or a demon. I am an *imandwa*—a changer-of-shape, a forest-spirit. Once, my kind lived among the people of the east, who revere cattle. We *imandwa* can be woman or man, cow or bull; whichever shape we choose. The easterners worshipped us, and they helped us to renew. . . .

"In time, however, the easterners learned new ways, and they turned away from the *imandwa*. Our kind drifted into the wilderness. Yet we still need to renew.

"I was in cow-form when I sensed you and Gbo nearby. At the time, my course was clear. I used my magic to attract Gbo to me. Gbo is the father of my child. He is the renewer.

"But you, Dossouye . . . I never intended to use you. I felt your need, and I tried to fulfill it, as my ancestors did for the easterners—until they needed us no longer.

"It is the same with you, Dossouye. You no longer need me.

"I renewed in cow-form. In that form, I must give birth. When you awaken, I will be gone.

"Good-bye, Dossouye. I hope your travels lead you to what you truly need."

The moment Marwe lifted her hand, Dossouye lost consciousness.

Dawnlight seeped into the *kwetu* when Dossouye opened her eyes again. It was the sound she heard that brought her fully awake—the cry of an animal in pain. . . .

Dossouye rose and pushed through the opening of the *kwetu*. Outside, the rain had relented, but the air was still laden with the damp of the wet season.

She saw Gbo standing over another animal: a beast that thrashed and groaned in distress. Impatiently pawing the ground, the war-bull looked expectantly at Dossouye.

Dossouye's feet carried her toward the two animals. She knelt by the side of Marwe. In cow-form, she had the same russet coat and ivory horns and human eyes Dossouye remembered. But now those eyes were filled with pain, and her flank bulged with new life struggling to emerge.

In Abomey, Dossouye had witnessed difficult birthings in the pens where war-bulls were raised. One glance revealed that Marwe's calf was turned the wrong way.

The *imandwa* gazed at Dossouye, the pleading naked in her eyes. Without hesitation, the *ahosi* reached inside Marwe and pulled at the calf until its head was in the proper position. Contractions rippled through the *imandwa's body until the calf finally lay in Dossouye's arms.*

Its hide was midnight-black . . . like Gbo's.

Dossouye stayed in the clearing until both Marwe and the calf were standing upright. As the long-legged infant took his first meal, its mother kept her eyes on Dossouye. The gratitude in those eyes shone so deeply there was no need for words to express it.

Marwe's eyes followed Dossouye as the ahosi dragged Gbo's gear out of the *kwetu*. Although he had not been saddled or bridled for nearly a rain, the war-bull remained quiet while Dossouye secured his gear. Then the *ahosi* donned her loin-protector and strapped her sword about her waist.

She looked again at Marwe. She was free, and she realized that the *imandwa*'s magic had imposed nothing on her; it had only enhanced desires that were already there.

Dossouye went to Marwe. She wound her arms around the *imandwa*'s neck and pressed her face against the long, elegant head of the shape-changer.

"One day, I will return," she whispered.

A moment later, she was in the saddle and urging Gbo out of the clearing. She did not stop riding until the trees grew straight again.

THE HUNTERS
Mavis J. Andrews

By the time a reader gets to the end of any anthology, he is usually suffering from overdosage, even of the best fiction. So I try always to end up with a very short story with a sharp twister in the tail, which will leave the reader wishing there were more.

Four days before the deadline, this one came in.

All we know about Mavis Andrews is that she has lived in various parts of Canada, now lives in a suburb of Toronto, has two young sons, and earns her living as a legal secretary. From this story we can deduce a sharp wit and a way with words. She too is working on a novel (isn't everybody?)

T he meager rays of day cast long shadows over the still white land. Jaed crouched silently by a cluster of bare-branched shrubs at the top of the hill and looked down over the frozen slope to where her boat lay on the ice. She had to reach it.

Jaed seemed to be a part of the gray-brown bush, unmoving as her dark eyes scanned the shadowed snows. She was dressed in torn buckskins, and her long black hair was tied back with a leather band. Her right hand clutched a long knife. Her left arm hung twisted and useless by her side.

Blood coated her clothing, and long blood-dried gouges marked her face.

It had been a routine hunt until the Morwolves attacked, the giant black wolves of the Northland. Not for countless years had the Morwolves come this far south so early in the winter. The Tribe had expected free hunting for another two moons. The northern lands must have been early strangled by the snows for the Morwolves to move south already, Jaed knew. They weren't due until the killing ice wind swept the lands; then, the Tribe stayed safe in the caves and left the frozen wastes to these dread hunters.

The Morwolves traveled in packs, but hunted in pairs. Jaed was fortunate that she had met no more than a pair on the eastern ridge that morning. She sighted them just as she reached the top of a rise, two massive creatures loping shoulder to shoulder far down the rock-strewn ridge. She knew them from the Elders' whispered tales, and she froze. They stopped and their heads whirled toward her. Taller than the height of a hunter they stood, with their sharp ears pricked forward. Their eyes were burning amber, and the force of their sighting struck her like a spear. They were still for only the blink of an eye, then they leapt and raced toward her.

Her ash bow was at the ready for the buck she was hoping to find. She had time to shoot off her four arrows in rapid succession, each finding its mark in the huge black chests. The poison from the arrows slowed them, but still they raced toward her with their yellow eyes gleaming hungrily. She imagined she could hear their hunting cry, their soundless mind-call.

The smallest stumbled, then dropped onto the hard-packed snow, felled by the poison. Briefly it struggled, then lay still. The other came on.

Jaed readied herself. The Morwolf leaped. Jaed stabbed out with her knife as she fell to the snow. Powerful jaws clamped down on her arms; claws tore at her. Jaed fought with all the fury of a cornered hunter. Suddenly the giant black body fell limp. The Morwolves were dead.

The poison had killed them. Jaed's knife saved her from dying with them, but not without cost. She was now being hunted by the entire pack. They would have heard the death cries; they would all respond.

Jaed kept her mind as still as her body, not allowing the fear that curled within her to loose itself and scent the air. Around their winter campfires, the old hunters of the Tribe whispered that to be captured by a whole pack of Morwolves meant a slow and savage death, but to be captured after killing one of their comrades would be worse than death.

She could see them, dark shadows moving silently on the darkening slopes, waiting for her.

She had to go. She leapt from the cover of the bushes and ran till her pulse was a drumbeat in her head and her lungs were on fire. Through the pounding of her heart she seemed to hear their silent screams. She could see the shadows gliding down the hills, closing in on her, but she held the thought of the boat in her mind like a shield. She only had to reach it. It would skim over the frozen lake as fast as the wind, much faster than even the Morwolves. She would be safe.

She was almost there. She knew she could make it. Then her foot caught on a protruding branch. It had looked like nothing more than a gentle wave of snow. It was frozen hard into the ground. The momentum of her flight hurled her face down in the snow.

She landed hard. The wind was knocked out of her. She twisted, struggling to get to her feet, but her left foot was caught tight. Pain shot up her leg and washed over her as she pulled.

Then the hot hungry scent of the Morwolves filled her nostrils as one by one the massive black creatures silently surrounded her. For a frozen moment her eyes met the yellow eyes of the gray-muzzled one. She tried to think of the prayer words her mother had taught, tried to picture her mother kneeling before the fire sending soft chantings out into the night, but all she could see were the gleaming yellow eyes and all she could hear was the sound of her heart mixed up with the sound of their breathing. The sight and sound filled her mind till nothing else existed.

Then she knew.

Jaed heard a scream as fiery pain ripped through her brain,

not even aware that the tortured voice was hers. The screams filled her ears and she fell into whirling blackness.

The young Morwolf licked at her injured left foreleg and gingerly got to her feet. She breathed in the clean snow-smell and the warm home-scent of the pack, and gave herself a satisfied shake. She felt good, even with the pain. It would soon be gone. The Healers would take care of it. Her father's gray muzzle nudged her gently, "Come, my child."

Her mind filled with the contented humming of the pack. "You are one of us now, Jaed," the voices sang. "It's time to go."

"Yes," Jaed sang back softly. Limping, she fell into step beside her father and, giving an incurious glance at the empty shell of what had once been human, she followed the pack up the hill to home.

DAW

DAW PRESENTS THESE BESTSELLERS BY
MARION ZIMMER BRADLEY

NON-DARKOVER NOVELS

☐ **HUNTERS OF THE RED MOON** (UE1968—$2.95)
☐ **WARRIOR WOMAN** (UE2253—$3.50)

NON-DARKOVER ANTHOLOGIES

☐ **SWORD AND SORCERESS I** (UE2359—$4.50)
☐ **SWORD AND SORCERESS II** (UE2360—$3.95)
☐ **SWORD AND SORCERESS III** (UE2302—$4.50)
☐ **SWORD AND SORCERESS IV** (UE2412—$4.50)
☐ **SWORD AND SORCERESS V** (UE2288—$3.50)
☐ **SWORD AND SORCERESS VI** (UE2423—$3.95)
☐ **SWORD AND SORCERESS VII** (UE2457—$4.50)
☐ **SWORD AND SORCERESS VIII** (UE2486—$4.50)

COLLECTIONS

☐ **LYTHANDE** (with Vonda N. McIntyre) (UE2291—$3.95)
☐ **THE BEST OF MARION ZIMMER BRADLEY** (edited by Martin H. Greenberg) (UE2268—$3.95)
